A Legacy Of One

A Legacy Of One

Kevin G. Chapman

Copyright © 2021 by Kevin G. Chapman
Second edition

Kindle Direct Publishing

This is a work of fiction. The events and characters depicted here are the products of the author's imagination and any connection or similarity to any actual people, living or dead, is purely coincidental.
All rights reserved. No part of this book may be reproduced or transmitted by any method without written permission from the author.
Cover design by 100 Covers

Other novels by Kevin G. Chapman

The Mike Stoneman Thriller Series

Righteous Assassin (Mike Stoneman #1)
Deadly Enterprise (Mike Stoneman #2)
Lethal Voyage (Mike Stoneman #3)
Fatal Infraction (Mike Stoneman #4)

Fool Me Twice (A Mike Stoneman Short Story)

coming soon:
Perilous Gambit (Mike Stoneman #5)

Visit me at www.KevinGChapman.com

To my wife, Sharon, with whom I spent my Columbia years and thirty-eight wonderful years since then.

"A legacy is planting a seed
In a garden that you never get to see"

-- Lin Manuel Miranda, Hamilton (the Musical)

Prologue

MAX FOSTER looked down on New York City through a massive floor-to-ceiling window. The brass buttons on the vest of his three-piece suit strained against the burgeoning bulk of his stomach. Far below, on the opposite side of Central Park South, the sidewalk teemed with men in business suits and women in heels hurrying home from another day of insignificant work. Insignificant; that's what Max thought. That's what they all were; living out their lives worried about their golf games, their hair styles, their mortgages, and what schools their kids would attend. They complained about the economy and the weather and fretted about world hunger and climate change, but they were powerless to affect any meaningful change in the world, and they knew it. To Max they were just shoes, walking where he dictated and doing his bidding if he wished it.

Max sipped his martini and pitied them. They were as the notes on the page, and he the conductor. He stretched out his right arm, wielding an imaginary baton, and briefly conducted the pedestrian symphony twenty-seven stories beneath him. The last golden reflection of the setting sun glinted off the

FAO Schwartz building on Fifth Avenue, casting a beam of light on the carriages parked near the corner of Fifth Avenue and creating double shadows in front of and behind the horses. Max was at the center of the universe – the sun shining towards him from both directions.

He glanced at the teak grandfather clock standing guard at his office door and frowned. The call he was expecting was three minutes late, and Max was not a man accustomed to being kept waiting. He walked past the mirrored backsplash behind his office bar and assessed his reflection. His suit was impeccably tailored. His Custom Shop shirt pinched slightly into the folds of his neck, but when he pushed his shoulders back and expanded his chest, the fleshy skin stretched enough to smooth out the lines. He frowned at the amount of scalp he could see through his combed-over hair, which was getting thinner each day. Then he shrugged and dismissed the thought. He looked distinguished and powerful, just as he liked it.

Max finished off his martini and placed the crystal glass on a silver tray sitting on the antique coffee table next to his overstuffed leather sofa. The office cleaning staff would have it washed and back in its place in his mahogany breakfront by the time he arrived for work tomorrow. The telephone on his desk rang, and he settled into a high-backed brown leather chair before answering on the fourth ring. No need to appear anxious.

"Yes. . . . I assume the situation is entirely under control? . . . Good. . . . Should I be at all worried here? . . . Your assurances are comforting, but I would prefer to simply see the results and not need the assurances. . . . I agree that he seems reliable, but there are times he's too soft on key issues. . . . See that he does. . . . Keep me advised."

Max pushed the END button on the console and sat back, still holding the handset. He swiveled around to face the window again and gazed out at the city, now lighting up in its incandescent glow as the sun died below the western horizon. Everything had gone according to plan, and yet he was inexplicably apprehensive. The boy's father was so solid. His father was so much smarter. His father knew exactly where he wanted to be and always moved clearly in that direction. The boy was more like a sailboat in a storm – capable of surviving if there was a steady hand at the tiller, but in danger of capsizing at any moment if the captain's attention wandered. Max wondered if his team was vigilant enough to avoid the Scylla and Charybdis. The boy seemed so vulnerable to temptation. Max hung up the receiver and took a deep breath. His team was good. They had been through the wars. He was confident. In any case, at this point he was committed. Doubt could not be allowed.

Max considered refilling his martini glass, but decided that an exercise of will power would be more appropriate. He congratulated himself for his self-control.

He hoisted himself out of the chair and walked briskly toward the door, took his hat from the ornate walnut rack in the corner and left the office. Nobody saw him leave except the old man emptying the trash. He smiled. At his age, he was still the last one out of the office. Then he frowned. Why weren't his younger underlings working harder than he? Then he smiled again; because, he thought, they were not in control. He was. If only he didn't have to rely on politicians. They could be unreliable; especially the younger ones.

Chapter 1

JONATHAN EUGENE PRESCOTT III casually leaned against the thick, taut rope supporting the white canvas tent and sipped his second Black Label of the evening. With the stiff vertical side of the event pavilion behind him, he was able to keep his back clear and keep the swirling crowd in view. His father always told him it was best to know where the sharks were. The nametag clipped neatly to the pocket of his Italian suit – dark blue with robin's-egg blue pinstripes – was slightly askew, matching the mop of curly blond hair in the freshman photo next to his name: "Jon Prescott – CC '91." Twenty-five years, he thought with a rueful smile. There had been a lot of haircuts over those years. His hair was now a sandy brown, clipped into a neat, conservative side-part. His eyes, though, were still the same steely blue as in his freshman picture.

Jonathan spied a slightly overweight, balding man bearing a similar nametag making a beeline toward him, with a serious sense of purpose. "JP, you dog, you!" the man thrust out a meaty hand toward Jonathan like a bayonet. "Nobody's surprised about your election, *Senator*." He emphasized the title, while winking obviously. Jonathan despised being referred to by his initials, as he had during his college years. None of his real friends ever attempted it.

Jonathan parried the assault smoothly, as he had thousands of others. He smiled broadly. "Mort! How the hell are you?" He shook his classmate's hand firmly and released quickly, steering Mort Zuckerman to his left and planting him next to the same support rope against which Jonathan had been leaning. Zuckerman was not a campaign contributor. Jonathan had memorized the list of those classmates who had donated to the noble cause of electing him as the junior senator from Connecticut eight years earlier, and of re-electing him in 2014. But there were more elections to come, and many of his classmates had the means to be future contributors. This fact had been drilled into Jonathan multiple times in the days leading up to his class reunion by his campaign manager, his chief of staff, and his wife. Jonathan had not really wanted to attend the event, but the fundraising opportunity could not be missed.

Jonathan exchanged reminiscences with Mort Zuckerman for the next few minutes, as a circle of well-wishers gathered around the senator. It was getting muggy inside the event tent, which was planted in the middle of the grassy field where Jonathan had played Ultimate Frisbee as an undergrad, safely within the walls of Columbia University. Looking out the narrow entranceway, he could see a neatly trimmed hedge and the ornamented portico of a student dormitory building. With a chamber quartet playing in the corner and the dull murmur of several hundred people talking, he could hardly make out the sound of a siren screaming up Broadway beyond the sheltering edifice of Furnald Hall. It was still New York City.

He was scanning the crowd, although trying not to be obvious. So many people, and so many years older than when he had last seen most of them. Was it really twenty-five years? He had been twenty-two when he had graduated in 1991; a lifetime ago. Jonathan had not been particularly friendly during his college years with any of the people in his current conversation circle. He had the sinking feeling this could end up being a very long night.

He was easily the highest profile member of the Columbia College class of '91. The thought made Jonathan smile to himself. Others from his class were doctors, lawyers, and business leaders – and one very prominent federal judge. But Jonathan was the top of the heap, even if he had not been at the top of the class.

He drained his glass, creating an excuse to disengage from the group of well-wishers who wanted so much to tell their families they hung out with the senator during their class reunion. He smiled and shook hands all around before excusing himself and heading toward the portable bar in the corner of the enclosure. He stopped to listen as a group of eight men and two women stood around a support pole and sang the college Alma Mater, "Sans Souci," to raucous applause. When the crowd broke out into a chorus of "Who Owns New York?" Jonathan skirted the edge of the revelry and continued toward the white-coated bartender, whose name was Juan. Jonathan had already tipped Juan twenty dollars to ensure prompt refills throughout the evening. He had also sworn Juan to a pledge to serve him no more than four drinks before switching him to Diet Coke, no matter how much he begged.

He ordered his third Black Label with a quick wave. He would have preferred a single malt. Juan was surrounded by a disorganized mob of revelers, most of whom were used to being first in line. As he waited for the fresh glass, he couldn't help but smile at the raucous bunch of singers, still at it mid-tent:

"Oh, we own New York!
Yes, we own New York!
C-O-L-U-M-B-I-A"

Jonathan could not help but join in on the final chorus.

As he cheered the end of the song, a hand grabbed his shoulder and a familiar voice cried out, "Jon! Still sober?" Prescott turned and recognized the face of his freshman year roommate, and best college friend, Frank Elkhardt. Jonathan marveled at how little Frank seemed to have aged in twenty-five years. His face had the same youthful look, complete with a pimple on his neck under his left ear. He had the same reddish-brown hair, but cut much shorter than as a teenager. The glasses were different – more updated, frameless lenses, which accentuated his blue eyes. Same smile. Same naïve, trusting face atop a thin frame that longed to reach six feet but fell a few inches short. Frank held out his hand, but Jonathan embraced his old friend in a full hug. His campaign manager would not have approved, but Jonathan didn't care whether he rumpled his perfect suit at that moment.

"Frank, you amaze me!"

"How's that?"

"You're a ghost! You look like you could still wear your old college clothes."

"These *are* my old college clothes, dummy. It's still the best I can afford." Frank winked and smiled.

"Oh, right, I forgot, public interest law doesn't pay. Have to struggle along, do you?" Jonathan enjoyed the repartee missing from his usual dull conversations with sycophantic aides and constituents. "But – now, correct me if I'm wrong here – there was a small class action litigation on behalf of the wait staff of a big cruise line. Wage and Hour violations, as I recall, wasn't it?"

"Oh, that," Frank replied sheepishly, blushing slightly, but still smiling. "Well, yes, there was that one, and one or two others that paid a few bills."

"A few bills!" Jonathan exclaimed, slapping Frank's shoulder, "I heard your fees were in the seven figures!"

"Actually, not quite," Frank lowered his voice, as if they were sharing a secret. "And I did have to share with my three partners but let's just say it did pay for a few new suits and a shirt or two."

"And a $2,500 donation to my Senate election committee," Jonathan whispered, enjoying the feeling of a secretive conversation in the midst of the crowd of people.

"Don't broadcast that, mate, I'm a registered Democrat. I can't be seen handing over campaign dollars to the enemy."

"Never an enemy, old buddy, only an adversary." Jonathan put on his senatorial face again and retrieved his new glass from the bar, where Juan had left it sitting during the conversation. "Let's get a table for a minute; I'd love to catch up."

The two wound their way between clumps of chatting classmates, Senator Prescott smiling and waving at a few who shouted greetings along the way, until they eventually found an unoccupied table near the side of the tent opposite the bar. The roof overhead was supported by three tall poles and rose thirty feet in the air, where cigar smoke was starting to accumulate. Cigarettes were banned from the event, but several men had broken out the stogies and security was not about to stop them. Not with alumni donations on the line. Besides, they were, technically, out of doors. Jonathan and Frank sat on flimsy plastic chairs, the legs of which were slightly wobbly and dug into the uneven ground when they sat down. The tables were barely bigger than a waiter's tray, and just as wobbly as the chairs. Jonathan steadied his glass by keeping his hand on the table. Frank was not drinking yet. Once again, things had not changed much since college; Jonathan was already two drinks ahead.

They chatted for ten minutes, with only a few brief interruptions. Jonathan let Frank do most of the talking. As with most conversations for Jonathan, the other person always knew his story, the story splashed all over the papers, the tabloids, the news magazines, and the television. His heritage, his famous family, his prestige, his wife, his two perfect daughters; everyone knew his remarkable success story. At least, they thought they did. This gave Jonathan the freedom of listening, rather than answering questions.

The two friends had kept in touch through law school – Jonathan at Columbia and Frank at Boston University. After law school, they had drifted apart, as Jonathan embarked on his brief law and lobbying stint, then slid comfortably and inevitably into his political career. Frank explained how he had toiled away building a resume as a public interest lawyer, while trying to repay his student loans. He had worked for three small firms and also for a city agency in New York before taking the risk of opening a small office with three other lawyers in 2001. The firm had struggled, but thanks to a few large class action victories, which in turn generated favorable publicity, the four partners were now drawing more than $200,000 per year each. Not a large salary by New York standards – indeed, first year associates at the largest law firms were making nearly as much right out of school – but a comfortable living for Frank. His loans were repaid. He was thinking about whether to purchase his one-bedroom apartment before his co-op option expired. Frank was enthusiastic and optimistic about his life and his law practice. Ever the optimist, Jonathan thought.

As Frank was just starting to ask Jonathan about the Senate, he stopped mid-sentence, his eyes looking beyond his old roommate into the crowd. "What is it?" Jonathan inquired.

"Ricky Menendez," Frank replied, lowering his voice.
Jonathan turned casually to look. He saw Ricardo Menendez, standing with a gathering of eight or nine classmates in a clump about ten feet away. Menendez, appointed by President George W. Bush as a federal district court judge in 2005, was the only federal judge in the class. His appointment was a

compromise deal and was intended to show Hispanic voters that President Bush was willing to appoint a minority to the bench. The Republicans who made the deal soon regretted it, as Menendez issued a series of decisions in environmental and employment cases that branded him a liberal "activist" judge.

Menendez stood in the center of a circle of well-wishers, smiling shyly. He seemed uncomfortable with the attention. He was shorter than most of the group, which nearly obliterated him from the view of those outside the circle. Frank and Jonathan could see his head between the shoulders of two blue suits. Menendez glanced briefly in Jonathan's direction and the two made eye contact. Jonathan smiled, but did not wave. He nodded imperceptibly, then looked back at Frank. There would be tension in the group whenever the two came close to each other.

Menendez had been appointed to the United States Court of Appeals for the District of Columbia Circuit by President Obama in 2009. His nomination was opposed by Senate Republicans, who did not like Menendez' track record of liberal decisions and feared that his elevation to the Court of Appeals was a precursor to a future Supreme Court nomination. At the time, there had never been a Hispanic judge on the nation's highest court. Jonathan Prescott was absent from the Senate that day and did not cast a vote, as the confirmation was granted by the Democratic majority.

President Obama had since nominated Sonya Sotomayor to fill the spot of first Hispanic Supreme Court Justice, pushing Menendez off the front pages. But his name had been thrust back into the spotlight when Justice Antonin Scalia died suddenly, opening up a seat on the High Court during the final year of President Obama's second term. Obama had taken his time, but in early May, just a few weeks before the class reunion, he had nominated Menendez.

Republicans now held a slim two-seat margin of majority in the Senate, which held the power to reject the nomination.

The leaders of the party had decided it was politically risky to reject a qualified minority judge who had been originally appointed by a Republican president. Therefore, they decided to block the nomination from ever coming up for a vote at all, and to not even hold hearings on the nomination. The justification was that it was too close to the upcoming Presidential election. The new President, they said, should fill the vacant seat. This stance had generated tremendous controversy, but the Republicans had the votes.

Jonathan hoped to survive the evening without speaking to Menendez. So far, mission accomplished.

After an awkward pause, Jonathan drained his glass again and was just about to get up and head back to the bar when a woman suddenly plopped down onto the empty chair at their tiny table. Her soft features were accentuated by the dim lighting under the tent. Her red hair, pulled back into a severe bun, glistened in the humid air like spun silk. Tasteful diamond earrings dripped from her lobes, drawing the eye to her long, slender neck and bare shoulders. Her dress for the occasion was emerald green with black accents. It was strapless, but showed only a hint of cleavage. Jonathan and Frank looked startled for a moment, and then both smiled.

"Well, well, well," she crooned, "some things really never do change. Twenty-five years later, and the two of you still stuck together like glue." The mischievous twinkle in her eye was matched by a sly smile. "Maybe the rumors were true after all about you two being gay lovers."

Frank burst out a guffaw and stood up, stretching out his arms and awaiting the woman's embrace. "Janice," he exclaimed, "you know you're supposed to have a name tag."

"Yes, but where would I put it on this dress?" she rose from her chair gracefully and sweeping her hands down the front of her strapless number, where there truly was no good place to pin a tag. "Besides, anyone I care to talk to will know me without one." She hugged Frank warmly, lingering in his embrace just a touch longer than necessary.

"True that," Frank laughed, breaking away and sitting back down while motioning Janice to do likewise. Jonathan had remained seated and had not smiled since the gay lovers remark.

"Oh, don't be such a Republican," she taunted, finally drawing a weak smile from the senator. "You know I wouldn't publish it, even if it were true."

"I know," Jonathan responded, fixing his eyes on hers and nodding slightly. "At least, I hope I do." Janice gave him a reciprocal smile and then turned her eyes toward Frank.

Janice Stanton's career since graduation was nearly as well-known as Jonathan's. Journalism degree from Columbia, then a splashy four years at *The Village Voice*, where she wrote an exposé on corruption in local New York City government at the age of twenty-seven that got her nominated for a Pulitzer. From there to *The New York Times*, with assignments in Israel, Iraq, and Hong Kong. Another Pulitzer nomination, and then the big piece on corrupt overbilling by a big government contractor that bilked the Treasury out of millions during the Gulf War. For that, she *won* the Pulitzer, and helped send several people to jail.

After a failed marriage to a high-profile New York real estate mogul, Janice then jumped from *The Times* to *The Wall Street Journal*. Her political reporting and liberal leanings seemed in conflict with the conservative editorial positions of the paper, but she had flourished for the past four years, albeit without any additional Pulitzer consideration. Her byline still could make a corrupt politician sweat, and could make even straight-laced public servants nervous.

"Did you know we're going to be neighbors, Senator?" Janice's smooth delivery made Jonathan wonder whether she was joking.

"You mean you're moving to New Greenwich?"

"No, Silly. I'm going to D.C."

"Actually, no – I hadn't heard."

"Yes. I'm a senior political writer for now, but I've been told the bureau chief position is going to be open soon, and I'll be in line for the post." She batted her eyelashes and rested her chin on folded hands, staring at Jonathan to see his reaction.

"That's terrific, Jan," he smiled and stretched out a hand of congratulations. "I think you'll like it in Washington. Lots of muck to rake." Jonathan met her stare calmly, with no hint of emotion. He was well-practiced.

Janice casually crossed her legs. The silk of her dress parted to allow her toned, bare leg to emerge up to mid-thigh. "Aren't either of you gentlemen going to offer to get me a drink?"

Frank started to get up, but Jonathan motioned him to sit, holding out his own empty glass and tinkling the ice cubes, now lonely for some liquid company. "What can I get for you, Jan?"

"Oooh, I just *love* it when you call me 'Jan,' Jon. Nobody calls me that at work anymore. It's just like old times. You can get me a scotch – straight up."

"Not exactly like old times," Jonathan quipped, as he started worming his way toward the bar. The crowd inside the tent had expanded as the cocktail hour neared its conclusion. He looked back over his shoulder and called to Frank, "Can I get you anything, old buddy?"

"Diet Coke," Frank called back, "with lime."

"Some things really never do change," Janice remarked as she re-crossed her legs, drawing an admiring glance from a classmate to her right, whose wife elbowed him in the ribs. "How the hell did you survive this place without drinking as hard as the rest of us?"

"I was too busy to get drunk, most of the time."

"Well, you were busy, all right. But you had time for a little fun along the way." Janice raised her eyebrows and winked. Frank turned away and waved in the direction of a group of men, none of whom seemed to see him. Janice frowned slightly. "Sorry, Frank. I didn't mean to embarrass you."

"Don't worry, I'm beyond embarrassment."

Janice smiled sympathetically and reached to grasp Frank's hand briefly. "I recall our college romance fondly, Mr. Elkhardt. I hope you do as well."

"Oh, yes," Frank responded, a bit more quickly than he would have liked. "Those were good times, mostly. You, me, Jon, and Gwen, although I'm sure you were happier when Gwen wasn't there."

"Hey, I never said a mean word to Gwen!"

"Not exactly, but things might have been different if she weren't in the picture." Frank paused, awaiting Janice's reaction, but she just looked away.

"Is Gwen here?"

"I think she's across the street at the Barnard dinner. Of course, she could show up at any moment."

"Thanks," Janice slumped back in her chair. "Way to kill the mood." The two sat silently for a moment, each lost in memory. Twenty-five years. A long time. But not so long.

They both looked up as Jonathan returned, balancing three glasses. "Why so quiet – you two planning something illegal?" He laughed as he set down the drinks. His was a double. Juan wanted to make it count, since it was his last of the evening.

"Actually, Senator, we were just wondering about the whereabouts of your lovely spouse."

"She's with the ladies tonight, over at Barnard. I don't expect to see her until after dinner."

"Perfect," Janice purred, "we get you all to ourselves."

"Well, us and two hundred or so of our closest classmates," Frank interjected.

Jonathan grimaced. "Oh, God, can you two please save me from my classmates?"

"Now, Senator," Janice scolded, "surely some of these good folks are supporters of yours. Isn't this a golden opportunity to glad-hand with your constituency?"

"Who knows," Jonathan responded dismissively. Jonathan knew exactly. Thirty-one; seventeen of whom had made the maximum $2,500 individual contribution. Three of those had coerced colleagues and business associates into making similar donations. He didn't want to know whether those contributions were somehow reimbursed, contrary to current campaign finance regulations. Two had contributed $5,000 each to his political action committee, and nine had purchased $10,000-per-plate tickets for a fundraising dinner. "I'm off duty tonight."

"Well, then can you give me a quote about the upcoming Menendez vote."

"Like I said, I'm off duty."

Janice pouted slightly, but then made a pantomime of putting her invisible pen and pad away in her purse. "OK, then – I'm off duty also – and the rest of the night is off the record." She took a large sip from her scotch and smiled sweetly across the table. "Besides, I'm too busy putting the finishing touches on a really big story that's going to run in a couple of weeks, so I can't be bothered with small-time politicians."

"Who's small-time?" Jonathan interjected, trying to sound hurt. All three friends laughed together.

"Who's the target of your latest investigation, Ms. Stanton?" Frank asked in his best cable news anchor voice.

Janice smiled mischievously. "Nnn, nnn – I'm not at liberty to disclose that information, Mr. Elkhardt. You will just have to read it in *The Journal* when it hits the newsstands, like everyone else."

"Oh, now, surely you can share some bit of inside information with old friends?" Jonathan cajoled.

Janice's smirk broke into a full grin as she leaned forward across the tiny table and whispered to the two men. "Do you remember when we went to Riverside Church to hear a speech by the Reverend Abraham Hawkins?" Frank and Jonathan both nodded at the memory. "Well, it may turn out that Reverend Hawkins is not as squeaky clean as his reputation and his television show would have everyone believe."

Jonathan and Frank sat back. Frank whistled softly. "Wow," he mumbled, "that is some high-profile material."

"Shhh," Janice hushed him and slapped his shoulder. "Secret, remember? Not a word to anyone. OK?"

"OK," Frank immediately replied. "No problem. Good luck. I'll be looking for it."

Jonathan said nothing, but stared over Janice's head, into the crowd.

"Well, then," Frank rose from his seat. "I propose a toast. To old friends, and to old days that always seem to get better and better in retrospect as we get older."

"I'll drink to that," Jonathan said, standing and extending his drink toward the middle of the table. Janice rose as well, and clinked her glass lightly against Jonathan's and Frank's. They each drank deeply as the glee club started singing another song, long forgotten by most members of the class of '91 but which they all tried to mouth the words to as if they could never forget the old college tunes.

The three friends smiled at each other. "It's been too long," Jonathan said over the growing din of off-key singing.

"Too long," Frank agreed. "Let's make sure it's not as long between drinks together next time." Jonathan nodded, and wondered whether seeing either of them again soon would be advisable. His father certainly would not approve, but only if he knew. He didn't need to know. None of them did.

Their college days were twenty-five years ago. Who cared what happened so long ago? He knew better, but at that moment, he didn't give a damn. Perhaps it was partially the Johnny Walker talking. He was a senator. Nobody could take that away from him. He had made it at age thirty-seven – even younger than his father. He was his own man now. Perhaps he'd get another drink, he thought. There were other bars on a campus filled with class reunion parties, where he hadn't given limiting instructions to the bartenders.

"Just like old times," Jonathan said, and tilted back his glass.

Janice tossed back the rest of her scotch and asked Frank if he would get her a refill. "How about you, Jon?"

Jonathan smiled. The bartender wouldn't know that Frank was getting the drink for him. "Sure," he said, smiling at Frank as he dove into the teeming crowd in the general direction of Jonathan's good friend, Juan.

Janice now had Jonathan alone, but it was only a matter of time before someone else came up to glad-hand him. "Jon," she began quietly, making eye contact, "you know your political career has made you quite a topic in our story meetings lately." Jonathan frowned and furrowed his brow as he tried to look her in the eyes, but she turned slightly away. "Since I'm going to be in Washington, covering national politics, I'm wondering when the time might be right for me to write a story about you."

"What kind of story?"

"The true kind."

"How true is true?"

"Oh, I don't know. I've been doing some preliminary research, but I have a long way to go. Maybe you could give me a few private interviews – to make sure I have all the facts straight?"

Jonathan looked down at the light blue tablecloth, collecting his thoughts before he spoke again. When he looked up, Janice was staring defiantly, and Jonathan had put on a calm face. "Not every story needs to be told."

"I know. But some do," she stated calmly. "Remember, Jon, the truth will set you free."

"You know that's not true. Sometimes the truth can really fuck you over good. Is that what you want? You want to hurt me?"

"No," she whispered, reaching her hand toward him involuntarily, before snatching it back. "That's not the idea. I just want to get some inside access. You can understand that, right?"

"Are you asking for exclusive access?"

Janice dropped her eyes to the table. "Yes, I'd like to do a big story, and if you can give me some exclusive material – material that would make a good story – then we wouldn't have to talk about anything else. You can give me some new angles that haven't been fully explored. Like whether you're planning a run at the White House in 2020 if the Democrats keep the Presidency this year. I haven't made up my mind exactly what I want to write yet."

"Are you sure I can't talk you out of doing this? In the old days, I used to be able to change your mind," he softened his tone and folded his hands together on the table top, in a praying posture.

"Not about everything."

Jonathan sat back in his chair and said nothing else. Now it really was going to be a long night.

One hour later, Jonathan, Janice and Frank were among ten alumni squeezed into folding chairs at a round table with a large sky-blue balloon centerpiece, trying to figure out which salad fork went with which place setting. This was made more difficult by the number of cocktails each of the revelers had consumed before dinner.

"How is your father?" Janice inquired between bites of Caesar salad – just trying to initiate some conversation. "He must be very proud of you."

Jonathan blinked. How did she know he was thinking about his father? "Well, isn't that the primary goal of every son; to make his father proud?" There was just a tiny hint of sarcasm in his voice, but Frank picked up on it.

"You always were too hard on yourself, old chum," Frank pointed his salad fork in Jonathan's direction, nearly poking Janice's hair in the process. She ducked backwards to get out of the middle of the two friends. "I mean, *you* got into Columbia Law, while I got shipped out to Boston for three years."

"Ha!" Jonathan spat, actually projecting a small bit of crouton into his water glass. "If there were any real justice in the process, it would have been you at Columbia Law and I would have been at Fordham."

"You see, you sell yourself short. Your undergrad grades were decent – and who got a better LSAT score?"

"I did," Jonathan said with a wry smile, "but if you had half the private tutoring I did you would have blown me away."

"We'll never know, will we? But who gives a shit. You got in, and you got the great job right out of law school, and you made something out of it."

Jonathan sighed. "Are you really that naïve?"

Janice decided it was time to jump in, or the boys would monopolize the conversation for hours. "Yes, Jon, I believe he was, still is, and probably always will be. Frank is Pollyanna, and I sometimes wish I could share his ability to keep that optimism. But Frank, darling, you hardly need to pump up Jon's ego. It's not as if he could help going to work for Lord & Wall out of law school. It was his father's firm, although I'm not sure the senior senator ever actually worked a day in his life as a lawyer." She glanced at Jonathan and saw his confirming smirk.

"Keep going, Jan, I'm enjoying this," Frank goaded her.

"Alright, if you insist," Janice said with a wink. She plowed ahead, enjoying the dissertation on one of her favorite subjects. She had been working on a story about Jonathan Prescott III in her head for many years. "A few years of paying dues as an associate lawyer, and then young Jon moved to D.C. where he joined the lobbying arm of Schweitzer, Marks & Little. With daddy's name and connections, it wasn't long before Jon was the assistant campaign manager for Arthur Lee, then Speaker of the House. Apparently, Daddy didn't want Junior to be lost in his senatorial shadow, so he sent him to a different campaign – am I right?"

Jonathan was smiling broadly now, and nodded. "My father does have a very large shadow."

The rest of the guests around the table were all sitting forward, listening closely to the conversation involving their famous classmate. "As I was saying before that interruption," Janice continued, "the post for Speaker Lee was perhaps the cushiest job on Capitol Hill. Lee had been elected to ten terms from a district that was 90% registered Republicans. His opponent was a 29-year-old college professor with a pony tail who had never held public office. The Speaker was re-elected with a mere 93% of the vote."

"It was good experience!" Jonathan protested playfully.

"Our boy worked on another successful Republican campaign in '98. Then, in 2000, with George Bush 43 standing next to his father, Jonathan Prescott III was announced as the Republican candidate for the House from the 4th district of Connecticut – a district once represented by Jonathan Prescott, Jr. and a House seat held by Republicans for the past twenty years in a predominantly Democratic state. Also a House seat that became suddenly available when the incumbent representative unexpectedly announced his retirement only two weeks before the deadline for candidates to submit petitions to the State Board of Elections."

"A happy, but entirely innocent coincidence," Jonathan insisted vigorously, attacking a hard roll with his butter knife.

"Coincidentally, the same former representative immediately took a six-figure job with Schweitzer, Marks & Little."

"Quite a coincidence," Frank chided, while Jonathan sat in silence, rather enjoying the recitation of his career.

Janice looked around the table and smiled at the classmates who were giving her their full attention. She took a sip of red wine and then continued. "With no serious Republican challenger interested in taking on the son of the senior senator, and no time for the Democrats to organize a candidate once the seat became unexpectedly open, Representative Prescott breezed into the House. With George W. Bush in office, our boy was re-elected easily in 2002 and 2004. His resume in the House during a short tenure is impressive: co-sponsor of more than thirty bills that eventually became law, youngest member of the Republican Leadership Conference, and not a hint of scandal or controversy.

"Finally, with the 2006 mid-terms approaching, Jonathan Prescott, Jr. announced his retirement from the Senate – once again at the very last minute so there was little time for the Democrats to mount a bigger challenge to what was a potentially vulnerable seat. The Democratic National Committee was already pissed off because their preferred candidate was being challenged in the primary by a Wall Street tycoon who was trying to buy himself a senate seat by spending millions of his own dollars. The upstart ran on an anti-establishment platform and, after winning the primary, got little support from the national organization during the general election. Meanwhile, the Republicans had raised plenty for the Prescott campaign and had cleverly not included the designation of "Jr." in its fundraising materials. All the funds technically qualified as available for use by Jonathan Prescott III, who breezed to victory."

"Bravo, Barbara Walters," Jonathan said, clapping his hands and standing at his seat. "People might think you've been paying attention to my career."

"I'll be paying even more attention from now on, since I'll be coming to live with you." Janice smiled, but Jonathan's face turned to stone.

"Jan, don't joke like that. Somebody listening might get the wrong idea."

"What? Worried Gwen will come storming across the street and we'll have a nice cat fight?"

"I'd pay to watch that," Frank interjected, attempting to defuse the situation, but nobody laughed. "C'mon, you two, we're all grown-ups here – well, at least two of us."

"Yes," Janice said mischievously, "but which two?"

The other guests at the huge round dinner table were all listening to the senator and his friends. There was an awkward silence for a moment, before one of the wives asked Jonathan why his wife was not with him. It was the seventh time he had explained that his wife, Gwendolyn, who graduated from Barnard the same year he finished Columbia College, was across Broadway at her own class reunion dinner. Why was everyone so worried about his wife?

"So, what should I expect in D.C.?" Janice asked, changing the subject.

"Well, that depends on whether you get invited to the right parties."

"I'll make sure to clear my social engagements with you in advance," Janice smiled. "Maybe Gwen will get me an invitation to the big gala for the National Association of Mothers for Morality. Wouldn't that be a hoot?"

Jonathan frowned reproachfully. "Gwen does a tremendous amount of good work. That organization, and others she is active with, are trying to rebuild the tattered fabric of our society's morals."

"Oh, please," Janice retorted. "Lobbying for abstinence education instead of teaching teenage girls about birth control is regressive. And advocating against morning after pills and available condoms is just denying the reality of teenage sex. And trying to limit access to safe abortions is medieval."

Frank cut in before the conversation got too politicized. "Jan, I know Gwen truly enjoys her involvement in conservative organizations like that one. It's expected of her, and I understand that she is really a rising star. She was born to be a party planner."

Jonathan then came to his wife's defense again. "She is much more than a party planner. She makes speeches, and visits schools, and truly is an asset to this country. I'm quite proud of her."

"And you should be," Frank agreed quickly. "But I don't think she'll be inviting Janice to share the dais with her at a banquet any time soon."

"Well, maybe you'll take me out to lunch sometime, then," Janice suggested.

Jonathan frowned at her, furtively glancing around the table to see whether the other guests were again listening in, but they seemed to have gone back to their own conversations. "I don't think that would be a good idea, Janice. I'm a happily married man and a public figure, and being seen in private company with an attractive single woman might raise eyebrows."

"Ooooh," Janice cooed. "I'm so glad you still think I'm attractive."

"Oh, please," Jonathan said with disdain. "It's not always about you."

"No," Janice shot back. "Usually it's about you."

Frank jumped in again by rising from his chair and taking Janice by the arm. "Look, Jan, there's Stu from the old

Spectator staff. Wasn't he your managing editor? Let's go say hello." Janice reluctantly allowed herself to be led away, glancing back toward Jonathan, who was left momentarily alone.

Chapter 2

JONATHAN SAT ON AN AWKWARDLY uncomfortable sofa, doing what he hated most in life, and which he did less and less since his election to the Senate. He was waiting. These days, people waited for him. His father had taught him that you should not keep a more powerful visitor waiting – unless you wanted them angry for the meeting. Those less powerful than you, the elder Prescott had preached, must be kept waiting an appropriate amount of time, so they don't get an inflated impression of their own worth. They must see that they need to see you more than you need to see them. It rankled Jonathan that he was still, apparently, in the inferior position.

The darkly decorated foyer of Max Foster's Manhattan office featured high-backed wooden chairs and an overstuffed maroon leather sofa. The ornate Persian rug on the hardwood floor matched the sofa's color precisely, as did the cherry-wood legs of the marble-topped coffee table. The table lamps in the corners were heavily shaded, as if straining to prevent any light from reaching the ceiling.

Jonathan wondered, as he often did, why his campaign organizer's office had to be in Manhattan, rather than in Washington. He should get himself a Washington-based manager. He also should get himself a new chief of staff, to replace the toady whom Max had placed in his office. He knew Ed Edwards was essentially a spy for Max, but he also knew deep down that he wouldn't be replacing Ed. He needed the guy, and would not know where to go to find someone as efficient and effective – even if he was a spy. Maybe next term – after the next election. He would get through this cycle, and that would be the time to assert his independence from Max Foster. One more election, and then he would be in a more powerful position. His next campaign would be in between presidential election cycles, when incumbents always had a huge advantage. Then, in 2024 – no, he would not even think about it. Not yet.

As Jonathan sank deeper into the soft cushions, he struggled to lean forward and shift his weight so he could cross his legs. As he foundered on the red leather sea, he glanced to his left. His father was staring at him disapprovingly. He knew that look. He had seen it so often. The elder Senator Prescott was sitting ramrod straight. The chair had a maroon cushion, but the elder Prescott looked as if he would have preferred sitting directly on the hard wood. His back did not touch the rear of the chair. His feet were planted firmly on the floor. Although he had recently turned seventy-five, he looked ready to jump from his seat and go ten rounds with any challenger.

Senator Jonathan Prescott, Jr. was the dictionary definition of "distinguished." His hairline was receding slightly and graying around the temples, cut short and combed straight back from his face. His Brooks Brothers suit, Custom Shop monogrammed shirt with French cuffs, and silk tie were immaculate. His shoes reflected the dim light in the room like a mirror. His dark, penetrating eyes were fixed on his son; his lips pursed together.

Jonathan, tired of battling the sofa, stood up and straightened his suit jacket. He paced across the small waiting room and stood under an oil painting of a rotund businessman in a brown suit. The man in the painting could have been a real estate mogul, or a politician, or a mob boss. There was no plaque to explain his identity.

"Sit down, Son," Jonathan's father said in a hushed, but sharp voice. "You look like you're nervous. Never let the other guy think he has succeeded in making you nervous or anxious."

"Dad, we're waiting to see Max, not the Minority Whip."

Jonathan's father had an endless supply of maxims and "rules of engagement" that had served him well during a forty-year political career. He had begun imparting his political wisdom to his son at the age of ten, complete with occasional quizzes during car trips. For a few years, after he was elected to the House, Jonathan had tried to end the lessons, but his father had been ready for the gambit. "Son," he had said, "I've forgotten more about politics than you'll ever know. When I think you've learned enough, I'll stop talking. Until then, you'd best keep listening. Not much of a price to pay for all the help and support you get from me, I'd say."

"Help and support" was code for fundraising, campaign management, advertising coordination, research, PAC connections, and general string-pulling. A nasty editorial had once referred to Jonathan's father as his "political pimp." The Republican National Committee could do most of the same for him, even without his father's direct intervention, but the RNC would not want to alienate a man whose connections brought in millions each year. It would have been a huge risk for Jonathan to break away from his father. Max's private polls showed fully twenty percent of those who voted for him considered it a "critical factor" that he would be getting advice from his father – as if electing Jonathan really meant electing the old man again. His father was right, as always. Listening to the sage advice was worth the price, and the alternative was not worth the risk.

So, Jonathan waited for Max Foster, the money man. It was never entirely clear to Jonathan what The Foster Group,

LLC did, nor what Max's formal title or job was. TFG was listed as a public relations firm, but there were no publicly-traded companies that listed The Foster Group as their PR support arm. There were easily forty bright-eyed MBA-types working for the firm, but the senator never met with any of them directly; he only saw them sporadically scampering across the plush carpeting of the office corridors or shuttling folders in and out of conference rooms. Jonathan didn't need to know what the minions were doing.

As Jonathan stood under the anonymous portrait, considering whether he should follow his father's advice and sit down, Max's assistant sauntered into the waiting area. She could have been on a Vogue cover in a sleek but conservative red and black dress, tight enough to reveal a well-conditioned body, but not showing any cleavage. Her hair and makeup were perfect, as was her red lipstick. She smiled like a Universal Studios tour guide and said, "I'm so sorry to keep you waiting, Senators. Mr. Foster is ready for you. Please follow me." She turned smartly and strode away down the carpeted hallway. She led Jonathan and his father to a large conference room. Jonathan had been there before and had stopped being impressed by the wall of television monitors and all the multi-media equipment.

Max Foster walked deliberately into the room a few seconds after the Prescotts. He held out his thick hand and shook with each man briskly. He asked Jonathan how he was and then, without waiting for an answer, turned to the senior Senator Prescott.

"The polling is showing good maintenance with the core support groups, and increasing trends with independents and women." Jonathan sat down quietly in a chair on the opposite side of the polished wooden table. The truth was that Jonathan had little patience for poll numbers, support trends, and election projections, and both Max and his father knew it well. His presence at the meeting was almost a formality.

After ten minutes of polling data, Max switched to money matters. A PowerPoint presentation, projected on a twelve-foot wide screen covering most of one wall of the room, showed graphs and charts of contributions, investment growth estimates, and schedules for future fundraising. Jonathan was looking forward to having another six-year term. He had been exhausted by having to campaign for his re-election as a Representative every two years. As a senator, he had four – nearly five – years of being a lawmaker before he had to run again. But, here he was, back in Max's conference room talking about campaign financing for the 2018 election, which was well over two years away.

Jonathan sat up and took notice only once – when he saw the fundraising goal. Twenty million dollars; an amazing number. Where would it all come from? Were they raising money for a Senate re-election campaign, or for something else; something bigger? Then he looked at his father. His eyes were wide and focused. He was sitting forward in his chair, his hands on the table in front of him and gesturing at Max as they spoke.

Jonathan knew moments like these were mental orgasms for his father. Indeed, Jonathan speculated that managing his political career would keep him alive forever. He would always be there, in that room with Max, as long as Jonathan was a senator. Or in the office-that-should-not-be-named. Jonathan knew Max and his father were planning for it. Maneuvering, plotting, waiting for the right year, the right opportunity, the right incumbent or opponent. Jonathan was only forty-seven. He had twenty good political years ahead. There was time. 2020 was an outside possibility, depending on whether there was a Republican incumbent running. The senior Prescott could never stop planning. Jonathan and his father never said the "P" word aloud.

While Jonathan was considering all these issues, he stopped paying attention to Max and his father, until he was startled into awareness.

"Jonathan!" his father snapped, then softened his tone after his only child made eye contact. "Time to pay attention, Son."

"Sorry," came Jonathan's sheepish response. Once again, he felt like the inattentive student called out by the irascible professor.

Max started a new series of PowerPoint slides. Now the images were not dollars, contribution statistics, and campaign cost estimates, but issue points and position summaries. On the one hand, these were things he really did care about. On the other hand, he felt the familiar pang in his stomach. Was it guilt? Frustration? He hated being told what his positions should be. He wanted to exercise his own judgment. Of course, he needed to know all the facts first. That was a rationalization, and he knew it, but it helped ease the feeling.

"Now, Jonathan, the Randall Institute's report on you is terrific. Your core constituency will be very happy. They give you a one hundred percent voting record on taxes, religious issues, education, and family values. You're doing great. But the polling on this chart shows that the voters aren't getting the message." Max directed his laser pointer to a bar graph showing the opinions of probable voters in Connecticut, broken down by Republicans, Democrats, and Independents. The chart showed their impressions of Senator Prescott on the question of whether he was "doing a good job of controlling taxes and government spending." The question itself was loaded, Jonathan thought, but he was puzzled by the fact that only 72% of registered Republicans rated him "excellent" on this question. How could anyone argue that he hadn't voted correctly on these issues?

"What this tells us," Max looked Jonathan right in the eye and pointed a finger at the screen, "is that you are not speaking out enough. Your speeches and social media posts are not letting the people know what you stand for and how you are voting on the issues. We need to do a better job there. And here," Max changed the slide. This one showed the results of a poll question on whether the senator was "doing a good job of protecting the rights of the unborn." Another loaded question. Here, 62% of registered Republicans rated him "excellent," but Jonathan's attention was pulled to the bar highlighted in red on the slide – 28% responded "don't know" to this question. Democrats, on the other hand, rated him "unsatisfactory" by 80% to 20%. No surprise there.

"Again, Jonathan," Max spoke earnestly, "the message is not getting out. You are voting correctly, but the people are not hearing the message from you, or from the media, and so they don't know what a great job you're doing. You need to speak out more on this issue. You need to get it out to your Twitter followers. It's vital to maintaining the core conservative voters."

"We've discussed this before," Jonathan replied evenly. "I don't want to unnecessarily alienate the liberal voters and Independents on this. If the literature and targeted email and media releases on this put the word out, then fine, but I do not want to make that issue a keynote in my speeches or my social media messages. The base who are inclined to vote on those kinds of one-note issues aren't going to go over to the other side. I'll answer the questions, but why emphasize that point?"

"Son, you don't want to look weak on abortion." The elder Prescott spoke with conviction. "This is a national issue. It's important to maintain an exemplary record."

"My record is one hundred percent, I'm told," Jonathan shot back a bit more emphatically than he had intended. "I mean," and he lowered his tone, "my voting record is fine. There is nothing there that raises any questions. Nothing anyone can use against me."

"Yes – but you need to be strong, not just right."

"What's 'right' anyway?" Jonathan threw out the question like a college student in a seminar.

"Jon!" his father sat bolt upright and stared at his son with piercing eyes. "Don't start getting queer on me."

"Dad, I hate that word, please." Jonathan spoke softly and looked down at the table, rather than meeting his father's eyes.

"Screw the word," his father pounded on the table, causing a glass of water to spill onto the polished wood. "I'm talking about a principle here! I know you have some liberal friends who like to worm into your head, Son, but there are some issues you cannot be soft on, and this is the most important. This is what defines a conservative these days. You cannot lose our core."

"Can't you just have Bailey say it for me?" Jonathan spat out.

Max pursed his lips slightly before responding. "Son, what Bryan Bailey says on his radio show helps establish the issues and solidify the support in our constituency groups, but unless you want to go on his show and play paddy-cake with him for a half hour, you need to speak with your own voice on this."

Jonathan stood up and put his palms on the back of a black leather chair to steady himself. His father had taught him the trick of moving, standing, or taking a drink of water while composing his thoughts at a critical time. "The conservative core voters are going to vote for me regardless, no matter what I say on abortion, because the alternative is to vote for the Democrat, so I continue to question why I should focus on making it more certain that those voters are going to vote for me, at the risk of losing out on other voters who might vote for me, but who will be less likely to vote for me if I emphasize the abortion issue."

There was a tense silence for several seconds. Max was waiting for one of the Prescotts to speak. Jonathan did. "Like I said, my voting record is one hundred percent, and it's going to stay that way. Don't worry, Dad. But don't expect me to go out and proselytize."

The elder Prescott scowled, but said nothing further on the subject. Max jumped in to ease the tension by moving to the next slide. "Here are the poll results on prayer in school." And the group moved on down the list of issues. Jonathan had pledged support for a Constitutional amendment allowing prayer in school. There was no chance the amendment would ever happen, but it was good to support it just the same. It looked good to the constituency.

"Now, let's talk about Menendez." Max looked apprehensively at Jonathan, then at his father. He knew this was going to be a problem, so he put it in the middle of the deck. That way he'd have something to move on to if things got heated.

"I have said nothing about Menendez," Jonathan kept his voice even as he looked at his father.

This time it was the senior Prescott's turn to use the water glass. He set it down gently, barely making a sound, then spoke in a similarly even tone. "You're going to have to take a position eventually, Son. The vote won't get delayed forever."

"I know. I'm having some discussions behind the scenes. My opinion hasn't changed on the merits. It's a terrible precedent to set. We have the majority now, but what about when that changes, and it will change. If we do this, the next time we have a Republican president and a Democratically controlled senate, we will get nobody confirmed. This is a nuclear missile and pushing that button is an act we can't reverse. But, I understand it's a party issue. If my vote is needed, I understand what I'm expected to do."

"Son, it's the Supreme Court. These seats don't come up often."

"Sure, but what if our guy doesn't win in November? Huh? Then they'll get their guy and we will have fired the missile for nothing. It's a nuke. It's a mistake. You know it as well as I."

"The party is behind this one. It's vital to keep this liberal off the Court. If we allow Scalia's seat to go to a liberal judge we will never get *Roe v. Wade* reversed. The people are behind it. The polling shows that. There's not a lot of room for discussion."

"Like hell there's not!" Jonathan let go of his chair back and waved his arms in the direction of the video screen. "At some point, I have to exercise some independent judgment. I'm inclined to vote in favor of allowing hearings. If we decide to reject him on his merits when he comes up for a full vote, then so be it. Hiding behind the procedural veil here isn't fooling anyone. The long-term consequences will be the same. Maybe, during hearings, information will come out that will give us a more principled basis to reject him. Then, maybe it will be too close to the election to start considering a different nominee."

Jonathan's father rose from his chair and began pacing. "We've been through this. There are three Republicans in vulnerable seats who don't need the heat of having to vote against a Hispanic judge. You know that. It could result in us losing the senate."

"And we think the voters are so easily swayed that those senators, who vote to block consideration, will get off the hook?"

Max jumped in. "Actually, Jonathan, our research does support that conclusion."

Jonathan fumed, but remained under control. "I already told you. I understand my obligations to the party. If I can't convince my colleagues, then I'll face it. Until then, I see no point in arguing about it further."

Max looked from one Prescott to the other. "Let's move on, shall we?" Both Prescotts nodded. They reviewed Jonathan's position on other key issues and the poll numbers for each. Jonathan was opposed to governmental taking of private property for private development, which seemed to be an easy call. He was opposed to increases in property taxes, which was an entirely local and state issue, not a federal issue, but Max felt it important for the senator to be on the correct side of the issue just the same. He was opposed to gay marriage, although there were no pending bills dealing with the issue after the Supreme Court settled the issue a year earlier. Jonathan wondered to himself if he was simply opposed to everything and not really "for" anything.

The poll results included seventeen key issues. They constituted the barometer of the conservative Republican platform. Some of the issues had little or no immediate impact on upcoming senate votes. Jonathan knew they were calculated to make sure he was properly positioned on "national" issues for the future.

Max finally wrapped up the meeting after nearly three hours. "All the summaries are in the briefing book, Jonathan." Max handed over a thick three-ring binder with neatly printed tabs separating each issue section. "Upcoming votes are flagged with yellow stickers. I've included analysis of expected amendments. If anything unexpected comes up, the staff will brief you as you go. I'll send copies to Harriett and Donna so we can make sure you're in Washington for the key votes."

Jonathan rarely knew his schedule more than a day in advance. Often, it wasn't until he was having breakfast and looked at his daily scheduling memo that he knew where he was going to be for lunch. It made his head swim. Thank God for all his advisors and schedulers and aides. He had a staff of twelve, which was above average for a senator. His father had managed with six. This sometimes annoyed Jonathan, but he told himself that times were more complicated than when his father was in Washington. The critical members of the team were Harriett, his personal secretary, and Donna, his press secretary. Harriett had been picked by Max, but Jonathan had no thoughts of replacing her. She was a miracle worker. Jonathan had picked Donna himself, although he could not recall whether she had been recommended by one of Max's people. It didn't matter; she was the most loyal and efficient staffer he had. Between Harriett and Donna, Jonathan never missed a meeting or a vote.

When the meeting finally broke up, Jonathan pulled Max aside near the marble-and-glass bar lining one side of the conference room, now littered with discarded glassware and melted ice cubes. "Max, I know you have a relationship with the Reverend Abraham Hawkins, right?"

"Yes," Max said slowly, wondering about the sudden introduction of this subject.

"Well, I think you'll want to know that *The Wall Street Journal* is getting ready to run a significant story about the reverend, and I don't think it's likely to be flattering."

"Really?" Max raised his eyebrows and bent closer to Jonathan. "How do you know this?"

Jonathan turned his head and looked toward his father, who was waiting by the door, looking impatient. "I'd rather not say, specifically, Max. Just trust me; it's a reliable source." Max nodded and walked away.

Jonathan and his father finally exited Max's building and got into their waiting black Town Car. Jonathan never worried about how the driver was always able to be right outside the door just at the right time, but he appreciated it. He loosened his tie and sat back against the leather seat. He was sure that lunch would be the next stop, and he really didn't care where, or with whom. He was tired, and closed his eyes for a quick nap, while his father selected a newspaper from a group neatly arrayed in a pouch attached to the seat back behind the driver.

Upstairs, Max arranged his notes on the meeting and entered a few comments onto a legal pad emblazoned with The Foster Group logo. His scribble was legible only to himself and his personal secretary, which was fine with Max. The bullet points were:

- On track – has his voting instructions. Don't expect any deviation from policy.
- Still a little soft on abortion.
- Have his father speak to him about Menendez.

Max buzzed for his secretary, who efficiently came in and scooped up all the binders and papers. She walked ahead of Max, out of his office and down the hallway to an unmarked door next to a water cooler. She keyed in a four-digit code on a keypad above the knob and waited for a click. Inside, Max placed his thumb on a scanner mounted on the wall and keyed in a ten-digit code on another keypad. A large metal door sprang ajar and Max's secretary walked in. Max returned to his office. The files would be neatly stored away in the confidential vault. Every night, Max closed the vault and set the lock. He trusted his secretary. Stella had been with him for fifteen years, and she received an annual bonus for her loyal service. The vault code was listed in Max's will, tucked away in his lawyer's office in case he was dead or incapacitated. Nobody else knew the code. The information was secure. That was what Max was all about; security and confidentiality – the bedrock of politics.

Chapter 3

SWEAT POURED OFF the tall, thin Black man's face like a small forward in the fourth quarter of an NBA playoff game, dripping to the polished hardwood floor in a procession of tiny splashes. Occasionally, he reached into his suit jacket for a white silk handkerchief and dabbed at his nose to avoid having a drop hanging off the end, which would spoil the next camera close-up. He was always careful to dab and not wipe, lest he smear his make-up. His powder-blue silk shirt would be sent to the cleaners after the show. The suit jacket, hand tailored in London, fully disguised the moist shadows under his arms, while the visible stains around his neck only emphasized his zeal.

Abraham Hawkins slammed his open palm on the solid oak podium and threw his head back violently as he shouted "Amen!" Perspiration from his flowing black hair exploded in a cascade picked up by the camera stage right. The spray was silhouetted against the bright stage lights – tiny streamers of moisture slowly bending to the force of gravity and descending into the darkness like the wisps of fading fireworks. Hawkins left his head in full back tilt position for a solid ten seconds, posing with his left hand outstretched toward the audience and his right still planted on the lectern.

You never know when someone in the audience was trying to get a snapshot.

He had finished his scheduled twenty-two minute sermon in nineteen minutes and forty-five seconds. Jimmy Abrams, the director in the studio perched high above the auditorium, had spoken into Hawkins' earpiece ten minutes earlier to let him know the show was running a minute-twenty over schedule and he needed to save at least thirty seconds at the end for a fundraising pitch that had been added at the last minute. Cutting two-and-a-half minutes off the sermon on the fly was a challenge, and he was pleased with himself when Jimmy's voice in his left ear confirmed that he had just enough time left to wrap up.

The preacher slowly raised his head and surveyed the seventy-three pre-screened supplicants of the First Church of the Modern Christ who had applied for free tickets to the taping. Each had waited a minimum of three months for the chance to worship with the famous reverend live and in person. Also in attendance were seven VIP guests who had ponied up one thousand dollars each for the special privilege of sitting in the front row. They were all in full rapture. Shouts of "Amen!" and "Praise Jesus" rang out randomly along with applause and whistles of satisfaction. It had been a good show.

Jimmy's voice crackled in Abraham's ear, "And we're in commercial. Ninety seconds." Out of nowhere, six people appeared on the stage, surrounding Hawkins in an instant. His hair was toweled off but not completely dried, his tie straightened, his brow, face, and neck mopped and powdered. He accepted a small bottle of water and downed it in one sustained swig.

Meanwhile, the audience handler was waving his arms and giving instructions to the crowd about what they were expected to do when the "on air" light came back on, and giving instructions for their behavior at the end of the show, when the reverend would be coming down into the congregation. Nobody was permitted to leave their seat, he told them, unless touched by Hawkins' hand first. No exceptions. Anyone seen leaving their seat without invitation would be intercepted by security. There had been a few problems in the past with unruly members of the public who had managed to infiltrate the live studio audience. Everyone nodded and smiled, happy for the privilege of being in the live presence of their hero, even if not permitted to touch the hem of his garment.

Hawkins muttered into his microphone, "Are we still off?" After confirming with Jimmy that he still had fifteen seconds, he snapped, "Can you tell Clarence to turn up the damned air conditioning!"

Jimmy did not reply except to count down to the end of commercial. "Four, three, two . . ."

When the lights went up, Hawkins broke into a huge smile and waved to the wild applause of the audience. He finished up with an impassioned plea to the television audience for increased donations to the church, which was in the process of constructing a new building in rural Alabama that would serve as both local church and preschool for needy families. Jimmy seamlessly cut the picture from Hawkins' face to the audience, where collection plates were being passed down the rows of seats, already overflowing with cash and a few checks. The plates had been nearly full when they were handed out, but the viewers at home didn't need to know such details. As the shot cut to a close-up of Hawkins' face, a web address and toll-free number scrolled across the bottom of the screen.

"You can help those less fortunate than yourself," he intoned. "Your generosity will not go unnoticed. God will know. You will know. You can go to sleep tonight knowing *you* are responsible for a poor child learning to read, and a community that desperately needs the loving hand of the LORD will have a place to worship in peace and safety. You must change your selfish ways. You must abandon your insincerity and your sins. You must slow your descent into Hell and the damnation of your eternal soul. Don't worry, my children. There is hope for you – if you will just look inside yourselves and find a penny, a nickel, a dollar. One dollar per day for one month is thirty dollars. Call right now, 1-800-FORGIVE and pledge $30 per month – this month and every month. It's not hard, my children. This is less than you spend on coffee and donuts every day. You can use that same Visa, MasterCard, or Discover you use to buy the Devil's goods you love so much. Or, you can give the volunteer disciple on the phone your checking account number and GOD will take the money from your account every month – a direct deposit into the eternal offering plate. Or you can visit our website, which is listed on the bottom of the screen. You will find that when you help others you sleep better at night, you feel better about yourself, and your heart will be lighter, your stress reduced, and you will start to make the slow, steady, arduous climb up that stairway to Heaven."

Shouts of "AMEN!" cascaded from the crowd.

"You are all angels. Jesus will be with each and every one of you. Good night, and God bless you."

Jimmy gave the cue for the choir to start singing the closing hymn. Flashing lights above the stage facing the audience blinked "AMEN!" Jimmy barked out, "Roll credits." The reverend slowly descended the six steps from the stage into the audience pit, where he shook hands and exchange hugs with his congregation. The big spenders each got a personal greeting. The production crew, as instructed, had also seated the best-looking young ladies in the front row, which was where Hawkins spent most of his post-show time.

He lingered over a particularly comely young woman in a thigh-high dress whose crossed legs had attracted his attention during the broadcast. He gave her an extended hug, his mouth near to her right ear, before waving to the rest of his live flock and slipping off stage right beyond a door marked "no admittance" into the corridor leading to his dressing room. As he walked, he shed his suit jacket, disconnected the small microphone clipped to his tie from its battery pack affixed to the back of his belt, and snapped both pieces of equipment neatly off their supports, handing them to an intern who appeared next to him and who accepted the gifts from the great preacher with a bow.

On his way down the hallway, he stopped for a moment to peek into the telephone room, where sixteen volunteers were all talking earnestly into their headsets. A bank of blinking lights on a master console held a stockpile of others on hold waiting to speak to a representative of the Church, their credit cards no doubt close at hand. He smiled and waved at the operators, who all waved back without interrupting their patter. His viewing audience gave more money over the phone than via the internet. Hawkins knew that needed to change soon, but for now, it was the phones that brought in the cash.

In his dressing room, Hawkins peeled off his sweat-soaked shirt, leaving him in a tank-style t-shirt and his suit pants, supported by red silk suspenders. He rolled his head from side to side, taking deep breaths and rotating his shoulder blades, trying to release all the tension of the last hour, his eyes closed in blissful solitude. He loved this room; his sanctuary. No one was allowed in the dressing room or the outer antechamber before or after the service. This was a rule drilled into the staff when they were first hired. Anyone so much as seen hanging around in the hallway outside the exterior door was summarily terminated, which had happened more than once – or so the new hires were told.

The sole exception to "the Golden Rule," as it was known among the employees, was Lucille, the reverend's personal assistant. Lucille was a very large black woman with a thick southern accent worthy of the original cast of *Gone with the Wind*. Lucille came and went as she pleased, and only people with Lucille's personal escort were permitted to approach the sanctuary.

The reverend opened a glass cabinet and extracted a crystal tumbler and a carafe of amber liquid, from which he poured a generous serving. As he sipped his seventeen-year-old Balvenie, he glanced at his watch. 4:45 p.m. He sat down in a well-padded armchair next to a small round table and picked up the telephone. He called his stock broker and berated him for being slow on the sell button on a particular stock that cost him $10,000. Then he called his lawyer to get an update on a land purchase, and demanded that he lean harder on the local zoning board.

"Tell them they may hear their names mentioned in my next televised sermon, closely linked to the Devil if they continue to block the building of this Church's regional headquarters." The lawyer suggested that if the building actually contained a small chapel, they would have more leverage since it would technically be a place of worship. They discussed the extra $100,000 that the chapel would add to the construction cost and the loss of 2,400 square feet of office space, but concluded it was not too much to sacrifice if it helped get the zoning permits – God willing.

He then called Max Foster's office and confirmed that, per Max's instructions, his sermon to the television flock included subtle opposition to pending legislation providing greater protection for gays and lesbians against discrimination in employment and housing. He had urged his followers to contact their congressmen, and especially mentioned two Democrats in vulnerable seats. He didn't ask whether either of those congressmen actually supported the pending bill. Max had mentioned them and noted that they were politically vulnerable in the next election. It would be fine if his tele-congregants believed that the congressmen supported the bill. It was supported by the Democratic National Committee, so any Democrat could fairly be associated with it.

If the congressmen ultimately voted against the bill, then Max's Machine would get the votes it wanted, and it would paint the congressmen as flip-floppers for changing their positions under pressure from the religious right. If they voted for the bill, then the message would be that the reverend was right and they should be damned to Hell. Either way, they would become more vulnerable. Max mentioned the names of the Republican candidates the Machine expected to put up for the seats, and Hawkins made a note on a small pad enclosed in a gold-leaf cover for future reference.

Max asked if Hawkins' people had tracked down the source of the leaks leading to the as yet unpublished piece in *The Wall Street Journal*, and the reverend said they had, indeed, made some headway, but that there was still work left to do.

After thirty minutes on the phone, there was a knock on the dressing room door. Hawkins downed the last swallow of scotch, enjoying the smooth finish on his experienced tongue, placed the empty glass in a porcelain sink and popped an Altoid into his mouth before opening the door. There, in the soft dressing room light, stood the girl with the long legs from the front row. She told him her soul was in need of healing. Hawkins glanced over her shoulder at Lucille's plump face and received a small nod, which meant Lucille had briefed the woman on the etiquette of a private meeting with the reverend.

It also meant that Lucille had confirmed her background check, and obtained a signed statement that she had come voluntarily to the reverend for counseling about a personal matter and that she received advice during a fifteen-minute meeting, during which the reverend was gracious and polite and never touched her except to shake her hand when she left. He invited her in, closed the door, and laid his left hand on her head.

"Are you willing to repent?"

"Yes"

"Are you ready to do God's will?"

"Yes!"

"Are you willing to supplicate yourself and give yourself fully and completely to GOD?"

"YES!"

He put gentle pressure on her head, pushing her slowly to her knees. He looked up at the small, high-intensity lighting embedded in the ceiling, shining down on him like electric sunbeams. He smiled and took in a deep breath, spreading his arms out to his side to form a cross.

Chapter 4

December, 1988

A BLUISH-GRAY CURL OF SMOKE drifted up from the small flame at the tip of the flag. As the red stripe melted into the white, a cheer arose from the small band of protesters perched precariously along the stone pedestal on which sat the venerable statue of Alma Mater, her arms outstretched and the green oxidized bronze of her robes flowing down toward the plaza. One of the young men kept himself from falling off by hanging on to her bronze breast as he waved a clenched fist at the swirl of bodies below. The crowd surged forward, epithets and curses filling the crisp December air. Even by Columbia University standards, this was a good show for a Thursday afternoon.

Frank Elkhardt stood on the marble-and-brass pedestal in the center of the main campus quad and watched the scene unfold. Across the plaza, the white dome of Low Memorial Library rose above a wide cascade of marble steps, which normally would be dotted with clumps of students lounging or reading. At the foot of the steps an Italian-modeled plaza spread out, forming a wide open space used as seating during commencement ceremonies. The bricks of the plaza, which formed an intricate pattern of rust-red and pale white around twin fountains with phallic spouts, were currently obliterated by the mass of people churning in the morning sun. The fifty-three steps leading up to the Corinthian columns guarding the building were similarly covered with humanity like a bivouac of ants. And in the center of the sea of faces stood the calm figure of Alma Mater, who had certainly seen worse during the tumultuous Vietnam demonstrations of the late 60s. But it had been a while.

The spot where Frank stood was still referred to as "the Sundial" despite not serving that purpose for more than forty years. The University had removed the cracked marble globe that served as nature's calendar in the middle of College Walk – a gift from the class of 1885. Frank's hands were dug deep into the pockets of his New York Mets jacket, which was clearly not warm enough for the winter chill. His head was exposed to the cold, save for a pair of black ear muffs bisecting his strawberry-blond curls. His cheeks were flushed with color, both from the cold and from the excitement of the moment, and contrasted with his steel-blue eyes, which were transfixed by the spectacle. He stood on tip toes, straining to get a better look at what was happening on the library steps, where the center of the demonstration had taken form.

"Come on, Jon," he said excitedly, the vapor from his breath visible in front of his face as he spoke. "We're missing it!"

Jonathan Eugene Prescott III, fellow sophomore and Frank's friend and freshman roommate, stood below Frank on the cobbled stones of the plaza. His hands hung limply at his side, clothed in fur-lined leather gloves. His mohair pea coat fell almost to his feet, a dark brown that was almost black, accented by a white-and-grey scarf wrapped fashionably around his neck and tucked into the front of the overcoat. His tawny hair waved slightly in the wind as he stared forward at the surreal scene.

The demonstration had started out as a rather dull peace rally, sponsored by some recently formed group calling itself "Friends of Democracy." The banal speeches and signs bearing hastily inscribed peace signs and anti-war slogans – "Keep U.S. out of War" and so forth – would not have drawn much attention if they had been left alone.

But the Young Republicans just couldn't stay away. A group of fifteen or twenty college men – all with very short haircuts, Frank observed – had marched onto the plaza, bearing a rather large American flag. They elbowed their way through the crowd and mounted Alma Mater, draping the flag around her sturdy bronze shoulders. Then they broke into an awful rendition of "The Star-Spangled Banner," although nobody could hear it. The anti-war group was peppered with socialists and even anarchists who were imported to boost the turnout, and who immediately turned ugly and started throwing anything that was handy at the counter-demonstrators.

As garbage rained on poor Alma, the counter-demonstrators started yelling obscenities, and the anti-war crowd started to assault the little fortress that the flag-wavers had formed around the statue.

In the mêlée, someone produced a lighter and ignited the tip of the flag, which was apparently made of polyester or some other synthetic, fabric which both burned easily and melted at the same time. Now the anti-war group fragmented, as those who were against the prospect of a future draft, but not so zealous about it that they would stand by and watch someone burn the American flag, shoved and pushed at the more radical factions in the group. The Young Republicans tried to douse the flames as pockets of fist fights broke out between the demonstrators and the counter-demonstrators, and between the radical factions and the Columbia students who had turned out for the event, but who didn't fancy these interlopers turning their campus into Tehran.

"Look at them," Jonathan muttered, shaking his head in disgust. "The liberals can't see the forest for the trees, as usual."

"Don't lump them all together as liberals," Frank shot back, in a voice harsher than he intended. He turned his attention away from the demonstration for a moment and toward his friend. "I mean, I don't support burning the flag, no matter what the cause. Don't put me in with those lunatics."

"If you mean that, then don't just stand there gawking – do something to show it." With that calmly delivered line, Jonathan started walking, almost marching, toward the milling throng in the direction of Alma Mater. Frank jumped down from the Sundial and fell into step, not really sure what Jonathan had in mind, but unwilling to miss any more of the excitement. When they reached the edge of the crowd, they each started elbowing through, which was a simple process at the outskirts, but became increasingly difficult as they neared the center of the mass.

Jonathan shouted over the cacophony, "Meet me behind Alma Mater," and waved a gloved hand in that direction. Frank waved and yelled back, not that Jonathan could hear. The noise was deafening. A group at the base of the steps was chanting something about war, while the rest of the crowd generally grunted and screamed at each other. Frank was carried to the right by the tide of people, but he kept fighting the current, trying to get back on course toward the statue.

Just then, Frank felt a wet slap across his face, and lurched backwards. He blinked and saw a young woman, wearing a red beret and scarf, staring up at him with blazing dark eyes. "You don't know shit!" she screamed. "You elitist pig! You and your snotty college-boyfriends! What the hell do you know about what's really going on in the world?"

Frank opened his mouth to say something, but instead ducked the girl's next swing and pushed her aside, moving away in the direction of his goal. He smiled wryly to himself, thinking that on a normal day on the steps of the library, he and red beret probably could have had an interesting conversation about the merits of socialism, the stratification of the social classes in America, and the potential social and political solutions to the problem. That kind of thing was routine banter on warm spring evenings on campus – but generally was not accompanied by fisticuffs.

Frank continued to swim through the sea of people like a salmon fighting the current of a mountain stream, not knowing exactly what he was going to do when he got there, but driven to succeed. He was exhilarated by the moment. As he got closer to the statue, he could smell the acrid smoke from the partially burnt flag, which had been torn by the crowd using it for tug-of-war.

"Commie bastard!" he heard one man shout.

"War monger!" came the reply.

"Oh, yeah? Well you like it fine when I go die fighting for your freedom, don't you, asshole?"

"That's right – you go kill some babies and rape some women and be a hero, dickwad!"

Such eloquent dialogue was likely not uttered at Columbia by Alexander Hamilton and John Jay. Of course, Jonathan mused, those founding fathers would never have been on these steps, which were not built until a full hundred years after the first classes graduated from King's College, as it was then known. Odd, he thought, that here in this near-brawl he would be thinking about Columbia history, as taught to every incoming freshman during orientation week.

It seemed like a lifetime ago, although it was only seventeen months since he had arrived in New York to fulfill a dream of attending an Ivy League college. Sure, the classes and studying and atmosphere had been great. But this! This, was what it was all about. He was not yet twenty years old, and felt like all the problems of the world were his to solve. Now he was part of something – not just debating socio-economic theory with other young future leaders, but actually doing something. These thoughts rolled through his head as he continued to push through the roiling sea of increasingly unruly demonstrators.

As he worked his way higher up the steps to a point beyond where Alma sat, still tranquil amidst the turmoil around her, the crowd thinned out and Frank was able to move toward the central cauldron of activity with less resistance. He saw Jonathan, standing several steps above the statue, pointing a finger at someone below him and shouting words Frank could not hear over the din. Frank yelled and waved, but couldn't get his friend's attention. Finally, when Frank was only six feet away, Jonathan turned and acknowledged Frank for a moment, before turning his attention back to where it had been.

"Your grandfather probably fought in World War II so you and your snot-nosed friends could be here today."

Frank couldn't hear the reply, but he could see Jonathan getting genuinely agitated, which was rare. Jonathan generally put up a calm exterior, as if he were above the fray. Frank didn't hold it against Jonathan that he acted like he was better than everyone else. Given his family and his upbringing, it would have been hard not to be a conceited ass at least some of the time. But this was a side of Jonathan Frank had not seen before, despite being roommates during freshman year and still living together in separate rooms in the same suite as sophomores. Jonathan's face was red, and there were wrinkles along the side of his eyes. A deep blue vein bulged and throbbed at his temple and his neck tendons stood out, straining against his scarf. He was pointing and thrusting his arm in the direction of his adversary.

Jonathan took a step down as the other man stepped up. They were two steps apart now. The object of Jonathan's wrath looked to be another student based on his apparent age. He had long brown hair tied back in a ponytail, which flowed out from under a maroon knit hat. Frank didn't recognize him. There were students at the rally from NYU and Hunter College, as well as others who came from the surrounding boroughs of New York, so the guy could have been from anywhere. He stuck out a finger in Jonathan's direction and yelled something that Frank couldn't make out. Then he lunged forward and shoved Jonathan in the chest with both hands. The motion caused the attacker to lose his balance on the steps and fall forward, as Jonathan fell back, but into the people standing behind him. Jonathan regained his balance and jumped down a step, landing with both feet full on the other man's back.

Maroon Cap emitted a loud grunt, but arched his back and tried to get up, supporting himself on his elbows and causing Jonathan to lose his balance and fall off to the left, away from Frank. Maroon Cap was now on his feet and swung at Jonathan with a roundhouse right hand, which landed on Jonathan's shoulder as he turned away from the blow.

Frank wasted no time leaping into the fracas. He stepped over someone else who had fallen on the steps and dove onto Maroon Cap's back. Surprised by the blind-side attack, the man fell over, with Frank on top of him. Jonathan wasted no time planting a solid kick to the man's side with his thick brown Bass loafers. The man tried to get up again, but Frank was straddling him and holding him down. Frank's heart was pounding so hard that he could hear little else in his ears. Jonathan shouted "Nice shot," and someone else let out a scream.

The tone and pitch of the crowd's buzz changed noticeably and suddenly. Frank heard a shrill whistle, then another blast, as people around him screamed louder and scrambled away from Alma. The counter-demonstrators were still hanging from the statue, waving the tatters of their flag. The police had arrived, some mounted on horseback, along with campus security.

"Crap," Jonathan exclaimed, looking at Frank with fear in his eyes. "Let's get the hell out of here." Jonathan turned and started to scuttle along with the rest of the crowd in the direction of the Broadway side of the steps. Frank got off Maroon Cap and started after Jonathan, but the man grabbed his ankle and pulled him down.

"Jon!" Frank shouted. Jonathan turned and saw Frank prone on the step. Maroon Cap was getting up. Jonathan turned and came back to Frank's aid, holding up a clenched fist menacingly. Maroon Cap was slightly smaller than Jonathan, but stood his ground. Frank scrambled to his feet in time to see Jonathan and Maroon Cap lock arms as each tried to grab the other. They stood, clenched, like two wrestlers, each trying for the take-down. Frank directed a kick at Maroon Cap's knee and delivered a glancing blow, which was enough to throw off his balance and send him falling, with Jonathan along for the ride, down the steps toward the back of Alma's pedestal.

They fell in a heap, and before either could get to his feet, two cops appeared from the side of the statue. One cop grabbed each of them and pulled them apart, then twisted the arms of each man behind their backs. "Break it up, boys," the cop holding Jonathan grunted, as he reached for a pair of plastic riot-control handcuffs and proceeded to bind Jonathan's wrists.

Frank vaulted down the steps, yelling "Hey, let him go! He didn't start anything. That guy swung at him, and tackled me." Frank looked into the face of the officer, which showed not the slightest interest in what he was saying. "Don't you understand?" Frank persisted, "You have to let Jonathan go."

The officer stared at Frank for a moment, then reached out and grabbed the top of his left shoulder, spun him around, and pushed him up against the back of Alma, planting a knee into the small of his back. Frank winced and cried out, "Hey!" but got no response. He felt his wrist encircled by a set of cuffs, which burned against his skin as they snapped tightly. "What the hell do you think you're doing?" Frank called out over his shoulder toward the officer.

"I'm busting your sorry ass," was the curt reply. "Move it!" The officer gestured down the steps to both of the handcuffed students.

"Man," Frank moaned, "do you believe this?" Frank then noticed Jonathan's face, which was ashen. "Hey, man, don't worry; I'm sure they won't charge us with anything. C'mon, badge of honor – arrested at an anti-war rally. Cool!" Frank was flushed with excitement, even as the cop pushed him forward down the steps toward other officers waiting at the bottom in the plaza, waiving at demonstrators who were disbursing. Frank saw one of the counter-demonstrators, the remnants of his flag protruding from his coat, sitting on the ground with his hands behind his back. Frank recognized him as Collin McDermott from Literature Humanities class, and nodded. Collin nodded back, smiling through a puffy lower lip, dripping blood from a small cut.

"Relax, man," Frank said in Jonathan's direction. "No big deal, right?"

"Right," Jonathan managed unconvincingly. "Unless my father finds out about this."

Chapter 5

THE STREETS OF NEW YORK CITY teem with people at all hours of the day and night. On a hot, muggy summer night, after the lights on the Empire State Building go out, the sounds of hurrying footsteps are still heard between the honking cabs and squealing tires. Hundreds – even thousands – of nameless people meander along the sidewalks and streets. In many ways, it's the most anonymous place on Earth.

Senator Jonathan Prescott III strolled through this labyrinth of humanity, stepping easily past a sleeping homeless man in front of the side door to an unmarked building, although he had no idea where he was going. This felt more like home to him than New Greenwich. Jonathan felt comfortable here.

"Just for a walk," he had told his security chief, Ramon Escavera. "Around the block a few times; alone. To give me a chance to think." He had consented to taking a cell phone in lieu of a personal escort. The line was open, and Ramon was listening through an earpiece. All Escavera heard from the phone was the clop of Jonathan's wing tips on the sidewalk and the muffled swish of his jacket pocket brushing against the microphone. Escavera was focused on the sports section of the *Post*. Matt Harvey had pitched a complete game shutout for the Mets the night before.

As he walked, Jonathan tried to focus on what had been bothering him since the class reunion. Was it Janice? Could she still have that effect on him? Were there still feelings there? Had there ever really been true feelings? He smiled ruefully to himself and dismissed the idea. He and Janice had been over for a very long time. In fact, he doubted she would be interested even if he was. Probably not, he concluded. Janice Stanton was, perhaps, one of the few women in the world who would not be intoxicated by the senator's legendary charm. No, it was definitely Frank. What was he – jealous of Frank? Frank had a pitiful little law practice. Frank was a nobody. Frank had wasted his life. But Frank was happy. That was it. Frank was truly, unapologetically happy.

Jonathan was happy also, wasn't he? He took stock of his life, as he waited for a woman pushing a baby stroller to clear his path. He had achieved so much, and there was still so much in front of him. He was on a road to even greater fame and power. He was one of the ruling elite. He was still among the youngest senators in Washington. He was smart, a great speaker, and had a storybook family and a hot wife who worshiped him. He was a prince. All his dreams had come true. Hadn't they?

He tried to recall whether he had ever actually dreamed about being a senator. He had certainly dreamed about Gwen. Of course, he also had dreamed about Janice, and Donna, and many others. The reunion had brought up memories of what he and Frank had talked about in school. But that was just talk; idle chatter from idealistic kids who didn't know anything about the real world.

Jonathan dodged out of the way of a man running up the sidewalk in the opposite direction, a thin windbreaker billowing behind him. He wondered where this man was going in such a hurry at this hour. He imagined that the man was late getting home from an appointment. His wife – or girlfriend – would be pissed at him. Max called them "shoes." They were the nameless, faceless voters whose opinions Max would mold and whose shoes they needed in the voting booths. Jonathan had far greater and weightier concerns. There were bills to consider, laws to make, great things to accomplish. What had Frank accomplished? Nothing. So why was he so fucking happy?

He rounded the corner and saw his Town Car, parked at the curb, with Ramon lounging against its side, reading the paper by the ever-present ambient light of the city. As he approached the red velvet awning of an upscale restaurant, a couple emerged through the heavy door and onto the sidewalk. The man looked to be about Jonathan's age, dressed in a business suit, the top button of his shirt ajar and his tie pulled down several inches. The woman was short and slightly plump, wearing a red dress. Her blonde hair blew wildly in the light breeze as she laughed at some just-told joke, leaning against her date and tilting on her high heels, gripping the man's arm for support as she laid her head against his shoulder. Her date looked down at the top of her head and slipped an arm around her waist. They walked past Jonathan, neither one giving him a passing glance.

Jonathan turned briefly to watch the couple lurch down the sidewalk. The blonde was a little on the chunky side for his own taste, he thought. He preferred Gwen's tight, athletic build. He smiled to himself and shook his head. He was not jealous of that man and his blonde date. He was not jealous of anyone. His life was exactly what he wanted it to be, and Gwen was exactly the wife he needed and wanted. Hell, Frank didn't have a girlfriend, or so he said. Frank lacked so much that Jonathan took for granted.

"Ready to roll, Boss?" Escavera asked casually when Jonathan approached the car.

"Ready," Jonathan replied confidently.

"Good walk?"

"Yes. Cleared my head. I'm good to go."

The car pulled into traffic and Jonathan sat back against the leather cushion. "I'm good," he whispered to himself.

Chapter 6

August, 1989

THE INTERNSHIP HAD BEEN POSTED in the student employment office in Hamilton Hall. It was a summer position working for a senior consultant for the Republican National Committee's New York office. Lots of students applied for it, but Jonathan was selected. He had interviewed for the internship in a new suit from Barney's that his mother bought for him. In fact, it had been his mother who mentioned the internship to him.

He had reported for work promptly at 9:00 a.m. on June first with a white button-down dress shirt and a conservative blue tie to go with his blue pinstripe suit and black tasseled loafers. His boss for the summer was a man he had never met named Max Foster, a senior consultant for the RNC who worked on the campaigns of Jonathan's father. Max introduced him around the office simply as Jonathan, taking care not to mention his last name, which Jonathan appreciated. He didn't want any special treatment just because his father was a senator.

The work was tedious and often difficult; mainly research on current political issues, compiling poll results, writing up summaries, and cataloging news reports to track the coverage and whether it was generally favorable. For weeks at a time, Jonathan toiled in the screening room, watching video tapes of national and local news broadcasts and noting the issue coverage slants. Around 3:00 p.m. each day, a pretty Asian girl, usually in a very short skirt, came around with a rolling trolley of pastries, cookies, and coffee. He often shared his cookies with Rodney, the technician who was assigned to show Jonathan the tapes. Rodney would rewind and re-play sections of the broadcasts that Jonathan wanted to review, and would skip ahead when the stories were unrelated to the political issues they were researching.

Rodney had another job at night, tending bar in a club in Greenwich Village. He invited Jonathan to come down and check it out some time. Jonathan said he would, but somehow never got around to actually doing it. It turned out that Rodney was a smart guy, and well informed about politics. He and Jonathan often discussed the issues while they watched together, and Jonathan got into the habit of showing Rodney the drafts of his reports before they were submitted to the head of the research department.

On Friday nights, Jonathan and Frank would get together back at The West End, the dive bar of choice for most Columbia students, and share a pizza and a pitcher of beer and talk about their summers. The West End was the kind of place most adults avoided. It was dark, cramped, and loud most of the time. The wooden tables were worn and covered with engraved graffiti and the floor was generally sticky from the remnants of spilled beer and ketchup. But the pitchers were cheap, the fries were crispy, and nobody cared how loud the students talked. It was a refuge from the libraries and the dorms. At The West End, nobody studied and nobody felt guilty about it.

Jonathan described the cookie cart girl, making her seem even hotter than she was. He lied about her coming on to him in the dark screening room. Frank bitched about the grumpy customers at the bank where he was working as a teller for the summer. The Chemical Bank at 113th and Broadway was the primary branch for all Columbia University payroll checks. The line of customers usually stretched around several turns of the maze-like barriers set up for crowd control. Frank liked the interaction with people all day long. Jonathan said he would go insane having to deal with the public and smile all the time. Inevitably, one night the conversation got around to the amount of money Jonathan was getting paid for his internship.

"I thought internships were unpaid," Frank said. "I'm pretty sure the posting in the job office for that RNC internship said it was for no pay."

"I don't remember that," Jonathan replied.

They talked about the issues Jonathan was researching, and as much as Frank disagreed with most of the Republican positions, he had to admit that the subject matter of the research was interesting, and writing the reports for which Jonathan was responsible sounded to Frank like much more fun than counting other people's money all day. Jonathan figured Frank would be a great asset to the RNC's research department and he promised to speak to his boss about getting Frank a job for the following summer.

On the first Monday in August, Max Foster sidled up to Jonathan's cubicle work space, a steaming mug of coffee in his plump hand. He sat his ample behind on the edge of a filing cabinet as if he were just one of the boys shooting the breeze during a free moment. Jonathan smiled widely and extended a hand, although in the back of his mind he noted how unusual it was for Max to suddenly appear like this without notice. Max didn't actually work for the RNC, so he didn't have an official office, although he was such a frequent visitor that he had an ID card. But Jonathan's vague apprehension was quickly overcome by Max's impressive presence.

"Did you enjoy the opera Saturday night, Son?" Max asked casually. "I always loved Aida when I was your age."

"Um," Jonathan hesitated, quickly attempting to decide whether to lie to Max about having skipped the Metropolitan Opera (and the $75 tickets he had been given for the event) in favor of a night of bar-crawling in the East Village. Did he recall the plot of Aida well enough to fake his way through a conversation if Max asked him any questions? On the other hand, why would Max care if he went or didn't? They weren't his tickets. "Actually, I didn't make it on Saturday – I got tied up somewhere else."

Max threw up the back of his hand dismissively. "Oh, well, no matter. It was a glorious weekend. I can understand wanting to enjoy the outdoors. Listen, Jonathan, how about taking a little walk, I have something I'd like to discuss with you."

Max had put down his coffee mug and was already halfway out of the cubicle before Jonathan said, "Sure," and rushed to follow him. Once again, a small voice in his head wondered why Max had shown up so unexpectedly, and without anyone else. Come to think of it, Jonathan couldn't think of any time he had been alone with Max for more than a few moments at the start or end of a meeting, and always when there were other people right outside a conference room door.

He started to feel anxious as he walked alongside the big man, making small talk about the mayor's latest television commercial and President Bush's upcoming appearance before the United Nations. Was he getting fired? Was someone mad at him? Jonathan searched his memory for anything important he had been involved in at the RNC that could have landed him in enough trouble to warrant a personal sacking by Max Foster.

They rode the elevator to the ground floor and walked out into the steamy puddle of humidity that passed for air during a Manhattan summer. The sweat started gushing down

Jonathan's neck. He looked at the side of Max's face out of the corner of his eye and detected a bead trickling slowly down beside his ear. He was human after all.

As they walked up Sixth Avenue, Max started talking, not looking at Jonathan, but as if he were speaking to a group at a business meeting. "There is a state senator in New York from an upstate district named Norman Coleman. Six terms in the state senate. No ambition for higher office, but a fixture in Albany. Chair of the appropriations committee. Republican, but fiscally quite liberal. He is up for re-election in November and the primary is in three weeks."

"There's a primary election in August?" Jonathan asked incredulously.

"Yes, but you're not the only one who doesn't know about it. It's not generally very contentious and has low voter turnout, especially in upstate districts." Max turned to Jonathan for the first time as he continued, "And normally incumbents don't have much if any opposition. But this time is different. Coleman has an opponent in the primary, and although we've been keeping a low profile, he has enough grass roots support that he could be a threat to Coleman – under the right circumstances."

Jonathan frowned, trying to puzzle out why Max was telling him all this without seeming to be dense. He stalled a bit, asking, "We?"

Max smiled. "Yes, you caught that, eh? Good boy. I said we have been keeping a low profile because the RNC has officially endorsed Coleman – pretty much have to since he's such an established Party man. The Committee can't do anything officially to back an opponent under these kinds of circumstances. It wouldn't look right – it sends the wrong message to the party faithful. But my people have been involved – off the record – with the opponent, a young man named Matthew Strickland. Not much older than you, Jonathan. A real up-and-comer, we think. Good family.

Raised in the district, out near Binghamton. He could be a real asset."

"To the Party, or to you, Max?" Jonathan tried to keep a cool expression, despite the moisture soaking his armpits and his heart pounding in his chest.

"Good question, Son. I knew you were as bright as your father. An asset to everyone – to the Party, to the State of New York, and also a long-term asset to both of us, and to your father. The boy has ambition – a likely candidate for Congress someday. Good district for him. Good, honest people."

"Why isn't Coleman an asset?"

"Mmmm," Max pursed his lips. "Let's just say Mr. Coleman is very . . . independent. He has shown an alarming tendency to break away from the Party and strike out on his own. He thinks he's untouchable and has no continuing need for the Party's support. We think he may be wrong, but as I said, the Party cannot, in the current circumstances, take any public position adverse to an incumbent in his position."

Jonathan walked along in silence for a few moments. They had walked north and were crossing 57th street, going toward Central Park. "Is there something in particular that worries you about Coleman?"

"Yes, Jon. I'm quite worried about a bill kicking around in his committee in Albany. He has the power to kill it, or allow it to move out of committee and reach the floor of the full Senate. I have lobbied for him to kill it, but he seems intent on allowing it some air."

"What's the bill?"

Max smiled again, but this time it was a wry expression. They crossed 59th street and passed through a gap in the stone wall surrounding the park, strolling in the shade of leafy trees along the winding path of smooth asphalt. "I'd rather not get into the details of all that, Jon. Boring stuff. Finances and appropriations and all. The point is that my people have a very strong feeling about the bill."

Max slowed and then settled himself onto a green wood-slat bench beneath a particularly thickly branched tree, stretching out his legs as if he planned to stay a while. Jonathan dutifully sat down beside him. "My boy, the point of this discussion is that I foresee Mr. Coleman encountering some trouble in the upcoming primary, which could very well result in young Mr. Strickland winning the Party's nomination. That would allow the Party to put its support behind Strickland, and would likely cause him to win the seat. The second ranking member of the appropriations committee is a very loyal man who would have less trouble making the correct decision to kill the bill next term and solve my problem."

"OK," Jonathan filled in the moment of silence, still wondering what part he played in this upcoming political drama, but not wanting to seem stupid in front of Max. "So, how do you plan to make sure Coleman doesn't win the primary?"

"That, my boy, is the reason for this little chat." Max's expression turned serious as he twisted his massive frame toward Jonathan. "I know you are the kind of young man on whom I can count. You are loyal to the Party, and you understand the big picture. I foresee great things for you, Jon. Perhaps greater even than your father. You trust me, don't you?"

"Of course," Jonathan responded immediately. There could be no other response.

"Yes. I have great confidence in you, which is why I am giving you a very special assignment. I'm sending you up to Binghamton for a few days. I need you to meet with a reporter with whom I'm acquainted. It's a small paper, but influential in the area. I need you to confirm a story the reporter already is working on. It involves Mr. Coleman, who has unfortunately acquired a taste for cocaine, and who has been observed in

New York City consorting with some unsavory types and engaging in illegal drug-related activity."

Jonathan's mouth fell open a bit at this news. "Wow! That's quite a bombshell. But I don't know anything about that. What can I say to a reporter?"

"You can say, Jon, that you were at a club called The Trading Post in lower Manhattan on Saturday night. You can say you recognized Mr. Coleman there, in the company of a very good-looking blonde woman in her late twenties, and that you observed him leaning over a small table. You can't say with any certainty he was doing a line of cocaine, but when he sat up he touched his finger to his nose and seemed to be inhaling heavily. You can also say the group he was with appeared to be very drunk and loud and that you saw white powder on the nose of one of the other people in Mr. Coleman's group, whom you saw later in the bathroom."

Jonathan was silent, staring at Max and wondering if this was some kind of test, or joke, or both. "But, Max – it's not true."

"I just told you it is true, Jon."

"But, I mean, I wasn't really there. I didn't see anything."

"Jon, you're not testifying under oath here. You are only talking to a reporter. I have it on very good authority that these are facts. We can't have Coleman getting re-elected without his constituents seeing the full picture. You are really helping do a great service to the electorate."

Jonathan was silent, staring into the waves of heat rising up from the pavement. "I don't know, Max. It seems like you are asking me to do something dishonest."

"I appreciate the bout of conscience, Jonathan," Max soothed. "But let's assume somebody really did see Coleman at that club on Saturday night, but that somebody is in a position where he can't personally come forward because it would be embarrassing to him to admit he was there. So, we need somebody else to serve as the beard – to provide the information as the surrogate. Keep in mind the reporter is already working on the story, there is other evidence of these facts, but the reporter needs corroboration. You provide the corroboration. The reporter doesn't have to use your name in the story. You are merely a reliable corroborating source. Coleman will never know where it came from, nor will anyone else. This is an important moment, and this is something you can do for me, in confidence. I need people I can trust, Jon. I need people on whom I can depend. I think you know I'm fond of you and I've done a lot to help your father, and to help you. I need a little help in return here." Max looked directly into Jonathan's eyes, with an unwavering stare.

Jonathan looked away. "I understand, Sir."

"Good," Max chirped, rising from the bench as if the conversation was over and he was ready to move along to his next appointment. "I'll send you a summary, along with the information about the reporter. This Wednesday, you can drive up to Binghamton. You should be back by Friday night. Thank you, Jon. I won't forget this."

He turned and walked down the path toward Columbus Circle, leaving Jonathan sitting, stupefied, on the bench. Had he agreed to Max's request? He spent the walk back to the office convincing himself that he had volunteered for the assignment, and that it was a noble purpose, and that Max would certainly repay him someday. By the time he re-entered the air conditioned comfort of the RNC office, he was dripping wet, but confident he would be riding off to Binghamton as a white knight fighting the good fight in the battle for goodness and right. He was looking forward to it.

The next evening, Jonathan met Frank at The West End and, over burgers and fries, described his upcoming trip to Binghamton.

"My God, you're not going to do this, are you?" Frank exclaimed, his mouth agape. "I can't believe you would even consider it."

"Calm down, Mister Morals," Jonathan smiled, having anticipated Frank's reaction and prepared his arsenal of arguments in advance. "What have you got against the truth?"

"Truth!" Frank exclaimed incredulously. "Truth?! We're talking about you lying here – it's got nothing to do with the truth."

Jonathan sat back in his creaky wooden chair and looked over Frank's shoulder at a cluster of co-eds sitting at a table across the room. He was calm and confident, with well-rehearsed lines. "But let's assume the facts are true, and there is a witness to them, but it's someone who can't come forward. If all I'm doing is providing the same facts that somebody else could provide, then the truth comes out, and isn't that the most important thing?"

Frank opened his mouth and pointed a finger across the table, over the dozens of names carved into the ancient laminated wood, then held his tongue and pursed his lips. After a pause, during which Jonathan sat with a Cheshire Cat grin on his face, Frank regrouped. "That's an assumption you're making based on what? This guy has an agenda, and he could make up any story. Why should you believe him?"

"If the situation were reversed and Max was supporting Coleman and asked me to suppress the story and tell the reporter I saw him at the opera Saturday night, would he be more or less believable?"

Frank frowned and took a long sip of his beer. "No. Either way the guy has an agenda and he's having you say whatever supports his end. He's still using you as a pawn."

"But if the end is just, does it matter what the means?"

"Machiavelli? Really, Jon? You've been paying attention after all!" Frank smiled broadly and raised his bottle in a salute. "But remember that Machiavelli was joking – he wasn't really advocating that the ends justify the means. He was being sarcastic."

"I disagree, my friend," Jonathan said in his best professorial voice, raising his own beer in a return salute and then taking a swig before continuing. "The author's intent is mere speculation. What is truly just if not to expose corruption and deceit? If this guy Coleman is a two-faced hypocrite, pulling the wool over the eyes of his constituency, is it not a noble cause to call him out? And if the means are less than ideal, is that infirmity not dwarfed by the rightness of the result?" Jonathan paused, his arm raised involuntarily toward the ceiling.

"Did you rehearse that?" Frank scowled.

"Well, actually, I may have been thinking about it," Jonathan replied sheepishly, lowering his arm.

"But what about your individual integrity, Jon? What about lowering yourself to carrying out this ruse like an errand boy? What if someone finds out you were a part of this?"

"I've thought about that, Frank. Don't underestimate me. But I don't think there is much chance of getting caught in a lie here. There's hardly anybody who could say with certainty that I was not there on Saturday. And even if somebody else wants to dispute the story, it's just a dispute – it's not possible to prove I'm lying."

"I could prove it," Frank responded darkly. "I was with you until you came home on Saturday night and I can say you're lying."

"Ah, my virtuous young Jedi, but you fail to understand that your so-called 'proof' is merely your word. You have no pictures. No physical evidence. No credit card receipts. How can you prove I was with you?"

"But it's true. You know it and I know it. I'm sure there were other people who saw us."

"Once again, it's only a question of eyewitness accounts. It was dark. They weren't really focused on me. They don't know me. I'm not such a recognizable guy. You may be able to convince people you're saying what you think is the truth, but you can't really establish that it is truth."

"What?" Frank asked, raising his voice slightly, then catching himself and reverting to appropriate table-talk volume. "Are you saying now that 'truth' is whatever a witness says it is? And if the witness is lying, then what?"

"You're once again speaking in absolutes. How do you know the witness is lying if the truth of the matter is merely a question of believing one witness as opposed to another?"

"The sophistry is intriguing, Jon, but what if it's all really a lie? What if the guy Coleman is really a good man and you are participating in a conspiracy to smear him and ruin his career?"

Jonathan frowned and sipped his beer to buy time, waving to their waitress – a perky redhead named Julie whose lower back was peeking out below the spaghetti-strap top she was wearing under her apron. "This is politics, Frank. People are always saying things about politicians during elections that aren't true. A good politician can deflect untrue statements and rise above them. If he's really innocent, then the real truth will come out eventually and he'll clear his name."

"How?" Frank challenged. "How is the guy going to clear his name with three weeks to go before the election? Even if he can round up some eye witnesses who can say he was somewhere else – it's like you said. Without some hard evidence proving beyond any doubt he was somewhere else, the lie sticks and the voters believe the sensational story in the paper and the guy is toast. Doesn't it bother you to be a part of that?"

"There you go again," Jonathan said in a mock Ronald Reagan voice. "You keep assuming that it's not true."

"So, you're willing to prostitute yourself for this guy, Max, based on his say-so that the facts are true, knowing that if you're being lied to you will ruin an innocent man's career. You're willing to do that all on faith?"

"We do a lot of things on faith, Frank. Max Foster is a trusted adviser to my father and he's a well-respected political consultant who has the ear of every Republican leader in America. If I'm not going to trust him, who am I going to trust? Besides, this is a favor I'm doing for Max. He has done favors for me, and I'm sure I'll need him again. This is good for me."

"That's another good end, then, Mr. Machiavelli?" Frank gave him a nod and spread out his hands in surrender. "The means, I believe, are questionable, and the consequences could be disastrous for this guy Coleman, but the personal end will be achieved. I hope you can live with this down the line, man. I don't think I could do it."

Jonathan nodded back at his friend, accepting his resignation like Anatoly Karpov. "I'm entirely comfortable." Julie arrived at that moment with two fresh beers. She beamed at Jonathan, who sat back in his chair and looked her up and down without any attempt to hide his lascivious thoughts. Julie only smiled as she leaned over him farther than was really necessary to retrieve the empty bottle at the far side of the table.

"Is there anything else I can get you boys?" she purred, looking only at Jonathan. Frank shook his head at his friend's uncanny ability to get every cute girl in a room to have eyes only for him. Jonathan just grinned and told Julie he was good. Frank hoped so, but couldn't shake the feeling that his friend was making a serious mistake.

Two weeks after his trip to Binghamton, Jonathan saw Max Foster entering a meeting at the RNC. Max had not spoken to him since he left him sitting on a park bench. The mission had been a success. The reporter seemed to already know all the facts Max had explained. Jonathan hardly had to speak – simply nodding and mumbling "uh huh" to confirm the reporter's questions. The only new tidbit, which intrigued the reporter, was Jonathan's account of the white powder on the nose of the man in the bathroom. "You're sure this man was at the same table as Coleman?"

"Yes," Jonathan had said confidently. That was all the reporter wanted to hear. No follow-up. No questions about what the man was wearing, or whether he spoke to Jonathan. The reporter dropped his notepad into a black saddle bag, shook Jonathan's hand quickly, and hurried out of the bar where they had arranged to meet, as if late for a deadline. Jonathan didn't stick around Binghamton long enough to read the article the next morning. He drove back to New York in one stretch, arriving at two in the morning. There was nothing in the *Times* or the *Journal* the next day, or the day after. Then, over the weekend, Jonathan caught a brief note on the television news on channel eleven about state Senator Coleman, who was involved in a drug scandal. Not big news in the city, but Jonathan smiled to himself, knowing he had played his role well.

Jonathan loitered outside the conference room, waiting for Max to emerge, then trailed him down the hall toward the elevator like a puppy following his mother's dripping teat. Max ignored him until the doors closed and they were alone for the downward drop to the lobby. "Well done, Son," Max said flatly.

"No problem," Jonathan replied, beaming and feeling a flush in his face at the great man's compliment, glad to be standing slightly behind Max so his blush couldn't be seen. "When you have a chance, I have something different I'd like to discuss."

"You can walk with me if you'd like, Jonathan."

"Great!" Jonathan spouted, a little more enthusiastic than he intended. They walked out of the building and headed east, toward the recently opened offices of The Foster Group. "Well, Max," Jonathan stammered, "you see, it's about next summer. I've been thinking about whether I want to come back again to the RNC internship."

Max turned his head as they walked. "I would advise you to seriously consider one more summer, Jon. You can make some excellent contacts there, and it will not raise any eyebrows if you do two summers. Then we'll need to find you something different – perhaps a summer in D.C. or out in the field working on a campaign."

Jonathan lit up at the prospect of some real political action, but then caught his enthusiasm, remembering why he wanted to speak with Max. "That would be great, Sir. But if I'm at the RNC next summer, I was wondering if there is any chance of finding a spot on the intern team for a friend of mine."

Max stopped suddenly, leaving Jonathan to stride forward several yards before realizing his companion was no longer with him. He hurried back, now worried about the expression on Max's face. "Jon, I appreciate the loyalty you feel toward your friend Mr. Elkhardt. However, I don't think the RNC is an appropriate place for him."

"What makes you think I was asking about Frank?" Max just stared at Jonathan without speaking. "Well, you're right, it is Frank. Look, he's a great guy, and really smart, and he's working his way through school and could really use the money."

"What he could use, Jon, is a change in his viewpoint. My advice to you, Son, is to spend less time with this boy. He cannot help you in your career. He has nothing to offer you."

"He's my friend," Jonathan shot back defensively. "He has saved my ass more than once. I owe him better than that."

"Suit yourself, Son," Max replied as he started walking again. "I'm not going to dictate to you who your friends are, but if you trust my advice, you'll make sure you expand your inner circle, and think about leaving Mr. Elkhardt on the outside."

They reached Max's building and Foster stopped again, holding out his hand to Jonathan and making it clear he would continue inside unescorted. Jonathan shook Max's hand and turned to walk back to his cubicle. He had tried, he told himself, although as he replayed the conversation in his mind he realized he had not made much of a case after Max had quickly shot down the idea of inviting Frank to work at the RNC. But he had tried. He kept telling himself that.

By the time he reached his desk, he was content that he had, indeed, tried. He had fulfilled his obligations to Frank. He wondered whether Max's advice about Frank was reasonable, but then dismissed it. He was his own man. He would choose his own friends. Frank was a friend. He just wouldn't be getting a cushy summer job next year.

Chapter 7

BRYAN BAILEY LEANED BACK in his low-slung chair, which creaked under his weight. He ran his left hand through his oily mat of gray hair. The caller on the line, Ray-from-Tuscaloosa, was rambling about immigrants and how they were ruining America. Bailey reached for his cigarette, smoldering in a crowded ashtray on the edge of his console. When Ray paused, Bailey leaned toward the large black microphone hovering in space in front of his face, blew out a blue curl of smoke and spoke to his 11.34 million syndicated listeners.

"You are *so right*, Ray. Now you need to make sure you vote in November for a candidate who will *do* something about it!" Bailey reached out and pressed a lighted button, extinguishing Ray-from-Tuscaloosa's virtual existence. He glanced at the computer monitor on his right, studying the options presented to him along with the digital clock counting down to the next commercial break, which showed forty-seven seconds. He had a guest in the next segment, which meant the two callers he didn't choose would be cut off when they cleared the lines and would be unhappy. But he also knew they would get over it. He chose Mary-from-Houston, who wanted to wish a happy birthday to her 90-year-old sister, which figured to kill off the segment without leaving anything hanging.

After wishing Mary and her sister a long and healthy life, Bailey removed his oversized headphones with a great sweep of his left hand and hustled off to the toilet. When he returned, he was not at all surprised to find his cramped studio inhabited by two other people. He recognized the old man. His eyes lingered on the young woman in the tight pink sweater. She was crushed into the space between the one guest chair and the glass wall of the studio. She smiled brightly at Bailey, who tried not to leer excessively. He quickly reclaimed his seat and deftly donned the headset as he saw his producer on the other side of the glass giving him the hurry-up signal. In his ears he could hear his intro music coming to a close, just as his red light sprang to life.

"We are back, America, and thank you so much for spending your afternoon with me once again. This is Bryan Bailey keeping it real and telling it like it is no matter what President Obama thinks. We are honored today to have in the studio one of the bright lights of the evangelistic community and a true American hero, the Reverend Abraham Hawkins. I will tell you, friends, that I have been listening to this man preach and speak on civil rights and on Christian family values since I was a young man about one hundred and fifty pounds ago, heh, heh. Welcome, welcome, welcome, Reverend."

"Thank you, my friend," Hawkins crooned. "It is as always a great pleasure for me to visit with you and your congregation."

Bailey chuckled into his microphone, not looking at the preacher. "Reverend, my flock spans the nation and we follow the Good Book and the Constitution of the United States – call us the Church of American Values. I'm sure you'll agree that we need everyone out there listening to get on board and see the light, am I right?"

"Amen to that," Hawkins said into his microphone, without a glance at his host. Both men were practiced at preaching to the imaginary audience they pretended to see in front of them, seeking an astral projection outside the dumpy radio booth and into a football stadium filled with adoring fans. "Now, you know I'm not a politician, but I do pay attention to the issues of the day. I'm sure you've been educating your listeners about some of the dangerous and evil things being proposed by godless members of Congress."

"You are referring, of course, to the so-called Free Access Act that we have spent some considerable time on, Reverend. My listeners will remember this bill in the House of Representatives purports to protect the right of women to unfettered access to abortionists anywhere in America and seeks to overturn by federal action the laws of our many states that have chosen to protect the health of young women and the rights of their unborn children in ways that even our often-too-permissive Supreme Court has held to be absolutely constitutional. Now, Reverend, what's your angle here – what do you want to talk about with the real American patriots out there listening today?"

Bailey rolled back away from his microphone, the chair's casters smoothly and silently gliding into the only available empty space. Bailey knew from experience that Hawkins was a talker and he could probably get in a full smoke before it would be necessary to start introducing callers. The four phone lines were already blinking expectantly.

Hawkins fanned the passions of the invisible audience, describing how Pennsylvania had enacted a law requiring a waiting period so any woman considering murdering her child could ponder her actions after a consultation with a doctor before proceeding with the abomination. Yet the Planned Parenthood lobby in Congress wanted to ban all state efforts to require information and a period of consideration to expectant mothers. And how Texas had passed a completely sensible state law requiring abortion clinics to be inspected by state health officials and to meet minimum standards for medical treatment facilities to protect the safety of these innocent and misguided young women who risked their own lives as well as the lives of their babies by choosing the brutal dissection of their unborn heirs. Bailey had to smile to himself as he finished the last drag of his butt. The man was a master.

"The phone lines are open, America. What do you think? Martha-from-Cleveland, you are on the air with the Reverend Abraham Hawkins." Bailey again leaned back and let Hawkins do the heavy lifting. His producer was very good at screening out total crackpots and liberal plants who would want to raise contrary points. His supplicants would feed Hawkins fuel for the fire and agree with everything he said. Abortion was a reliable topic on the mid-week shows – guaranteed to generate fierce opinions, heartbreaking stories, and solid ratings.

After fifteen minutes, Hawkins had drained two bottles of water and was mopping his brow between sentences. The producer motioned there were five minutes left before the end of the segment, which would bring Bailey a twelve minute break between commercials, the top-of-the-hour national news, and a five-minute station break for the local affiliates to fill in with traffic reports and local news along with a few local commercials. Then one more hour and the day would be a wrap. *Good show, so far*, he thought.

"Jenny-from-Connecticut, you are on the air with the Reverend Abraham Hawkins."

"Hello?" squeaked the caller, hesitantly. "Am I on the air?"

"Yes, my child, you are with me on the air," Hawkins soothed. "What is your story, Miss Jenny?" His voice was comforting and encouraged the young woman to relax and speak. Years of experience gave him a quick sense of how to get a stranger to confess their sins, even live on national radio.

"Well, I – I had one, when I was very young. An abortion. It was awful and I wish I had never done it." The caller choked back sobs, prompting Hawkins to jump in.

"There, now, don't you worry about weeping over your dead baby my little Jenny. It's good to cry. It's good to mourn. There is no shame in having regrets for your sins and begging Jesus for forgiveness. If your story can help one young girl make the right choice in her life then you will have redeemed yourself. Tell us – tell us."

Jenny was openly crying now, but choked out her tale. "My boyfriend, he was the father, he said nobody would ever want to marry me if I had a kid, and that he was not going to marry me no matter what. . . . He said I had no choice, that I had to, and that I better not never tell nobody. He drove me to the clinic and waited outside. It all happened so fast. I never had time to think. I wish, I mean, if I only had more time . . . ."

"Now, Jenny, I know exactly how that happens – it's a story I've heard so many times before," Hawkins looked over at Bailey, using hand signals to ask whether the host wanted to get to any other callers. Bailey shook his head, but gave Hawkins the rotating fingers sign to wrap it up quickly. "Your sad, sad tale is not unusual. It's not your fault. Your boyfriend will burn in eternal Hell fire for what he did, and you are living proof that young women need to be given the time and space and information needed to make the right choice about not killing their babies. If this bill gets passed, there will be so many more poor girls like you, Jenny. Am I right, Mr. Bailey?"

"Reverend, you are so very right, and I am crying my own tears here in Nashville for Miss Jenny-from-Connecticut. But don't you worry, now, Jenny, because I know in your state we have a senator who will stand up to this wicked liberal lobby and fight for the rights of unborn children. Senator Jonathan Prescott the Third is a rock who will help block this bill. Do you know Senator Prescott, Reverend?"

Hawkins was caught off guard by the question, thinking his duty was concluded. He quickly leaned back toward his microphone. "Well, Sir, I have not personally met the man, although I have heard very good reports about him from people I respect and I think he has a great future in front of him in Washington D.C., if he chooses to continue his noble cause."

"I think you're right, Reverend, we need men like Jonathan Prescott to step up and lead this country to better times and uphold our American morals and traditions. Let's hope Jenny and her fellow voters in Connecticut will make sure that happens. That's all the time we have this afternoon with Reverend Hawkins. I thank you, Sir, for gracing us with your wisdom and guidance and I wish you all the best in your continued ministry."

"Thank you, Bryan. It is always a pleasure to be here, and thank you to the American people for listening to an old Black preacher on a White man's radio show. It truly is a wonderful day."

Bailey laughed heartily at the comment as his producer counted down to zero and the red light faded out.

Chapter 8

JANICE STANTON STEPPED OUT of the black Buick that had driven her home from her mid-town office. The summer night still dripped with humidity – even three in the morning. She had been up working on the Hawkins story. She cursed her editor for being such a stickler for source checking and fact verification, but she knew in her heart he was right. The story was a hot potato and the paper needed to be 100% sure of every detail. She was tired, and she didn't look forward to going home to her castle of cardboard.

She had been packing for the impending move to Washington, D.C. and most of her belongings were in boxes. She paused in the stillness of the early morning, glancing up and down the quiet block, lined with little trees encircled by knee-high wrought-iron fencing to keep the Manhattan dogs away. There were brownstones up and down the street, none more than four stories tall. Few had any lights on at this hour. She wondered whether Georgetown would look similar.

She trudged up the steps to the front door and into the tiled lobby, stopping at her mailbox to retrieve a few stray bills and a flyer from a new Chinese restaurant around the corner on Columbus Avenue. She idly looked over the mail as she approached her door on the lobby floor, which was the second floor of the building. She had her key ring looped around her little finger and stuck it into the heavy lock without looking, feeling for the entrance of the metal into the keyhole. When the door pushed forward before she had turned the key, she dropped the mail, along with her briefcase, and backed quickly away into the corridor, gasping for breath, her heart racing.

She thought about screaming, but at this hour she wasn't keen on the reaction of the old lady who lived across the hall and who was always peeking her head out of her door and scowling disapprovingly when Janice made noise in the hallway late at night. Instead, she picked up her briefcase and fished out her cell phone as she hurried back to the stoop. She knew better than to dial 911 and instead punched in the number of her local precinct house, which was only a few blocks north. She calmly explained the situation and asked for a patrol car to be sent over. At three in the morning, it didn't take long for the car to pull up, with lights flashing but no siren.

When the officer pushed open the apartment door, Janice followed behind and flipped on the hallway lights. The officer told her to wait at the door while he checked inside to make sure the intruder was gone. Janice wondered how he could feel safe entering the unfamiliar apartment with no back-up, but New York City budget cuts had reduced most night patrols to single officers. When he came back and gave her the all clear, she entered to inspect the scene.

It was hard to tell how much things had been displaced, because the apartment had looked like a disaster area when she locked it up the prior morning. Janice explained she thought some of the boxes had been moved, and the more she surveyed the contents of the cardboard, the more she was convinced many of them had been disturbed. Not the ones with dishes and clothes, but certainly the ones with books and papers and folders.

In the small bedroom she could instantly see that her desk had been ransacked. The drawers had all been pushed back in, as if the intruder thought she might not notice, but the papers and stationery supplies had definitely been moved around.

"Is there anything valuable missing?" the officer inquired, pulling out a small notebook. Janice thought it was quite similar to the one she used for taking notes during an interview.

"It's hard to tell for sure, Officer," Janice replied slowly as she surveyed the damage.

"Did you have any cash or jewelry in the apartment?"

"No, not really. Everything is in the boxes by now, so I'm not certain where it all is."

"Well, if you determine there's anything valuable missing, you can call the precinct and we'll come back to take a statement for the report." He was clearly eager to get back to whatever he had been doing when he got the call to investigate a break-in.

"Well, my laptop is gone. That's for sure." The officer wrote it down. She gave him a description. It was encrypted and protected by a password, so she was not particularly concerned about her credit card information, which was probably listed somewhere in her email and internet records on the computer. It was more than two years old, and she had been thinking about getting a new one anyway.

"OK, Miss. You call the precinct if you figure out what else is missing. I'll file this report and someone will call you in the morning with the case number."

"Thank you, Officer." Janice saw him to the door, then realized the lock was still broken. Drilled. A pretty professional job, the officer had said. She shut the door and secured it with the interior dead bolt, which was still intact. She would call the locksmith in the morning.

Sitting on her ratty sofa, she stared out the window onto the quiet street, totally unable to sleep despite her exhaustion. Who would break into her apartment and steal her laptop?

This was not a random break-in. Somebody had drilled out her lock, searched through her papers and desk, then took her computer, pushed in the drawers, and closed the front door on the way out. She wracked her brain trying to think of what stories she had recently published that might generate such cloak-and-dagger activity, but she came up empty. The Hawkins story might generate a big reaction in some circles, but it had not been published, so nobody knew about it yet. She was going to be glad to get out of New York.

Chapter 9

EDWARD EVANS WAS BORN AND RAISED in Alexandria, Virginia, which may as well be called South Washington, D.C. His father was a career government man, starting out after World War II in what would later become the Veteran's Affairs Department under President Truman. Then he moved up to a low-level State Department job under Eisenhower, which he managed to hold onto even under Kennedy. By the time of the assassination, Archibald Evans had an office at the Pentagon and was one of the established veterans who Johnson needed around during Vietnam.

Nixon loved him, and even invited him to the White House along with a dozen others who were marking their twenty-year anniversary in public service. After Watergate and the sad end to the war in Southeast Asia, Archibald was asked to resign and start collecting his pension. But he was back four years later when Reagan's team decided they needed some old-school consultants back in the Pentagon. He retired for good in 1992 after almost forty years on the inside in Washington. For most of those years, his oldest son, Edward, got nightly briefings on the inner workings of the most complex government in the world.

Ed Evans became the chief of staff for Senator Jonathan Prescott III because Max Foster gave him the job. Jonathan was happy to allow Max to make those kinds of decisions, in consultation with his father, because he had no better suggestions and really didn't want to do the research necessary to make different choices. It had always been that way for Jonathan's political career, which bothered him only in fleeting moments when he met a new staffer and mused about how nice it would be if someone consulted with *him* before hiring another person for *his* staff. But his father and Max had always made good choices, and they had always taken good care of him. Why should he be bothered with the mundane details of hiring staff? And why should he not have the very best talent available? Why not rely on those around him who had expertise? That was a mark of a good politician – the ability to surround himself with talented, smart people who could help make decisions. Max always said that. So did his father. It was gospel.

Max Foster received weekly reports from Ed Evans, sent via a secure, encrypted email account directly to Max's private fax machine. Max read the reports, then either shredded them himself or placed them in a confidential envelope for storage in the office vault. The report from the previous week, however, was now sitting on top of a bright orange file folder, which was splayed open on the grand mahogany desk in his twenty-seventh floor office. Ed fidgeted slightly in the crushed velvet seat of his Louis XIV armchair opposite the desk, waiting for Max. It was something he had grown used to over the years – waiting for Max.

"How concerned should I be here, Ed?" the large man asked in a low voice, suggesting a distant thunder storm.

"I don't think it's anything we should be greatly concerned about, Max. It was only a committee vote, and it's a minor bill. I know Jon is quite friendly with Senator Stevens and we have discussed the possibility that we might need Stevens to vote with us down the line on our oil exploration bill. We even discussed throwing Stevens a vote – like this one – to help him get one of his bills out of committee, without necessarily committing to a 'yes' vote on the floor. If he had come to me to discuss this, we would have decided to go along with the idea, don't you think?" Ed looked at Max, waiting for his agreement, but all he got was the side of Max's face, one jowl hanging loosely and silhouetted against the bright window behind the desk.

"I'm worried about the pattern," Max grumbled. "How many votes has he had this term?"

"On the floor or in committee?"

"Both!" Max snapped, swiveling his chair and facing away from Ed, looking out at the green canopy over Central Park.

"Well, Sir," Evans rifled through notes in his leather portfolio, quickly pulling out a summary chart. He had personally prepared it the day before in preparation for this meeting, which Max had called unexpectedly. "There have been a total of three hundred twenty-six."

"On how many of those did we give him a position?"

Ed suspected Max already knew these numbers by heart, but he quickly scanned the columns of numbers. "Two hundred seven," he responded.

"And how many times in two hundred seven did he vote contrary to our instruction?"

"Four, Sir," Ed responded without looking at his sheet – that one *he* knew by heart.

"And in his first term?" Max continued the interrogation without looking at Ed, "How many times in his first term did he vote contrary to instructions?"

"Zero, Sir."

Max swiveled back to face Evans, who tried hard not to feel like a truant high school boy sitting in the principal's office. He had been doing his job quite well and had nothing about which to be ashamed. He was simply giving his boss a routine briefing. He needed to relax. He tried to control his breathing, but the air in this office always seemed heavy.

"Does that suggest a pattern to you, Ed? Does it suggest the boy is getting more independent minded on us?" Max leaned forward as he spoke. Evans could smell onion on his breath from the half-eaten bagel sitting on a linen napkin on the small side table behind the desk.

"Sir," he began haltingly, sitting up a little straighter in his chair and trying to sound more confident than he was. "While I certainly do wish the senator had discussed this recent vote with me in advance, and I plan to discuss it at an appropriate moment, none of the four rogue votes were on significant items. None of them were votes where I had any substantial discussions with him. We did go over the votes each time in our morning briefings, but in each case there were more important issues on the agenda those days we discussed more specifically. None of the four rogue votes resulted in passage of any bills we oppose. In retrospect, Sir, you can argue Jon made good decisions about siding with Democrats on minor votes where he can show a little bi-partisanship and earn some favors across the aisle. I did not condone them, but looking back I can't say I would not have supported the decisions if he had asked." Ed rushed through the last statement and then looked up at Max for confirmation.

"Hmmff." Max snorted, but did not immediately object, which Evans took as a good sign and as an opportunity to continue.

"Max, he wants to feel like he's in charge. He wants to think he's running the show every once in a while. It's only natural he should want to make a few deals on the side. He may talk to a colleague in between votes and be persuaded to change a position without having time to discuss it with me first, particularly when we haven't made the vote a point of emphasis in advance."

"We have given him votes, Ed." Max thumped the palm of his hand on the desk for emphasis as he made his point. "We allowed him to vote with a liberal block on that forest preservation bill."

"Which we knew was going to fail anyway," Ed interjected.

"Of course, but he wanted to score some points with Senator Greenstein from California, and we let him. And we gave him that pointless alternative energy development appropriations bill he was so keen on."

"Which was going to pass whether he opposed it or not. You're right, Sir. But you can't expect him to be one hundred percent with us on every minor vote. You have to give him a little slack in the line."

Evans fell silent, but Max did not immediately respond, instead reaching for a sip of his Earl Grey tea, which sat on an electronic warming pad in a blue Delft china cup. "Perhaps you're right, Ed. Perhaps I'm seeing ghosts. The boy is likely to have a mind of his own every once in a while, I suppose." Max paused for another sip. "But you need to make sure he is one hundred percent in line on anything big – anything important. That's what I'm paying you for, Ed. You understand?"

"Oh, yes, Sir," Ed responded quickly, now sitting forward on the edge of the high-backed chair. "You can be sure that on any priority items, I'll be sure to have Jonathan in line."

"And if you get any indication from him that he's not rock solid, you call me. You got that, Ed?"

"Yes, Sir."

"And watch his social calendar, too. I know you're not technically in charge of that, but I don't want him appearing at any gay rights fundraisers by mistake."

"Sir, the Sierra Club event was an error. He was invited by Senator Kerry and he thought it was for Kerry's Muscular Dystrophy Society. I know it raised a few eyebrows, but it was only one dinner."

"But Jonathan tends to socialize with some of the more liberal Republicans, and that spills over to some of the barracudas across the aisle, too. He's impressionable, and impetuous. We need to keep him out of trouble. I don't want there to be any doubts about him up the chain. We're going to need everyone's support if we make a run at the White House. His voting record needs to be spotless on everything important. You know how critical that is. And the impression he leaves when he attends a liberal fundraiser is not what we want. Make sure Harriett is on top of it."

"I understand, Sir."

"Good." Max paused, considering whether to bring Evans into his confidence concerning his worries about Jonathan's vote on Menendez. He decided Ed did not need that information. "I'll let you know if there is anything in particular I need you to discuss with the boy. For now, I guess I'm just a little jumpy. He's a colt sometimes – just getting his legs. He's liable to run somewhere we're not expecting. You keep a close eye on him. Ya hear?"

"Yes, Sir. Absolutely." Evans half-stood, watching Max for an indication of whether the meeting was, indeed, over. When Max looked away, Ed knew it was safe to stand all the way up and collect his things. "You can depend on me, Max. You know that."

"I could depend on your father, Ed. He was as solid as they come. And Jonathan's father is the same. You younger men worry me sometimes. But you've never done anything to make me doubt your loyalty, Ed. Thank you, I suppose I don't say that often enough. You're a good man. I don't mean to suggest otherwise."

"No problem, Max." Evans smiled, although he quickly suppressed it when he saw that Max was not returning the expression. "I'll keep you posted."

"Hmmff," was Max's only reply, as he reached for his bagel and looked back out the window. Ed let himself out, making sure not to let the door slam behind him.

Max chewed his bagel, fighting the sense of unease he had about Jonathan. Perhaps he was just getting old. Jonathan Prescott III was probably his last shot at the White House. There were others in his stable, but none as promising. No one who had Jonathan's breeding; no one with the name recognition; no one as handsome. Jonathan was his best shot. He tried not to want it so much. He reminded himself that he could screw the pooch if he tried too hard. It was like Ed said, the fish needed some play in the line. Don't rush it. He sipped his tea, which was not hot enough, even with the new warming device he had received as a present from his nephew. He buzzed his secretary to ask for a fresh cup, but told her not to rush. Patience, he said to himself, was a virtue.

Chapter 10

"**S**ENATOR PRESCOTT, YOU MAKE ME PROUD to be an American."

Jonathan smiled across the small table at Milton Coombs. "That's very kind of you to say, Milt. I appreciate it." Jonathan finished swallowing a slightly over-cooked shrimp and reached for his water glass. He didn't really care much for the food at Big Bob's Oyster House, but it was close to the Capitol building and the constituents liked to go there for lunch because there were so many other congressmen and senators there on any given weekday who could be waved at or glad-handed. And the waitresses were hot.

Milt Coombs was rail-thin and always looked like he could use a good meal. Jonathan marveled to himself at Milt's success in business, despite not seeming to be all that bright. He had founded Hobby Heaven in Tulsa only ten years earlier as a local supply outlet for his wife's scrapbooking obsession. He filled the store with Christian icons, posted the Ten Commandments on the front door, and advertised the store as a haven for good Christians who wanted a wholesome, family-oriented place to shop. The decorations in the store for all the yearly holidays were over-the-top amazing. For Christmas it was a galaxy of lights, but no Santa Claus allowed. He was so successful that he had expanded throughout Oklahoma and then nationwide and now had two hundred thirty stores coast-to-coast.

When the EEOC scolded him for having a Christians-only hiring policy, he tried to have the company re-formed as a religiously affiliated non-profit, but the IRS wouldn't go for it. It was the IRS's unsympathetic stance that prompted Milt to contact Jonathan, who was highly recommended by conservative radio talk show host Bryan Bailey. Milt had twelve stores in Connecticut, so Jonathan could legitimately consider him to be a constituent.

Over the years, Max Foster convinced Milt to contribute toward a super-PAC that financed advertising and lobbying efforts for conservative Christian causes. The Hearthstone PAC, as it was called, also produced political advertising in favor of particular bills and positions, and attacked politicians who were opposed to those bills and positions, but without expressly endorsing any candidates for office. In Max's parlance, Milt was a "whale" – a huge contributor who could be counted on for significant money when needed.

"Now, how's it going on that bill to allow religious hiring, Senator?" Milt was wiping his mouth with a cloth napkin he then let fall carelessly onto his empty plate. Mealtime and small talk were apparently over and it was time for Milt to get down to business. He stared across the silk rose sticking up in the middle of the table in a while porcelain vase, waiting for an answer.

"The bill is drafted, Milt, and we're working on getting co-sponsors for it in the House before we submit it to committee." Jonathan pushed aside his half-eaten plate of seafood pasta, happy to have an excuse to stop eating. "The more co-sponsors, the better our chances will be, although I have to tell you there will be a problem trying to explain how the bill doesn't conflict with the anti-discrimination laws already on the books."

"I hope it does conflict, that's the whole point, right – to repeal those laws?" Milt tapped his index finger on the table for emphasis, making the golden cross lapel pin on his jacket shake.

"Milt, it's not that easy. What we're trying to do is carve out a very small exception to the otherwise generally applicable anti-discrimination law to allow some flexibility in hiring for church-based private employers. If it looks like we're trying to give everyone in the country *carte blanche* to discriminate against Jews and Muslims and anyone else based on religious beliefs, we'll have no chance." Jonathan breathed in and counted to five, then breathed out to the same count. A relaxation technique designed to help him remain calm and not get too argumentative. Milton Coombs was a man who wanted what he wanted and he did not take failure well. His donations were important enough that Jonathan's assignment was to keep him happy – without promising success.

"Just as long as Hobby Heaven falls into the exception," Milt spat out, folding his arms across his chest. "We're clear on that, right?"

"Very clear, Milt," Jonathan soothed. "When we're in committee, we will make sure to mention several times that Hobby Heaven is an example of the kind of business our bill is intended to address, although we also need to be clear that it's a more broadly applicable law – it's not just a special treatment bill for your business."

"Yeah, I understand that," Milt replied, pouting slightly. A specifically targeted piece of legislation was exactly what he wanted. "And let me ask you, Senator, what are you doing to help us out on those abortion control laws the Hearthstone ads are always talking about? Is there anything on the table on that front?"

Jonathan was caught a bit off guard by the question, so he reached for his water glass to buy some time. He knew the

Hearthstone PAC was funding television and radio commercials supporting state laws in Texas, Oklahoma, Kansas, and a few other places that placed regulatory burdens on abortion clinics. He wracked his brain trying to recall the details, but quickly figured he would just let Milt give him a briefing, since it was clearly a pet subject of his. "Milt, why don't you remind me of where Hearthstone is on those issues, to jog my memory."

"Well, you know we're supporting the Texas Family Values Foundation that is funding the litigation defending the clinic licensing law against the Planned Parenthood bastards."

"Yes," Jonathan nodded.

"We got the bill passed in the state legislature and signed by the governor – I really wish Rick would run for president again. Anyway, we're all good there and we're ready to shut down those abortion holes but they went to court to challenge the law and the lower court agreed with the liberals and so we're now on appeal and the law is on hold until the appeals court makes a decision. We're running ads in support to put pressure on the judges."

"Good idea," Jonathan agreed. "You never can tell what will motivate a federal judge when making decisions on these kinds of issues. Having public opinion against you can be intimidating. But these kinds of laws are very much state and local issues, there isn't a lot we can do on a national level on that."

"Why the hell not?" Milt exclaimed, sitting forward in his chair and lowering his voice. "These bastards have to be stopped, and we found a magic bullet, see. We make 'em conform to all the requirements of an out-patient surgical hospital, and they can't do it, so they have to close down. And it's all legal and neutral, like you said – it has to seem like it's a general law to protect health and safety, which is bull of course because it's targeted to shut down only abortion clinics, but who cares if we get it done? Why can't we have that at a national level?"

"Because requirements for medical facilities are not made on a national level – they are state laws enforced by state inspectors and state health departments. It's not the federal government's place to be telling states what standards to have for their hospitals." Jonathan tried to keep his voice calm and with a hint of regret that he couldn't do more to help Milt.

"You could try," Milt noted, pleadingly. "You could have a bill in Congress for it, even if the courts won't enforce it. It would set a good precedent for other state fights."

"You might be right about that, Milt. Let me bring it up in the next Republican Caucus on the Hill and see if I can get any support for the idea." Jonathan was hoping for a quick end to the lunch meeting so he could get back to his office, but Milt didn't seem in a hurry. Their waiter had brought the check in a black leather cover and placed it next to Milt, but he had made no move yet to pay it.

"And what about Planned Parenthood? They're the biggest sponsor of abortion clinics in the country, why can't we run them off – cut off their federal funding? We should nail those bastards to a cross." Milt looked around him, worried that someone might have overheard.

"Milt, federal law already prohibits Planned Parenthood from using any federal money to fund abortions. That comes from private donations. All the other money they get is part of general appropriations for health services organizations. They provide health care and cancer screenings to women who qualify for federal Medicare, so there's not much we can do without dismantling all of Medicare. You can fight them in the media and try to convince people not to contribute their money. I think that's a more productive approach." Jonathan removed his suit jacket from the back of his chair and stood up to put it on, signaling, he hoped, that the meal was at an end. But Milt waggled a finger in Jonathan's direction, inviting him to sit back down and come closer, as if he had some secret to reveal.

Milt leaned toward the middle of the table and spoke in a hushed voice, "What if we could catch them Planned Parenthood bastards in a real scandal?"

Jonathan joined in the conspiratorial posture and leaned over the table toward Milt. "What kind of scandal?"

"Let's just say I know some folks who are working on it. We know they're doing late term abortions against the law, and coercing girls to give up their babies' organs for transplant and research, which is illegal. And we're pretty sure they're selling off the baby parts for profit. We're going to prove it."

Jonathan sat back and whistled silently to himself. "Well, that would be a bombshell indeed, Milt. Do you have some mole inside the organization giving you information?"

Milt blushed slightly and shook his head. "I can't say anything more, Senator, but just you be watching. We're gonna have some humdinger commercials coming out once we get all the dirt on 'em. Then we'll see whether there's anything you can do in Congress."

"Well, if they violate any federal laws along the way, I'm sure we can try to get the federal prosecutors on them."

"You'd better," Milt said, finally reaching for his credit card. "We're gonna shut them down and make sure there's no place in America that will perform an abortion."

Jonathan softly bit into his lower lip, knowing he should not get into any kind of discussion with Milt Coombs on the subject of whether there were some circumstances when a safe abortion procedure should be made available, or whether the perils of unlicensed and illegal abortion providers was actually worse than Planned Parenthood. This was not the time or the place. He heard Max Foster's voice in his head, telling him, "Just feed the whale and keep him happy." Jonathan stretched out his hand to Milt and gave him a solid shake, explaining that he had a vote on the floor in less than an hour and he really had to run.

At the table next to him, William Schook, the junior senator from Rhode Island, was having lunch with a man Jonathan did not recognize. Schook looked up at Jonathan and said, "Oh, hey, Senator Prescott, is that vote today?" Schook winked imperceptivity toward Jonathan.

"Oh, yes, Bill, it's this afternoon, you'd better not miss it."

Senator Schook began making his apologies about having to cut the lunch meeting short as he gathered his things. Jonathan met him on the sidewalk outside the restaurant and they walked at a hurried pace back toward the Capitol complex.

"Thanks, Jon. I needed an exit strategy there."

"No problem," Jonathan responded, without making eye contact. "Are you coming to the DAR Gala next month? My wife is the co-chair and she's looking for a few more senators to be on the receiving line."

"I'll let you know, Jon," Schook said, as he peeled away and made a right turn toward a Starbucks. "I owe you lunch for getting me out of that one."

"Any time," Jonathan said to himself as his colleague strode away. "Next time maybe you'll save me from Milt Coombs."

Chapter 11

MAX REALIZED HE WAS SLOUCHING. The soft leather seat on which his bulk rested was well worn and its springs were lazy, allowing him to sink deep into the cushions. When he reached toward the small black table for his glass of Jamison's, he realized he could barely reach it because he had sunk so far down. His grandmother would scold him for such poor posture. He struggled forward, scooched his butt against the back of the settee and arched his back, while planting the soles of his $350 Gucci shoes firmly on the stiff carpeting. He was less comfortable, but he looked better. He smiled to himself, thinking of the Billy Crystal character from the 80s saying, "It is better to look good than to feel good." True, he thought.

He glanced down at his Omega wristwatch, then glanced toward one of his two companions on this little excursion. His name was Earl. Max didn't know his last name and didn't really care. The security operation that handled his trips, Knapp & Company, was the best in New York. He trusted Earl to do his job, because he knew and trusted Charlie Knapp, who had been chief of detectives for the NYPD before he got his pension and launched his own private security operation, taking two dozen of New York's finest with him. Earl was seated at the corner of the bar, with a split view of Max's booth in the back and the front door. Earl's back was to the restrooms and the kitchen. Anyone coming or going would have to pass him. He was wearing a gray pinstriped suit and a burgundy tie, which was lagging an inch under the unbuttoned collar of his Custom Shop dress shirt. He had the hang-dog look of a tired business executive, killing time in the bar of the airport Marriott after a long day of dealing. Max smiled again, because Earl was so very good at his job. He didn't look a bit like a private security operative. Max didn't like the word "bodyguard." It made him nervous. He knew Earl's partner, a shorter, stouter man who went by the name "Bud," was outside, watching the lobby.

Max hated traveling to these meetings, but it was necessary. It was part of their deal. Twice a year in Max's office in New York, and twice on the road. Like a basketball team's schedule; balanced. Any emergency meetings that became necessary would be worked out *ad hoc*, but this was the regular meeting. Second quarter. Road trip. Max barely recalled what city he was in. The airport Marriott – could be anywhere. That was the point, although it didn't make Max smile. He'd already had two smiles in five minutes. He was over his limit. And his man was late, which soured Max's mood even more than having to sit up straight on the damn booth seat.

When Earl straightened up on his bar stool, Max tensed, knowing the party was starting, even though from his seat in the dark corner, Max could not see the bar entrance. The place had been scouted thoroughly, and they had met here before, so there were no surprises. On a Tuesday afternoon at 5:15, the crowd was light. The back booths were sheltered around a corner from the doorway, and no patrons had yet attempted to occupy any of the two surrounding booths. Earl had already tipped the two bored waitresses twenty dollars each to make sure they didn't bother the man in the back. There were already two glasses on the table. Like most things in Max's life, it was like clockwork.

Abraham Hawkins slid into the seat across from Max with barely a ruffle of his suit jacket, which he tossed down on the seat next to him as he straightened his cuffs and reached for his drink. After a small sip and a deep swallow, he said, "Hello, Max."

"You know, I could have poisoned that whiskey. You should be more careful. Might want to consider having one of your boys get you your own drink." Max stared at the reverend, with no outward sign of mirth.

"Well, now, Max, I s'pose that's true," he added a little extra southern drawl for the occasion, "but now why in the world would you want me dead? Am I not your best and finest partner in our joint work for the Lord?" Abraham took another, larger, sip from his glass. It was room temperature, twelve years old, and so smooth he barely felt the burn on the back of his throat. "Can I not trust you, my old friend?"

Max's stare never left the preacher's eyes. He pursed his lips in a wan smile, then offered, "It's a strange world, Abraham. You just never can tell."

"Well, then," Abraham replied, losing all pretense of the southern accent now and putting on more of a Samuel L. Jackson attitude voice, "I suppose it's also possible you had the whole bottle of The Glenlivet poisoned, and even if my boy had gone behind the bar and poured it his own self my glass would still be a killer. Isn't that about right, Max?"

Max now allowed himself a genuine smile, and broke his stare-down eye contact with his table mate. He raised his own glass and offered it across the table. "A toast, then. To trust." Abraham smiled back, and softly clinked his glass with Max's. "To trust." Both men drank a good belt, and Max signaled subtly to Earl for another round. He wanted Abraham well lubricated tonight.

"So," Abraham inquired, "how are we doing?" It was the end of the small talk and the beginning of the business portion of the meeting. Abraham had places to be, and Max was planning on making the 6:55 back to New York. The bulk of the discussion was fairly routine for both men, but they agreed face-to-face meetings were essential to their dealings. No chance of bugs or interception of telephone calls, plus each man could place himself with the other at those particular times and places so each knew they depended on the other's discretion. Abraham didn't know that when Max traveled, his name was Morton Armstrong, and that he had a driver's license, passport, and photos of Mort's three kids to prove it. Abraham also didn't know that Max Foster was on a conference call with business clients in Hong Kong, which would not end for another twenty minutes. The man who imitated Max's voice so well that not even an FBI voice print over a telephone line would be conclusive was named Vince DiVincenzo, and he lived on Staten Island. Abraham didn't need to know.

The meetings had started in 2002, after The Foster Group had been providing business advice, program planning, and fundraising support for the reverend's ministry for several years. Abraham had over-extended his finances to open satellite ministry offices and his cash flow was weakened by a drop off in contributions after September 11, 2001. Abraham needed some credit help, and Max wanted support for a Republican congressman from northern Florida who had suffered through a sex scandal involving a Black prostitute. A hooker alone, or the cocaine by itself, might have been manageable, but a White congressman with three young kids caught in the company of a Black drug-addict prostitute in a Tallahassee motel was a doomsday scenario.

But the guy was next in line to be the chair of the Armed Services committee, and seniority like that was hard to come by. Max needed the man to repent his sins, gain forgiveness, and curry favor with the Black evangelical population of the second congressional district of Florida in order to make up for lost votes among White independents. He was willing to offer support for a federal fair housing loan program for inner-city single parents and he was offering up a half-million dollar line of credit at prime minus 2 points arranged through a bank that owed the congressman a favor.

A week later, the most disgraced member of the House of Representatives made an appearance on nationally syndicated television in the House of the Lord, care of Abraham Hawkins. Max had to admit later that it was a damned fine show. The guy had wept openly. He had torn the knees of his Brooks Brothers suit crawling across the wooden stage, prostrated himself before the altar of God, and begged Abraham for forgiveness. Abraham twice denied him, and berated him for his sins, for his shallowness, and for his transparent attempt to fool his congregation into believing that such a wretch could actually repent. The reverend had walked away from the sobbing man and scorned him.

Then, out of the audience came a Black woman. She had long, braided hair. She shouted at Abraham, with her arms outstretched. She said her daughter, Rhonda, had succumbed to drugs, and had walked the streets as a prostitute. That Rhonda had almost died until she came home, and then she found the church, and she was *saved* and she was getting well and she was right there in the pew, and the woman said that *Rhonda* could forgive the man; that *Rhonda* knew how hard the Devil could work on us; and that if *Rhonda* could find it in her heart to give the man another chance at Heaven, then surely Abraham could.

There was not a dry eye in the house when it was over. The congressman vowed to return to his wife and kids, which he did until three months after the election when she moved out and signed a very comfortable divorce settlement, which Max had arranged shortly after the televised repentance. The congressman moved into an apartment in Washington, having won forty-eight percent of the Black vote against a liberal Democrat and sailed to re-election. The Democratic National Committee would think long and hard about financing a strong opposition to him again in that district. His seniority, and eventual chairmanship, were safe. Max had a chit in his pocket. A big one. Abraham's financial crisis was soothed. Everybody was happy. Just the way Max liked it.

Since then, The Foster Group had provided Abraham's ministry with consulting services of various kinds. The bulk of services were provided under an arrangement where Foster's company made tax-deductible donations to Abraham's registered section 501(c)(3) charity in the same amount as the ministry paid. In some cases, the value of the services, and the time records supporting those services, were somewhat inflated as compared to similar services provided to fully paying clients, but Abraham never complained.

When the IRS investigated the accounting practices associated with the church's merchandise sales, and why such a large portion of the $19.4 million in gross revenues in 2003 had been transferred to a subsidiary corporation, which was not registered as a tax-exempt entity, The Foster Group ran interference for Abraham. Max called in a favor he had coming from the assistant Secretary of the Treasury and the investigation was closed after Abraham paid a nominal fine and agreed to either shut down the subsidiary or get it properly registered. Since the construction company had finished the work on Abraham's new house, it was not a problem to close down the subsidiary and transfer all assets to Abraham's newly formed charitable foundation.

When three employees of the ministry were arrested on charges of using the Abraham Hawkins "On the Road for God" busses as a distribution network for cocaine trafficking in four southern states, Max made sure the press coverage was muted. He fed the inquiring reporters information about the ring leaders, who were ex-cons who had duped the well-meaning regional supervisor of the ministry's rural outreach program by using false identification to get their jobs as bus drivers. Abraham was never implicated. One of the three was Hawkins' first cousin, but his identity was never made public.

Max had done well by Abraham, and Abraham had always understood the value of a favor. The ministry now had sixteen separate tax-exempt corporations that operated in forty-seven states. The reverend was far too busy to actually monitor his organization, and so he had long since turned over that tedious chore to Max, who had three staff members spending a significant amount of their time managing Abraham's empire. The Foundation paid for these services. When Max needed to get out a message to the Black community, he had a conduit far more effective than the six o'clock news or the internet. He had Abraham fucking Hawkins.

Max finished up the financial report in fifteen minutes. Just the highlights. The full financials would be sent in writing, not that Abraham would bother to try to read them. Now it was time to get down to the real business of the meeting.

"I gotta get confirmation that the Selma situation is under control," Hawkins stated, trying his best to sound calm.

Max frowned. "Abe, you know you're wasting your money with that church in Selma, and the museum. It's a white elephant. You'll be pouring money into that hole for years without any return."

Hawkins shifted in his seat and slicked back his hair with his left hand, a move his father had taught him to use before beginning an oration. "Max, I know, you've told me before and I'm sure you'll tell me again. But it's not a business deal. Those folks lost their church in a fire and they are good people. Some of them marched with Doctor King. I promised I would help them rebuild and that I would finance the museum to make sure that The March was never forgotten in Selma. I gave them my word, and they need me."

"C'mon, Abe. What's the angle? What's in this for you?"

"Nothin', Max. Not one thing other than knowing that my ministry is doing good works. I need that, Max."

"What, so that the IRS won't start taxing your television revenue?"

"No," the reverend was quiet for a moment, then continued. "No, Max, because the Lord works through me and I am responsible for those people. There's a little girl in that congregation who is twelve years old and who sings like an angel and she could be a star someday, but she needs a choir to sing in. And those people have nothin' but dirt and debt and they need their church. I know the pastor there. He's a good and decent man. Never took no money from nobody. He works his ass off for his flock, and he's the most humble man you'll ever meet. He reminds me of my papa."

Max didn't have a snappy comeback for that one. He opted for a small sip of his Jamison's. "Abe, I didn't mean to imply—"

"That's OK," Hawkins interrupted. "I know. I know I got some repenting to do on my own. But God has blessed me with this ministry and this voice and it is my duty to use that to help folks and to praise His name. I do that every night, but I gotta do it in other ways, Max. This is one of them. This is not a corporation trying to maximize profits. It's a ministry, Max. Don't forget."

Max bowed his head slightly, acknowledging the rightness of the statement. He also knew what the balance sheet looked like, and knew good works were not the only item on the reverend's agenda. "Now, Abe, I have something for you." Max leaned back, smirking, allowing the anticipation and curiosity to get the better of his companion.

"What you got?" Abraham leaned up to the edge of the small table, his eyes alive. At these moments, Abraham looked like a drug addict whose dealer was reaching into a pocket, ready to bring out the dope. Anticipation. Hunger. Abraham thrived on the rush that came from power. He didn't seem to care what Max wanted done, as long as he could, in his own mind, and in these quiet conversations with the fat man from New York, take credit for shaping the world.

"This is long-term, Abe," Max began, looking directly into the reverend's eyes. "I believe we may have an executive candidate. Maybe for 2020, or 2024. It needs to be cultivated carefully. We're talking here about every federal judicial appointment, including the Supreme Court, and every executive appointment from the NLRB to the Federal Reserve Board."

Abraham's eyes widened even more than normal, showing white all around the dark circle of his brown irises. Max could see the fine red lines of blood vessels bulging. The reverend looked away and let out a soft whistle, then blurted out "Oooh-wee, are you serious? The mother-fucking President of the Yoo-nited States?"

Max deadpanned his response. "Yes, that's exactly what I'm talking about. But, like I said, it's a long-term opportunity. You can never predict these things. Even you and I working together can't make it happen without a lot of other help. But we have a seed and I want it planted and nurtured. I'm going to want small references. Not too often. Just every once in a while. A mention of some legislation he got passed, or something he said in a speech. My writers do good work for him. I'll give you copies and excerpts. See if you can work a quote or two into a sermon every once in a while, and attribute it to him. Get his name out there so people start to know who he is in the Black community. Make sure the associations are positive. Nothing specific – we're not asking anyone to vote for him yet. We just want the subconscious minds to hear his name and feel good about it. Understand?"

Abraham nodded. "Shouldn't be a problem. What's the dude's name?"

"Senator Jonathan Prescott."

"The old fart?" Abraham spat out, incredulous. "Man, that mother is half a step removed from being a slave owner. Damn! What are you thinkin'?"

Max smiled a gentle, reassuring smile for Abraham. "No, Abe, the old fart is his father. Jonathan Prescott III is forty-seven. He's good-looking and he's smart. He actually has a bit of a liberal streak in him, which will help you sell him, but I think we can manage that on my end. He gives a good speech, and his father's name holds him in good stead in the conservative world. What we need is the ability for him to win votes in liberal states, and particularly in the Black community. He polls at twelve percent positive among Blacks of voting age, and only fourteen percent even know who he is outside of Connecticut. We need to get those numbers up. The good news is that we have some time. Years. Like I said, this is a long game."

Abraham sat back in his seat. "Man," he sighed. "The fucking president." He took a deep drink from his third glass of scotch and drifted off into his own thoughts. Max let him go, watching the wheels turn in Abraham's head. Max was certain that the preacher was envisioning himself giving the invocation at the inaugural ball. The elder Senator Prescott would have a heart attack, of course, if a Black preacher from Alabama so much as entered the room at his son's inaugural. But the seed had been planted. The meeting had been successful. It was time to catch his plane home.

Chapter 12

December, 1988

THEY WERE ON THE WAY HOME from a night out to celebrate the completion of final exams. Janice, Gwen, and most of Frank's other friends had ganged up on him and dragged him out of the suite of dorm rooms in Hartley Hall. Jonathan even got Frank to let him pay for dinner as a thank-you for Frank's help with their economics class. They all needed an excuse to blow off some steam. A mid-December chill was in the air, and the holiday lights were up on all the poles along Broadway.

They were all exhausted after a week of finals, but it was a festive gathering as fifteen college students talked excitedly about their plans for the upcoming winter break. Gwen's family was going to the Caribbean for two weeks. Janice was staying on campus to work on *The Spectator*. Frank was going home to visit his family on the west coast for the first time since starting school. Everyone was feeling optimistic about life. By the end of the night, it was just Frank, Jonathan, Janice, and Gwen closing down the place.

Janice was in a particularly good mood, supported by three Mai Tais, and was hanging onto Frank for support as the four friends stepped onto the Number One train, headed uptown. The Hunan Balcony was on 99th Street and Broadway, and the walk down to 96th Street to catch the subway had been an adventure, between Janice swaying across the sidewalk and Jonathan insisting on singing Christmas carols as loud as possible at 1:30 a.m. Frank had suggested they could just walk back to campus – it was only 16 blocks – but Jonathan had insisted the subway would be much warmer. He was right. Out of the biting wind, it was quite a bit more comfortable underground.

Gwen was pleasantly buzzed after finishing off most of a bottle of cheap champagne over dinner, and was clutching Jonathan's elbow like a barnacle. The group rushed through the turnstile when they heard an approaching uptown train, knowing it would be a long wait for another at that hour. Jonathan dropped a token on the ground and just stuffed another into the slot and ignored the stray coin. They rushed into the car closest to the entrance just as the doors closed and Jonathan pumped his fist at their good fortune.

"Merry Christmas, everybody! Got lucky, eh? Good day indeed!"

Frank smiled and raised an imaginary glass to toast Jonathan's statement. "A good day indeed, my friend."

They sang "Let it Snow" as the train rattled past 103rd Street and 110th Street. They were having so much fun they hardly noticed they were the only passengers in the car, or that they were in the next to last car on the train. They spilled out onto the platform at 116th Street and staggered toward the exit at the far northern end of the station like two entrants in a three-legged race. Janice was glued to Frank's arm, and Gwen was hanging off Jonathan, who had broken into a chorus of "God Rest Ye Merry Gentlemen." None of them noticed the two figures pressed up against the wall halfway between them and the stairway. It wasn't until they were a few feet away that they all pulled up short as if a traffic light had suddenly turned red.

"Give it up, motherfuckers!"

It was the smaller of the two men who spoke. He was barely five feet tall, but he made up for it with menacing eyes. He was dark-skinned, with a black hooded sweatshirt covering his head, creating a shadow across much of his face. Frank couldn't tell for sure if he was Black or Hispanic. His baggy jeans were stained and frayed at the bottoms, but his sneakers were shiny white, like they were just out of the box. His companion was at least a full foot taller, and weighed twice as much. He was Black with a bald head that reflected the lights fifty feet above them on the ceiling of the subway tunnel. He wore a dirty letterman's jacket from some high school with a large letter "H" on the chest in maroon, fringed with white. He never said a word, but his presence was like the proverbial 800-pound gorilla in the room. The smaller man pulled out a switchblade and popped it open with an ominous click.

Frank's mouth dropped open, but he could not speak. He stared up at the big Black man, then down at the smaller man with the knife; then stepped back, dragging Janice with him. Jonathan stood still, in mid-song, then burst out, "What the fuck?"

The smaller man thrust his knife out toward Jonathan. "You're fucked, asshole – now gimmie your fucking wallet." He glared at Jonathan and stuck the knife out farther in his direction.

Jonathan's shoulders drooped and he pushed Gwen behind him with his left hand. "I can't fucking believe this."

"Believe it, motherfucker."

"Great vocabulary," Jonathan muttered, as he reached into his jacket pocket and withdrew his wallet. The short man reached out and grabbed the wallet, then grabbed Jonathan's arm and pulled him forward hard, making him lose his balance and fall to the cold concrete platform. The short man then kicked the side of Jonathan's head, causing him to groan as blood spurted out of his lip.

"You, too," the short man barked, as he turned his blade in Frank's direction. "Bitches too!"

Frank reached into his jeans pocket and took out his wallet. He opened it and held it out toward the small man, showing him the money inside and pulling it out. "Hey, no problem, dude, here's my money – take it – but why not let me keep my ID and shit, OK? No good to you, right?"

The small man grabbed the money, and knocked Frank's wallet away with his hand. It flew over the side of the platform and down onto the subway tracks. "Shit!" Frank ejaculated.

"Hurry up, bitches!"

Janice and Gwen were frozen for a moment, but they both began to fumble for their purses. Meanwhile, the small man stuffed Jonathan's wallet into his pocket. Neither Janice nor Gwen could seem to locate their money. Janice was whimpering and her hands were shaking so badly she could hardly manage to get her clasp undone.

"Fuck this," the big man said in a deep baritone. The short man nodded, and both turned around and ran toward the stairs, leaving the group of friends stunned in their place. They watched as the two dark shapes reached the top of the stairs and turned left, toward the Barnard campus.

Jonathan dragged himself up off the ground, wiping blood away from his mouth. "God damned niggers!" Jonathan spat out. "I can't believe that!" Jonathan looked at Frank with his eyes blazing.

Frank stared back, not believing what he had just heard. Janice's mouth was agape. Gwen was staring at the ground. Frank was hoping Jonathan would apologize, but he kept going. "We fucking pay for their bastard children and they suck up our welfare and do they appreciate it and make any effort? Fuck no, they just put it up their noses and keep on stealing. We should just send them all back to fucking Africa." Jonathan was breathing hard and kept wiping the trickle of blood away from his mouth.

"Hey, that was pretty intense, dude," Frank offered. "I'm shaking. I know you don't mean that shit."

Jonathan just glared back at Frank, then turned to Gwen. "You all right, Sweetie?"

Gwen was still trembling. Jonathan put his arm around her shoulders and supported her. "I – I think so," she stammered. "Can we just leave?"

"Sure," Jonathan said soothingly. He started walking toward the exit, with Frank and Janice following along in silence. Nobody spoke as they emerged above ground into the still, cold air of the early morning. Up and down Broadway the green lights dotted each intersection like a line of Christmas ornaments, with only one lonely cab zooming northward past campus. Frank suggested they report the robbery to campus security. Jonathan only grunted, which Frank figured was close enough to an affirmative response, and so he steered them in that direction.

The sleepy security guard took their information and advised them to cancel any credit cards that were in their wallets. Jonathan nodded, looking impatient. "Oh, crap!" Frank exclaimed. "My wallet. It's still down on the subway tracks." The guard frowned, while Jonathan just glared at Frank as if he'd forgotten to feed the dog.

After the guard told them they would have to wait until the next day to get new student ID cards, Jonathan said he'd walk Gwen back to her dorm. He asked Janice if she would want to come along, but she quietly declined and said she'd stay with Frank while he went back to the subway to try to retrieve his wallet. "Okay, I'll see you back at Hartley." Frank waved at Jonathan, who was already walking out with Gwen.

After walking in silence halfway back to the 116th street gate, Frank figured he should say something. "Man, I guess we pretty much walked right into that situation, didn't we?"

"Yeah," Janice mumbled, her head down; hands stuffed deep into her coat pockets.

Frank pressed on. "I mean, if I live in New York long enough, I'm bound to get mugged eventually, right?"

"Getting off the subway at the end of the platform at two in the morning probably increases your odds."

Frank smiled, then burst out laughing – glad Janice could still get out a quip like that after what they had been through. Janice joined the laughter, then pulled her right hand out of her pocket and slipped her arm through Frank's elbow, pulling herself against his body as they walked along the bricks of College Walk. "It sucks, but it could have been worse."

"Yes, definitely could have been worse. Except for Jon's reaction."

They stopped laughing and looked at each other. Frank offered, "It was just the heat of the moment. I'm sure Jon didn't mean that. I've never heard him say anything like that before. Nothing close. Aberration."

"Well, people's true colors tend to come out when they're under stress. His father's a closet bigot, you know."

"What?" Frank stared incredulously at Janice.

"Oh, yeah. Back in the early sixties, during the beginnings of the Civil Rights movement, Jon's father supported George Wallace's barricade of the University of Alabama. Made some very nasty speeches about the propriety of segregation. Later he claimed to see the light, but some people think he was always a racist."

"Wow, I didn't know that. But Jon is not his father. He doesn't even like his father."

"Yeah, well, apples and trees, you know."

Frank pondered the possibility that his best friend really believed the bile he had spewed forth an hour earlier. He shook his head, not wanting to consider the prospect.

Chapter 13

ABRAHAM HAWKINS SAT, slumped slightly forward, in front of a huge mirror ringed with soft light bulbs. He leaned even closer to the mirror and focused on the small gray hair extending from his left nostril. Reaching up and pinching the errant protrusion between the manicured nails of his thumb and index finger, he tugged sharply, wincing at the pain. He gazed for a moment at the extracted hair, holding it up to the light and wondering exactly when his nose hairs had turned white. The pompadour of thick black hair on his head, he knew, was chemically enhanced – both for volume and color – which was why he always appeared with a close shave. A white beard simply didn't suit his image, although every so often one of his well-meaning aides suggested that a little gray around the temples would project a wise, scholarly look.

When was it? He continued to stare at the nostril hair, then looked back at the mirror, searching for new lines in his face – under his eyes, where he regularly applied Lancôme anti-wrinkle cream. At $110 per ounce, the crap had better do the job, he thought ruefully. At his income level, he could afford the best that cosmetics had to offer. He had considered surgery, but if it were to come out that he had a face lift, he would appear vain – something he constantly preached against. Bad form.

He closed his eyes and reached for the stubby rock crystal glass on the dressing table, half-filled with amber liquid and two semi-melted ice cubes. A slow sip, then a gulp. He sighed. These moments of melancholy were getting more frequent. Perhaps he needed a break. Perhaps he just needed a new cause – something to really get excited about and sink his teeth into. Like the old days.

Abraham Ray Hawkins was born July 31, 1944 in a small town outside of Montgomery, Alabama, the son of a country preacher. He was the eldest of seven children. His mother worked hard to keep their three-room house clean and put food on the table, much of which was donated by members of the church congregation. She always wore a starched dress and a simple string of white pearls, which accented the deep black skin of her slender neck. At least, that was how Abraham remembered it. Never a dumpy house dress. Never pants. Never a night shirt. Even when cleaning the house or bathing the smaller children. Always one of those stiff dresses, which she washed by hand and hung out to dry before ironing. She was keenly aware of her appearance, being the preacher's wife.

Thaddeus Horacio Hawkins, his father, was the son of a share-cropper and the grandson of a slave who had lived on a South Carolina plantation. Abraham's grandfather had moved to Alabama seeking a free life, but instead found only a quick death working in the textile mill. Abraham's grandmother then died in childbirth, leaving one still-born daughter and a two-year-old orphan son. Thad was adopted by the pastor of the Baptist church; a free Black man, college educated, who had moved to Alabama from Chicago in search of a mission. Pastor Horacio Hawkins later moved outside of town – away from the increasingly violent racist attacks against Black families – where he established a little congregation in the town of Cecil, Alabama. He adopted the abandoned boy and gave him the name Thaddeus after St. Jude, whose last name was Thaddeus, and his own surname. Thad had grown up in the church, and became the pastor after his adopted father died in 1939. Pastor Thad married a local girl and proceeded to fulfill the biblical edict to be fruitful and multiply.

Pastor Thad also explained to his son, as they took long walks to visit the members of the congregation, how the Church would provide help and comfort to those in need. He encouraged his flock (for that's how he thought of them) to seek him out and ask for help, and he would always give help – at least some – to all in need. That was God's work. The more people received help from the Church, the more they appreciated the love of God, and felt connected to the community, and the more their friends and neighbors and relatives would then give, because they could see the good works. Abraham understood the economic model his father had established.

But why, Abraham had asked, did they live in such a drab, cramped little house, when the church had enough money to build a fine, proper house for its pastor and his family? His father had explained that, too. He explained how the pastor could never appear to be rich, and could never seem to be taking advantage of the money given to the church. The leader of the church must be humble, like Christ, and must suffer as much as the most unfortunate member of the flock in order to truly understand their pain and their need. Abraham never fully understood this lesson, but accepted it.

In February of 1965, Dr. Martin Luther King Jr. delivered a sermon at the First Baptist Church of Montgomery. The Cecil Choir sang, and Abraham Ray Hawkins was invited to sit on the dais behind the pulpit. Dr. King's speech moved the crowd to wild shouts of approval, and sobs of despair. Abraham was mesmerized by the power of this man's oratory. He watched from behind as Dr. King swelled the crowd, then brought it down, only to build slowly up again toward an emotional climax. This was the master, and Abraham wanted desperately to be the student. He approached Dr. King after the event and shyly introduced himself, asking whether he could possibly participate in the next rally.

On March 7, Abraham was one of the 525 marchers who set out across a bridge in Selma, Alabama, only to be turned back by the Selma police and the National Guard. Abraham was bitten twenty-one times by an attack dog and spent a week in the hospital. When he returned home, he was a legend. The people of Cecil and all the surrounding county flocked to him. Was it true? Was he really there with Dr. King in Selma? He finally got tired of showing off the scars from the dog bites, and it wasn't long before Cecil was too small a town for the legend that was Abraham Hawkins.

Abraham was officially ordained as a Baptist Minister on July 4, 1966. Some of the formalities of his education and religious training were overlooked in the process. Dr. King himself attended the brief ceremony, where six ministers of the word of God were officially proclaimed. He was a member of the Southern Christian Leadership Conference, and bigger things lay ahead. Abraham seldom made it back to Cecil.

He had been on the steps of the Lincoln Memorial when Dr. King said he had a dream, but he was off at a reception for new Black college students at the University of Georgia the day Dr. King was murdered. He was shocked, and enraged, but he also knew the cause must march on. But with Dr. King gone, leadership and direction were hard to come by. He went to Washington, D.C. to meet with activists and made an appearance on a Black-owned radio station, WVOL, with

Stokely Carmichael, who had been involved in the riots following Dr. King's death.

Abraham delivered a passionate appeal for action, and responded to calls from listeners with such poise that the station owner invited him back the next day. Within a few weeks, Abraham Hawkins had his own program four days per week, featuring evangelical preaching, calls for civil action and enforcement of the Civil Rights Act, and guest speakers from the movement and the SCLC. He was popular, and he enjoyed the spotlight. People recognized him around town. He was invited to parties with influential guests. He was named one of the top ten eligible bachelors in D.C. by a local Black magazine. The legend of Abraham Hawkins was growing.

The radio show became so popular locally that it was syndicated on five stations in Virginia and North Carolina. Then to twenty more stations throughout the South, and finally coast-to-coast. Abraham was the voice of Black America.

In 1970, he went on television for the first time at a rally and choir concert to raise money for the NAACP college fund. He wept openly on camera during his appeal, and the flood of callers to the telephone lines swamped the system and shut down phone service to the entire city for twenty minutes. Black leaders started calling him "Midas" behind his back; he could raise money faster than anyone else.

When he was twenty-one years old and marching with Doctor King, he was young and there was so much to do that he did not have time to start a family, or even have a girlfriend. Folks said he was so dedicated to his cause. When he was twenty-five, he was a young firebrand, crisscrossing the South with the civil rights parade, and he was too poor and too unsettled to think about settling down. But there were some rumors that the reverend was not as diligent in following the seventh commandment as perhaps he should be. There were also other rumors that folks only whispered about.

By the summer of 1971, nearing age twenty-six with his radio ministry blooming and his television career just getting off the ground, several of his closest friends and advisors told him that remaining a bachelor was not in the best interests of his image as the father of his congregation. And so, Abraham took a wife. He found a nice girl from Alabama named Sophie Williams. She was beautiful, educated, submissive, and knew her place.

Abraham told everyone he wanted a family with many sons who would follow in his footsteps and spread his ministry even wider in the world. Early the following summer, Sophie became pregnant. This was a truly joyous event that was known to Abraham's entire listening audience. The arrival of Abraham Hawkins' son, or daughter, was greatly anticipated, and Sophie was flooded with gifts that arrived at the apartment daily.

Five days before Christmas, nearing the end of the sixth month of Sophie's pregnancy, Abraham was out of town delivering a sermon in a football stadium in Louisiana. After the sermon, he received a telephone call. Sophie was in the hospital. The details were not disclosed to the press. She remained hospitalized for three days. There would be no baby. Abraham wept openly on the air during his radio show the next day. He talked about his father, the preacher, who had inspired him. He said being a father was his most treasured dream. It was not disclosed whether the Hawkins' unborn baby had been a boy or a girl.

By New Year's Day, Sophie was back in the hospital, having developed what would only be characterized for the public as "complications." Abraham arranged to set up a mobile studio in her hospital room and broadcast his daily radio show from her bedside for six days. Abraham asked his growing radio congregation to pray for his bride. He talked about the child who had been lost, and who would never sing in the choir for him. His producer said later he had never seen Hawkins so emotional and sincere on the air.

On January 10, 1973, Sophie Hawkins died. The hospital confirmed that her death was the result of an infection following the miscarriage of her pregnancy. Hawkins gave a grand eulogy, and told his followers Sophie had been the one true love of his life. From that day forward, he said, his congregation was his family, and the members of his flock were his children. Abraham Hawkins vowed to never marry again, and he held up his deep grief over the tragic death of his young wife as a shield whenever anyone suggested the reverend should not remain a single man. Eventually, he was able to say he was simply too old to start a family.

After Sophie's death, Hawkins worked with a renewed fire and energy. The weight of the world was on him, and there was so much to do. "One step at a time is the only way to walk. Even Jesus walked the Earth one step at a time," his daddy had always said, when they were trudging five miles toward some dusty farm house where an old woman was ill and had called for spiritual support from her pastor.

On January 20, 1973, while he was still mourning Sophie's recent death, the Supreme Court of the United States handed Abraham the best present he would ever receive: *Roe v. Wade*. Despite the rising tide of pregnancy for single Black females in the inner cities of America and the growing number of Black children living in single-parent households, Black ministers across the country denounced the sin of abortion and the unholy court that had legalized the practice.

Here was another cause for Abraham. The Civil Rights movement had started to deflate, but abortion was a cause for the ages – protecting the unborn – like his own unborn child who never had a chance to live. It was God's work, and Abraham took it up with a vengeance. There would be other social and political issues, including school prayer, obscenity, and assisted suicide. Abraham told his flock that Satan wore black robes and sat on a High Court. Eventually, other Black preachers softened on abortion and recognized the relative benefit of avoiding unwanted children, particularly those born to young and impoverished women. Biblical scholars argued about the scriptural foundations for opposition to abortion. Hawkins, however, never gave up the abortion fight. It was his most sacred cause. He had lost his only chance at fatherhood. He felt the pain of every father whose child was taken away under the abortionist's hand. He pleaded with his followers not to ever take for granted a human life, no matter what the circumstances. They may never have another chance at creating life. Abraham knew that pain. He turned it into a sword.

Over the next twenty years, Abraham's gospel was broadcast to more people in the United States than any other Black preacher's. Only Billy Graham had a larger following. His congregation was spread out around the nation and the world, making it less important for him to live a life of poverty like his father. At least, that's what Abraham told himself. Or perhaps his father had simply been wrong about that one. Too bad Thaddeus Horacio Hawkins never had a chance to visit his successful and famous son before he died of a sudden heart attack in 1970. No, Abraham thought, his father would not have approved. So it was just as well he did not have to argue with his father about the issue.

Abraham's stroll down memory lane was abruptly interrupted by a sharp knock on his dressing room door. "Five minutes, Reverend Hawkins," the young stage assistant called.

"Yes," he croaked back, not realizing how dry his mouth was. He took another sip of his scotch, then reached for a bottle of Scope mouthwash and rinsed thoroughly. He brushed his teeth with whitening gel, sprayed antiseptic throat spray onto his tongue, combed back his shining black hair, and pushed away from the dressing table. He looked back at the mirror one last time, and his eyes were drawn to a faded postcard, stuck into the frame in the lower-right corner. It was addressed to him at his old radio station in Washington, and postmarked 1970. It was from his father, and said simply, "Do the Lord's Work." He smiled to himself. He had always kept that postcard in his dressing room, and carried it from studio to studio as his television ministry had grown. It offered him inspiration and comfort.

"I'm doing it, Daddy," he whispered to himself. Then he turned and walked out the door toward the bright lights. "I'm doing it."

Chapter 14

January, 1989

THE THIRD SATURDAY AFTER the mugging, Jonathan was awakened from a very sound sleep by the knocking on his dorm room door. He was uncharacteristically rumpled and disoriented when he cracked open the door and squinted into the light to see Janice sporting a bright smile, holding out a cup of Chock-Full-o-Nuts coffee and offering up a cheery, "Good morning." Jonathan, who was wearing only boxer shorts, quickly shut the door and glanced at the glowing red numbers on his digital clock. 7:22. After a Friday night that hadn't ended until Saturday morning, Jonathan had been planning to sleep until at least ten o'clock.

He wracked his brain, trying to recall what appointment or event – involving Janice – he could have forgotten about. He drew a complete blank. Winter break was half over. His suite was empty except for him. What could Janice possibly want? As he pondered all this, he was startled by another rap on the thin, hollow wood of his door.

"Just gimmie a minute," he mumbled through the door, looking around the floor for some pants. He found a pair of gray sweats which he quickly pulled on, and then re-opened the door. Janice was still there, and still smiling. She handed him the cup of coffee and as he accepted it, she breezed past him into his darkened room. "Now hold on a minute there, Miss Manners. I don't recall inviting you into my room."

Janice sat lightly on the edge of his desk chair and looked up at him. Jonathan wondered why her smile made him so suspicious. She was wearing a thick wool cowl-neck sweater under her winter coat, which was unzipped. The pink and blue threads of the sweater were covered with thin wisps of wool that stood straight out with static electric charges. She had on jeans and black boots. Her red hair was tied back in a neat ponytail and her cheeks were flushed slightly, as if she had just stepped in out of the cold.

"I want you to come with me this morning for a few hours," she said very matter-of-factly, looking directly at his eyes and holding his gaze. "I know you didn't expect me, and I'm sorry for waking you, but I decided this morning that it's important for you, and for me. So get some clothes on and get ready to go. I'm not taking no for an answer, and I'm not leaving until you agree to come with me." She finished in a rush, almost out of breath by the time she got it all out.

Jonathan stared at her in silence for a moment. He couldn't help but admire the way she filled out her sweater, and she looked awfully cute in those boots. He then asked, "You're serious, aren't you?"

"Yes. Quite serious."

"Which is going to be easier for me: arguing with you about this, or just doing what you want?"

Janice smiled even bigger. "Just do what I say, and nobody gets hurt."

Jonathan burst out with a quick laugh. "OK, you win. I'll get dressed. Where are we going?"

"I'll tell you on the way."

Jonathan rolled all the possible explanations for Janice's early-morning raid around in his head as they walked out of Hartley Hall into the cold morning air. As Janice led him out the Amsterdam Avenue side of College Walk and turned left – uptown – he had to ask. "Where, exactly, are we going?"

She shook her head slightly and wrapped her arms around his elbow, partly huddling for warmth, and partly clutching him so he couldn't break away. "You always need to know everything, don't you?" She tugged playfully on his arm. "You just can't stand not being in complete control of every situation."

"It's a reaction to my upbringing. I never had any control over anything in all the years I lived at home. My father, or my mother, always had every detail worked out in advance. Now that I'm on my own here, I guess it's true I like to call the shots. That's not so bad, is it?"

She paused to consider her reply as they skipped across 121st Street just when the light turned yellow. "I suppose it's neither good nor bad. It's just you. But for now, just let me lead, OK?"

They walked along in silence for three more blocks before turning right on 125th Street, heading east. Jonathan glanced around and behind them, but the sidewalks were deserted at this hour on a Saturday. Only a few cars swished by them. "Um, Jan," he stuttered, "you realize this is not a very nice neighborhood, right? I hope you know what you're doing."

Janice set her mouth in a thin line, as if scolding him for the comment. "For your information, this is actually a very nice neighborhood, which you might know if you ever came here."

"It's Harlem," he replied, emphasizing the name as if it were self-defining. "I don't come here, because it's fucking dangerous. At least for people like us."

"That's what you don't understand," Janice shot back, now actively frowning at him. Then her eyes softened, and she tried to smile again – not wanting to get him pissed off and have him bolt back to campus. "We're almost there." She guided him across the street to the north side of 125th, just east of Adam Clayton Powell Boulevard. There, on the corner, was an immense black stone building, with high arches and ornate figures carved into the ancient-looking marble. The sign at the corner of the structure read: "First Baptist Church of Harlem. All are Welcome Within These Walls." Janice led him up the many steps leading to the arched portal into the imposing church. The massive wooden doors were fifteen feet tall, yet swung aside easily at Janice's touch.

Inside the vestibule, it was still and dim. A few candles on a table provided barely enough light to see by. Jonathan looked up and could dimly make out the painted ceiling, illuminated by what light could penetrate a dirty stained glass window set into the stone above the doorway. He could make out clouds and trees among the colorful images. He thought he saw a cow, but didn't have much time to study the fresco. Janice tugged on his elbow and led him to the side of the foyer, down a stairway, and into the basement of the church. "You're not taking me down here to kill me, are you?" Jonathan joked.

"You never know," Janice replied playfully.

When they reached the bottom of the stairs, the illumination level increased tenfold. There, in the bright light of industrial fluorescent bulbs, was a scene familiar to Janice, but which to Jonathan looked like something out of a Salvador Dali painting. The room was massive, at least two hundred feet long and fifty feet wide, with a black-and-white tile floor that looked like an immense chess board. Long tables were set up in neat rows running the length of the room, with gaps every twenty feet forming aisles for the people to walk through. The walls were bare, except for religious icons hung at intervals on the dirty surface that Jonathan guessed had once been white.

At the far end of the room, Jonathan could see the shiny steel of kitchen equipment – serving trays mounted on tables, bins of silverware, stacks of plates, and stacked plastic containers with drinking glasses. Huge steel coffee urns stood on a separate table, flanked by a multi-peaked mountain of Styrofoam cups. The smell of the brewing coffee merged with eggs, bacon, body odor, and wet newspaper. The buzzing of voices, the clanking of plates, and the squeaking of metal chairs against linoleum tiles created a cacophony in stark contrast to the quiet of the church foyer. All this bombarded Jonathan's senses at once as he struggled to absorb the scene.

It was the people who caught the bulk of Jonathan's attention; the mass of people. The immense room seemed to move like a single living creature as the individual figures writhed within it, like a hive of honey bees. Although the room was quite warm, most of the people were wearing coats – or at least multiple layers of clothing – as if they were still outside in the winter chill. Four men at a table very close to the stairway were huddled together playing dominoes, while several more men watched intently. Nearby, three women were talking together while their children played under and around their table. One boy, who looked to be about two, had a red-and-white toy fire truck. He rolled it back and forth while attempting to make a noise like a siren, which added a high note to the auditory symphony. There must have been three hundred people in that basement. There may have been a white face, but Jonathan couldn't make one out. It was a sea of dark faces, dark hair, and dark eyes. Jonathan froze; unable to move. He could feel dozens of eyes staring at him. What in the hell was he doing there?

Gently, Janice pulled his elbow forward, whispering, "Welcome to a part of my world." She led him slowly down the side of the room, between the brightly painted cinder-block wall and the first row of tables. They had to step over one man who was asleep on the floor in a pile of rags and dodge several children who were playing a game that involved throwing a rubber ball against the wall. Jonathan looked around the room, trying not to stare. He thought about making a run for it, but Janice had his elbow in a vice and he didn't want to have to knock her down to break free. They moved in slow motion, as if in a dream. He half expected to wake up any moment, but then realized that in his dreams he never smelled things this strongly.

As they neared the back of the room, Jonathan saw Janice waving at a very large Black woman standing behind a line of people waiting to be served food. She smiled broadly at Janice and motioned her to come back behind the line of tables.

When they wormed their way between the wall and the end of the table setup, the big lady was right there, putting a bear hug on Janice and then turning to Jonathan. Janice made the introductions. "Jon, meet Miss Hattie. She runs this place. Miss Hattie, may I present Jonathan Fitzsimmons."

Jonathan did a quick double-take as he looked at Janice, then smiled, realizing she was protecting his identity. He extended a hand toward Miss Hattie, who grabbed it in a sweaty grip and shook it up and down hard. "Any friend of my little Jan is a friend of mine, and welcome in my kitchen." Then, turning to Janice, she said, "Darlin', we're pretty well off on the line for now if you wanna show Prince Charming here around."

"Thanks," Janice replied quickly, "I'll do that." She turned Jonathan around and led him back into the mosh pit. The next hour was a blur for Jonathan. He trailed after Janice, watching and listening. Some of the people knew her and went out of their way to greet her and spend a few minutes talking. She easily engaged them, sometimes asking about their mothers or sisters as if they were old friends. He saw how they drank up the attention – like they had been dying for some human interaction and relished three minutes of conversation with Janice the way Jonathan had seen business executives relish three minutes of conversation with his father at a $1,000-a-plate fundraiser.

He watched Janice talk to children, both with and without their mothers. She talked to an old man with a scruffy beard who smelled so bad that Jonathan had to work hard not to gag. She spent five minutes with a woman who was so incoherent that Jonathan had no idea what she was saying, yet Janice smiled and nodded like she was making perfect sense.

As they walked away, Jonathan whispered, "Did you understand that?" Janice shook her head slightly and winked at him.

Eventually, they sat down at a table in the corner farthest from the stairway. It was at the very end of the food line, where the people picked up their paper napkins and then turned to go back to a table with their scrambled eggs, bacon, and toast. Janice sat down, greeted a young woman named Denise, and asked her how her son, Harold, was doing. Jonathan thought how WASPish the name was.

Denise and Janice talked for a few minutes, Janice asking about how she had found a job. Denise perked up and explained that she was working as a receptionist at a small law firm in midtown. Janice was thrilled. They talked about the public housing project where Denise and Harold lived. Denise's shoulders drooped at that subject, as she explained that the man who was her daughter Hillary's father (but apparently not Harold's) was giving her a hard time about not being allowed to live with them. The man had shown up drunk at the door, demanding to be let in at three in the morning the night before.

Janice then pulled Jonathan down to the floor, where a boy sat with his back against the wall. He was small, with skinny legs and short, curly hair. Jonathan judged him to be about seven or eight years old. He was squinting at a newspaper and had a stubby pencil in his hand.

Janice squatted next to him. "Whatcha doing, Harold?"

Harold looked up at Janice and smiled in recognition, then said in a soft voice, "Puzzle."

Jonathan looked down at the newspaper in the boy's hand, which was folded neatly into a rectangle about eight inches by six inches. It was *The New York Times*. He glanced at Janice, who nodded that it was alright for him to talk to the boy. "Hey, Harold. My name's Jon."

Harold looked up at Jonathan suspiciously, then looked at Janice, who nodded. Jonathan pressed forward, "You mind if I take a look?"

Harold shrugged and handed the newspaper to Jonathan, who was squatting down now, next to Janice. He turned the folded paper to reveal the crossword puzzle. The tiny boxes were mostly filled in on the left side in neat block capital letters, and blank on the right side. There were no signs of erasures. The clues were crossed off with slashes where Harold had filled in the answers. Jonathan unfolded the paper to see the date. It was that day's Saturday *Times*. He folded the page back to its original state and handed it back to Harold. "Do you like doing the crossword puzzle?" Harold nodded. "Do you do it every day?"

Harold cocked his head and said, "Most days, except when we can't find a paper."

"What grade in school are you?"

"Third."

"Do you like your school?"

"It's alright, I guess. Most of the kids like to goof off a lot."

Jonathan laughed, trying to put the boy at ease. "I remember doing that a lot when I was in third grade, too. You keep on doing those puzzles and you'll do just fine." Harold didn't respond. His head was buried behind the newspaper and he was scratching out an answer with his pencil. Jonathan stood back up, stretching his legs, which had been in a squat for longer than was comfortable. Then he turned to Harold's mother and asked, "Has he been tested?"

Denise looked questioningly up at Jonathan and replied, "We go to the clinic down on 110th Street twice a year. He gets all his shots and stuff there."

"No," Jonathan smiled, "not medical tests, I mean intelligence tests. He seems quite gifted for a third grader. What is he, eight years old?"

"Seven. I put him in the kindergarten early so I could work." Jonathan looked at Denise more carefully. She had soft features and small, delicate fingers. She had a pouch of knitting supplies in her lap and she was working on what looked like a sweater. She didn't look to Jonathan to be much older than Janice. He wondered how she could possibly have a seven-year-old son and also a daughter.

"Well," Jonathan stammered, not really knowing what to say or do in such a situation, "I'd make sure Harold is enrolled in the gifted and talented program in his school. He seems to have a very high IQ."

"Ha!" Denise blurted out, setting down her knitting and staring up at Jonathan. "You think P.S. 127 has a gifted students program? What planet are you living on?" Her voice was loud enough to be heard at the adjoining table, and several people looked up to see the commotion. Jonathan blushed and sat down at the table opposite Denise.

"I meant no disrespect, Miss. I just assumed—"

"Well you assumed wrong. This ain't no fancy suburb. I'm happy when he has a book to read."

Jonathan apologized again and looked at Janice, pleading with his eyes for her to save him from this conversation. She came to his rescue and spoke with Denise for another minute, while Jonathan stood silently. He tried to imagine what it would be like not knowing whether you would be able to find a stray newspaper so you could do the puzzle – not having the extra forty cents to buy a paper of your own.

Jonathan and Janice stayed in the shelter for two hours. At Janice's prodding, Jonathan even had a conversation with the group of men playing dominoes. He learned that two of them were Vietnam War veterans who, Jonathan thought, were both paranoid and possibly suffering from serious mental trauma from the war, or from their lives since. Still, they had stories to tell and were glad for a new audience. Eventually, Janice said good-bye to Miss Hattie, who assured her that they hadn't needed her to scoop eggs.

As soon as they were out of the church and back on the street, Jonathan said, "So, that's how the other half lives, is that the point?"

"Fortunately, I don't think it's half the population that needs a soup kitchen to get a hot meal."

"You know what I mean."

"Yes, I know what you mean," Janice grinned playfully. "I just wanted you to see that there are people out here who are not thugs."

Jonathan only grunted in response, then walked along in silence for a few minutes. When they were back on Amsterdam, walking South, Jonathan said quietly, "What a bright little boy Harold is, huh?"

Janice smiled quickly to herself and then responded, "Oh, yes. I've seen him there ever since I've been going."

"How long is that?"

"Since last spring."

"How did you get involved with a place like that?"

"It was through Home Front. A senior named Lisa Kelly brought me with her one day and I've been going back ever since. Miss Hattie does such a great job, and on a shoestring budget. They get some small amount of money from the city and the rest is private donations – and support from the church. Sometimes all the people need is someone to talk to for a minute. It's not that much for me to offer. I guess it makes me a bleeding-heart liberal, eh?"

Jonathan turned to look at her face, searching for traces of sarcasm, but found none. "Yeah, I guess so."

"Welcome to Sergeant Stanton's Bleeding Hearts Club Band."

"Look," Jonathan stopped short on the sidewalk, "I came along because you ambushed me this morning. That doesn't mean I'll be coming back."

"No, I suppose not." Janice was working to control her voice. "I didn't tell anyone who you are, so you can protect your precious family image of being snobs and never associating with any poor lowlife minorities like Denise and Harold."

Now it was Jonathan's turn to control his emotions. "I never said Harold was a lowlife."

"But he breaks your stereotype that all poor Black kids are hoodlums and criminals, doesn't he?"

"I never had that stereotype."

"Oh no? I suppose you'll tell me you had lots of friends growing up who spent Saturday mornings in a soup kitchen."

"Of course not."

"Well, now you know one. His name is Harold. Do you think Harold will grow up to be a criminal?"

"No. He seems like a sweet boy, and so smart! I couldn't do the *Times* crossword at his age – not one clue."

"The only problem is how he's going to cultivate that intelligence in a New York City public school, while living in the projects with a single mom and surrounded by every bad influence you can imagine – and some you can't."

"Yeah, I guess that's the problem," Jonathan said absently, as they started walking again. "That kind of intelligence has to come from somewhere. His mother seemed nice enough, but not really that bright. The father must be intelligent."

"Could be a grandfather, or grandmother," Janice replied. "We'll probably never know. Hell, for all we know the guy who mugged us in the subway is that boy's father."

"No. It just doesn't work that way," Jonathan shot back – a little too sharply and more quickly than he intended. "Not possible. A son is the product of his parents. The apple doesn't ever fall so far from the tree. That boy's father must have some brains. I can't believe he could be that scumbag from the subway."

"Sounds like your father talking."

"That doesn't make it wrong."

"But we'll never know, will we?"

"No." Jonathan was silent for a few steps. "So what's the solution? It's not as if pouring government money into public housing projects and welfare programs is going to make all those issues disappear."

"No, you're not wrong about that," Janice conceded. "I don't claim to have all the answers. I just keep going back there to help. It's only a little help, but damn it, if every person helped just a little, it would at least be something. I just hope someday Harold gets to go to Columbia, or Harvard, or MIT, or wherever to use all his potential."

"I can't argue with that," Jonathan said, and then paused. They were stopped at a red light at 118th Street, waiting for some cars to make the turn onto Amsterdam. He turned to face Janice, and said quietly, "Thanks."

"For what?"

"For taking the time to help, and for bringing me with you."

"Don't mention it."

"Don't worry. I won't. And I'd appreciate it if you would also – not mention it, I mean."

Janice sighed in resignation and said, "I figured you would say that."

Chapter 15

It was after 7:00 p.m. and the office staff had gone home. Jonathan's desk was stacked with briefing binders. The sun cast a long shadow of the Washington Monument toward his window. Gwen had a DAR planning meeting that night, so there was no rush to get home for dinner. His necktie was loosened and he had his feet propped up on the corner as he talked with Max Foster, who was on the speaker phone.

"And Jonathan, what were you thinking with that reporter from the Catholic League?"

"What do you mean?" Jonathan replied innocently.

"You know damned well what I mean," Foster blurted, before checking his anger and his tone of voice. Jonathan smiled to himself. He enjoyed pissing off the big man every once in a while and getting a reaction from him. "Jon, you are a solid politician and you know your way around an interview. You give them what they want and let them go on their way. This was a softball interview with a magazine trying to give you a glowing story about how you and Gwen are such a lovely couple and your daughters are adorable and model children and you are all God-fearing Christians. I assume you don't have any problem with that, right?"

"None whatsoever, Max," Jonathan deadpanned, extracting his legs from their elevated position and beginning to pace around the desk as he listened to Max's tinny voice come over the speaker.

"So, your assistant press secretary tells me that when the reporter asked you if you believe in God, you asked her to define her terms. Where do you think you're going with that?" Max's voice suggested hopelessness and wonder.

Jonathan smiled at the memory. The young reporter had been completely flummoxed by the question. "I'm sorry, Max. I was just having a little fun with her. She was so cute and sincere and young and I just couldn't help but poke her a little bit. It didn't matter. She just went on with her list of prepared questions and it never amounted to anything."

"This time, yes," Max grumbled. He was in New York. He hated having to have these kinds of conversations via conference call, but he loathed the trips to Washington, and as much as he might have wanted to summon his senator to New York, he realized there were limits to his power to insist on command performances when Congress was in session.

Max paused, then continued in a calm voice. "I know it was not a big deal this time, but what if that had been CNN, or Barbara Walters? You can't just throw that shit around casually. You're playing with fire. I can still get you re-elected if you screw your housekeeper, or if you get caught doing drugs. I can save your ass if you slip up on policy questions or if you can't remember the name of the Prime Minister of Canada. I can probably get you re-elected even if you convert to Judaism. But the one thing you can't get over in this country is not believing in God. You get that, right, Jon?"

Jonathan paused his pacing before responding. "Do you believe in God, Max?"

"It doesn't matter one whit whether I believe in God. Hell, it doesn't really matter whether *you* believe in God in the privacy of your own home or in your private office. What matters is that the good voters of Connecticut and Nebraska and Kentucky and Iowa and just about every other Goddamned state believe in God. Their preachers tell them to believe in God and they had better damned well believe Jonathan Prescott the Third believes in God or you can kiss your political ass goodbye." Max stopped talking but Jonathan refused to fill the silence. "Now you're just playing with me, aren't you?"

"Of course," Jonathan replied, a wry smile on his face. He knew Max could not see it, but somehow he worried it would be given away by his voice, so he suppressed it. "I'm just having a bit of fun at your expense, Max. I'm sure you'll forgive me. And don't worry, Barbara Walters will not have me admitting to being an atheist on national television."

"Good," Max grunted. "Now, can we try to focus on your upcoming foreign policy votes?"

"Sure, Max," Jonathan agreed, sitting back down in his plush desk chair and opening a black binder, which was tabbed and color-coded according to the issue and its designated political importance. "Let's focus on what's coming up soon. We'll leave the existential discussions for the old age home."

Jonathan tried to focus on the position briefing, but he kept trying to remember a particular quote from Rene Descartes about truth, which Jonathan mentally linked to the question about the existence of God. He had studied it in school, but it was gone from his memory. Max, of course, would be no help. He put it out of his mind, promising himself he would look it up later.

"If you would be a real seeker after truth, it is necessary that at least once in your life you doubt, as far as possible, all things."
   — Rene Descartes

Chapter 16

April, 1988

"**FRANK, DO YOU BELIEVE IN GOD?**" Jonathan's tone was very matter-of-fact as he gazed across the tousled dorm room at his friend, who was lying on his bed reading *Don Quixote*.

Frank marked his place and rolled onto his side, facing Jonathan. He furrowed his brow and asked, "Are you serious?"

"Yes," Jonathan replied. "I mean, it seems we're being asked to question everything. Descartes was trying to make an argument for the existence of God, but he didn't really get there, did he? But I've been raised to believe in God and I just want to know what you think. Do you believe in God?"

Frank paused for a moment, placed a bookmark in his Cervantes, then replied, "OK, let's have a discussion. So, define your terms."

"What?" Jonathan responded, puzzled.

"Define what you mean by God." Frank stared at Jonathan, waiting for an answer.

"What do you mean? God is, well, God. You either believe God exists or you don't."

Frank smiled as he sat up and swung his legs down over the edge of the bed. He leaned forward, placing his elbows on his knees and cupping his chin in both hands. "You, see, Jon, that's the first problem. You may have in your mind an idea that you call *God*. You then ask me if I believe in God – which means you are asking me if I agree with your idea, which is in your mind. You want me to say 'yes' or 'no' to something when I don't really know what your idea is. It's like me asking you if you believe in Don Quixote but you have never read the book – how can you answer the question?"

Jonathan cocked his head to one side and curled his lip into a smirk. "OK, Professor Elkhardt, game on. I get it. I'm talking about God, as described in the Bible." Jonathan reached onto a shelf above his desk and pulled out a Bible, Revised Standard Edition, which had been a gift from his church upon the completion of Sunday school when he was fourteen. His name was spelled out in gold leaf letters on the front cover. "This God," he said, pointing to the book.

"Alright," Frank said as he thought about his next reply. "Let's start by talking about the book, then. Old Testament? The Hebrew Bible? Just the first five books – the original Torah, or the whole group of additional books in the Old Testament?"

"What about the whole thing, including the New Testament?" Jonathan retorted.

"Let's take it one step at a time," Frank said. "Remember that the New Testament is mainly about the Son of God – there are few references there to the old man. In the Old Testament, there are many different descriptions and depictions of God, right?"

Jonathan pursed his lips and nodded slowly, "I suppose there are, that's true."

"There is a God who created the universe. There is a God who told Noah to build an ark. There is a God who wanted to destroy Sodom and Gomorrah, but was convinced by a human that he was wrong, so he changed his mind. There is a God who played around with Job. There is a God who appeared in a burning bush to Moses and who caused the Israelites to be freed from slavery in Egypt."

Jonathan broke in, "Let's focus on that God, OK? I know those stories. I've been hearing them since Sunday school. That's the guy. That's God. He heard the cries of the Israelites and caused the plagues upon Egypt and set them free to find the Promised Land."

"Good," Frank agreed. "So, we have an omnipotent being, existing outside the bounds of time and space, able to cause frogs to fall from the sky and to kill off the first born sons of an entire culture. So, the omnipotent being called God was, at least for some period of time, interested in the course of human events to the point of interceding and taking specific actions. God caused the global flood, and freed the slaves from Egypt. So, is a belief in God dependent on a belief that God did, in fact, cause those events to occur?"

Jonathan cocked his head to the side, then responded, "I suppose it is possible for you to believe in the existence of God, but not to specifically believe the literal stories in the Bible."

"Good!" Frank exclaimed. "Now we're getting somewhere. So, Jon, can we agree that the stories in the Bible were intended to illustrate God, and to set forth a set of moral principles and behavioral expectations?"

"Well, it's more than just that. There are specific commandments and laws in the Bible."

Frank smiled and pointed to the book in Jonathan's hand. "Do you know how many specific laws and edicts about behavior there are just in the first five books of the Old Testament?"

Jonathan shook his head. "There are a bunch."

"Six hundred thirteen," Frank said confidently. "At least that's what I read once, I don't claim to be an expert on scripture. And how many of those six hundred plus rules do most people actually follow in twentieth-century America, even among church-going Christians?"

"Is that a rhetorical question?" Jonathan posed.

"Yes," Frank responded quickly. "The answer is only a few. Most of them are archaic and outdated, and many of them we would find to be abhorrent, cruel, or just stupid, so we ignore them. We don't sacrifice live animals, we don't allow fathers to sell their disobedient daughters into slavery, we don't fast and celebrate the holidays as commanded by the Bible, and we don't even observe elements of the Ten Commandments, such as not committing adultery. So why should we pay any attention to any of it?"

"We're getting off the point," Jonathan said, waving his hand dismissively toward Frank. "I'm not talking about whether you believe the text of the Bible is literally true or if you think we should all be living our lives by the exact teachings of the scripture. I'm talking about a broader concept of whether you believe in God at all."

"Fair point," Frank conceded, which made Jonathan smile. He enjoyed the verbal sparring with Frank and always got pleasure out of scoring rhetorical points. "So, based on the definitions we have been discussing, I have to say I don't believe in your idea of God."

"But then, what do you believe in?" Jonathan persisted. "What is your definition of God? Aren't you a Christian? You once told me you grew up attending a Lutheran church."

"I did," Frank stated without emotion. "I spent my childhood there, attended Sunday school, was the leader of my youth group, sang in the choir – heck, I spent more time in that church building than in my high school. But in the end, all it did was make me aware that I didn't buy in to what they were selling. What do I believe about God? I have to say that I don't know. I don't have every answer.

"I look at the sunrise and how lovely it is, and how perfect the world seems to be sometimes, and I marvel. Could it all be random? Could my existence be merely the chance confluence of eons of evolution without any guiding influence? It's possible. I don't have enough data to make up my mind either way. I believe in nature – in gravity and photosynthesis and the laws of thermodynamics. I believe the world is a place worth taking care of. If that's God, then I'm fine calling it by that name.

"But I don't believe there is an omnipotent alien being who exists outside of time and space in a parallel dimension called Heaven and who periodically peeks in on planet Earth and manipulates events to his – or her – particular whim. I don't believe a supernatural God determines who lives and dies, who gets sick and who recovers, or which team wins the Super Bowl. I don't believe that the events of my life are predetermined based on a master plan hatched by God, or that the events of my life are at all influenced by decisions made by God. I certainly don't believe my future actions should be influenced by what some modern-day humans think is the correct interpretation of a five-thousand-year-old book. And if there is a God, I don't believe any human knows what God's plan is, or what God's will is, and anyone who says otherwise is a charlatan."

"Wow," Jonathan sighed. "It must be difficult living in your world."

Frank chuckled, "Yes, sometimes it very much is. It must be comforting to you sometimes to be able to take refuge in the belief that if you go to church and say the right prayers and avoid murdering anyone you'll spend eternity in Heaven, and that your life on Earth really doesn't mean much."

"Hey, I never said I believe that," Jonathan objected. "My life is important. Your life is important. Besides, the moral teachings of the Bible are the point, right? Not so much the literal truth?"

Frank paused for a moment before responding. "I certainly agree, Jon, but the question is whether the same moral teachings can and should exist outside the trappings of religious faith, and whether the religious aspects of some things corrupt the morality."

"I disagree," Jonathan quickly responded. "The element of faith makes the moral teachings that much stronger."

"Sure, but sometimes too strong."

"What do you mean?"

"Well," Frank said as he got up from the edge of the small bed where he had been perched. "Take, for example, abortion, which is a moral and political issue, but has been made into a religious issue when it really shouldn't be."

Jonathan frowned. "It's an issue for religious people because it's a moral issue, Frank."

"That may be true for some, but the various churches and religious fanatics who have seized on the issue try to make the religion piece the most important – as if God has said 'thou shalt not abort a pregnancy.'"

"Well, the Bible does say that," Jonathan interjected.

"You see, there's the problem. You're an intelligent person and your immediate knee-jerk on the subject is to think your religious teachings say that, when it's not true."

"What do you mean?" Jonathan was genuinely puzzled. "'Thou shalt not kill' is a pretty big one, isn't it?"

"Sure," Frank agreed, "but it's really 'thou shalt not murder,' where 'murder' means an unjustified killing. There's plenty of killing in the Bible, including stoning to death a girl who has sex outside of marriage. That's another one we don't follow anymore."

"True," Jonathan conceded, "but intentionally terminating a life without justification is wrong, morally and religiously."

"So that leaves us to debate what is a 'life' that has the right not to be terminated, and when does 'life' begin, which is *Roe v. Wade* in a nutshell."

"But if life begins at conception, then the Supreme Court's view about life not counting until after the first trimester is not necessarily correct." Jonathan was leaning forward now, intensely enjoying the discussion.

"So, what if I told you that the Bible says to the contrary – that an unborn life does not have rights equal to a living, breathing person?" Frank held out his hand, motioning for Jonathan to give him the Bible, which Jonathan was still clutching.

"I'd say you are crazy," Jonathan responded, handing over the black leather volume.

Frank opened the book, which crackled as the bindings stretched, as if for the first time. Frank flipped a few pages before finally stopping and reading silently for a few moments. Then, he pointed his finger at the page and read aloud. "Exodus, chapter twenty-one. We can skip over all the rules about treatment of slaves for now," Frank said, moving his finger down the page. He then continued, "'Whoever strikes a man so that he dies shall be put to death. Whoever strikes his father or his mother shall be put to death. Whoever steals a man, whether he sells him or is found in possession of him, shall be put to death. Whoever curses his father or his mother shall be put to death.'" Frank paused again. "I guess that pretty much settles the biblical stance on the death penalty, huh?"

Jonathan grunted his acknowledgement.

Frank continued reading aloud. "'When men strive together, and hurt a woman with child, so that there is a miscarriage, and yet no harm follows, the one who hurt her shall be fined, according as the woman's husband shall lay upon him; and he shall pay as the judges determine. If any harm follows, then you shall give life for life, eye for eye, tooth for tooth, hand for hand, foot for foot, burn for burn, wound for wound, stripe for stripe.'"

Frank stopped reading and looked up at Jonathan.

Jonathan looked back, puzzled. "Right, it says if you cause a woman to abort an unborn child then you must pay life for life."

Frank pursed his lips and shook his head slightly. "This is why you have to read carefully. I'm pretty sure this is the only specific reference in the original Hebrew Bible that mentions the termination of a pregnancy. The passage actually says that if the woman loses the baby – 'so that there is a *miscarriage*, and yet no harm follows, the one who hurt *her* shall be fined' – so if there is no harm to the mother – 'her' – other than having a miscarriage, but the unborn child is lost, then there is a fine. Cursing your father or mother is punished by death, and smiting a man and causing his death is punished by death, but causing a woman to lose her baby is a fine – not death – which means that the 'life' of the unborn child is not equal to the life of the mother, or even equal to insulting a parent."

Jonathan frowned and furrowed his brow. He snatched the Bible away from Frank and re-read the passage to himself. "I didn't think it said that," he mumbled. "But really, what difference does it make? I can still have a moral position without needing to rely on scripture as its foundation."

"Absolutely true," Frank agreed eagerly. "You can indeed take a moral position without the Bible as its underpinning. It's just that most people on that side of the debate don't do it and don't really try to do it."

"Well, I still think aborting a pregnancy is wrong," Jonathan stated matter-of-factly, as if it ended the discussion.

"I would call it tragic, in many cases," Frank responded, "but not morally wrong. I can accept the idea that a woman has a right to make a choice about whether to carry and deliver a baby or not. It's sad when it happens a lot of the time, but it's a legitimate choice. We only magnify the tragedy when we brand the woman as 'sinful' for doing it so that now she's damned to Hell for all eternity.

"I don't think the religious threat helps the moral discussion. It's such an absolute – it's the order of the God, so it now is beyond question or examination. It's an intellectual cop-out. The preacher or priest tells his followers that God made the rule and they must follow it upon penalty of eternal damnation, so they believe it whether it's actually there in the Bible or not and they pass the rule along to their children. I sometimes think all our morality discussions would be better off without any reference to faith or God. We just teach children to act with compassion and brotherhood toward all other people and to behave within the moral bounds of civilized society because it's a good idea, instead of because it is the command of a supernatural God. How would that be?"

"It would be chaos," Jonathan responded smoothly. "We would certainly have more war and conflict. It would be every man for himself and hedonism would be the norm for everyone with no fear of Hell and no worry about the consequences of our actions in the eyes of God."

"You really think so?" Frank asked simply. "Hasn't there been more conflict and war caused by humans fighting over whose idea of God is the right one than would be caused by the absence of God?"

Jonathan paused in thought for a long time, while Frank stared at him, waiting for his answer. "I don't know about that," Jonathan conceded. "It's a hypothetical without any answer. We have religion in the world, and we always will – at least in our lifetime."

"On that, we can agree," Frank said, picking up his copy of *Don Quixote* and finding the place where he had left off. "Some changes will take more time than we have on this Earth, that's for sure."

Jonathan fumbled on his desk for his homework, eventually settling on his macroeconomics textbook. Before starting to really study, though, he said, "Thanks, Frank."

"For what?"

"For being honest."

"How do you know I wasn't bullshitting you the whole time?"

Jonathan laughed. "You're right. You were probably just wasting my time."

Frank looked up from his book. "No, Jon, the one thing I never waste is time. We have so little of it, and we can never get it back once it's gone."

"True," Jonathan nodded. "I'll try my best to never waste your time – or mine."

"Now you're talking about a religion I can get behind," Frank said. "The church of the ticking clock. Come one and all and hear the truth – your time is running out, so get the fuck out of here and go do something meaningful with your lives!"

"Amen to that," Jonathan agreed, as he popped the top off his highlighter pen and smeared its yellow tip across his economics text. Under his breath, not even loud enough for Frank to hear, he said it again, "Amen to that."

Chapter 17

JANICE STANTON PUSHED OPEN the heavy glass door of the conference room on the sixth floor of the News Corporation building. She was running a few minutes late. When she saw who was in the room, she stopped cold, still holding the door half open. Marcus Brockman, the managing editor, was seated at the far side of a glass-topped conference table. Next to him was the paper's chief first amendment lawyer, Stuart Karlan, along with Janice's editor and mentor, Cathy Pantell, and Richard Firestone, the Page One editor who was working with Janice on the Hawkins piece. The table was littered with an assortment of papers and notes. It looked to Janice like they had been hard at work for a while before she arrived.

"What's all this?" Janice asked sincerely.

"Sit down, Janice," Brockman said seriously, gesturing to a chair across the table. She sat down carefully, assessing the situation and telling herself to stay calm.

Karlan, the lawyer, started the conversation, which Janice knew was not a good sign. "Janice, there's a problem with the Hawkins article."

"What sort of problem?" Janice interjected, unable to hold herself back, despite knowing better.

"For starters, your two primary inside sources both sent us emails this morning saying they were unhappy with your reporting on the story. They say they have been misquoted and that their comments to you have been distorted."

Janice was stunned. She shook her head. "Wait, how? That's not possible. I mean, I haven't shown them the story."

Brockman stepped in. "You must have sent them excerpts to verify their quotes and the substance of their information, though, didn't you?"

"Yes, of course," Janice looked toward Cathy, her friend and chief advocate, who shrugged her shoulders slightly as if to say there was nothing she could do. "I verified their quotes, of course. I spoke to both of them. I have my notes." Janice began digging into her satchel of papers, but Brockman stopped her.

"Don't worry, Janice, we know you did. We're not doubting you. But, nevertheless, the witnesses have recanted. They say you pressured them and made up statements you attributed to them."

"What?!" Janice was now getting angry. "I did no such thing!"

Cathy attempted to come to the rescue. "Nobody thinks so, Janice. Really. Nobody."

"Are you sure the emails are really from Dorothy and Jeanine?" Janice offered a possible way out.

"We already thought of that, Janice," Marcus cut in. "We verified the email addresses from your notes and Cathy called them both personally and spoke to them."

Janice stared at Cathy, with her mouth slightly open. "What? You looked at my notes? You called my sources? When?"

"This morning," Brockman continued. "I'm sorry we had to do that, and I'm sorry we couldn't bring you into the process sooner, but there was an allegation here of some pretty serious potential misconduct. We felt it was necessary to verify the information independently. Cathy accessed your notes and got the emails, and she insisted on making the calls herself."

Janice looked at Cathy, who nodded seriously, then smiled weakly at Janice. "Janice, we never really doubted you, but we had to check. I called the two girls myself."

"And what did they tell you?" Janice was getting agitated, but worked hard to maintain composure.

Cathy frowned, then continued. "They both told me the same thing they wrote in their emails. Exactly. In fact, it was as if they were reading from a script. They were both extremely nervous and hesitant, and I'm pretty sure there was someone in the room with both of them when I called. I asked them some follow-up questions, but they refused to answer anything. They both said they didn't want you to call them or contact them and they both said they would not agree to be mentioned or quoted in the article, even if their names were not used. They both said it exactly that way." Cathy looked down at some hand-written notes. "They both said 'I will not agree to any mention of me or any quote from me in the article even if my name is not used.' Exactly the same quote from each of them. Word for word."

"That's crazy," Janice exclaimed. "Those girls barely have a high-school education. Neither one of them could have formed that sentence on their own. They were obviously being coached. They were reading. Somebody was pressuring them. It's Hawkins! He found out about the article. But how..." Janice trailed off her sentence.

"We know," Cathy interjected. "It's obvious. He got to them. But now they have recanted. We have no sources for the piece."

Karlan jumped in. "Janice, how did Hawkins find out? Who did you tell about the story?"

"Nobody!" Janice shouted. "My God. Maybe one of the girls told somebody they spoke to me. I don't know. I told them they had to be careful and not tell anyone. But then why did they need my laptop?" Janice said this last statement more to herself than to the group, but Cathy picked up on it.

"You mean your break-in?"

"Yes," Janice looked out the glass window of the conference room, trying to remember what was on her stolen laptop. "I had notes on my home laptop. I think also a draft of the story."

"It was encrypted, though, wasn't it?" Brockman asked.

"Yes, of course it was. And password protected. It was secure."

"Not for a professional hacker," Karlan said. "If someone with the right equipment has that laptop, they would be able to break those encryptions and get to the data. If Hawkins knew you were working on a story, he could have arranged for the break-in looking for your notes."

"Well, then we'll break that story!" Janice fumed, knowing she had no proof and could never write that story.

"Janice, I'm afraid there's more," Karlan continued. "We received a letter from a law firm in Birmingham, which represents Hawkins. They advised us that they believe we are preparing to publish an article and have threatened a libel suit. They named the two source witnesses and say if we go with the story, they have sworn affidavits from both girls stating that they were coerced into talking to you and that you fabricated information and misquoted them."

Janice put her elbows on the table and held her head in her hands. "This isn't happening."

"Unfortunately, it is," Brockman soothed. "We know this is all a set-up and that Hawkins got to your sources and strong-armed them into recanting their stories. We know you didn't do anything wrong, but they have sworn statements, and we can't run the story without sources."

Janice looked from one face to the next across the table, hoping for some encouragement. "Well, we can run the rest of the story – without the girls."

Brockman shook his head slowly. "No, Janice. Without the sources, there is no story. We can't run the rest without a punch line. You know that."

"I know," Janice conceded. "I know. It's just that I've been on this story for six months. I can't believe the bastard got to the girls, after I was so careful with them." Janice was on the verge of tears as Brockman and Karlan stood to leave. They both gave Janice a pat on the shoulder as they exited, leaving her with Cathy.

"I'm so sorry," Cathy offered, knowing it was small comfort.

"So am I," Janice replied, without making eye contact. She packed up her satchel and went back to her desk, where she sat in silence, staring at a distant window and the glass of the building next door. She had told nobody outside of the paper about the story, except Frank and Jonathan at the reunion dinner. But they had no connection to Hawkins – and they wouldn't say anything to anyone anyway. It had to have been one of the girls who said something. Nobody at the paper would have leaked this.

She was devastated. She was supposed to go off to Washington on a high note after the publication of this bombshell story about Hawkins and his shady financial dealings and tax evasion – and about his sexual abuse of female supplicants. That was the big hook – the tax and financial issues were small potatoes and not entirely clear-cut. So much work. Gone.

Janice shut down her desktop computer, packed up the few personal effects she kept at her work station. One of her office friends, Monica Peoples, stopped by and asked her if she had anything else in the pipeline that she was working on. "Yes," Janice replied. "There is one other pretty big story I've been thinking about for a while."

"What's it about?" Monica asked.

"I think I'd better not say. After what just happened, I may not even tell Marcus until the final draft is done."

Chapter 18

SENATOR JONATHAN PRESCOTT III was standing beside a conference table the size of a Cadillac on one of the lower floors in Max Foster's office.

"How many?"

In his hand was a glossy tri-folded flyer, with his own smiling face on the front flap. It was a masterpiece of subtle innuendo mixed with carefully crafted facts. Nothing in it could be called false, and explaining why the impressions it left in a reader's mind were not entirely consistent with the actual facts would take so long that no politician or television news pundit would even consider taking the challenge. It was the product of a team of media specialists, public relations experts, and researchers. Max was quite proud of the group effort.

It created the impression that Jonathan was the senator toughest on crime, toughest on government corruption, and independent of special interest influence. At the same time, he was a rock of moral principles, a fighter for justice, and a protector of the middle class. It also carefully cast negative aspersions on his next likely opponent without mentioning his name. It was brilliant.

"One hundred thirty-five thousand," Max replied. "All being sent to targeted Connecticut voters via direct mail. This is an important time for you to get some positive messages out to the base."

"Who's paying for that?" Jonathan asked, as casually as he could muster.

Max gave a muffled snort and then composed himself quickly. "Jonathan, don't you worry. Your campaign chest is well stocked at the moment and Ed and I both think this is money very well spent. Plus, as a policy document for your constituents, it qualifies for free postage. It is not a problem."

Jonathan pursed his lips, but remained silent. Later, he asked Max for a moment alone. He always felt like a sixth grader in the principal's office when he was alone with Max, sinking into the leather sofa and being forced to look up at the fat man in his raised desk chair. He was half down into the plush leather when he changed his mind and stood back up, preferring to pace the Persian rug while they spoke, which also allowed him to look away from Max's probing eyes without seeming to be backing down from a staring contest.

He paced and spoke softly, as if someone might be listening. "Max, I know you're working hard on my behalf and that fundraising is a part of that, but it is *my* campaign and ultimately my responsibility if there is anything, umm, unethical about the funds. I feel I have an obligation to monitor the fundraising activities – and the spending. So, I'm sure you understand, right?" He looked directly at Max for the first time since he started talking.

The fat man was leaning back in his chair, with a faint smile on his face. "My boy, you are one hundred percent correct, and I admire your conviction and your concern about ethics. You are right that you are ultimately responsible and you deserve to know everything you want to know about every dollar we have raised, and spent, on your behalf."

Max swiveled his chair and raised his great bulk off the damp leather into a standing position. He sauntered to the bar and poured himself a Jamison's straight up into a rock crystal tumbler. "I will be happy to give you the name of every donor, the background check on every fundraiser and solicitor, and the breakdown by age, race, income level, and occupation of every person who has written a check. But," and he paused to take a quaff of the whiskey, "let me tell you that no matter how diligent I am about checking my people, and no matter how careful our people are about confirming the source of every donation, my long experience in this business leads me to the conclusion that there is no way for any politician to have a significant fundraising effort that would be entirely clean and worry-free. It's like a health inspector coming into a five-star restaurant. If he looks hard enough, he'll find something to cite as a violation of the health code. That doesn't mean the restaurant is a health hazard – it just means you can't run an industrial kitchen without a few mice in the corners.

"If you dig hard enough, I'm sure you'll find there are two checks from family members that technically exceed the $2,500 per household limit for individual contributions, even if the husband and the wife have different last names, and he cut his check from his business account while she used the joint checking account. And I'm sure you'll find a few donors who happen to be employees of one of your stronger benefactors who purchased a $10,000 plate at a VIP dinner, and although there may not be any evidence that the employer put pressure on the employee to make a contribution, someone who was interested in slandering you could make it seem that way.

So you see, Jonathan, the question isn't whether there is some possible violation, or the appearance of some violation, of strict ethical rules. The question is whether there is any systemic problem or widespread evidence of impropriety. And the more significant question is whether the candidate has plausible deniability if anything is ever brought to light."

"I don't want 'plausible deniability,' I want to know the truth."

Max's face flashed a quick smile, the settled back to its usual impassive and unreadable calm. "I'll hold myself back from saying 'You can't handle the truth' and simply advise you that there is no such thing as 'truth' when it comes to fundraising."

"What kind of doublespeak is that, Max?"

"Jon, I can assure you your fundraising activities are entirely legitimate and even a rigorous investigation would reveal probably only minor and technical violations of the impossible-to-comply-with election funding laws, all of which you would be entirely able to say you didn't know about and did not sanction, and all of which are sufficiently minor that they would not cause a ripple in the media."

"Why doesn't that make me feel better?"

"I don't know, Jonathan. It should make you feel fine. I have never had a candidate suffer any kind of fundraising issue and you certainly will not be the first."

Jonathan paced across the plush carpet without speaking for a full minute, deep in his own thoughts. He suddenly turned back toward Max and said, "Well how about this, then. Just explain to me exactly how it is that all those fancy flyers are being sent out to my constituents using my congressional postage exemption without violating the rules about such postal usage being limited to non-campaign literature?"

Max pursed his lips momentarily, giving away his annoyance with his young senator and his persistent questions. More annoying, to Max, was Jonathan's streak of conscience and integrity. They would have to be dealt with, and he thought that perhaps this was the right time. It was a risk, he knew, particularly since it had not been scripted this way at this time, but he made the leap of faith that it was as good a time as ever. He sat back down and leaned back in the soft, yielding leather of his chair and put his shiny black shoes up on the corner of the desk. He reached into the top middle drawer and extracted a small, foil-wrapped chunk of dark chocolate – his treat of choice during stressful times.

"OK, Jonathan. You want to face the music and take responsibility, then now is as good a time as any. Those flyers have already gone out. There is nothing we can do about that. They have been written very, very carefully by my staff – your staff – so that they are informative regarding policy issues and pending legislation. They do not mention any specific campaign issues or your potential opponents in the next election. There is no actual campaign going on, at the moment, and I believe they are entirely legitimate under the regulations.

"However, they are pretty obviously intended to bolster your support for the next election, they include veiled shots at your most likely opponents, and although they don't specifically discuss a campaign, they are designed to encourage the recipients to send money toward your election war chest. I have no doubt that if they were given a close going-over by someone liberally inclined in the media – and we know there are plenty of them out there – they could be seen as potentially violating the spirit, if not the letter, of the regulations under which you are permitted to send postage-free mail. They certainly could be spun as an attempt to give you an advantage in the next election, even greater than your general incumbency will give you. If somebody wanted to do a hatchet job on you based on this, they certainly could do it.

"However, I believe the chance of such media attention is extremely small. The election is so far away that nobody has officially entered the race against you, and so there is no opposed candidate to complain to the Federal Election Commission. You are not high-profile enough for anyone in the national media to care about a mid-term mailing to your constituents. There is not enough juice to the pamphlets or to the story to make it worth any journalist's time or any TV network's air space. Plus, you'd be able to deny responsibility and say that any violation was merely a technicality and you'd get off Scott free anyway.

"Your mailing costs, although substantial, are a drop in the bucket for the Post Office and won't be picked up by any audit within Congress. You can bank on that.

"So, Jonathan, that's the truth. Now, I can give you the number of the Federal Election Commission and the auditor of the Congressional Budget Office who is in charge of monitoring mailings by senators. You can feel free to self-report a violation, or request an audit. You could even offer to pay the full cost of the mailing out of your campaign coffers. We have the money. So go ahead – fall on your sword and shine the spotlight on yourself, and on me and on your staff. If you must do it to ease your own conscience, then go ahead. We're all adults. We'll get over the shame. If that's what you want." As he finished, Max eased his legs down from their reclined position, turned his chair, and stared directly into Jonathan's eyes, like a poker shark daring his opponent to call his bluff.

Jonathan stared back, but only for a moment before lowering his eyes. "I'll think about it, Max. I'll think about it and let you know if I want to self-report this and pay the ticket."

"That's a thoughtful and appropriate response, Jon. It's what I expect from you."

"But just do me this favor, please," Jonathan returned his gaze to Max's face, which stared impassively back at him – impossible to read. "Before you send out anything like this in the future, I would like to review it in advance."

"Of course, Jonathan," Max smiled back, a black speck of chocolate still stuck to one of his lower teeth. "You're the senator. I will make sure Edward gets the message."

"Great. And please copy me on the message to Edward. I appreciate that he does a fine job, and you certainly did make a good choice when you recommended him to me, but I want to make sure he understands he works for me, not for you, Max."

"Of course," Max replied smoothly. "As I said, you are the senator."

"Fine." Jonathan turned and padded across the noiseless floor to the door and exited without turning back.

Max Foster sat in silence, savoring the moment. It had been a risk, but the bluff had not been called. Jonathan Prescott III had folded, as Max knew he would. The boy was impetuous, but predictable. Max reached into the middle left drawer of his desk and pressed a black button. He then donned a pair of Bose noise-reducing headphones and listened intently, while he manipulated a large knob and watched the digital time index readout on the machine wedged into the cramped space. After fussing with the equipment for a few minutes, he flipped two side-by-side switches, then pressed the "play" button and the button marked "dub" and listened to the playback:

I can give you the number of the Federal Election Commission and the auditor of the Congressional Budget Office who is in charge of monitoring mailings by senators. You can feel free to self-report a violation, or request an audit. You could even offer to pay the full cost of the mailing out of your campaign coffers. We have the money.

After a few more manipulations, he dubbed the next segment:

I'll think about it, Max. I'll think about it and let you know if I want to self-report this and pay the ticket.

Max smiled to himself as he hit the STOP button.

He saved the fragments of conversation and archived them to a master disk, then erased the original recording, made from seven microphones hidden around the office and all quite invisible. If ever he needed to ensure the senator's loyalty, the recorded digital voices would come in handy. He had a vault full of such recordings, but had occasion to use them only a few times. The thought of each instance, however, brought a smile to Max's face. He enjoyed the hunt, the play, and the catch. Even if the quarry never knew he was being hunted, or had been bagged.

Chapter 19

JONATHAN'S EYES WERE FIXED like ball bearings of blue-grey steel across the small table. "You can't be serious, Jan!"

Janice looked away and sighed. "Of course I'm serious – haven't you been listening?"

Jonathan glanced around the room. They were in the back corner of a Thai restaurant on E street. It was 3:30 in the afternoon and they had the place to themselves, but considering the conversation, Jonathan wanted to make sure nobody was listening. He looked back at his old friend. She turned back and met his gaze. Then he sat back in his chair, suddenly realizing he had been leaning over the table. He forced himself to relax, going through one of his reliable breathing exercises, taught to him by his debating consultant, hired by Max during his last campaign. This was a time to go into full defensive posture. He forced his voice to be smooth and controlled. "I can't believe you would even ask that."

Janice pressed her lips together, her own defensive mechanism to prevent her from saying something she might regret later. She folded her arms and willed herself not to show any sign of emotional reaction. How had they come to this?

The interview had started out so well, and so friendly. They had ordered appetizers and hot & sour soup at 2:00. Jonathan had been there when Janice arrived, which in itself was a surprise to Janice, who was used to the senator always running late. There were no aides or security officers. Janice had walked up from her office at the Washington Bureau of *The Wall Street Journal*. She had called Jonathan's office two weeks after the class reunion dinner to schedule an interview. He had requested that she dress conservatively, so nobody would think it was a romantic encounter.

The first half hour went swimmingly. She told him there was going to be an article and wanted his cooperation. She wanted to have multiple meetings, to which he had not committed. She snapped on her digital recorder and placed it on the table so she would not have to scribble notes while they talked. They chatted easily about his years in the Senate, about his wife and kids, and about his favorite pet bills winding their way through Congress. They ordered shredded duck with garlic sauce and spicy tofu. They smiled. They laughed. He was comfortable. He let his guard down a bit.

The first indication of trouble was when Janice steered the conversation to their old college days – harkening back to the discussion they had at the reunion. She reminded him of the trip they took to Ellis Island with Frank, and how Frank had been obsessed with tracing his genealogy. He had been so disappointed when he could not find the specific record he was looking for of his ancestor passing through the immigrant processing facility. Personal heritage and genealogy had become an important subject for many people, and with internet resources and DNA tracing constantly expanding, it was becoming easier for individuals to trace their family histories. "Do you know if Frank has kept trying?" she asked.

"I don't know. I suppose he probably has. You know Frank. He never gives up." Jonathan laughed at their mutual memory of Frank.

"Do you think it really matters, though?" Janice asked casually. "I mean, does it change who we are whether our great-great grandfather was a prince or a pauper? Whether our ancestors came to this country on the Mayflower or were refugees from the potato famine? We are who we make ourselves, aren't we?"

Jonathan pondered the question for a moment, wondering whether it was really as innocent as it seemed, but he was in a good mood. He had ordered a scotch with his main course and was considering ordering a second. "Jan, I think it does matter," he leaned forward as he spoke, feeling the opportunity for a good quote for her article. "We all have free will, and we all have the opportunity to make ourselves better in life. Look at Frank as a great example. In America, no matter what your background, you have the opportunity to be a prince – a prince of industry, or a scholar, or a political leader. You don't have to be born into royalty or aristocracy in this country. That's one of the things that makes us so special."

He paused, contemplating the exact words he wanted to be quoted on. "Jan, make sure you let me edit this before you write it, OK?" She nodded, not wanting to break his rhythm. "But knowing your roots, knowing your family background as I do, can provide a focus and direction that might otherwise not be there. I've known all my life who I am based on my family. It has always been something I've been proud of, but it has also been a kind of burden – but in a good way. I've known I have a responsibility to my father and to my family name. I have an obligation to be a leader, to use the power and wealth with which I have been blessed to better the world. Failure has never been an option for me. I have worked hard to live up to my family's expectations and to be a strong link in the Prescott chain. I love my children very much, and I have instilled in them the same family sense of obligation and honor. We are Prescotts, and we must protect that and guard our family and work for the betterment of the United States of America."

Jonathan sat back, smiling a pleased-with-himself smile at the turn of phrase he had come up with spontaneously. Who needed speech writers, anyway? He took a bite of tofu and held up his empty glass so the waiter could see he wanted a refill. Janice smiled, too. Then she changed the subject in a way Jonathan had not expected.

"Jon, those are terrific quotes. I really do appreciate your sentimentality on the subject. I know you have always lived with the burden of your father's expectations. But have you considered the possibility that Senator Prescott, Jr. is not really your father?" She allowed the question to hang in the air as she scooped up some noodles with her chopsticks.

"What?" Jonathan laughed and at the same time cocked his head to the side. "What have you been smoking, Janice? Not my father? Who put that crazy idea into your head?"

The first fact that had raised Janice's eyebrow was Jonathan's blood type. It came up when his cousin Thomas had visited him in college and needed emergency surgery for a ruptured spleen. It wasn't that Jonathan's blood type could not occur in the same family as Thomas's, but it would take an unusual combination of factors.

"Is that it?" Jonathan was incredulous, and a little angry, but he was still trying to control himself. "Jan, I can see, I suppose, how that could raise a question in your mind, but really, it's nothing. That can't possibly be the basis for any serious suspicion that – what? That I was adopted? Preposterous."

Janice pressed forward. "That's not all, Jon. You said yourself all the other Prescotts have large families. All your uncles have what, four or five kids? I remember Thomas saying that. Your father was the exception, having only one child – you." She paused to see if he was showing any signs of cracks in the Prescott veneer. "I did some research, Jon. I spoke to some neighbors and friends of your mother. Did you know she had a difficult time conceiving?"

"Of course I did," he shot back quickly, becoming annoyed with the line of questions. "That is why my parents could never have any other children. My mother had difficulty conceiving. Mother told me it was medically unlikely that I was born at all. They tried very hard, but she couldn't get pregnant. Finally, they were blessed by God and she bore me, for which I am quite grateful. Where are you going with this?"

"You may be interested to know, Jon, that according to three separate sources, your mother went to several doctors. They all told her she was perfectly fertile. I believe it was your father who had trouble producing a child, Jon, not your mother."

"So what?" Jonathan exclaimed, looking toward the bar and wondering what was taking the waiter so long to bring him his scotch, since they were the only ones in the restaurant. "Let's assume for the sake of discussion that my father, and not my mother, was the one who had trouble producing a child. So what? I suppose it might be slightly embarrassing for my father to admit he had a low sperm count, and so he told me and others that it was mother's medical problem, and not his. Male ego. Understandable and really not a big deal, right?"

"Well, I would agree with that, Jon." She smiled, and he smiled back, hoping the subject was finished. "But," she continued, then paused as the waiter brought Jonathan his drink. He took a long sip, then looked at her with a skeptical gaze. "But all of your genetic markers come from your mother, not your father. Your eyes are blue, like your mother's. But your father, and your grandfather, and all your uncles, and all your cousins have dark eyes."

Jonathan's brow furrowed momentarily. "Janice, I will give you credit for doing your homework, but you and I both know dark eyes are a dominant trait. Since my father's family has dark eyes, most of my relatives have the dark eyes. But surely there must have been a blue-eyed gene somewhere in my family tree."

"Yes, Jon. It's possible. I haven't been able to determine the eye color of all your paternal ancestors going back more than one generation. It's possible your grandfather could have passed on a blue-eyed gene. But two of your aunts have blue eyes. They have, between them, nine children, all of whom have dark eyes. If there is a blue-eyed gene in your family, it would have been passed down to your uncles, who would have one blue-eyed gene and one dark-eyed gene. That means each time they conceived a child with one of those blue-eyed aunts, there was a 50/50 chance that the child would have blue eyes. The statistical odds of nine such children all having dark eyes is more than 500 to one."

Jonathan sat in silence for a moment, thinking. "Jan, that is a very small statistical sample from which to draw such a significant conclusion."

"Yes, it is," she admitted. "But there is also the blood type."

"We already covered that."

"Yes, we did," she nodded, reaching for her small cup of tea and holding it gingerly with her thumb and index finger. When she had slurped a small sip, she continued. "But – "

"No more 'buts,'" he interrupted. "I'm starting to get annoyed by your 'buts.'"

She smiled ruefully. "Jon, it is so very simple. You can put all this speculation to rest by simply asking your father to take a DNA test that would conclusively prove he is your biological father."

This was the statement that prompted Jonathan to exclaim, "You can't be serious, Jan!"

After another pause, and another pull on his scotch, Jonathan shook his head slightly. "It's preposterous. It's ridiculous. It's the lowest kind of tabloid sensationalism. You can't possibly print something like that!"

"I don't know what I'm going to print, Jon. That's why I'm talking to you. I want you to be able to dispel any doubt here by taking the DNA test."

"Ha! Can you imagine me asking my father to supply a blood sample so I can have a DNA test run to prove that he's my father? Are you out of your fu – your mind? Can we turn that thing off for a moment?" Jonathan gestured at the small silver machine lying quietly on the white table cloth, silently recording their conversation.

"Sure," she said, reaching to push the pause button. "Look, Jon. I'm not trying to do a hatchet job on you. I really think this could be a great piece for you and for me. But I have this information, and it bugs the shit out of me. I can't shake the idea that maybe, just maybe, your father was unable to conceive, and so your parents arranged for an adoption, or maybe used artificial insemination so your mother could have a child, then doctored the birth records to make it seem like it was a natural pregnancy. I'll admit my sources did tell me they recalled your mother being pregnant and they didn't recall anything unusual about it. She didn't go away for months and then come back with a baby. The hospital records also show a normal birth, although I think those records, at that time, could have been manufactured by someone powerful and rich enough."

She paused to gauge Jonathan's reaction, then continued, wanting to get all the information out on the table. "This could be a big story for me, Jon. I have to be honest with you. Even based on speculation, there is enough here to justify some ink. I would kill it entirely if a DNA test proved it wrong. On the other hand, if the DNA test proves it right, it would be significant. You said it yourself – you feel like you have a responsibility to your family name. What if it really isn't your family?"

"Jan, even if this fantasy of yours were possible, it wouldn't matter to me. I have one mother and one father, and I have been raised as a Prescott forever. It would not make a bit of difference to me."

"Wouldn't it?" She stared into his eyes, questioningly. "And there is also the abortion."

Jonathan's eyes widened. He reached out his hand toward the recording machine and snatched it off the table. He examined it carefully and confirmed that it was not running. He pushed the power button and watched as the red light faded out. "That's off limits, Janice. You know that."

"Why, Jon?" she said defiantly. "Just because you say so? Just because it's something you don't want to see made public? Just because it would hurt you and your family and your career? Just because it would expose you as a hypocrite on the issue?"

"I'm no hypocrite!" he snarled, keeping his voice to a rasping whisper. "You were the one who wanted to abort. I never told you to do it. I never said I supported it. What could I have done to stop you?"

"You and I both know it was the right decision. Right for me and right for you – and for Gwen."

He bowed his head slightly. He could not have married Janice. His father would not have entertained the prospect, even if she was pregnant. And Jonathan wasn't sure what Gwen's reaction would have been if she had known he had slept with Janice. He had been in an impossible situation, and Janice had solved it for him; for them both.

"Jan, I'm not saying it was not the right decision for you, but you swore to me you would keep it a secret. How can you even think about printing something that happened twenty-five years ago? Just to get some attention? I thought you had some ethics."

The words hung in the air like smoke from a lit fuse. "I do have ethics!" she said, raising her voice more than she intended. She lowered to a proper tone before continuing. "I am as ethical a journalist as you will ever meet. That's why I'm here talking to you. That's why I am giving you a chance on the paternity thing. If it turns out you're not really your father's son, then I have a big story and there is no need to mention the little indiscretion in college."

"Are you threatening me?" Jonathan stood up, without really thinking about it. He looked around sheepishly, then sat back down slowly. "Are you seriously telling me that if I don't prove that my father is my father you'll run with this tripe, and you'll break your vow to me and print a story about your aborted pregnancy?"

"I'm not sure what I'm saying, Jon," she dropped her eyes to the table, unable to look directly at him. "I'm in a bind here. I need a big story. You remember I was working on a really big story when we were at reunion; about Abraham Hawkins? Well, it's dead. The bastard got to my sources and forced them to recant. Six months of research down the drain. Now my editor is hounding me. I haven't had a really big story in a couple of years."

Jonathan blinked, momentarily losing his poker face as he recalled telling Max about Janice's upcoming article on Max's client.

"I need something for Page One. I can go several ways here. The research isn't done yet. I'm giving you a chance, Jon. I actually think a properly presented story about your family history could really humanize you and make you more likable and appealing to liberal voters."

"Sounds more like you're giving me an ultimatum."

"Call it what you want. I'm doing my job."

"That's bullshit and you know it! You can write about anything you want. You're doing this because it's easy. It's a cop out, Janice. You're better than this. I thought you were beyond this. What do you think, that you publish this and then Gwen will leave me and you can swoop in and take her place?"

"No, of course not." She looked at him now with a tear developing in the corner of her eye. "I know that was an adolescent fantasy. I know you never loved me, and I never loved you. But maybe what happened twenty-five years ago was important. I haven't had a child. I may never have a child. Maybe that was my only chance."

"Then why don't you write about *your* story and leave me out of it?"

"Because nobody gives a rat's ass about my story except that it connects to yours, Jon."

Jonathan said nothing. He drained his scotch, letting the ice cubes rest against his lips as he strained the liquid into his mouth. "Jan, I'm your friend. You can't do this to me."

"Jon, would you take a political position for me because you're my friend? Would you support a bill allowing same-sex marriage, or suppressing anti-abortion laws? Will you vote in favor of confirmation for Menendez?"

"That's different."

"No, Jon. It's not different. It's different to you because *your* job and *your* political future would be at stake. Well, this is my job and my career at stake. Why shouldn't I go for the gold ring? Why should I spare you and sacrifice myself?"

"I'm not asking you to sacrifice yourself. I'm asking you to do what you promised to do. I'm asking you to keep your word, and not to hurt me just to get yourself ahead."

"Are you going to take the DNA test?"

"No. Are you going to publish this so-called story?" She was silent. "I hope that means no, Janice. I really do." He stood up again, this time with purpose. He removed the napkin from the waistline of his suit pants and walked away from the table, without looking back. Janice moved the noodles around on her plate with her chopsticks. Was she really so desperate for a story? Why shouldn't she do it? Why should she protect him? Would he ever do the same for her? She motioned to the waiter for the check.

Chapter 20

March, 1990

THOMAS PRESCOTT ALWAYS SAID his cousin Jonathan should have gone to Yale instead of Columbia. He said it to Jonathan every chance he got. In March of Jonathan's Junior year, Thomas – one year older and cruising toward his graduation in New Haven – came down to the city during his spring break and stayed in Jonathan's dorm for two nights. Although Thomas's father – Jonathan's uncle – was not a particularly impressive person and had never made anything of himself that didn't involve being Senator Prescott's younger brother, Thomas had always carried himself with an air of superiority toward Jonathan. He insisted on being called "Thomas" and never "Tom." Jonathan found it pretentious, and always made it a point of having his friends call him "Jon" as a protest against Thomas's adherence to formality.

As children, Thomas and Jonathan hung out together at family gatherings. Their fathers were two of the four sons of their grandfather, Jonathan Simpson Prescott, who immigrated to the United States in 1927. He was decidedly not of aristocratic stock in England. The elder Jonathan Prescott had left home and set out for America, which at the time was the land of plenty where a young man with some ambition could make a life for himself. He took to lying about his family back in England, making it seem as if they were minor royalty and he had left his family's estates to make a name for himself because he was tired of living in his older brother's shadow.

Jonathan Prescott knew how to talk and he knew how to work a system. He figured out quickly that if people in New York thought he had aristocratic roots in England, he could work that angle without ever having to actually prove anything. Transatlantic mail was notoriously unreliable, so the letters he sent home to his father, "the Duke," never seemed to get answered.

Jonathan hooked up with the political establishment running the City of New York and hustled his way to a position of minor authority. Within a year, folks were calling him the Governor of the Battery. He traded favors on the wharves and gladly took bribes from the ship captains who wanted their cargo given priority in the off-loading process. Two years after arriving, he was making a decent wage, and doubling it with gratuities from his charges. At that point, he was able to take a wife.

The woman of young Jonathan's desire was from a genuinely aristocratic Boston family. She had been sent to New York to attend Barnard College. Her father was a patron of the arts, and it was her father's visit to New York on a steam ship that brought Elizabeth Wentworth to the pier in lower Manhattan where she met Jonathan Prescott – an exotic foreigner with a smooth way of talking and a hustler's ambition. Jonathan courted her for several months, including taking in several art galleries and one opera, which he hated. But he understood people and he understood that this family was American aristocracy and could help him advance in this new country. He spent his money on new suits and shoes and made himself look more like the British royalty he claimed to be. He even arranged for a friend in England to forge a letter to him that supported his stories about his family's pedigree.

When the Great Depression consumed the country starting in 1929, Jonathan suffered no financial losses because he had no money invested in the stock market. Elizabeth's father was affected, but his business interests were mainly in manufacturing and shipbuilding in New England. Jonathan married Elizabeth in June of 1929 at a lavish affair on Cape Cod, then returned to New York, where he parlayed his new familial relations into an actual political post. As a municipal commissioner, he was charged with collecting tariffs and enforcing regulations on the docks where he had been working since his arrival. He quickly doubled his bribe income and was able to keep Elizabeth in relatively good comfort.

Because of the condition of the economy, Jonathan and Elizabeth were not keen on starting a family right away. This was more Elizabeth's idea, and Jonathan was happy to oblige. On the docks, he was able to discretely satisfy his manly appetites, and Elizabeth, while lovely and refined, never excited him sexually anyway. She was happy to enjoy the cultural and Society events of New York, which continued even during the Depression for those who had the money to keep up appearances.

The election of Franklin D. Roosevelt in 1932 was a boon to the country, eventually. For Jonathan Prescott, it was an immediate bounty. Through his connections at New York's City Hall, and through his father-in-law, he took a low-paying job with the Roosevelt administration coordinating New Deal federal worker projects. With money pouring in from Washington in an effort to boost the economy, new construction projects sprang into being. Jonathan secured a position doling out federal dollars to construction contractors and suppliers. His bribe income increased tenfold, and without any meaningful oversight from the federal government, Jonathan was able to put himself on the payroll of four different government contractors.

By 1935, he had moved Elizabeth out of Manhattan into a massive house north of Poughkeepsie – near Roosevelt's own estate – and Elizabeth gave birth to their first son, Jonathan Prescott, Jr. Over the next six years, Elizabeth produced three more sons, and had two miscarriages.

The Prescott family thrived as Jonathan Sr. increased his political connections and his wealth. Elizabeth settled into a role as mother to her boys and was the brightest star in the social circles of their small town. She and Jonathan attended the occasional Broadway opening or social affair in New York City, but they both grew comfortable in the country. Jonathan gradually drifted away from the Roosevelt administration as he solidified his own clout in New York. By 1946, he was a fundraiser and strategist for the Dewey campaign. He was in line for an ambassadorship if Dewey had been president, and was heartbroken when the election did not go as everyone expected. Jonathan consoled himself by burying himself in his business interests and building up his fortune as he raised his sons. He gradually gave up on the idea of further political office for himself and started dreaming about making his sons into a dynasty.

In 1953, Jonathan Sr. kept a promise he had made to his father-in-law and sent his first son to Columbia College, where Jonathan, Jr. was an academic star, a decorated football and baseball player, and the president of the Class of '56. Jonathan Sr. understood the value of connections and sent his other sons to different schools, trying to spread the Prescott tentacles as far as possible. William, the second born, was accepted to his grandfather's alma mater, Harvard. Charles was sent south to the College of William & Mary. Edward, the baby, was the rebel and ignored his father's wishes by enrolling at hated Yale. Jonathan's brothers each graduated and used the family connections to place themselves in lucrative positions with different businesses. They all quickly married and began cranking out grandchildren for Jonathan and Elizabeth. All but Jonathan, Jr.

Jonathan, Jr. focused his attention on satisfying his father's hunger for political power. Jonathan was a born politician. His oratory was unmatched. His charm and good looks allowed him to mingle with the highest of society, but his rough-and-tumble years on the sports fields made him comfortable in a middle-class bar. Jonathan took to politics like a thoroughbred to the track and quickly became his father's pride and joy. The elder Prescott nurtured his son's political career and advised him about whom to meet, whom to avoid, and whose favors to accept.

As the country lurched through the turbulent sixties, the Prescott clan grew and solidified its wealth and status. In 1964, the family gathered at the estate of Jonathan Prescott Sr. for the wedding of their progenitor's oldest son. Jonathan, Jr. had chosen for a bride the daughter of a wealthy and well-connected Connecticut family. Sylvia Elizabeth Fitzgerald was eight years younger and barely graduated from Smith College. They had courted only briefly, and only after Sylvia's father had informed her he had found her a husband. Jonathan moved Sylvia to Connecticut at the advice of his father, to a town in a congressional district where the voters were conservative and the incumbent congressman was nearing retirement.

When Jonathan, Jr. was elected to Congress, none of the accomplishments of his brothers mattered. Jonathan was the winner of the family competition. Jonathan, Jr. and Sylvia shuttled back and forth between Washington, D.C. and Connecticut, and made excuses about why they had not yet had any children. They were so busy, and Sylvia was still young. But as the decade neared its close, Sylvia was in her late twenties, and Jonathan Sr. often mentioned how far ahead his other children were in the grandchild derby. Finally, in April of 1969, Jonathan Jr. and Sylvia had their first and only child, Jonathan Prescott III.

At family gatherings on the Hudson, young Jonathan frolicked with his numerous cousins, but most of his male counterparts were much older. There were a few girls near his age, but the only boy was Thomas, the only son and youngest child of Jonathan, Sr.'s youngest child, Edward. They fished in the river together, learned to sail small boats together, and rode horses around their grandfather's grounds. They were friends, but also rivals, as were their fathers. But as they were stuck with each other based on their similar age, they hung out and became close. Thomas went off to his father's alma mater, Yale, while Jonathan followed his father's path to Columbia.

And so, when Thomas came to New York to visit Jonathan in the spring of 1990, the two cousins picked up their friendship and rivalry. Over two days, they painted the town and pretended that neither cared how well, or how poorly, the other was doing in school. They talked little about their fathers, but gossiped greedily about their older cousins. Gwen was invited to join in some of their festivities, but Frank and Janice were excluded. It was Frank, however, on whose door Jonathan pounded at 2:30 a.m. on Sunday morning when Thomas needed help.

Thomas had fallen into bed after a night of drinking. He had been complaining about stomach pain since he made a diving catch of a football on South Field the previous afternoon and landed on the ball. He had the wind knocked out of him and shrugged off the pain, not wanting to admit he was hurt in front of Jonathan. During the evening, Jonathan had chided him about not being able to hold his liquor and he had ignored the growing pain in his abdomen. But when Thomas awoke and doubled over on the way to the bathroom, Jonathan knew this was not just a hangover. Thomas could barely move when Frank arrived and immediately called 9-1-

1, over Jonathan's objections. The ambulance rushed him to the nearby St. Luke's Hospital, where he was quickly diagnosed with a ruptured spleen and taken into surgery.

The doctor came out to the waiting room to talk with Jonathan, who had called Thomas's father already. Thomas was in surgery and needed to receive a blood transfusion. Thomas, the doctor told Frank and Jonathan, was type B-positive. The doctor asked Jonathan if he was a compatible blood type, but Jonathan was type A-negative. Frank was no help either, as a type A-positive. There was a flurry of activity and phone calls as Jonathan, his father, and several contacts in New York City scrambled to get the correct blood for Thomas. The necessary strings were pulled and Thomas came through the surgery in fine shape.

After Thomas went back to Yale, Frank told the story to Janice, who had taken a class in genetics. She said it seemed odd that Thomas and Jonathan, who had the same grandparents, could have those blood types. In order to have a negative blood type, both of a child's parents must have negative blood. This means that both of Jonathan's grandparents had to have negative blood types, and that Thomas's mother must have a positive blood type. And for Thomas to have B-positive blood, while Jonathan had A-negative, there would have to be an interesting combination of genes coming from Thomas's mother.

"Well, it's not like that's impossible, right?" Frank had asked.

"No, it's not impossible, of course – it happened. There are lots of different chromosomes that get passed down even if you don't have the specific blood type. That's why a child can have a different blood type from either parent."

"Really? So the mother can be type A and the father type B and the child can be type O?"

"Yes, that can happen. I think," Janice frowned, trying to remember information from years earlier.

"So, it just reconfirms that our family is truly exceptional," Jonathan chimed in.

"Yes," Frank added, "even your blood is special." They all had a good laugh and for months afterward if Jonathan got a cut or scratch the others would pretend to scramble to save the precious special blood. Jonathan got tired of the bit and they eventually dropped it, but every once in a while Jonathan still made a comment about his very special Prescott blood.

Chapter 21

THE OFFICE LOBBY LOOKED LIKE a cross between the waiting area of a 1960s pediatrician's office and a late 90s AIDS clinic. A man with a three-day growth of beard, dirty blue jeans, and a sweatshirt that was more sweat than shirt slouching in a chair with orange cushions and varnished wood arms. He had Band-Aids on several fingers, with blackened nails protruding from beneath the coverings. He appeared to be sleeping most of the time, but every once in a while when Janice peeked in his direction, his eyes were wide open and staring at her.

In the opposite corner sat a large Black woman wearing a tan dress, a red-and-black plaid scarf wrapped lightly around her neck. She swatted the bottom of a small boy of three or four years who continually disobeyed her directive to stop running back and forth across the floor. Then, she wiped the nose of a slightly older girl who sat sniffling in a green chair, her eyes scanning the pages of a Dr. Seuss book.

Janice looked longingly at the plexiglass partition behind which sat the office receptionist, busily filing her blood-red nails into sharp edges. She did an outstanding job of ignoring Janice's fierce stare.

On the rickety table loaded down with a haphazard assortment of magazines, some even published within the past month, there sat a gold-plated business card holder, out of place among the rubble. The edges of the cream-colored cards were gilded with gold-colored ink. The firm's name, Elkhardt, Baker, Goldstein & McGuire, was prominently displayed, along with its telephone number. Below the firm name, a cursive inscription read:
Saving the world, one person at a time.

Janice smiled silently, remembering how Frank always said he was going to save the world.

After twelve minutes of waiting, Frank finally appeared behind the glass. He waved to the receptionist and there was a jarring buzz, followed by a loud click. The heavy door opened into the reception area, drawing the attention of the two children. Even the nearly comatose man in the corner looked up in anticipation. Frank went over to the man and shook his limp hand, explaining that his partner, Nelson Baker, would be with him shortly.

He then walked to the woman and the runny-nosed daughter, patted the girl on the head, and addressed the mother by name. He asked how her father was doing and assured her that Marty, his partner, was on a conference call but should be able to speak with her soon. Frank smiled at her and squeezed her hand more sincerely than any politician.

Finally, he turned to Janice and held out his hand to help her up from her chair. He escorted her to the door and opened it for her, ushering her out first into the brightly lit hallway.

They walked without speaking down the two flights of stairs to the street and out onto the hot Broadway sidewalk. It was the first week of August, but for a change the humidity level was tolerable. Frank had not strayed far from campus; he had set up his little public interest law firm on 98th Street, twenty blocks south of Columbia. They exchanged small talk about the weather as they walked to the Hunan Balcony and ascended to the upper level, with a view of the traffic whizzing through the yellow lights below.

"Do you remember coming here . . . that night?" Frank asked.

"Oh yes, I remember," Janice replied dreamily. "We never came back. I don't think I've been back since."

"Well, there are not that many good places in the neighborhood, so I come here all the time," Frank smiled. "So far, I haven't been mugged on the subway after eating here, so I'm pretty sure there's no jinx on the place." Janice smiled back at him as they sat down and accepted their laminated menus from their young Asian waitress.

After ordering hot & sour soup and lunch specials, Janice asked about the people she had seen in his waiting room. Frank cheerfully explained that Bobby Hendrickson, a recovering heroin addict, had been evicted from a rent-controlled apartment while he was in rehab and was fighting his landlord to get his home back. All his belongings had been left outside on the street in boxes and had been ravaged by the street people before Bobby got out to claim them. He was now living on the sidewalk in those same boxes and arguing daily with the police, who keep shooing him away with threats of arrest for vagrancy. Bobby, he explained, actually had an MBA from Stanford and had worked for an investment bank before he succumbed to the drugs.

Mrs. Florence Dupree's father had fallen off a city bus when the driver neglected to fully retract the disabled access ramp back into stairs. If that were not bad enough, when an ambulance showed up and the driver found out he didn't have medical insurance, the driver refused to transport him to the hospital without receiving payment in cash in advance. This caused a twenty-minute delay while two good Samaritans passed the hat among the bus passengers. During the delay, her father went into shock and suffered a minor stroke. He was now out of the hospital and receiving home health care courtesy of the City of New York while Frank's partner worked out a settlement.

"Doesn't it bother you, being an ambulance chaser?" Janice chided playfully.

"Well, in this case, I think the ambulance deserved to be chased. Then beaten and publicly humiliated." He laughed lightly at his small joke, which had made Janice smile. "The good news is that we only take cases we think are worthy. We're doing fine financially and we can afford to be picky."

"I wish I could say the same about my stories," Janice sighed.

"You can't decide what the news is. You have to report the facts, right?"

Janice looked down at her soup. "I wish it were that easy. Sometimes you know the facts, but not everyone wants you to write them."

"Don't tell me your editors at *The Journal* are covering up a story?" Frank perked up, suddenly more interested. "What is it? Some liberal politician caught at a KKK rally?" He smiled at his joke, but it quickly faded when he saw that Janice was not amused and had a somber expression. "Sorry, Jan. Is it really so bad?"

"I had a great story – a Pulitzer-worthy piece. I had that two-faced bastard dead to rights and I would have exposed him for the hypocrite that he is."

"Jon?"

"No!" Janice exclaimed. "No, I'm not talking about Jon – I'm talking about Abraham Hawkins."

"What does he have to do with Jon?"

"Nothing." Janice sat back, frustrated. "It was my story on Hawkins my editor killed. Not that I can blame her. I had two terrific witnesses. I worked for months to get them to tell me the truth about him, and it was good. It was really good. Then, at the last minute, they both recanted their stories and claimed I had coerced them. It was total bullshit. No question that Hawkins got to them and forced them to recant. He's such a scumbag."

"Can you find other sources and try again?" Frank offered hopefully.

"No, I don't think so. The story is so tainted now I don't think I could make it work. Plus I doubt I'd be able to get to any girls that he has abused now without Hawkins seeing me coming. That story is just dead." Janice took a sip of her tea and looked up at the ceiling before continuing. "Frank, you think exposing the truth is always the right decision, don't you?" She looked up with her brown eyes large and longing.

Frank was about to agree, but then found himself hesitating. "Well," he hedged, "I suppose it depends on what 'truth' we're talking about. You may have advance notice of troop deployment in Iraq, but it probably wouldn't be a good idea to publish it, even if it's true. Right?" He raised his eyebrows, now wondering what it was they were really talking about.

Janice frowned. "Never ask a lawyer a simple question. He'll always find a way to make it complicated."

"Why don't you tell me what your story is about and maybe I'll be able to have an opinion. That is what you wanted to talk about, right?"

Janice fished a square of tofu out of her soup with a pair of coarse wooden chopsticks and popped it into her mouth to buy herself some time before responding. She looked up at the ceiling fan above their heads, then glanced out at the Broadway cityscape, taking a deep breath. Then she turned back to Frank and said simply, "It's about Jonathan."

Frank blew out the breath that Janice had taken in. "Has he done something? Is he in trouble?"

"No. Well, not now."

"So, what's the story?"

"It's not about a present issue, Frank. It's about the past." Her words hung in the air between them. Frank's eyes widened. "I'm thinking that it's about time somebody finally exposed what happened. Plus, there's something else I've found. At least, I think I've found."

"Whoa," Frank held up both hands in front of him, his napkin dangling from his left hand like a flag of truce. "I thought we all agreed we would not speak about that, Jan. It was a promise. You can't just decide to change your mind about something like that."

"Why not?" Janice shot back, defensively. "If he's going to be a national political figure, doesn't the country have a right to know about his true past?"

"C'mon, Janice. This isn't about anything the public needs to know or has a right to know. What difference does it make what happened twenty-five years ago?"

Janice had hoped Frank would be more sympathetic. "Don't you think I should expose the hypocrisy of Jon and his Republican buddies continuing to crow about being opposed to abortion rights when he had a child aborted himself?" She gave Frank a defiant stare and brushed back her hair as she sat back in her seat, as if putting some distance between her and the table would insulate her from Frank's reply.

"No, I don't. It's not like you wanted to have the baby and he coerced you into aborting. As I recall it, he was trying to talk you into keeping it, but you were adamant. In fact, I recall that you didn't even want to allow him to discuss your decision and try to talk you out of it. What am I not remembering?"

Janice pouted, looking down again at her soup and fishing around with her chopsticks for another lump of tofu. Her reply was in a much softer voice. "It still happened. He still knocked me up. Shouldn't the country know that?"

"And who would that help, besides you?" Frank had dropped his napkin and now was leaning across the small table, nearly putting his chin in the tea light candle burning in the center, next to a silk flower in a clear glass vase. "Would that help Gwen? Or their girls? Do you think the fact that a politician had sex out of wedlock when he was twenty-one years old is really relevant to his current policies or fitness to serve? Lord knows, Jan, I'm not a fan of Jon's political positions, or his party's, but I would not want anyone to do a hatchet job on him, least of all you! Aren't reporters supposed to be able to keep sources confidential? How do you explain to your confidential sources that you chose to breach a promise you made to Jonathan to not talk about this?"

Janice was silent for a full minute. During the pause, their waiter brought plates of food and removed their soup. Frank scooped up some broccoli and started chewing. Janice looked at her plate, but made no move toward eating anything. "I need a big story, Frank." She looked for a moment like she was going to cry, but she sniffed once and caught herself before any tears formed. "I need a Page One feature. My editors are all over me because I haven't had a real scoop or a good investigatory piece since I joined the paper. The Hawkins piece was the goods. I was psyched. It was my big one, and the guy stole it from me. I need a big story, and Jon's story needs telling."

Frank's face was blank. He had practiced his poker face for many years. In negotiations with high-powered partners from the biggest firms and with the Corporation Counsel for the City of New York, his opponents could never read his true emotions. As hard as she stared, Janice could not tell whether he sympathized with her plea about needing a story.

"I can't tell you it's okay for you to do that to Jon," he said flatly. "If you were hoping for my blessing, I'm afraid I have to disappoint you. It's not right. You know that, I think." Janice was silent as she began to mix her chicken and cashews into her brown rice. She didn't look up.

Frank continued to look sternly at his friend. "I have respect for your journalism, Jan. I really do. You've done some good pieces. I'd hate to see you throw away a great reputation on a sensationalistic story. It would hurt you, and it would hurt Jon. Are you still bitter because Jon chose Gwen and not you?"

Janice bristled. "Oh, please. That is so over. You think I held a grudge for that long?"

Frank's eyes softened a bit and he leaned toward Janice. "I know you shouldn't. We all had to get over our little heartbreaks, didn't we?"

"Well, I was never heartbroken. It's not like I ever really thought Jon was going to run away and marry me, right? Even if I kept the baby. We all knew that was never going to happen."

"Of course," Frank agreed soothingly. "And it's not like you were ever going to settle down with anyone and start a family, right? Isn't that what you told me?"

Janice was silent for a moment. "Yes, that's what I told you, and it was true. You accepted that. You were so supportive when it happened – even though you were still hurt. I didn't mean to hurt you or Jon. I wanted a career, not a family."

"Well, you got it, Jan. You got the Pulitzer and the great job and the high profile. Does it make you happy? Or is this article on Jon your chance to lash out at him because you aren't really happy?"

"Don't psychoanalyze me, Frank," Janice shot back. "And you're one to talk. You told me you wanted a more serious relationship; that just having fun and screwing wasn't enough for you. So, Mister Serious Relationship, how come twenty-five years later you're still not married and don't have a gaggle of kids waiting for you at home? Were you just waiting around for me to finally come back to you?" Janice chuckled and scooped up a mouthful of rice and chicken.

Frank stared down at his food. "No, Jan, that's not it." He tried to sound casual, but the emotion in his voice trickled through. "I got over that long ago. I just got caught up in my work. The right girl just never came along."

Janice looked sympathetically at her friend and former lover. "If you were looking very hard, I'm sure there would have been dozens of women lined up to take a run at you. You're quite a catch, my dear. Maybe you just weren't really interested?"

"Now who is psychoanalyzing who?"

"Whom, actually," Janice corrected, and they both chuckled. "I'm not trying to stir up old wounds, Frank. Sometimes I'm sorry things didn't work out differently, but that's life. You can't go back again. It's not as if you and I would have lived happily ever after. You had your save-the-world law practice, and I have been all over the world reporting and writing. I could never sit still long enough to settle down. We would never have worked."

Frank took another bite of beef and broccoli and stalled while he formulated his next response. "I know that's right. And it's pretty much what you told me twenty-five years ago. I know it was true then, and it was certainly true for a long time. Do you think it will always be true? You think things can't ever change?"

"I used to think things never really change. People never really change. We are who we are and we can try to hide sometimes, and pretend we're something else. But that's just deluding ourselves. Have you really changed at all since you were twenty-one?"

Frank smiled shyly. "No, I guess not really. And neither have you, really. You're older and more traveled and I'm sure wiser, but you're still Janice Stanton. You take no bull, you get what you want, right?"

"Right," Janice mumbled, more to herself than to Frank. "And I never wanted Jon. I could never be Gwen, the perfect politician's wife. I could never entertain the suck-ups and donors. I could never be the happy homemaker and mother and organize the women's teas and the school bake sale and host the Daughters of the American Revolution fundraiser. She's perfect for that. It's what she was born for – and what she always wanted. She has the happily-ever-after life she always thought she'd have. It would drive me insane."

"So, why would you want to destroy that by writing an incendiary article about Jon and dredging up the past?" Frank was back to his disapproving voice. "We never told Gwen about what happened. Why not?"

"Because Jon didn't want us to," Janice shot back quickly.

Frank gave her a knowing look, as if they both knew better. "True, Jon didn't want her to know, but you and I also know it would have devastated her, and neither of us wanted that. There was just no reason to hurt her. She was our friend, too, right?"

"Right," Janice replied without much conviction.

"So, if you decided then, before she married Jon, that it was something you didn't want to tell her, why is it important now to dredge it up and tell the world? What will it accomplish, except to give you a big, splashy story?"

"Isn't that enough?"

"I hope not," Frank said softly. "If there's something about Jon's current life or his political positions that's worth a story, then fine. But this is not a story, it's ancient history. You think I'm going to come out now and spray around dirt I have on Jonathan from our college years just to get headlines or to promote myself? There are some places we just shouldn't go, Jan."

Janice stared hard across the table at her friend. "What dirt do you have on Jon?"

"Oh, for goodness sake, Jan, it really doesn't matter. We all have skeletons in our closets."

"I know," Janice responded meekly, "but if Jon were running for president and you had something important that nobody else knew, would you keep it to yourself? Doesn't the public have a right to know?"

"No, Jan, the public has no right to know private and personal secrets about everyone." Frank put down his chopsticks and took a sip of his tea. "The media frenzy around all celebrities and all politicians is not a good thing. We have to understand as a society we don't have a right to peek through the curtains just because someone is in the public eye. I don't think anything that happened twenty-five years ago could ever be significant enough that it has to be repeated now if it's going to hurt Jon. We all fuck up when we're young. We all make bad decisions. If I thought for a minute that it was relevant, I would say something, but it's not, so I'm not going to, and neither should you." Frank realized he was leaning forward in his chair, and so he relaxed and sat back, picking up his abandoned chopsticks. "Didn't you say there was something else you were looking into?"

"What? Oh," Janice hesitated, "it's also tied to the past, I'm afraid. You remember how you were always trying to trace your family's roots?"

"Uh huh," he mumbled and nodded through a strip of beef.

"Well, you remember that Jon was always so proud of his family's pedigree and how his grandfather was this great entrepreneur and self-made millionaire? Well, what if I told you Jonathan Prescott, Jr. may not be Jon's real father?"

Frank nearly dropped his noodles. He swallowed heavily and replied, "Jan, I hope to hell you have some rock-solid evidence before you make a claim like that."

"Well," she hedged, "I'm not ready to go with that story quite yet. That's why the other story is more tempting. I *know* it's true. This other one I think could be true, but I'm still working on it."

"Well, since you don't write for the *National Enquirer*, I'm happy about that. You can't just throw out that kind of allegation willy-nilly. And why would you? People will think you're on a witch hunt for Jon."

"I'm not on a witch hunt!" She raised her voice, glancing around to make sure she didn't draw any unnecessary attention before lowering her voice again. "It's just that Jon is getting to be a pretty important figure, and the paper is interested in his background, and since I know him – at least I knew him once – I've been trying to angle to get some ink on this. It could be pretty important. I don't want to hurt Jon. But if it's true, and it might be, then it's something maybe he doesn't even know."

"Have you asked him?"

"Actually, yes. I did ask him. He said it wasn't true, but he refused to get his father to take a DNA test to prove it."

"What in the world makes you even think this?" He now dropped the veneer of his blank expression and looked interested again. She gave him the explanation between bites of lunch and sips of tea. Frank probed a bit at her assumptions, but in the end he had to admit there were enough facts to raise a legitimate question.

"Would you be able to convince a jury?" she asked.

He hesitated, thinking about how he would present statistical testimony from an expert who would explain how improbable it was that these facts could have occurred if Jonathan was, in fact, his father's biological son. It wasn't proof, exactly, but it would be persuasive. Then he shook his head. "If it were a trial, we'd just have the DNA test done by court order and that would finish it."

"Couldn't he dispute the DNA test?"

"Well, I suppose, but in conjunction with all the other evidence, there would not be much doubt if the DNA was not a match."

"Can you help me convince him to take the test?"

"I don't think I could do that, Janice. Why? What purpose would it serve, except to help your career?"

"Why is *his* career more important than mine?" she asked with flashing eyes. "All our lives we've all been conditioned to the fact that Jonathan Prescott's precious career is the most important thing in the world and everybody else has to fall in line and do what is best for Jon. Why not let *my* career take precedence for a change? Hell, I could force him to take the test if I publish the story. He'd have no choice."

"But what if you're wrong?"

"Then I'm wrong and we apologize and it's no big deal."

"Oh, I think it would still be a big deal."

"Not if I leave out the abortion. Now *that* would be a huge story."

"I thought we covered that."

She flashed her defiant green eyes again. She was energized by her speech about wanting to further her own career instead of Jonathan's. "If I go with either, I might as well go with both."

"Jan, you had better think long and hard about this."

"You're not going to help me out here, are you?" Her eyes were pleading with him, but Frank maintained an impassive countenance. "If I go with this, I may need a friend's shoulder to cry on if it blows up on me."

"I don't think you should do it, Jan. But if you need a shoulder, I'll still be here."

Janice reached across the table and grabbed Frank's hand again. "How come you are such a damned good person?"

Frank smiled and squeezed Janice's hand. "I'm not nearly as nice a person as you think I am. I just never gave you any reason to start investigating me." He winked and released her hand.

"Just don't go into politics," she smiled and winked back.

They finished lunch, including sharing a bowl of lychee fruit. The topic changed to Frank's family and Janice's tormented love life. By the end, they were both laughing, but the tension of the earlier conversation cast a pall over the table. On the walk back to Frank's office, Janice became quiet. She slid her right arm into Frank's left and hugged it as they walked. When they reached his building, she declined the invitation to come up, saying she needed to get back to her own office before heading back to Washington. He kissed her on the cheek and squeezed her hand again.

"Think about what you're doing, Jan. Actions have consequences."

"I know," she said. "I know." She turned and flagged down a cab. Frank stood and watched her from the doorway, noting the line of her calf as she stretched her arm upward. The consequences of past events were sometimes a long time coming, he thought. A very long time.

Chapter 22

March, 1989

IT WAS A FEW MONTHS AFTER Jonathan had first started going with Janice to the shelter in Harlem. Miss Hattie had taken to calling him "Slick" because he was always well dressed. He had been bringing in the magazine section from the Sunday *Times* for Harold. He had even accepted the invitation to join the game of dominoes once. He always felt the same way as he walked home afterwards – sympathy mixed with loathing, and a profound sense of futility.

What he was doing made him feel good while he was doing it, but he wondered if it was really doing any good or just giving morphine to a terminal patient. Except for Harold. That was what really kept him coming back. He had given Harold's mother a hundred dollars on his second visit. She gave it back, explaining that she was just there for the meal and to get out of her apartment for a while, and that there were many others who needed the money more than she did. Jonathan was dumbfounded, and put the bill back in his pocket. During subsequent visits, he always asked if Harold needed anything.

The answer was always the same – just bring the puzzle again next week.

Janice said he was dangerously close to allowing a liberal thought to creep into his Republican head. He laughed, but he also wondered whether she was right. Republicans didn't withhold money from charities. Plenty of Republican organizations helped the poor. It wasn't as if his father hated poor people. Everyone deserved their chance to excel in life. He was certain that helping the people at the shelter was something any good Republican would be proud of.

Neither Janice nor Frank mentioned Jonathan's diatribe after they were mugged in the subway. Janice was hoping Jonathan's recent experiences at the shelter had tempered whatever prejudices he might have had lurking deep in his subconscious.

That month, Jonathan invited Frank to come home to Connecticut with him for the weekend. It was the first day of spring, and Jonathan's mother had been pestering him to invite Frank to their house. Gwen was coming, too. Janice was off to visit her own parents, so it would be just the three of them for the trip. Frank was happy to get away from the city for a few days, and despite Jonathan's uncharacteristic modesty about the legendary Prescott Estate, Frank was duly impressed.

The house sat on five acres, with the entrance set back two hundred yards from the quiet road, sheltered by a stand of tall oak and maple trees through which a long, curving driveway ran like a creek up to the house. The trees were in full bloom and had just started raining white and pink blossoms onto the newly green grass. From the road, through the wrought-iron gate linking the ivy-covered brick walls around the property, you could not see the house. It was the ultimate in privacy. The house itself was a stately colonial design, with Corinthian columns guarding the front porch and a huge crystal chandelier hanging in the foyer you could see from outside through a picture window. It was mid-afternoon when their taxi rolled up to the front entrance, which was brilliantly lit by the sun overhead as they passed out of the shadows.

It was unusually warm for mid-March and the temperature was already in the upper 70s. Frank emerged from the cab and collected his overnight bag from the trunk. He slowly ran his eyes across the front of the house, counting ten sets of windows on the second floor. He gawked for so long Jonathan nudged up behind him and whispered, "You should see the summer castle."

Mrs. Prescott greeted Jonathan with a long hug and then welcomed Frank and Gwen into her home. She gave them a quick tour around the ground floor, showing the locations of the bathrooms, how to get to the kitchen, and where the back stairs were leading up to the bedrooms on the second level. There were six guest bedrooms, each decorated in a different color, and which Mrs. Prescott referred to as "the Blue Room" or "the Green Room" so everybody in the house knew exactly what she meant – except the guests, of course. She escorted Gwen and Frank to their rooms and left them to change clothes before whisking Jonathan off down the long hallway.

Frank was assigned to the Burgundy Room at the end of the hall, which he assumed would have been called the Red Room except for the communist overtones. It was bigger than the entire common room back at the dorm, with a four-poster bed piled high with an extra thick mattress so Frank practically had to high-jump onto it. There was a bathroom with two sinks and a shower next to his room, with doors opening from the Burgundy Room and also into the Gold Room, giving the guests a semi-private bath, with both burgundy and gold plush towels hanging on the wall.

Since the Gold Room was vacant for the moment, Frank had it all to himself. He thought mischievously that he would use the gold towels later. A double-wide window looked out on the trees lining the side of the house. He couldn't see any other sign of habitation, as if they were in a castle in the middle of a forest. Frank imagined a procession of horses prancing across the turf between the high trees, flying banners bearing the Prescott family crest carried by knights in full armor. No wonder Jonathan always said it was the most intimidating environment in which to grow up.

Frank changed into shorts, sandals, and a Columbia t-shirt in celebration of the warm weather and wandered through the downstairs rooms until he found the back door. Beyond was an enclosed sun room, with windows on three sides that were now all open except for insect-proof mesh wire. The iron-and-glass table in the sun room was set for lunch, with cloth napkins and what looked like crystal stemware and silver utensils. Out the door from the sun room was an expansive brick patio with two levels leading down to the pool, where Jonathan and Gwen were sitting with their bare feet dangling into the cool water. There was no sign of Mrs. Prescott. Frank quickly kicked off his sandals and joined them. "Will we be having tea here by the pool at four?" Frank asked with his best British accent. Jonathan just splashed him and laughed.

The next day was like a Club Med vacation for Frank. The food was plentiful and excellent. Although Frank had never developed a taste for wine, he assumed what he was drinking was top quality. There was a fully stocked bar by the pool, with a small refrigerator full of beer and soda pop. Frank still it called "pop" rather than the proper Eastern vernacular, "soda," just to make Jonathan and Gwen chuckle. The festivities were not interrupted by Jonathan's father, who called to say he was stuck in Washington on some last-minute meeting on Friday night, and then for some reason couldn't make it home on the early flight on Saturday either. Jonathan didn't seem to be missing his dad.

Senator Prescott arrived late Saturday afternoon and greeted the guests politely before disappearing into his private study, not to be seen again until dinner. That evening, the temperature had cooled into the 60s as Jonathan got set to do battle with the Prescotts' barbecue grill. He had insisted the first weekend of spring would not be complete without a proper cook-out. The mouth of the monster was fully six feet across, with a silvery hide shined to a mirror surface. Jonathan struggled to open the great maw, then was blown backward by the bellow of fire that erupted from the beast, singeing the hair on his arms above the cover of two plaid oven mitts. Eventually, he beat the dragon into submission and filled the air with the aroma of sizzling meat and, for Gwen, portobello mushroom caps smothered in garlic and olive oil. Jonathan's father emerged from the house dressed in casual slacks and a polo shirt and smiled at his son, remarking that he was doing an excellent job with the grilling.

"At least they are teaching you some useful skills at the old Alma Mater," he chided.

"Actually," Jonathan replied, "the cooking skills I've been learning from a woman named Miss Hattie at the Baptist Mission Shelter in Harlem."

"Really?" the senator responded with a raised eyebrow. "Is that part of the core curriculum these days?" Frank couldn't tell whether Jonathan's farther was amused or sarcastic. Jonathan explained about the shelter on 125th Street, and the people there. The more he talked, the more animated he got about the work Miss Hattie and the other volunteers at the shelter were doing and how important it was. Frank glanced at Jonathan's father a few times during the dissertation, noticing how quiet he was and how his eyes seemed to bore into his son.

When Jonathan paused to take a bite of his steak, his father turned to Gwen and casually asked whether she was also participating in what he called "this little laboratory class." Gwen explained she had heard about it, but had not gone there with Jonathan and Janice.

"Don't you worry about Jon spending so much time with Miss Stanton?" he needled, looking at Jonathan rather than at Gwen.

"Not at all, Sir," Gwen replied coolly, "I trust Jon. And besides, I've seen him at that hour of the morning and he's not very attractive."

Frank burst out laughing, grateful for a break in the tension, but unhappy about how far a bit of burger meat had flown across the table out of his mouth. Jonathan smiled, while Gwen and Mrs. Prescott giggled happily. Gwen reached over to Jonathan and tousled his hair a bit, which he quickly swept back into place with his hand while giving her a reproving look.

"Janice is a good person," Jonathan said, after swallowing.

"Have you read what she writes in that newspaper?" the senator shot back.

"It's still called *The Spectator*, Dad, which you ought to remember since it was there when you attended." Jonathan put just a bit more emphasis on "Dad" than he intended.

"Well it's turned into a liberal rag since then. In my day the editors had some perspective."

"We have plenty of perspective, and I'm getting more all the time, and Janice is one of the people helping me see things from different angles." Jonathan pushed his chair back from the table and stood up so he was looking downward at his father across the table. There were several steaks growing cool on a plate in a pool of red juices, a stack of uneaten hamburgers and a smaller stack of mushrooms, bowls of salads, a plate heaped high with corn on the cob, a platter of tomato and onion slices, and several open bottles of wine. On a small table against the wall of the sun room, a three-tiered platter of pastries, candy, and fresh fruit slices waited patiently. Jonathan waved his hand around the room. "You see all this food? This would feed twenty people at the shelter.

We take so much for granted. We waste so much. Sometimes I just feel so guilty about how lucky I have it in life."

"That's enough!" Jonathan's father snapped, throwing his napkin down on his plate for emphasis. "I will not apologize for my success in life, and neither will you. And I won't listen to that commie tripe at my dinner table."

"I'm not a communist, Dad, I'm not suggesting that the government should take our assets and distribute them to the poor. I'm only saying that we have so much, and we're so fortunate. We should appreciate it, and try to give back something to those who are not as fortunate."

"Don't tell me I don't give back to society, young man." Jonathan's father now stood also, so they were facing each other across the table. Frank and Gwen cowered in their chairs and slid sideways – out of the line of fire. "I have been a public servant for twenty-three years and I have worked very hard for what I have."

"And you got most of it from your father, who made his money by taking advantage of government programs and trading on political favors."

"Your grandfather was a great American, and you will not sully his memory with that kind of nonsense." The senator was actually shaking with suppressed rage, and pointed his index finger at Jonathan, who stood his ground – albeit on the far side of the table. "He made no apologies for his success, and I make none for mine. I've worked hard, and I expect you to work equally hard, and I expect you will be as successful as I, if not more so. That's not something to be ashamed of – it's the American Dream."

"Well, lots of people have that dream, Dad, but not everyone has the opportunity to make it real. I know a little boy named Harold whose mother works harder than you and mom have ever dreamed of, and that little boy is smarter at age seven than half the students at Columbia, but he's probably never going to live the American Dream because he's poor and Black and lives in the projects in Harlem."

"Is this one of your new friends from the soup kitchen?"

"They don't call it a soup kitchen, Dad. That was during the depression. It's a shelter."

"I don't give a good God damn what they call it, boy! It's a hand-out line for people who don't want to work hard enough to make a decent living for themselves. I know. I've been funding them through the federal welfare agencies ever since I've been in Congress. I'm not trying to stop them, but I'm sure as hell not going to have my son being corrupted by the kind of people that go there."

"Well, Dad, I guess you'll just have to hope I'm smart enough to tell the difference between a malingerer and someone who's just had a bad break in life. You can't stop me from going there and trying to do something to earn my entitlement to all this excess," he gestured again at the bountiful meal they had all just shared.

"I'm beginning to wonder how smart you are if you are so easily influenced by people like Miss Stanton."

"Dear, why don't you sit down," Mrs. Prescott pleaded, reaching up to touch her husband's arm.

"Don't worry, Mom," Jonathan interjected, "I'm about done here." He nodded at Frank and Gwen and then stormed out of the sun room into the house, disappearing beyond the kitchen.

Frank and Gwen sat in awkward silence for a few moments before Gwen excused herself and followed Jonathan into the house, leaving Frank to fend for himself with Senator and Mrs. Prescott. Mrs. Prescott asked Frank about his family in order to change the subject, and they talked for several minutes about Frank's home town and his father's job as the sports editor of the local newspaper and announcer on the local radio station. "In sports, there are no politics," Frank offered.

"Young man," said the senator, who had been silent through the conversation to that point, "everything is politics." With that, he stood abruptly and exited the sun room toward the interior of the house. Mrs. Prescott just smiled and offered Frank a chocolate éclair.

Fortunately for everyone, the Prescotts' house was so big it was easy for Jonathan and his father to avoid each other for the rest of the night. Frank suggested they go out to catch a movie, and even agreed to let Jonathan pay, just to get them out of the house. By the time they arrived home, Jonathan's father had gone to bed.

Later, Frank found himself very thirsty – probably from all the salt on the movie theater popcorn – and went down to the kitchen to find a can of soda pop. He went down the back stairs, which exited into a small hallway off the kitchen. As he walked back up the stairs, he saw Gwen flash across the hallway at the top, wearing her bathrobe. When he reached the penultimate step, he looked down the hall toward Jonathan's room and saw the door close quietly. Frank smiled to himself at Jonathan's daring. He would never try to sneak his girlfriend into his room in his own house, with his parents at home. Then again, Frank's house was quite a bit smaller than this one.

The next morning, Frank awoke and went down to the sun room to find it empty – but still with a full breakfast service waiting for him. He munched on a croissant and sipped fresh orange juice while glancing at the *New Greenwich Record*, which was among a small pile of newspapers lying on a side table. He found himself thinking he could get used to this lifestyle pretty quickly if given a chance. Gwen eventually arrived with her hair wrapped in a towel, suggesting she had just taken a shower. "Feeling a little dirty this morning?" he said over his orange juice, without looking directly at Gwen.

"Well, I just like a nice morning shower," she replied with a knowing smile.

Frank smiled back, still not looking into Gwen's eyes. He wondered aloud when Jonathan might be expected to emerge from his lair, but a few seconds later Jonathan breezed in, giving Gwen a bright "good morning" and a peck on the cheek before slathering what seemed like a half jar of jam onto an English muffin. "Make sure you're ready to go by two o'clock," he said between bites. "Taxi will be here so we can make the 2:36 back to the city."

"That barely gives me time to pack," Frank quipped, "but I suppose I can make it work. Where are your folks?"

"My dad and mom went to church, and then the senator has an appointment at the VFW hall. They are dedicating a plaque with the names of all the soldiers from New Greenwich who died in World War II. They are probably there by now."

"Shouldn't you have gone along?" Frank asked.

"Nah," Jonathan said dismissively, "it's Dad's gig. He's the star of the show. I'd only threaten to take away some of his attention. I'm sure he'd rather I not be there."

"Do we have time for a dip in the pool?"

"Suit yourself," Jonathan laughed, "it's way too cold for me. You act like you've never been in a pool before."

"Actually, I've never been in a pool before that didn't have a hundred other people in it at the same time."

"No shit?" Jonathan asked, incredulously.

"Backyard private pools are not very big in my home town," Frank responded simply. "The only time I got to swim was at the lake, or in the ocean, or at a hotel, or in the town's public swimming pool. Having this all to myself is a luxury."

Jonathan put on a heavy English accent, like he was Alfred, the butler from *Batman*, and said, "It's what we live for, Sir – to provide you with all the luxuries of life."

"And I appreciate it," Frank called out over his shoulder, already halfway out the door toward the pool.

At 1:58 p.m., Frank was sitting on a white wooden bench on the porch outside the front door of the Prescott house. His small overnight bag was at his feet and he was leaning back, eyes closed, letting the afternoon sun wash over him and listening to the sounds of the birds and insects in the surrounding trees. Gwen arrived and sat next to him just as a black Lincoln Town Car crunched over the white stones lining the driveway and came to a stop in front of them. Frank recognized the man who exited the vehicle and held the rear door open for the students. He had been working around the grounds, trimming hedges and weeding in the flower beds. Now he was dressed in a neat black suit with a white shirt and thin black tie.

Frank tossed his bag in the trunk and hoisted Gwen's suitcase in also. He shook his head at the weight of the things Gwen thought she needed to have for a two-night stay. He then got into the back seat and rolled down the window, happy to feel the breeze blowing on his face. Gwen was escorted through the opposite side door by the driver. Frank wondered what his name was, but nobody had ever introduced the guests to the house staff.

They sat in silence, waiting for Jonathan. After a minute, Mrs. Prescott came out and leaned into the front passenger window. She told the driver to take the kids to the train station. Then she turned to the rear window and said Jonathan would be staying for a little while, and that they should go ahead without him. When Frank asked if anything was wrong, she said nothing was wrong, Jonathan was fine, but he had some things to take care of. Frank offered to wait and take a later train, but Mrs. Prescott insisted they should go ahead and that Jonathan would be able to get back by himself.

"I'm not you, Father, and you can't expect me to be like you just because I'm your son!" Jonathan's voice filled the library of the Prescott house. He was pacing down the middle of the aisle between two large sofas. His father was seated on one, his legs crossed casually but his eyes steely and fixed on Jonathan. "You have to let me live my own life and find my own way."

Frank and Gwen had been gone for only about twenty minutes, and already Jonathan and his father were deep into this conversation, which Senator Prescott would describe as a discussion, and Jonathan would later refer to as The Argument.

The senator uncrossed his legs and rose from the sofa slowly, keeping eyes on his son, who was now standing at the far end of the library, leaning against a bookcase filled with dusty volumes. The older man's voice was always controlled and guarded, with little emotion. But here, in his private library, he was visibly angry, although he still did a fine job holding it in.

"I'll tell you what I have to do and what I don't have to do. I have to provide for your wellbeing until you are eighteen years of age, which you passed quite a while ago. Beyond that, I have no legal obligation to do anything for you, including paying for your tuition, or buying you a car, or arranging for you to get tutoring when you can't get your own act together in psychology class. So, what we have here is what I call a mutually beneficial arrangement. I provide for you what you want, and you do for me what I want. What I want is for you to put yourself in a position to be successful, and the place where you are going to be successful is in the kind of position I can provide for you."

The older man softened his tone and walked toward his son. "You're a smart kid, you've got good looks, and you speak well. You have such a natural place in politics. Think about what you can do in Congress, or even in higher office. You are my only child, and I've been preparing you for this since you were old enough to read *The Wall Street Journal*. I'm not going to sit by and watch you throw it all away."

"I'm not throwing anything away. Did it ever occur to you that someone else in the world might have a good idea? Did you ever think I might be advancing my future political career by going beyond your narrow view of the world?"

"That's just liberal college balderdash," Senator Prescott responded, easing himself back down onto the sofa. "The people I can connect you with won't be interested in that."

"Then maybe I need to meet other people to be connected with."

"Listen, Son, there are things you can do now, when you're young, that will be overlooked later – or will even be seen as part of building your character. You can go get stinking drunk at a frat party. You can go out and sow your wild oats with as many girls as you want – as long as you don't get them pregnant. But hanging out at a soup kitchen is not going to help you in your future career."

"I could do worse."

"Nonsense. Eventually, there will be a transition. I'll retire and step aside so you can take the family legacy. And you will hand down that legacy to your sons."

"Or daughters."

"Yes, well, I suppose that's possible, too. By the time your children get to that point, a woman could find her place," the senator mused, more to himself than to Jonathan. "But the point is that you are a link in a chain – from my father, to me, to you, to your children and to your grandchildren. That's my legacy – your children – my grandchildren. You need to take the long view, Son. What did the Bard say? 'To thine own self be true.'"

Jonathan paused, not sure whether the line was from *Hamlet* or *King Lear*. He decided not to take a guess. "I'm trying to be my own self, Father. My own person."

"That's fine – but be your own person in the way that will make you most successful. Think about where you want to be in twenty years. You have an obligation to this family."

"What about an obligation to myself? What about an obligation to better society?"

"I'm giving you a chance to better society."

"Yes, but only based on your definition of 'better.'" Jonathan shot his father a glare. "The rich get richer and more powerful, at the expense of everyone else. Dog eat dog. No mercy for anyone less fortunate. Let the religious fanatics control the morals and you control the money and everyone at the top of the pyramid is happy and the rest of the country and the world be damned."

"That is just tripe."

"You wish."

"Now, there's a masterful response. Perhaps we do need to get you onto the debate team to sharpen up your rhetorical skills."

"So I can carry the Republican banner for you? What if I don't want the job?"

Jonathan's father started to respond, and then stopped himself. He walked over to a small glass-and-copper rolling cart stocked as a bar, and slowly poured himself a scotch. Neat. Johnny Walker Black label. He took one small sip and then faced his son again, suddenly more somber and less angry. "It's not a job, Son. It's your destiny, and my legacy. It's a gift that I offer. It is the greatest gift I *can* offer."

"What if I don't want it?"

"Then we'll have to discuss what your goals in life are and how you plan to achieve them without my help, because I'll be damned if I'm going to support you and help you ruin your opportunity."

"Well, maybe you'll just have to be damned, then!" And with that, Jonathan stormed out of the library and went to his room.

But the conversation – or argument, or discussion – didn't end there. It went on, in spurts, sometimes lasting ten minutes and sometimes more than an hour, off and on for the next two days. At one point Jonathan called a cab to take him to the train station, but his father sent the car away from the gate. He thought about taking his bag and walking to the train, but his mother pleaded with him to talk with his father and not to leave when they were both so angry.

His father reminded Jonathan about all they had done over the years together. How much Jonathan had enjoyed the time they spent in Washington, and how much he had respected and been impressed by the people to whom he had been introduced: the power brokers of the Republican party. All through prep school, Jonathan had talked about how he wanted to follow his father's footsteps to Washington. Had he totally abandoned those dreams in two and a half years of college? For what? Because he wanted to help poor people in Harlem? He could help poor people in Harlem as a congressman, or a senator, or in even higher office.

In each round of The Argument, Jonathan's father succeeded in scoring rhetorical points, showing Jonathan how it was in his best interest to follow his father's advice and making it clear that if Jonathan strayed from the chosen course, he would be completely on his own – cut off from all financial support. Jonathan had never, ever been separated from the Prescott umbilical cord. He didn't know how he could possibly manage on his own. He would have to drop out of Columbia. He would have to find a way to pay for college. He would have to get a job. It was clear that his father really meant it.

"And I don't want you to see that girl Janice anymore," his father had said casually, near the end, after Jonathan's defenses had been mostly wiped out.

"I can't avoid her, Father – she's friends with Frank and Gwen, too."

"Well, you can stop spending time alone with her."

"Why, are you worried she'll corrupt me?"

"I'm worried she'll cloud your judgment."

"Some people would say that if your argument is sound, you needn't worry about opposing views."

"I'm not worried about her politics, Son, I'm worried about her tits." Jonathan's father stood stock still, looking directly at his son, who was shocked to hear his father use such vulgar language.

"What?" was all Jonathan could muster as a response.

"I'm worried she has designs on you, Son. I would feel better if you and Gwen announced your engagement soon and you made it clear to Janice – and any other potential gold digger on campus – that you are not available."

"She's not a gold digger. I'm sure she's not interested in me romantically."

"Take it from an old goat, Jonathan, you cannot be sure of that. Ever. She could be trouble for you. Mark my words."

"Well you don't have to worry there."

"I worry. It's my job." Jonathan's father actually smiled as he made that remark, and Jonathan smiled back. That was, for all intents and purposes, the end of The Argument. The next several sessions were more reinforcement and ego-building sessions. By Tuesday afternoon, Senator Prescott was confident his son's priorities were back in order, and that a true crisis had been avoided.

Jonathan thought that no matter what his friends might say, his true allegiance was to his father and his family. He vowed to concentrate on school and keep his eyes on the prize, as his father liked to say. He put thoughts of Janice out of his head, although she still occasionally appeared in his dreams.

He planned to go shopping for a ring for Gwen, who was exactly the right girl for him – as his father had said. She was from a fine family, had all the right breeding, and was very pretty. She would bear him fine children. His father was right about that. She was also great in the sack – a fact Jonathan chose not to share with his father. Yes, his course was clear. He convinced himself of that. He also convinced himself it was his decision – he had listened to his father and had made up his own mind. He had a choice, and he made it. True, it was based on the absence of good alternatives, but still his own choice. He would stick to it. He had to. He was a Prescott.

Sunday evening at dinner in the cafeteria, Frank and Gwen explained to Janice and a few other friends what a great time they had over the weekend. Frank described the food in great detail, contrasting it with the serviceable, but certainly unspectacular, fare of the John Jay Hall meal service. Nobody had seen Jonathan yet, but they shrugged it off. He was probably having dinner at home before taking a late train.

When he didn't show up for breakfast, or for classes, on Monday, Gwen got worried enough to telephone the Prescott's house. She was told Jonathan was fine, but was going to spend a few days at home. He finally showed up back at Hartley Hall on Tuesday evening. He didn't say anything to Frank after a quick "Hi" on his way to his room.

After that, Jonathan's behavior was noticeably different. He stopped going to the Harlem shelter with Janice. He stopped hanging around the offices of *The Spectator*. He said he needed to concentrate on his studies and that the newspaper was a distraction. Frank and Janice both tried to get him to explain what happened during those two days, but he wouldn't give any details. He would only say that he and his father had a long talk and he had re-focused himself toward achieving his real goals of law school and a career in politics. Anything that distracted him from those goals, he said, was a waste of time.

In every political discussion, Jonathan took the most conservative position available. Gwen said, "I'm sure it's just a short-term thing," but Frank and Janice weren't sure. After three weeks, there seemed to be no crack in the armor. Frank remarked to Janice that Jonathan had been taken over by space aliens who had sucked out his brain. Janice smiled and said, "It seems that way, but don't give up hope – yesterday he gave me his copy of the Sunday *Times* magazine."

Chapter 23

IN THEIR TOWNHOUSE IN GEORGETOWN, Senator Jonathan Prescott III, his lovely wife, Gwen, and their two daughters sat down to an informal dinner. If his political handlers could have had a camera in the room, the scene would have made a terrific campaign ad. Two girls, each bearing a striking resemblance to their mother, sat straight up in their chairs, napkins in their laps and holding their silverware deftly. Each of the girls had a black silk ribbon holding her hair back. They took turns talking in animated tones about their latest school triumph, battling for their father's attention and praise. Jonathan and Gwen both beamed at their beautiful princesses, and exchanged proud glances and smiles with each other.

An hour later, the girls were bouncing up the stairs to their second-floor bedrooms, wearing matching nightgowns. Elizabeth, nine years old and a bundle of energy, wore pink bunny slippers. Marilyn, eleven, opted for white fuzzy slippers without discernible eyes or ears. After the teeth had been brushed and the lights put out, Jonathan and Gwen walked arm-in-arm back down to the study for a nightcap. Then the mood changed for the worse.

Jonathan told Gwen about his conversation with Janice Stanton. She was threatening to publish a story in *The Journal* suggesting that his father was not really his biological parent. He did not mention the abortion, still hopeful that Janice would keep her promise not to publish that aspect of the story and not wanting to create an unnecessary crisis at that particular moment with Gwen.

"She wanted me to get Father to take a DNA test to prove he is really my father. Can you believe that? Can you imagine me even asking him?"

Gwen sat silently with a glass of California cabernet in her hand, the dark liquid sloshing slowly from side to side in no immediate danger of being consumed. She looked at the maroon Persian rug covering the blond hardwood floor and said, in a voice barely more than a whisper, "Is it true?"

"No, it's not bloody true," Jonathan spat back, visibly annoyed with her for asking.

"Then why would she make such a claim?" Gwen asked, raising her eyes to his and pleading with her expression for some assurance that her life and social standing were not really in jeopardy.

"I told you, it's based on speculation and a series of assumptions that can't possibly hold up to scrutiny."

Gwen took a small sip of her wine and paused to swallow. "What will we say to people when they ask?"

"We will say the story is wild speculation without any proof or substantiation and that we expect this kind of sensationalistic crap from *The Village Voice*, but not from *The Wall Street Journal*."

"That sounds like Max talking," Gwen said with a hint of disdain for the man who was largely responsible for her ability to attend the very best Washington parties.

"Well, get used to it, Honey. I'm afraid we'll both be called upon to answer that question if Janice decides her need for a sensational story is more important than her journalistic ethics."

"Would you consider preempting the story by getting your father to take the DNA test?" Gwen stood up as she spoke and walked to the bay window overlooking the trees lining the quiet street. She loved this home, which was a perk of Jonathan's Senate seat. They couldn't possibly afford the place on a standard senator's salary, but the landlord was vice-president of an association of real estate speculators that had an interest in killing an amendment to a tax reform bill. Max had suggested giving Jonathan and Gwen a good deal on the place would go a long way toward demonstrating the need for reasonable tax rates on capital gains resulting from commercial real estate transactions.

"Are you nuts?!" Jonathan drained his scotch and walked quickly to the bar to refill his glass. "Even if I wanted to, do you think for a moment that Father would agree to the humiliation?"

"But," Gwen turned and faced him, "if the test comes back and proves he is your father, you can get *The Journal* to kill the story before it prints and we can avoid the entire mess." She paused for a moment, considering whether to continue the argument, but decided to press on. "And if the test shows he's not your biological father, then at least we'll know, and we can say so and who the hell will care?"

"I'll care! And you know damn well Father will care. How can you even say that?" Jonathan dropped an ice cube on the floor, but made no move to retrieve it. "And don't tell me you wouldn't bloody care if I wasn't really a Prescott. Your mother would disown you."

Gwen raised her hand with her index finger pointing at her husband and opened her mouth to shoot back a snappy reply, but stopped suddenly, spun on her heel, and stormed out of the room. It was true that her mother had worked hard to set her up with Jonathan in school. The idea of being a part of this historic and important family had buoyed Gwen's mother through all their courtship. Her father had taken out a second mortgage on their house to pay for the elaborate wedding. Her parents had moved to a condominium in Boca Raton in retirement, making it clear they couldn't wait to have the grandchildren visit – long before there were any grandchildren.

They never missed the summer Prescott family picnic, mingling with the famous, the rich, and those who had glommed onto one of America's aristocratic clans. They were always pleased to say they were the parents of Jonathan The Third's wife, Gwendolyn. It was true. Her parents, who had reveled in the celebrity of being part of the Prescotts, would be crushed if it turned out Jonathan was somehow not really the true son of the famous senator.

As Jonathan stood silently in the study, pondering how he was going to handle the trip up to the bedroom later that night if Gwen was still in a mood, he caught motion out of the corner of his eye and looked up to see her standing in the doorway. Her eyes were puffy and her mascara was slightly streaked by her left eye. They looked at each other in silence for a few moments. Jonathan took a step toward her, but she held up her hand, signaling him to stop.

"No," she whispered. "Let me say what I want to say. You know I love you. I've always loved you. It doesn't matter to me whether your last name is Prescott or Smith. And it won't matter to the girls. I know you always wanted us to have a son to carry on the Prescott family name and I'm–" she paused, her lower lip trembling, fighting to not cry.

She wiped a tear from the corner of her right eye, further smearing her make-up. "I'm so sorry. I know it's nobody's fault, and the doctor said there was no choice after Marilyn was born. I told you we could adopt a boy, but you always said it wouldn't be the same. Well, maybe not, but I'm still willing. No matter what happens, your name is still Prescott, and your children's name is Prescott, and my name is Prescott and nobody can take that away from you no matter what any DNA test or anything else says."

She rushed across the few feet separating them and buried her face in his chest, wrapping her arms around his waist as he encircled her shoulders and hugged her tightly. They rocked gently back and forth without speaking for what seemed like a half hour, but which was really three minutes. "Thank you, dear," he whispered into her ear as he stroked her hair gently. "That means a lot to me. I hope everyone else feels the same way."

"If they love you, they will," she said convincingly. "You are a senator in your own right and a great man and nobody can take that away from you."

"It's nice to know you'll always be there, no matter what."

"I will, darling. No matter what." She looked up at him with dark mascara circles still wet with tears, and she smiled at him before sinking back into his chest.

Jonathan hugged her tighter, wondering if this was the right moment to discuss the prospect of Janice going with the abortion story, and whether Gwen's pledge of unshakable love would survive the shock. He decided to keep it to himself and enjoy the moment.

Chapter 24

March, 1988

JONATHAN PRESCOTT III SAUNTERED up to the bar on the ground floor of the Omega Tau Upsilon fraternity house on 114th Street, across the street from the main Columbia campus. Frat row at Columbia was a half-block long series of brownstones, each one painted a different color and with its Greek letters proudly displayed. On the campus side of the street was a fire hydrant that on this night was painted blue and white, the colors of Alpha Epsilon Pi, but the Omega Tau Epsilon boys had plans to repaint it by the end of this particular Saturday night. It was the main sport of the frats – repainting that fire hydrant. Nobody seemed worried about whether the nut would turn if there were ever an actual fire.

On this night, Omega house was hosting a party at which freshmen who had pledged to join in the fall were officially welcomed into the exclusive club. Jonathan's father had suggested this frat would yield good connections, even if he didn't live in the cramped building. Jonathan didn't care much about connections on this night – but he was happy about the open bar.

Frank greeted his roommate with a formal, "What can I get for you, Sir?" Frank had signed up for the Columbia Bartending Service early in their freshman year as a way to earn some extra money on the weekends to supplement his weekday job in the library. This frat party was a particularly good gig since the frat boys were all trying to one-up each other and impress the sorority girls from Barnard by generously tipping the bartenders.

There had been women at Columbia College since 1984, but there were still no Columbia sororities. The Barnard girls were decked out for the occasion. An invitation to this event was a tough ticket, and the room full of eligible bachelors was worth digging out the best dresses and shoes. Frank enjoyed watching the flow of young men and young ladies mixing and milling as they tried to find a suitable partner with whom to start a private conversation. Jonathan, he had noticed, was the center of many circles, and had been approached by several very attractive girls.

"Red wine," Jonathan ordered, "and make it a good pour." He winked at Frank as he dropped two dollar bills into his tip jar.

"Thank you, Sir," Frank deadpanned, handing the glass across the portable bar. "Would you like anything else?"

Jonathan leaned one arm on top of the bar, which for the moment was not a mob scene; the president of Omega Tau Upsilon had just announced that all the freshmen should gather in the library, which was actually the only common room in the building and normally served as the main hang-out and pizza consumption area. "Now that you mention it, I would very much like to get the phone number of the blonde in the red dress."

Frank chuckled with Jonathan for a moment. "I'm afraid that is a professional secret." Frank winked.

"No way," Jonathan blurted out, dropping the veneer of formality. "You don't even know her name, I bet."

"Well, Sir, you just never know what people will tell their bartender." Frank turned away to fetch a Coke for another patron, leaving Jonathan staring and wondering. Jonathan wandered off in the direction of the common room, scanning the crowd for the red dress.

When Frank turned around, he was greeted by a bare knee, sitting on a sturdy table next to the bar and connected to a very attractive woman dressed in a demure black dress, wearing white gloves, and holding a silver serving tray. On the tray, lonely mini crab cake sat among an assortment of crumbs, a partially consumed pot of tartar sauce, and a disheveled stack of cocktail napkins. Frank tried not to stare at her legs while asking, "Can I get you a soda, Miss?"

"What I'd really like is a big glass of that chardonnay," the woman responded, "but we have to wait until after the party before the servants get to drink, so I'll take a Tab." She stretched her arms out in front of her and arched her back, trying to shake out the kinks of her muscles, inadvertently emphasizing the curve of her chest for Frank. "How would you like to break a few rules and take this last crab cake so I can go back to the kitchen and rest a minute?"

Frank gladly grabbed the crab cake and popped it into his mouth without sauce or a napkin. He waved a hand at the empty tray and mumbled as he chewed, "Your wish is my command." The girl giggled slightly and accepted his offer of the glass of soda pop. After handing over the glass, he summoned the courage to risk an introduction. "I'm Frank," he said crisply, extending a hand, then realizing both of hers were occupied with her tray and drink.

She raised her glass in his direction and replied, "Janice."

Frank struck up a conversation. He was pleasantly surprised that she was also a freshman. She was a commuter student, but she said she was hoping to get into a dorm for her sophomore year, if she could scrounge up enough money – hence the job with the catering service. She said she was a journalist and had already published a big story for *The Spectator* and that she planned to be the first female Columbia College grad to win a Pulitzer Prize. Jonathan laughed and wished her luck, but chided her for having such modest life goals.

During the rest of the evening, Frank followed her with his eyes as she circulated around the room, serving appetizers and flirting with the frat boys. She seemed particularly friendly toward the upperclassmen. Although her uniform was conservatively cut, there was no disguising her athletic body, slim legs, and ample chest. More than one gentleman turned to watch her walk away after receiving her service.

Jonathan, meanwhile, found the blonde in the red dress, but was disappointed to discover that she did not recognize his name. She said she was trying to recruit Omega Tau Upsilon men to support the Barnard Gay and Lesbian Students Association. He politely extracted himself from the conversation and was heading back to the bar to torment Frank some more when he was intercepted at the doorway of the common room by a girl in a purple silk dress cut just above her knees. Jonathan noticed her high heels and her bare shoulders, although he wished the dress had shown off a little cleavage. She shyly introduced herself as Gwendolyn, but said he could call her Gwen.

He started to introduce himself but she cut him off. "Oh, I know who you are. My father is a huge supporter of your father, the *senator*." She placed an emphasis on the word "senator," as if Jonathan should be impressed by his own father's title. She told him she was also a freshman, at Barnard, and that she hoped her sorority and Jonathan's new fraternity would be having more mixers for the new students. She told him she had not had much success meeting nice Columbia guys in her first semester.

"Now, I find that very hard to believe – Gwen, you said, right?"

"Yes, it's Gwendolyn, but you can call me Gwen. All my friends do."

"So, I'll count myself as your friend, Gwen," Jonathan replied smoothly.

Gwen blushed and nodded. She said she wasn't entirely sure what she wanted to major in yet. She walked with Jonathan when he went to the bar. There he totally ignored Frank, who served them both drinks. Jon made a big show of dropping a five-dollar bill into the tip jar. Gwen clung to his elbow as he walked back to the common room, and lingered on the periphery of his conversations for the rest of the night.

She did not say she had a photograph of him in her dorm room, cut from a local Connecticut newspaper where his graduation from prep school and acceptance at Columbia College had been published at the request of his mother. She did not tell him that she had seen him in the cafeteria and at several college functions, but had not been able to get up the nerve to approach him until that night, after two of her sorority sisters had urged her to "take a chance."

At the end of the evening, Gwen discretely handed Jonathan a slip of paper with her name and phone number. He smiled brightly and promised to call her. He helped her on with her coat and watched as she walked down the sidewalk with three other Barnard women, and noticed that the blonde in the red dress was not one of them. It took all of Gwen's willpower not to peek back over her shoulder to see whether Jonathan was watching.

Frank and Janice both cleaned up their work areas and clocked out from their work shifts at about the same time. Frank asked if she was going home by subway, since she had explained earlier that she lived in Queens. "No," she said. "It's too late at night to be taking the subway. I'll stay here tonight." When Frank inquired where she would stay, Janice was vague, and he didn't press it. He offered to walk her to her destination, but she declined, claiming she needed to use the ladies' room and that he should not wait for her. He was pretty sure he was getting the brush-off, although he thought they had hit it off pretty well during the party. As he turned to go, she reached out and grabbed him by the arm.

"Hey, Mister Bartender Frank," she said, "how would I contact you if I were looking for somebody to pour me a drink sometime?"

Frank smiled and searched for a pen. He gave Janice his dorm room phone number. She took it and tucked it into a pocket in her dress that he would never have guessed was there, and said "Thanks. Maybe I'll see you around." Frank said he hoped so, and didn't press her for her own number. She smiled and then disappeared in the direction of the kitchen.

Later, in their room, Frank told Jonathan about the hot serving girl he had met at the party. Jonathan claimed not to have noticed her, but Frank did not buy it. Frank asked who the girl in the purple dress was who had been latched onto Jonathan for most of the night. "I think she said her name is Gwen," Jonathan gave a nonchalant answer. "I believe she's a Barnard girl." Jonathan cut off the conversation and left to head for the bathroom down the hallway.

Chapter 25

JANICE SAT IN A WINDOWLESS CONFERENCE ROOM on the eleventh floor of the office building housing the Washington Bureau of *The Wall Street Journal*. She had an annoying sense of déjà vu as she looked across the conference table at Marcus Brockman, the managing editor, and Stuart Karlan, the in-house lawyer. They had both come down on the Amtrak from New York. Janice's Page One editor and mentor, Cathy Pantell, was on the speaker phone, which made Janice a little nervous – why had she not come in person? Also in the room was a large man in an expensive suit who Janice did not recognize. She had known this moment was coming, but her throat was still dry and she had to clasp her hands together on the table top to keep them from shaking.

Stuart started the meeting in his usual business-like manner. "OK, we're all here. Marcus, I believe you know Max Foster," he gestured to the fat man, who made eye contact with Brockman without any apparent reaction. Nobody offered to introduce Max to Janice. "I have taken the liberty of showing Mr. Foster a draft of Ms. Stanton's Page One piece scheduled for next Saturday."

"Why him?" Janice couldn't help but ask. "Did you show it to Senator Prescott also?"

Stuart glared at her. Brockman reached for her wrist and patted it to tell her to stay calm and limit her comments to the facts of the story and answers to specific questions, as they had discussed just before coming into the meeting. Stuart continued, "Obviously, there are some facts stated here that are somewhat new and could conceivably be considered controversial." Stuart had a way with understatement.

Max grunted, suppressing a laugh, and sat forward in his chair, "Mr. Karlan, I can assure you these scurrilous lies will not only be controversial, they will result in this newspaper changing its name to the Prescott Gazette after the court awards the senator ownership of the company as damages for this outrageous libel." Max's voice was never raised, but his eyes burned as if trying to send laser beams through the paper's lawyer.

Karlan was not fazed. "Mr. Foster, we are here today and you have been invited to this meeting to make sure we all understand the basis for the story and to reassure you and the senator that we have verified all the facts. Let's start with the medical information and the family's genetic markers. Does the senator dispute any of the facts in the story?"

Max shifted slightly in his chair before answering. "The facts in that portion of the story are not in dispute, as you well know, Marcus." He turned his attention away from the lawyer and to the managing editor, who he obviously knew from some past association. Janice watched the back-and-forth like she was at the U.S. Tennis Open in Flushing.

"Only knowingly false facts can support a libel claim, Max."

"It's just as actionable to make libelous claims deduced from those facts."

"The story makes no claims."

"Like hell it doesn't."

"I've read it seven times, Max. The story does not claim the senior senator is not Jonathan III's father."

"What do you call this?" Max opened the portfolio on the table in front of him and peered down to read. "I'm quoting here, 'The statistical probability of these biological events happening if Jonathan Prescott, Jr. is the current senator's father are so small as to be nearly impossible.' Now, you tell me that is not a libelous statement."

"It's not a libelous statement, Max, because you didn't read the whole quote. That statement was attributed to a noted professor of mathematics, who was merely giving his opinion of the probability of random chance explaining the facts you do not dispute. You think the professor's calculations are incorrect?"

"It's an opinion, and it's as good as making an assertion that it's true."

"Not just as good, Max. It's an extrapolation from the facts, and it's the professor's opinion. We all know that opinion cannot be libelous."

"Well, it's damn scurrilous, Marcus. It's beneath the dignity of this paper. It's beneath your ethics!"

"Max, since when do your candidates question other people's ethics?"

Max blurted out a guffaw and everyone in the room exhaled, laughing along with the two combatants. Point to Brockman.

Foster, however parried the thrust. "Are you going to make me go to Rutherford on this?"

The room went silent at the reference to Rutherford Xavier Warren, the CEO and Chairman of the Board of the multinational entertainment corporation that had purchased *The Journal* several years before and who was a noted conservative supporter. Although Rutherford normally took a hands-off approach to the paper's news content, he certainly had the power to kill the story, and Janice wondered whether there was any chance Foster carried enough clout to actually get Rutherford to step in.

Marcus, however, was ready for the gambit. "Actually, Max, Rutherford loves a good bout of mudslinging as much as anyone and welcomes the publicity and the controversy. If you make this into a circus, he'll stand outside the tent urging the public to come take a look at the freak show."

Max contorted his plump face into an appropriate sneer and said, "What about the other . . . thing?"

"You mean the pregnancy, and the abortion?"

Max winced as if physically injured by hearing the word "abortion." "Yes," he hissed, "there cannot possibly be any support for this kind of sensationalistic claim. You know this is nothing more than outrageous tripe intended to discredit the senator. There is nothing, nothing in the world, that will save you from the judge on this." Janice imagined she could actually see smoke coming out of the fat man's ears.

Stuart broke into the volley at this point, "If I may . . . allow me to interject at this point. Janice?" Every head in the room turned to Janice, as if she had only just entered. Stuart asked the question they had rehearsed a few minutes earlier. "Janice, do you have a source for the allegation in the article that Jonathan Prescott III got a girl pregnant when he was in college, and that the girl had an abortion?"

Janice hesitated, despite all the preparation, then looked at Stuart, nodded her head, and said, "Yes," without as much conviction as she had intended.

"That's it?" Max bellowed, standing up and slapping the table for emphasis. "That's your support? The girl says 'yes' and that's it? Who is the source?"

Marcus jumped back into the game, keeping his voice even and low. "Max, I can assure you I have fully examined the source material here and we are confident it's genuine and supportable."

Max fumed and stared at Janice. "Who – Is – The – Source?" He could barely control his anger as he leaned over the table toward Janice, directing his rage point blank at her.

Janice recoiled involuntarily, but said nothing, as she had been coached. "The source is confidential," Marcus stated flatly. You know very well in a case like this the source would be in for a ton of trouble, from you and others, if we disclosed her identity."

"So," Max snapped his head toward Marcus, "it's a woman, that at least narrows it down."

"Yes, it certainly does. Now you're down to only 155 million people."

"Why did you drag me down here if you have nothing to tell me?"

"Max, we wanted you to see Janice in person and know that she has a solid source. We also want you to ask your man, the senator, whether he really has any reason to doubt that Janice is solid on this. He won't have any actual doubt. He'll certainly deny the facts publicly, but he will not sue over it, so I think we're done here." Marcus stood up, with Stuart right on his heels. Janice trailed the group out of the conference room, leaving Max sitting at the table, alone.

Later, Marcus tapped lightly on the cubicle wall of Janice's work space in the newsroom. He sat down on the edge of a small table strewn with paper and discarded coffee cups and waited for Janice to finish typing a sentence and press control + S to save her work before speaking. "Are you sure you want to do this to yourself, Jan?"

"It's a little late to be getting cold feet, isn't it?" Janice said calmly.

"You know I won't think any less of you if you decide there's too much heat here."

"That's bullshit, Marcus, and you know it," Janice smiled ruefully as she replied. "You would think I don't have the balls to be a political reporter and you would never again trust me with a big story."

Marcus smiled back. "True. But aside from that, I would support you all the way." They both laughed, breaking the tension. "Seriously, though, you realize the right-wingers are going to crucify you personally for this."

"I guess that's their job. That never bothers us, right?"

"Normally, I'd agree with you. But this one might be different. You are taking a point-blank shot at their golden boy. It could get rough. I wouldn't put it past them to come after you in ways you might not be able to anticipate."

"Senator Prescott won't do that," Janice said flatly, shaking her head slightly as she spoke.

Marcus eased himself off the table and walked toward the open space beyond Janice's desk. "You keep saying that, and I hope you're right. But I don't know how you can be so sure."

"I'm sure," was all she said, turning back to her keyboard. The editor mumbled something inaudible to himself as he walked out. He strolled down the aisle between work stations, smiling or exchanging a glance with most of the reporters who were toiling away as the day's deadline approached. He reached the end of the row and crossed into a conference room, where a short, thin man who looked to be in his mid-eighties, wearing casual slacks and a sweater vest, was talking on a cell phone. He waited for Rutherford Warren to finish the conversation he was having and look up at his chief editor.

"She's sure."

Rutherford nodded and dialed a new number. Marcus turned and walked back to the temporary office he was using while in D.C., still muttering to himself and wondering whether any of them really understood what they were getting into.

Chapter 26

THE NIGHT BEFORE THE STORY RAN, Jonathan sat with Gwen after the girls had gone to bed. Gwen was wearing slacks and a light blouse, and Jonathan noticed she was wearing the diamond-and-silver "G" necklace he gave her when they were still dating. He imagined it was a show of solidarity with him about the paternity claim.

She was such a good wife to him. She had done everything a politician's wife could do. She never complained when he had to take long trips, or spend nights away at fundraisers and campaign stops. She met him on the road whenever he called for her, and left him alone when he needed to focus and work without the distraction of his wife and family. She was the perfect hostess, and had a smile and a kiss on the cheek even for men and women she couldn't stand. She reveled in being Mrs. Senator Prescott.

Jonathan had never needed to fire anyone – Edward Evans took care of that for him. He had not developed a feel for giving out bad news. He made himself a strong drink and hoped the dull throb of the alcohol might help him get through the ordeal. He told himself it was long ago and that Gwen would understand and not really care.

Gwen was sitting on the sofa with a glass of white wine in her hand. Jonathan was pacing. He told her Janice was going to run the story about his supposedly questionable paternity. Gwen nodded and reached up her hand toward him, but he didn't take it. He then told her what Max had relayed to him – there would also be an allegation about an abortion of his baby dating back to his college days. Gwen asked if it was Janice who had the abortion. Jonathan nodded.

"Was it after we were engaged?"

"Yes," Jonathan replied simply.

"And you kept this from me all these years?"

"Yes," he confessed.

"You should have told me before we were married." she said quietly, trying to keep her composure, but feeling the welling of coming tears.

"You didn't want to know, if you recall. You never asked me about other women I had been with."

Gwen stood up now, spilling a little wine on the rug, but ignoring it. "I never wanted to know about the women you slept with before we were engaged, but this is different and you know it! And a child? You didn't think that was important enough to tell me about?"

"What good would it have done to tell you?" Jonathan asked, maintaining his calm with difficulty. He knew he had no high ground to which he could retreat here, but he could not help but defend his actions.

"It would have been honest, and shown that you trusted me enough to know I would still marry you."

"Would you have still married me?"

Gwen paused and stared at her husband of twenty years. "I think I would have, yes. But how can I trust you now? Are there any more? Any more lovers? Any more aborted babies?"

"No!" Jonathan exclaimed harshly, then caught himself and softened his tone. "No. None. I have been entirely faithful to you since we have been married."

"How can I believe that now?"

"You can because it's true. I can't say anything else. That one night with her was a long time ago. It never meant anything. I was angry with you because you didn't want to spend the weekend with me when you went home to see your parents. Janice and I went out for beers. She and Frank had just cooled off – you remember – and we got a little drunk and ended up in my room. That was it. We weren't in love. It was just sex."

"And it's just trust," Gwen said bitterly. "That obviously means more to me than it does to you." Jonathan moved toward her with his arms out, but she turned away. "Don't," was all she said. She turned and walked out of the room, climbed the stairs to their bedroom, and locked the door behind her.

After his talk with Gwen, Jonathan called his father to alert him to the latest developments. There was a lot of silence on the phone line. In the end, the elder senator only told Jonathan to remain calm and firm in his denials and he would rise above the story in the end. Jonathan told his father that the abortion story was true, but that it had happened before he and Gwen were married. He had tried to talk the girl out of the abortion, but she went ahead without him. The elder senator did not ask who the girl was, which spared Jonathan the dilemma of deciding whether to lie or face his father's lecture about how he always knew Janice was a woman he needed to stay away from. Neither man mentioned taking a DNA test.

That Saturday, on Page One of *WSJ Weekend*, above the fold, Janice got the byline of her life. The headline was typically understated for *The Journal*: "**Senator Prescott Bombshells: Pregnancy, Abortion, and Questions**

About Paternity." The subhead read "**Politician's past at odds with stance on social issues.**" The article set out the detailed facts leading to the questions about his paternity in the manner of a scientific journal, culminating in the statistical analysis explaining how improbable it was that all these facts could be true if Senator Prescott, Jr. was, in fact, the father of Jonathan Prescott III. Janice wrote that the senator was offered the opportunity to submit to a DNA test, but he declined. The story about Jonathan's college dalliance, resulting in an unwanted pregnancy and an abortion, was attributed to "reliable and confirmed sources and medical records obtained by *the Journal*." The identity of the girl was withheld for reasons of privacy.

The story hit the streets at about 4:00 a.m. in New York. At 6:00 a.m., Senator Prescott issued a statement that was faxed and emailed to every radio and television station in New York, New Jersey, Connecticut, and Washington, D.C., along with all the major networks, all the network outlets in the top ten markets, all the cable networks, and all the big political bloggers. The statement denounced the allegations about the senator's paternity and called the pregnancy and abortion claims unsupported lies planted by political enemies.

The cable news outlets picked it up first, starting with the 7:00 a.m. early news and rolling through the day and into the 10:00 a.m. Sunday political talk shows the next morning. *Face the Nation* interrupted its scheduled lineup to devote a half hour to Senator Prescott's situation. Tim Russert devoted his introduction entirely to the issue, and speculated that if the allegations about the pregnancy and abortion were true, it would be a blow to the Republican Party at a time it was struggling to redefine its conservative base, and would seriously damage any presidential aspirations for Senator Prescott. But, given recent allegations against other presidential candidates, it might not be fatal.

Janice received a stream of congratulatory telephone calls and even a telegram from the chairman of the Democratic National Committee, telling her that she had done a great service for the principles of freedom in America. Her former editor at *The Voice* even called to wish her well.

Marcus called to suggest that she get started on a follow-up piece on the senator's reaction to the story and the fall-out throughout the Republican Party. Janice was not as enthusiastic about the follow-up as she thought she would be, but she got started.

Chapter 27

THE NEXT TWO WEEKS WERE DIFFICULT for Jonathan. He couldn't hide entirely from the press, and so he granted a few specific interviews with reporters and television correspondents who were hand-picked by Edward Evans, at Max's suggestion. The FOX News interview was particularly well-planned, focusing on core conservative issues and only touching on the recent controversy long enough for Jonathan to state his party line.

On the pregnancy and abortion issue, he was advised to make a total denial. The theory was that the girl, whoever she was, would not come out publicly now if she was not willing to use her name in the original story. That would allow Jonathan to deny its truth with little fear that there would be any actual evidence or even a live person to contradict him. Max was angry when Jonathan told him that denial was not the way to go in this case, and furious when Jonathan refused to explain why he was so sure of himself on this particular issue. In the end, however, it was going to be Jonathan's interview, and Max could only pick the forum and questioner, not the answers Jonathan chose to give.

He was not a saint, he told Betty Berkley, a very pretty brunette whose low-cut blouses created a large viewership, few of whom could have correctly identified her eye color. When he was younger, Jonathan certainly did a little partying, and drank a little beer. He loved his wife, with whom he had been tremendously happy and to whom he was entirely faithful. But it was not beyond the realm of possibility that there could have been an unplanned pregnancy back then, in his distant past.

If he had known about it, he certainly would have done what he could to convince the girl to keep the baby. He believed all life was sacred from the moment of conception, and if the girl chose to abort the pregnancy, she made a lawful choice. Although it was a tragedy, there was most likely nothing Jonathan could have done about it. It pointed out, he said, the difficulty of the permissive laws now on the books, which gave the baby's father no opportunity to intervene and act in the interests of his child, and which allowed young girls to make hasty decisions about such an important matter. But this incident had only strengthened his resolve to fight for the rights of the unborn, and to fight for the rights of fathers, and to make sure the rights of the child were as protected as they could be within whatever legal framework existed.

When asked whether he thought the Supreme Court should overrule *Roe v. Wade* and allow states to ban abortions, he said he did. When asked whether he was planning to go along with the Republican plan to block the nomination of Ricky Menendez, he changed the subject.

On the subject of his paternity, he praised his father, Senator Jonathan Prescott, Jr., and his mother, Sylvia. He held up his birth certificate, proving he was born on March 17, 1969 at Mercy Hospital in New Greenwich, Connecticut at 6:09 a.m. His mother had given birth by vaginal delivery and spent three days in the hospital after the birth, and the medical records were undeniable proof of those facts.

He held up pictures, taken from his baby book, showing him coming home from the hospital in his mother's arms with his father standing proudly at her side. He showed a photo from his first birthday party at his parents' home in New Greenwich, one of him on his first day of kindergarten, and one of him sitting atop a pony looking to be about seven or eight, with his father standing beside him. There was no doubt, he said, that he was born to his mother and that he was the natural and legitimate child of his parents. No further proof, nor any DNA test, could shake that truth. Any innuendo or speculation to the contrary was merely political mudslinging and no serious media outlet would give it credence.

The Wall Street Journal, Jonathan opined, had abdicated its responsibility to journalistic ethics and had chosen to run a story he would expect to see only in supermarket tabloids. He was sad that Marcus Brockton would have allowed such a story to run, and he was deeply disappointed in his old friend, Janice Stanton, who had gone with the story despite having no foundation for it. He understood the pressure on a reporter to come up with sensational stories, but he had expected better from Janice. It was a cheap shot, and he was sure that years from now he would be in some campaign (he didn't say for president, but he was thinking it) and the story would surface again, as if it had ever been true or substantiated. But in the end, it was a non-issue.

Despite words of encouragement from most of his Republican colleagues in the Senate and most of his primary supporters and contributors, including Max, Jonathan could feel the freeze coming on. One week after *The Journal* story ran, Gwen called him at his senate office – something she rarely did – to let him know that Senator Stevens' wife had called her to say she and her husband, who was the second-highest ranking Republican, had decided to cancel the small dinner party scheduled for the coming weekend.

Senator Stevens was from North Carolina, a notoriously conservative state, and was up for re-election that fall. Gwen was told the Daughters of the American Revolution had decided to go with a different speaker for their monthly luncheon in October. Gwen was still invited to attend, of course. And the National Association of Mothers for Morality executive board had decided it would not be best for her name to appear among the list of organizers for the annual fundraising gala, on which Gwen had worked for six months. When Jonathan walked into the Republican caucus lounge, a cluster of aides suddenly stopped their conversation and scattered like cockroaches from under a lifted bowl. There was no mistaking that the mood around Jonathan had changed.

In his own office, a few of his staffers seemed unusually formal, while others seemed to disappear for hours without notice. Most of them had been referred by Max right out of Georgetown or hand-picked from the best law schools. Jonathan realized how few of his staff he had actually chosen himself, and how little he really knew about most of them. When he walked into the office one morning, he noticed that his chief policy analyst changed the screen on his computer as soon as he saw Jonathan. He couldn't be sure, but it looked like the analyst had been looking at a resume.

The exceptions to the growing chill were his long-time personal secretary, Harriet Barlow, and his press secretary, Donna Ward. Harriett had been with him since his first congressional campaign. She was a widow of about sixty, although the kind of old-fashioned woman who would never talk about her own age. She wore her hair in a perpetual gray bun and always wore a smart business suit, no matter what the weather, with a pressed skirt, pantyhose, and conservative one-inch pumps. She looked like a character out of a Humphrey Bogart film, and she was efficient, courteous, and loyal as a Labrador.

Donna, on the other hand, was a modern woman. She had started working for Jonathan when he was elected to the Senate eight years ago, and they developed an instant connection and friendship. She dressed in exotic outfits resembling middle-eastern robes some days, and buttoned-down men's dress shirts the next. She was the smartest person on his staff, and he always kidded her about when she would be leaving to take a job in State or at the CIA. She had blonde hair which she always wore up in some kind of clip or knot so Jonathan could never really tell how long it was. She was athletic and slim, owing to the daily rowing on the Potomac that she bragged about and hard workouts in the Senate gym. Since Jonathan never frequented the gym, he was never treated to the sight of Donna in a sweat-stained jogging bra and skin-tight running shorts. The male staff members, however, often commented.

Despite her renowned body, however, Donna had shot down advances from every male staff member. She had been married, but she didn't talk about it, and although she often mentioned her boyfriend, he never came to the office, and nobody ever seemed to meet him. This naturally led to speculation that the boyfriend was mythical and that Donna was a closet lesbian, which only made the men hotter for her.

Jonathan would have tried to ease her off the staff to avoid Gwen's occasional remarks about his sexy assistant, but she was too damned good at her job. Max had sent her over, saying she was well connected. Jonathan quickly came to appreciate exactly how well connected she was. He never asked how she knew every executive producer of every political television show in town and on the major networks, or how she seemed to have the phone number of every key reporter in her head. Jonathan was just happy she did. She was also tremendously well organized and worked with Harriett to form an impregnable wall between Jonathan and unwanted press coverage. She helped keep his legislative schedule on track, and made sure he was never late for a meeting.

Once, when Jonathan had spilled coffee on his shirt and tie just minutes before he was supposed to make an opening statement at a subcommittee meeting live on C-SPAN, Donna dashed out of the room and returned moments later with a fresh shirt and tie. She was still removing the tags on the tie as Jonathan was changing into the new shirt, which still bore the creases from its packaging. She helped Jonathan button the cuffs (he preferred French cuffs, but in a pinch he could hardly be picky) as he thanked her and asked how she had a new shirt and tie so handy. "It's my job to make sure you look good on camera, Boss," was her simple reply.

Over the years they had worked together, Jonathan and Donna had worked late more times than they could count. They had traveled together to every corner of the globe, including two weeks in Iraq and Israel where Jonathan had made a great impression on the Israeli Prime Minister. He had come across as a great supporter of the Jewish State and appropriately hawkish on the war.

His traveling group had stayed in tents, barracks, and cheap hotels. Jonathan wanted to make sure he was not perceived as living in the lap of luxury while the troops were struggling. They had washed in rivers and relieved themselves behind sand dunes. Jonathan had marveled at Donna's ability to pull a roll of toilet paper out of her backpack.

In all that time, and all the close quarters they had shared, there had never been a hint of attraction between them. Donna had never given Jonathan any indication that she was interested, and Jonathan had always been a perfect gentleman. In fact, Jonathan had often discussed his home life with Donna, who served as a traveling psychiatrist and sounding board whenever there were issues between Gwen and Jonathan. In many ways, Donna was his closest friend.

In the aftermath of *The Journal* article, Jonathan took refuge at the office, working harder than ever on a tax reform bill he was co-sponsoring. He was also doggedly pursuing a corruption investigation involving a Democratic senator from California whose campaign had received an unusually large number of donations from employees of a power company that would be the beneficiary of a regulatory change being championed by the senator. Jonathan could not abide corrupt politicians, nor peers who took bribes or kickbacks or sold their influence to the highest bidder. Perhaps it was his own family fortune and the deep tradition of honor instilled into him by his father, but no matter which party's legislators were involved, Jonathan was a bulldog.

As he worked later and longer, Donna worked at his side. As Gwen became more and more distant at home, still hurt by Jonathan's dishonesty and sulking because of their fall in social stature in the Washington elite party set, Jonathan shared with Donna his sadness that his wife was not as able to shrug off the controversy of The Article as he was. Donna, as always, was sympathetic and understanding.

It was the Friday before the long Independence Day weekend and Jonathan was working in his office after six o'clock. The summer sun was starting to descend and the Washington Monument cast a long shadow toward the Capitol building. Harriett had gone home at 5:00, while the rest of the staff who hadn't taken the whole day off had left shortly after lunch to beat the traffic out of town. Except for Donna.

She was wearing a wrap-around skirt emblazoned with a red and black pattern that was vaguely African and a light, cream-colored blouse with puffy shoulders that was loose at her waist, occasionally exposing a glimpse of bare belly when she reached up for a folder located on a high shelf. She sauntered into Jonathan's inner office, the door of which was open, and planted both palms flat on the front of his desk, bending over slightly as she loomed over him. "Boss, it's time for you to leave that investigation for the weekend and get home to Gwen and your girls."

Jonathan took off his reading glasses and looked up, blowing out a breath more heavily than he intended. "Gwen and the girls are at her mother's for the long weekend. I offered to meet her there tomorrow after the weekend traffic cleared out, but she said she would be just as happy if I stayed in town." Jonathan's head sagged toward the desk as he finished the statement. "Seems like spending extra time together is not as much of a priority as it used to be."

Donna straightened up and walked around behind the desk chair, putting her hands on Jonathan's neck and massaging his shoulders lightly. She had done this many times, sensing when Jonathan was tense and needed to relax. Jonathan leaned back in his chair, groaning happily as her fingers pressed into his tight muscles. "Mmmm, that's nice. Thanks, Donna." She smiled and returned the compliment by digging in harder with both thumbs. "Ohh, wow . . . aaahh . . . Ohh . . . it's a good thing that, ohh, there's nobody else here to listen to this or they might get the . . . aahh . . . wrong idea."

Donna laughed brightly and ceased the intense pressure, just letting her hands run gently over his shoulders, pinching the back of his neck softly at a pressure point she knew from experience. "Boss, if anybody were inclined to get the wrong idea about us, they would have done it a long time ago."

"True," Jonathan responded without turning. "So I guess I'm safe from the rumor mill, at least this time. Although maybe a rumor about an office romance would make Gwen jealous and get her to snap out of the deep freeze."

"I'm sure you two will work things out," Donna said, still resting her hands on his shoulders, but not really massaging them anymore.

"Ha!" Jonathan blurted out, turning his desk chair so he could look at Donna. "I'm not sure if I'm being punished because of the paternity scandal or the twenty-seven-year-old affair, but one way or the other Gwen has been treating me like I have a sexually transmitted disease that I contracted during an extended affair with a hooker." He gave a weak half-smile and pushed the chair back toward the desk, separating himself from Donna.

She remained standing, silhouetted against the window and the sinking sun on the horizon. Some wisps of hair hung randomly down her neck, loosed from their carefully constructed constrictions during the long work day, and made to stand out by the back-lighting of the window. A bead of sweat hung precariously in the hollow of her neck, poised to drip downward between her hidden breasts. Jonathan turned away, not wanting to focus on the femaleness of his press secretary.

"Come on, Jon," she said, using his first name, which she seldom did and never in public. "It can't really be that bad, can it? I'm sure you and Gwen have been through tough patches before. You'll work this out." She turned and walked away from him, around the desk and back into neutral territory. "Why don't we go get some dinner, then, and you can get back to the Doolittle investigation fresh tomorrow – I assume you'll be working the weekend on this?"

Jonathan agreed that some dinner would be a good idea. He packed up his files and hefted his briefcase, while carrying his suit jacket draped over his off arm. Donna met him at the outer office door and they left the building together, which raised nobody's eyebrows since it was a frequent occurrence. They strolled in the warm twilight air to a small Italian restaurant, which was a hot lunch spot for workers on Capitol Hill but quiet on a Friday night. Donna ordered them a bottle of Chianti and fried calamari to nibble on. She had the waiter pour ample portions into the oversized wine glasses and offered a toast to the continuing fight for justice and right in a corrupt and cynical world. Jonathan laughed heartily and took a long sip from his wine. He unfastened the top button of his shirt and loosened his tie.

They drank Chianti Classico, ate pasta and talked about Donna's ex-husband. She had paid for his degree from Georgetown business school. After he graduated, he got a terrific job offer from Goldman Sachs in New York and they had fought for two weeks because he wanted her to go with him to New York just because he was the man of the family. In the end, she stayed in D. C. and they split. She didn't even try to hold him up for alimony, although she now regretted that decision.

They ordered another bottle of wine. Donna laughed at a joke Jonathan told, which she had heard several times before. Jonathan took off his jacket and laid it down on the padded bench next to him. Then he spilled a little Chianti on his tie and Donna had him take it off so she could soak it in some sparkling water for him. When the bread ran out, they both asked for espresso and Donna suggested they could share one piece of cheesecake, which she ordered and allowed him to eat most of.

When the waiter brought the check and the senator's Gold Card had done its magic, they wobbled out into the cool night air together and walked down the Mall. Donna lost her balance and had to lean into Jonathan to catch herself. She linked her elbow into his to steady herself and leaned her head onto his shoulder as they walked. Jonathan could smell the fragrance of her shampoo.

"How long have you worked for me?" Jonathan inquired, sitting on a plush sofa in the living room of Donna's small apartment.

"Eight years and three months," she responded, a bit more quickly than she had intended.

"Not that you've been counting?"

She blushed slightly and turned away. She was standing by the kitchen counter, which had a cut-through to the living room, forming a kind of bar in front of which were four high stools. She was filling two cheap wine glasses from a bottle of red that was not nearly as good as what they had been drinking at the restaurant.

Jonathan looked around. "So, how come I've never seen your apartment?"

"I'm sure it would have been inappropriate for you to have come home to my apartment unless my husband had been here, and he was never here." She crossed the hardwood floor, her heels tapping loudly with each step, leaning down to hand Jonathan his glass. Her starched white blouse fell slightly as she stooped, revealing the lace fringe of her pink Victoria's Secret bra. She raised back up, then lowered herself onto an over-stuffed chair. A polished end table separated them, providing a landing place for the wine glasses and creating a neutral zone as they talked.

Jonathan leaned back, putting his feet up on the glass top of the coffee table in front of his chair. He leaned his head back and exhaled a long, slow breath, as if the weight of the world were being expelled from his body. "Don't you hate having to worry about appearances all the time?" he asked to the ceiling. "Wouldn't it be nice if we could just do whatever the fuck we want and not give a shit what the press had to say about it?"

She smiled, but didn't respond, knowing from her years of working with Jonathan that such rhetorical statements did not need an answer. "If a politician fell in the woods and no reporter was there to record it, would he make a sound?"

Jonathan laughed loudly and sat up in his chair, reaching for his wine glass and taking a healthy draught. "That's why I keep you around, Donna, because of your sense of humor."

"Thanks," she said, smiling seductively, "but I always thought it was my killer legs."

"That, too," Jonathan laughed. "No denying it. You know all the interns are hot for you?"

"Those boys would be hot for anything with two legs and a pussy," she said, holding her hand up to her mouth as she finished the sentence. "Sorry, Boss, I didn't mean to be vulgar."

"No offense taken, Ms. Ward," Jonathan responded, sitting back in his chair again and closing his eyes. The wine had made him dizzy and relaxed. The pressure of the past weeks had left him exhausted. He thought he might fall asleep right there.

"Excuse me a minute, Boss," Donna said, getting up from the sofa and walking across the room toward the bathroom. John didn't open his eyes, listening to the clicking of her heels, then the snap of the latch to the door.

He allowed himself to drift off for a moment. He kept his eyes shut, focusing on the swirling patterns of the insides of his eyelids and trying to hold the patterns in his mind as the floaters in his eyes meandered across his consciousness. He wasn't sure how long he stayed in a half-awake state. He heard the flush of the toilet, then the sound of water running in the sink, and then the click and squeak of the door opening. He waited for the clicks of Donna's heels on the hardwood, but they didn't come. After a few moments, he opened his eyes, curious why she had not walked back into the room.

When his eyes focused, he saw that she had, indeed, returned. She was standing directly in front of him, with the glass-topped coffee table between them. The lace fringe of her pink bra was no longer hidden behind her white starched blouse. Instead, it was prominently displayed, along with the curve of her cleavage, pressed together by the taut fabric. She wore matching pink panties, with lace edges that playfully curved around the milky whiteness of the skin of her thighs, then merged into a tiny string that disappeared around the back of her hip. Jonathan thought she seemed shorter, but then realized she had removed her high-heeled shoes, which accounted for her silent return.

"I hope you don't . . . mind," she said softly, as she slid the index finger of her right hand between her breasts and down the smooth, tight muscles of her abdomen, displaying the body that all the men on Jonathan's staff speculated about regularly. When the meandering course of her finger reached the top of her panties, she looped the string of pink silk deftly around its tip and pulled up the fabric, tightening it through her crotch and then letting the string snap back against her hip. "Do you like what you see?"

The erection already throbbing under Jonathan's pants probably rendered Donna's question rhetorical, and Jonathan saw her smile playfully when she glanced in that direction. He contemplated an answer for a few seconds, before saying, "That's like asking if I like the Venus de Milo."

She sauntered around the coffee table, then turned and walked behind the sofa, at which point Jonathan's eyes could no longer follow without turning his head, which he did not do. As she disappeared from view, he admired the curved profile of her fully exposed ass, and traced the path of the string of pink silk that disappeared between her perfect cheeks. He closed his eyes again and took a deep breath, shaking his head to ward off the effects of the wine. Had he fantasized about Donna? Of course. She was gorgeous and smart and always around. Had he noticed her lingerie from time to time when he caught a peek? Oh, yes. Was this a good idea?

He opened his eyes again when he caught a whiff of her perfume, very close, and felt the heat of her breath against the back of his neck. Her fingers crept around his shoulders slowly and she pressed down into a massaging motion. Donna had rubbed Jonathan's tired neck muscles many times in the office, or on an airplane, but never while wearing only a bra and V-string.

He melted back into her hands, closed his eyes, and groaned softly. He felt the moist, hot caress of Donna's tongue on the back of his neck, and then the soft pressure of her lips, and the gentle suction against his skin.

"I think I can help you relax, Boss," she whispered into his ear, her warm breath making all the tiny hairs on his neck stand at attention and sending a tingle shooting down his side into his groin. "If what you need is a blow job and a fuck, then I'm here for you."

Jonathan sat forward, away from Donna's soft hands and hot breath "I appreciate the company tonight. I needed it. And I'm truly flattered that you don't think I'm too old to screw. But I have a wife, who loves me – at least I hope she still loves me. I know I love her. I'm not ready to throw that away."

Donna reached for a blanket draped over the edge of the sofa and covered herself. "I'm sorry, Boss. I thought you needed a good lay to loosen you up. I'm not trying to take Gwen's place. I'm sorry."

"Don't worry, Donna. I won't be telling anyone."

"I appreciate that," Donna replied sincerely. "The interns would be in a tizzy."

"Let's just pretend the evening ended when I dropped you off at your apartment. It was truly a night when I did relax and forget about my troubles for a while, which I did need. So I'll say good-night."

"Good-night, Boss," Donna responded softly.

Jonathan grabbed his suit jacket from the arm of a chair, picked up his briefcase, which he had left in the front foyer, and let himself out without looking back. He walked back to his empty apartment, the night air clearing his head somewhat after the plentiful wine of the evening. When he went to bed, he could not get out of his head the image of Donna standing nearly naked in front of him. He focused on the small picture of himself and Gwen on their wedding day, which stood on the night table. She was smiling and waving at someone. He reached over her head, switched off the light and watched her face disappear into the blackness.

Chapter 28

ED EDWARDS SAT on the maroon leather sofa in Jonathan's Senate office wearing a dour expression. If he'd had a fedora, he would have looked like a B-movie gangster. Ed had just given Jonathan a briefing, on Max's instructions, about dealing with the media and their strategy for rehabilitating his now tarnished image back in Connecticut so the voters wouldn't remember any of the scandal by the time of the next election cycle in 2018.

"Listen to me, Jonathan, you must get back to basics here. Your base is nervous. They hear this stuff and they start to wonder. You remember what George W. Bush did, right? Cleaned up his act and leaned farther right than a stripper on a bar stool."

Jonathan sat back in his chair and inhaled slowly, trying to keep his temper in check. He exhaled just as slowly before speaking. "I know what I have to do. I'll be there for every Rotary Club charity fundraiser and I'll appear on the Christian Radio Network's Sunday show, just like Max has it scheduled. I'm not an idiot, so why are you treating me like one?"

"Sorry, Senator, I was only trying making sure the message was received."

"Consider it received loudly and clearly." Jonathan stood now and walked across the dull government-issue carpet to his cherry wood bar and poured himself a seltzer over ice. He liked the cold feel of the glass in his hand and the pressure he could exert on the thick walls of the stout high-ball while he spoke. He set his glass down on a coaster bearing a picture of the main Library at Columbia – an alumni donation present – and looked down at a folder, hoping Ed would get the hint. When Ed made no attempt to get up to leave, Jonathan asked, "Is there something else?"

"I don't know, Jonathan. Is there?"

"What the hell does that mean?"

Ed now got up, buttoned his suit jacket and smoothed his silk tie. When he spoke, he didn't look Jonathan in the eye. "Max wants to know from you – is there anything else? Are there any more surprises in store? Any more secrets out there waiting to be reported on by Miss Stick-up-her-ass from *The Journal*?"

"No," Jonathan said more loudly than he intended. He inhaled slowly again, wondering what it was about Ed that always got his dander up. "There are no other misadventures to be reported on. Was I ever drunk at a frat party? Sure. But no more abortions. No children born to girls I slept with in college will come crawling into town making a big splash. No more skeletons in my closet."

"You sure?"

"Yes, I'm sure!" Jonathan was visibly annoyed now.

"Hey, just making sure. I'll let Max know."

"You do that." Jonathan picked up the receiver to his phone and buzzed Harriett before Ed closed the office door behind him.

When he hung up a moment later, without actually speaking with Harriett, he gazed out the window onto the lawn of the courtyard outside. He wondered – could there be some little Prescott out there somewhere? He had always made sure the girls used birth control whenever he had slept with someone back in the days before he and Gwen had become exclusive. It had only been Janice after that, and then only the one time. But what about the girls before then? Was it possible? Wouldn't they have told him?

What if they weren't sure it was his? What if there were a child out there – not even a child now. The child would be more than twenty years old. His son, or his daughter. A Prescott who didn't even know it. And him – a Prescott, or maybe not really a Prescott. Things in his life that had been so certain, so rock solid, were now twisting like the Tacoma Narrows Bridge in a storm.

The electronic tone of his telephone snapped him out of his mini-daydream and back to the business at hand. It was going to be a busy day. Under pressure from several vulnerable senators, and some behind-the-scenes arguments about setting a bad precedent for the future, the Judiciary Committee voted to hold hearings on the Ricardo Menendez nomination. The maneuvering had begun to block his confirmation. The Party hoped a conservative justice appointed by the next president might tip the balance toward reversing *Roe v. Wade*. There was no doubt that with Menendez filling Scalia's seat, there was no hope of reversing the now 40-year-old precedent.

Jonathan knew Menendez. They had been classmates at Columbia all those years ago. He was brilliant. One of the finest minds and one of the freshest and most original thinkers Jonathan ever knew. True, he was far too liberal, and far too willing to bend precedent in order to achieve what he considered socially desirable results in certain cases. But his opinions were always well reasoned and flawlessly logical. His breaks with precedent were always subtle and incremental. On economics, taxation, contracts, and intellectual property, he was a stalwart of support for business and free commerce. On individual liberty issues, he was almost a Libertarian.

Jonathan had a hard time disagreeing with him there. But on social issues – abortion, affirmative action, government entitlements – that was where he was dangerous.

There had never been a nomination to the Court – election year or not – where the Senate refused to even hold hearings. It was one thing to reject a nominee on principled grounds. It was quite another to refuse to even consider the nomination. Jonathan had supported holding hearings, but he carefully preserved the expectation that he would still vote against confirmation when the vote came to the floor.

Jonathan was startled away from his thoughts by the buzz of his phone. Harriett advised that Xavier Richardson, the chief of staff for the Republican majority leader, was holding.

"No, X, not at all . . . yes, I know the vote is scheduled . . . of course . . . How many votes do you have committed to block? . . . That close, is it? . . . Well, I think you know where I stand . . . Really? They're not as solid? . . . Oh, now surely Harry can lean on a few of them . . . Let me see what I can do on my end and I'll let you know . . . OK . . . Goodbye, X."

Jonathan leaned back and smiled ruefully to himself. He had done an impressive job of failing to commit definitively one way or the other on how he would vote, without allowing Richardson to pin him down. They had a two-seat majority. If no other Republican flipped, his vote would not be needed. On the other hand, if two other Republican senators refused to go along, then the Democrats would get their man and Jonathan's vote wouldn't matter. But he also knew that scenario wasn't likely. He wondered whether there was a third option.

Chapter 29

ABRAHAM HAWKINS LIFTED HIS EYES toward the ceiling as his arms raised toward Heaven, ballooning his flowing robe into the shape of a snow angel. He bent his neck back and arched his pelvis forward, swaying to the music of the choir behind him. The choir members were clapping and swaying themselves to the gospel beat that they had arranged to an old standard.

*Jesus loves the little children,
all the little children of the world.
Red and yellow, black and white,
they are precious in his sight.
Jesus loves the little children of the world.*

When the soloist stepped forward and raised the microphone to her lips, the song sounded nothing like Abraham remembered it when he had been taught a sing-song version as a child by his Sunday school teacher in a drafty little room in Alabama. The world had changed since then, so why not the songs also?

The preacher found himself so lost in his thoughts that he did not notice his stage director motioning to him to move stage left to be in position for the next camera shot. He just stood there, in the center of the stage, forcing the choir soloist to move around him as if he were a statue. Finally, the soloist lightly tapped her boss on the shoulder at the stage manager's insistence, getting his attention and pointing into the pit between the stage and the congregation where the short man with the headset was frantically motioning Hawkins to move to his left, toward the pulpit.

When he reached his appointed place and stared into the teleprompter at the first lines of his sermon for the day, he snapped out of his momentary trance and remembered where he was. When the red light glowed on the top of camera number three, he didn't miss a beat. He was a professional, and that was more important to him than his reminiscence about a long-ago Sunday school teacher.

"My children," he began with a flourish and a broad smile, "Jesus loves you, and I love you. *All* my children. Yes! Hallelujah!" As the preacher's arms went up, the congregation began shouting out "Hallelujah!" in response. After a few moments of random shout-outs, Hawkins went to work. The subject matter was love and tolerance for all peoples of the world, just like the song said. But the message was more about how the members of Hawkins' flock, although loved by him and by Jesus, were victims of a white-dominated society in which they had been oppressed for two centuries. Like the Israelites seeking freedom from the yoke of oppression in Pharaoh's Egypt, the good Christian Black community of America had to cast off the bonds of oppression and seek freedom. But the oppression of which he was speaking was not slavery. No, his flock labored under the yoke of economic oppression.

"We must not wait for the oppressors to save us from our plight and expect hand-outs and alms to sustain us. God may provide, but God provides best by giving us the will to provide for ourselves." Abraham paused, peering out over his audience and searching for a face on which to focus. He found a young man in the second row, bright-eyed and rapt in his attention to the minister. Abraham looked down at him seriously, and then pointed with an outstretched arm. "You must work harder! You must be more diligent, and more honest in your work, and more thrifty in your lives. Look around you. There is a Black man in the White House. Do you think anyone is feeling sorry for the Black community? Look at the Asian-American community – hard working, making sure their kids go to school and learn math and science and moving into good neighborhoods and getting ahead in the world. Why? Why can the Asians do so well in a white world? Why can't you? Why can't WE? The answer is we CAN! You can! Don't feel sorry for yourself and wish your life was better. You go MAKE it better!"

Hawkins' speech writers had melded together the twin threads of religious fervor and economic policy in a clever weave that left the fervent listener with the desire to get active in his local chamber of commerce. As he neared the end, Hawkins turned directly to politics.

"And do not, my children, be led astray by false idols and false prophets. Scrutinize carefully all who come before you and claim that they love you and that they want to protect you. Do not be fooled by their dress or their banners. Democrats as well as Republicans can be our friends, or can be the agents of the Devil. Jesus has no party. Jesus is a registered member of the party of Love, and the party of Peace, and the party of Justice. We must look beyond parties and labels and look into the heart and soul of each man and each woman who claims to love you and who claims to want to protect you.

"There is a man who works in our Congress named Desmond Mason who I met recently and into whose soul I have looked. Here is a man who cares about his people – our people. Here is a man who abandoned wealth and power in the corporate world and went back to his home town, where he poured out his soul and his sweat to help young men –

Black, Hispanic, White, no matter what race. He took them off the street and got them into the gym, and into the library, and into the classroom. He changed their lives. I don't care about his party or where his money comes from or whether the Sierra Club endorses his voting record. I can tell you this man is a good man and a man who cares about you. You should care about men like Desmond Mason.

"And I know a woman in San Jose, California who sits on the local school board named Juanita Jones. She is a good woman, and a woman who loves her people and who loves Jesus." Hawkins went on to call out the names of four other individuals, briefly mentioning the background and accomplishments of each. "And don't think every Black man or woman is automatically on your side just because he or she is Black. Not every brother or sister is your friend, and not every white man is your enemy.

There is a fine man in the Senate named Jonathan Prescott. Not the old man you may have read about. No, sir. His young son, Jonathan the Third, is a progressive thinker, and a man who wants all to succeed in the American Dream. Here is a man you would think you would never vote for, but you would be wrong to think that just because of the color of his skin, or the heritage from which he comes."

In the end, only Mason and Prescott, among eight people called out by Reverend Hawkins, were politicians. They were passing references. Few in the congregation would have been able after the sermon to recall even two of those who were named. But in the offices of The Foster Group, two video recorders were humming away, taping the broadcast. Editors would select excerpts from the sermon, paying particular attention to the praise meted out to Desmond Mason and Jonathan Prescott, and filing away the footage for future use. A memo would appear the next day on Max Foster's desk, summarizing the content of the sermon. The memo would be shredded.

Chapter 30

February, 1990

IT WAS LATE FEBRUARY, but the clear sky and sunshine bore the promise of the coming spring. Many of the investment bankers and stock brokers were outside at lunch, wearing their overcoats but attempting to enjoy the above-freezing temperature by eating grilled vegetable wraps and drinking Perrier while they sat on the marble sides of the fountains at the base of the World Trade Center towers. A tall man with very short red hair wearing large, braided gold balls on his shirt cuffs was sitting on a bench with a much older woman in an Yves St. Laurent suit and too much makeup. Everyone seemed to be smiling – at least everyone sitting outside eating lunch that Friday.

Maybe it was only the upcoming weekend they were happy about. Jonathan certainly was happy. Not many 21-year-olds who were juniors in college got internships at Goldman Sachs. But not everyone had a senator for a father. Jonathan's internship, which could barely be called work, brought him downtown on Fridays from January through March. He got no pay for his time, but he had the opportunity to pal around with the rich and powerful and get a bird's eye view of the empire builders at work.

This particular Friday, Jonathan strode confidently across the plaza, his tie loose and the top button of his Brooks Brothers button-down open. He had on his suit jacket, but eschewed his overcoat on this sunny day on the assumption that he would only be outdoors for a short time. He smiled flirtatiously at a blonde wearing a tight skirt that was hiked up to mid-thigh level as she lounged on a bench, watching him walk by. He liked it when women noticed him. But he quickly looked away, scanning the plaza for Janice.

Once he spotted her she stood out, but not for the usual reasons. She was clearly not one of the happy young masters of the universe. She looked like the third runner-up at the county fair beauty pageant. Even Jonathan, who had trouble reading women's moods, could see immediately that something was wrong. He sped up his stride and placed a look of compassionate concern on his face, which he thought was most appropriate at the moment.

"Hey, Jan, why the sour puss?" He figured he could make her smile and she would snap out of whatever little funk she was in. It didn't work.

"Let's walk," she said in a monotone, hardly looking at him before turning away and walking west across the plaza, toward the river.

"What's up?" he tried to ask in a more serious and concerned-sounding voice.

"I don't think you want to talk here," she replied flatly. She didn't turn to look at him, but just kept walking. She was wearing jeans and running shoes that stuck out beneath her down jacket, which was unzipped and revealed a bright red, high-necked sweater. She set a brisk pace, her red pony tail flipping back and forth with her steps and brushing across her neck. Jonathan watched her hair bob as if mesmerized by a hypnotist's gold watch.

Before they crossed West Street, he was starting to sweat and loosened his collar even farther. They walked to the marina, where hundred-foot yachts were moored next to smaller sailboats owned by the affluent residents of the expensive downtown apartment buildings on the water near the financial district. Here, the lunch crowd was thinner. She kept walking, all the way to the iron rails that ran along the concrete bank of the Hudson River. She leaned forward with both hands on the sun-warmed metal, her back to Jonathan. He sidled up next to her, but she spun around and faced him. He had his back to the river now, and she squinted into the early afternoon sun.

"I'm pregnant."

The words lingered in the air for several seconds before Jonathan fully processed them. His squinting eyebrows furrowed farther, nearly causing them to meet above the bridge of his nose. His expression was blank – he couldn't think of the proper emotion to show. He started to speak, mouth slightly open, but stopped himself, not knowing what to say. Then, realizing he must look foolish, he blurted out the first coherent thought that came to him: "How did this happen?"

"Oh, brilliant question." Janice snapped coldly. Her eyes were studying him very closely, searching for the thoughts behind his blank face. Her eyes bored into his. She had always tried to read him, to figure when he was being sincere and when he was bullshitting her. Most of the time he was good at hiding his true emotions.

Jonathan blushed slightly, and set his mouth in a tense line. "I mean, we only did it that one time, on New Year's Eve. Jesus, Jan. I know I was pretty drunk, but I used a condom. It had been in my wallet for a while, but that shouldn't have made a difference."

"Well, I guess it fucking made a difference," she shot back. "I guess you're not happy for us, then?" She stared at him as his face changed quickly from hurt to annoyed, and then to resolved.

"Well, Jesus, Jan, this isn't exactly an invitation to the beach. You seemed upset on the telephone when you called, and you don't exactly look like a glowing mother, do you?" He didn't mean to sound angry with her, but that was the way it came out. "And how do you know . . . I mean, are you sure—"

"Yes, it's yours. The doctor is pretty sure I'm eight weeks along. It had to be New Year's. Frank went home two weeks before and I had my period after he left." She paused to see his reaction, and could see his mind working toward another question, which she preempted. "I haven't slept with anyone else, if that's what you are thinking about asking. The fact is I haven't had sex with anyone since that night." Janice paused, then smiled ruefully. "To think I told Frank I didn't want to get married and never wanted to have kids, which is why we're not sleeping together anymore. So now, look what happens. Anyway, it's yours."

Jonathan stood frozen in thought, not sure how to react. "This is going to be very complicated."

"Sorry to mess up your afternoon. I shouldn't have even told you. What the hell was I thinking?" She threw up her hands and started to walk north along the river.

"Wait, Jan," he called as he jogged after her, catching her in a few strides and grabbing her elbow. "C'mon, you hit me out of the blue here. Give me a break. Let's sit down and talk." He looked at her with his sincere eyes, and she relented and allowed herself to be guided toward a wooden bench. "I don't know what to think here. I mean, neither one of us planned this or wanted it, right?" He waited for an affirmative answer and got a nod, which was good enough for him to keep talking. He was thinking fast and talking slowly, trying to keep his brain two sentences ahead of his mouth. "What did you mean you weren't going to tell me? How could you not tell me? I mean, I may not be a genius, but I would have figured it out, right?"

"I doubt it. Anyway, it's not like I'm trying to trap you into marrying me or anything. We both knew right away it was a mistake to sleep together, right?" It was Janice's turn to pause, awaiting some response from Jonathan. He fumbled out an affirmative grunt, and Janice nodded and continued. "I appreciated that you invited me to spend New Year's Eve together since we were both in town and both Gwen and Frank were away. I'm sorry I got so drunk. I'm sorry I came back to your room. It was a bad idea. I know we said we wouldn't ever talk about it, but under the circumstances I figured the subject was unavoidable."

"Does Frank know?" Jonathan asked hesitantly.

"No, and he won't know. I assume you aren't going to tell him."

Jonathan agreed quickly. "And you're not going to tell Gwen." It was a statement, not really a question, but he waited for some sign of agreement.

"No, Jon. I'm not going to tell her. I'll let you tell her – unless you want to keep it a secret."

Jonathan pursed his lips and ignored the comment. He would decide later whether this was something he wanted to confess to Gwen.

Janice broke into Jonathan's thoughts. "Listen, Jon, we're both adults and we can handle this. I just wanted you to know. I don't need money. You don't even have to come. I'll be fine. I'm responsible for my own body." She got up and turned to start walking north again.

"Whoa, whoa, wait a minute. What do you mean? Where are you going? We need to figure this out here."

"There's nothing to figure, Jonathan. I'll take care of the abortion myself."

Jonathan reached out to take Janice's hand, but she pulled it away. "I mean, shouldn't we at least think about keeping the baby, here? I mean, Christ."

"No, we don't need to think about it, because I have already thought about it quite a bit. I found out for sure on Wednesday. I've been thinking about it ever since, as you might imagine. I've got a career ahead of me and I'm not ready to be a mommy – not by a long shot. Having a baby is not an option. Not with Frank, and certainly not with you. I'll get the abortion, you'll go back to your perfect storybook world and your happily-ever-after life with Gwen, and that will be the end of it."

"What about the baby? I mean, God, I don't know. This is a big deal. I can only imagine what my old man would say."

"Well, boychik, unless you plan to tell him, I doubt very much he'll be finding out."

"Of course," Jonathan said blankly, like he was thinking about something else. "But, isn't this kind of hard to keep a secret?"

"No," she replied matter-of-factly. "There's a clinic in Harlem where I volunteer sometimes. You should come visit. They do abortions every day. It's very simple and safe. Nobody is going to know. It will be like it never happened."

"Don't I get any say-so on this?"

"No. Actually, you don't." Janice's eyes were sharp now. She stood up and turned to face him as he sat on the cold bench. "If you proposed to marry me and start an early family, and if I accepted, then you would have some say-so. If you had used a better condom, or maybe if you hadn't been too drunk to put it on right, then you would have had some say-so. But as it stands, it's my body, and my future, and my decision. I wanted to at least tell you, but that's the extent of your involvement now."

"What makes you think I'm not going to want to marry you?"

"Ha!" She snorted and smiled for the first time that afternoon. "Get real, Jonny Boy! You and I both know you'll be marrying Gwen. I'm not in your future, and you're not in mine. We happened to both be in need of some companionship that night and we got a little drunk and we had our fun and games, and now it's back to reality for both of us. I don't expect anything from you. I'm responsible for this pregnancy and I'll take care of it."

For a long moment she stood there, looking down at him. She was defiant now. He looked shell-shocked, and Janice actually thought, for a moment, that she saw his real feelings. Finally, he said in a low voice, "When would you do it?"

"Have the abortion? It's OK, Jon, your father isn't listening, you can say it: a-BOR-shun. Probably tomorrow. The clinic has Saturday hours."

"Can you wait a few days? Just to let me let it sink in. Maybe I'll be able to work it out and go with you."

"Don't soil yourself."

"Really, I would go." Jonathan looked at her with sincere eyes this time.

"OK. I can wait until Monday. Call me later."

"I will." He watched her turn and go, walking briskly again as if exercising would prevent the pregnancy from showing. She didn't look back. Jonathan walked slowly, as if in a trance, back across the marina and toward the Trade Center. He was thinking hard and fast. He told the intern supervisor he wasn't feeling well and he needed to go home. She winked at him and wished him a good weekend. He started to protest her assumption about his motives for leaving early, but thought better of it and just left, still thinking. There was a lot to think about.

At eight o'clock that night, Jonathan stood in the hallway outside the apartment on Riverside Drive where Janice's aunt lived in the summer and where Janice stayed during the winter months when her aunt was in Florida. The doorman had announced his arrival, so there was no point in delaying ringing the bell, but he hesitated. He was rehearsing the speech he would make to her – anticipating her reactions and formulating his responses. It would be delicate. He rang the bell, but when the door opened, all thoughts of a planned conversation ran from his mind the instant he saw Frank standing in front of him.

"C'mon in." Frank's voice was flat, as if he, too, had been rehearsing. The narrow entrance hall opened up to the single room of the studio apartment. Janice was sitting on a tasteful maroon sofa. On the coffee table in front of her was an elegant tea service, complete with matching cups and saucers. Decidedly not student fare. Janice's aunt Bettina had some taste, if not a large living space. Janice had a saucer in her hand and a slightly embarrassed expression on her face.

"I told Frank," she said simply.

Jonathan had been thinking about what questions he might ask casually that would allow her to tell him surreptitiously whether Frank knew their secret, but once again his planned conversation was quickly rendered useless. "I kind of figured that."

"I should probably slap you and challenge you to pistols at dawn," Frank mocked, "but since you'd probably miss me and kill some poor innocent bystander, I figure I'll have to settle for turning you in to the Dean of students for violating the student Code of Conduct."

"You wouldn't!" For a moment, there was true fear in Jonathan's face.

"You're right. I wouldn't. But I have thought about it a few times this afternoon. Don't blame Jan. I dropped by unannounced and I could tell she was upset about something.

I wouldn't stop pestering her until she came clean. I know I told Jan that I wanted to take a break, so I have no right to feel jealous." Janice flashed a slightly hurt pout, but then resumed focusing on her tea cup. "She can do what she wants, with whomever she wants. So can you. I'm not your judge. Hell, I'm not even sure I'm your friend. But I'm more concerned about Jan than I am about my own hurt feelings here, so sit down and have some tea and let's talk."

Jonathan hesitated, then sank into the chintz armchair opposite the sofa, leaving Janice and Frank sitting next to each other. They talked, and cried, and shouted a few times over the next four hours. Jonathan wanted Janice to consider giving the child up for adoption, but Janice would have none of that. Going through a pregnancy during her senior year of college, having a baby, and then having to give it up for adoption was too much for her to even consider. They talked about when and where the abortion would happen. Jonathan wanted to pull some strings and get her into Mount Sinai medical center for "the procedure," as he took to calling it, still unable or unwilling to use the word "abortion."

"The clinic is fine, Jon. They do this every day. They're very good. Plus, how are you going to check me into Mount Sinai without your father finding out?"

Jonathan had actually already been thinking about how he might accomplish that, although he didn't want to admit it to Frank and Janice. "Why should I care?"

"Oh, come off it, Jon," Frank blurted out, standing up and pacing across the small room to the window overlooking the Hudson. "You know he would flip out."

"You're right, of course. Do you really think me so shallow that I'd be more worried about that than about Jan?"

"Yes," both Frank and Janice said together, and then burst out laughing. Jonathan joined in – it was the first light moment of the evening.

The cold wind bit through Frank's jacket as they walked along Morningside Park that Monday morning. Janice was on his left, hands pushed deep into the pockets of her tan leather bomber jacket. Her head was down and she had been uncharacteristically quiet. The unusually mild temperature that had prevailed the prior week had disappeared and winter had returned with a vengeance. As they crossed 121st Street, Frank could see the streak of sunlight piercing through the crevasse between buildings on the East Side and bathing them in a crisp morning glow, sending shadows dancing out from each tree branch in the park. Frank shaded his eyes with his palm and whistled softly, "Man, that's a pretty sight."

Jonathan grunted, without looking. He was swinging his arms as he walked, his black leather gloves protruding from beneath his grey wool overcoat. The three sets of feet tromped on along the dull concrete sidewalk over the sewer grate at 125th Street, ringed in abandoned candy wrappers and a single used condom. Frank stole a peek at Janice, whose sullen eyes did not glance back.

The clinic was on 127th Street, two blocks north of the church and shelter where Janice volunteered and where Jonathan had met Harold. He wondered momentarily which public school Harold attended and what class he might be in at that moment. Then he dismissed the thoughts and tried to focus on the events at hand. The trio had just crossed over Dr. Martin Luther King Jr. Blvd, next to the church, when Jonathan stopped short.

"Whatsa matter?" Frank spat out, annoyed with Jonathan's sudden halt. Jonathan didn't say a word, but stared ahead, down the sidewalk.

Frank then focused on the sidewalk farther ahead. Beyond a baleful beech tree enclosed in an iron planter, he could see a small group of people, maybe six or seven. Several were carrying signs mounted on long sticks, although Frank could not make out the writing. One had a large camera with a long telephoto lens protruding from his chest is if he had been impaled by a telescope. They were all chanting something Frank could not make out and waving their fists in the air. They seemed to be marching slowly on the sidewalk. "Are they usually here, Jan?" Frank asked.

Janice appeared to snap out of her self-absorption and shook her head, blinking at Frank. "Them? Oh, fuck them." She dismissed the group with a wave of her hand. "It's just the anti-abortion nuts. They come out every day and march around and chant their silly slogans and try to harass the girls who are coming in. The clinic sends out chaperones to help them through the gauntlet. They take pictures of the girls, like they are going to put them on milk cartons or post them in the subway: 'Baby Killer Wanted for Murder.' Self-righteous assholes!" Janice was getting worked up, which Frank considered a good sign, signifying that she was more her normal self instead of the zombie he had been walking with.

"Do you think they'll give us a problem?" Frank asked.

Janice turned to him with a wry smile, "I'd almost like them to touch me so I can sue their asses, but no, they probably won't give us any problem. They just shout and chant and yell at the girls, like they are going to convince them to change their mind and go home and have the baby. I like to ask them whether any of them are willing to adopt the baby, which usually shuts them up for a minute. They are happy to tell other people to go through childbirth and suggest giving the baby up for adoption, but they don't want to take on that responsibility for themselves. Jerks."

"Bet they would take yours, though, if they only knew." Frank laughed and Janice smiled, reaching out to encircle her arm in his and squeeze it, which made Frank feel warmer than he had all morning. But the warm moment was short-lived.

"Shut the fuck up, you moron!" Jonathan snapped, pivoting on his left foot to face the other two and block the sidewalk in front of them. "God damn it! Somebody could hear you say something like that." Jonathan's eyes were wide with terror and rage.

"Like what?" Frank shot back innocently. "I didn't say anything. I didn't say your name, or—"

"—And you'd better not!" Jonathan was seriously agitated.

"Yeah, we know. We get it. No names. Nobody knows anything. Right." Frank took a step forward, easing Jonathan's body out of the way to make room for him and Janice.

"Yeah, let's just get going," Janice murmured. She also took a step past Jonathan, then turned back to look at him.

Jonathan was frozen in place. He looked plaintively toward Janice, then lowered his eyes to the sidewalk and said, almost too softly for her to hear, "I can't go there."

Janice stopped and squeezed Frank's arm harder. "You're worried about *them*? Fuck them. They're nothing. We walk right past them. Just follow me."

"No!" Jonathan exclaimed, more loudly than he intended. Then more softly, "No, I . . . I know you – we – can get past them, it's just . . . that guy has a camera. What if one of them recognizes me? I can't have my picture in the paper walking into an abortion clinic! What would . . . " his voice trailed away as his eyes searched the sidewalk for cracks, or a life boat.

Frank stared at his friend, incredulous. "You're fucking serious, aren't you? You would really leave Janice and me, after everything you said about why you wanted to come and support her and 'do the right thing' for her, just because you're worried about how it might look?"

Jonathan didn't answer immediately. He didn't meet Frank's eyes – or Janice's. He turned away from the protesters. "I can't," he whispered.

Janice tugged on Frank's arm and started walking up the sidewalk toward the clinic. They left Jonathan standing alone, with his back to them. After a half-block, Frank stopped and disengaged Janice's arm from his own, as much as that pained him. He rushed back toward Jonathan's retreating figure. Jonathan heard the approaching footfalls and turned, just in time to receive the full force of Frank's forearm in his chest. Jonathan tumbled backwards, landing on his ass and sliding four feet along the pavement on his coat tails. Frank gathered his balance and stood over him, his breathing hot and heavy, blowing puffs of steam from his nose like an angry dragon. Before Jonathan could compose himself to say anything, Frank launched into him.

"Listen, I'm sorry. No. Fuck! I'm not sorry. I know you're a self-absorbed asshole and I know you're scared shitless that something you do will embarrass your big shot father, or God forbid tarnish your Golden Boy image and prevent you from being president someday. If you want to run away, then fine. Run. But don't say you'll come and be supportive because it's important to Janice and then back out at the first sign that it might have a personal cost to you. I thought you came for her, but it's clear you came for yourself, so you could make yourself feel better, or so you could maybe fuck her again. Because if it's about her, then you'd stand by her and not turn tail like a coward at the first sign that there might be some risk for you."

Frank paused and looked down at his friend, still lying on the pavement. "I thought you were better than that. I thought you were developing some personal integrity. I guess not. But someday, you're going to have to make choices in life about what you believe in, and whether you give a damn about anybody but yourself."

Jonathan was staring up, eyes wide and mouth slightly ajar. Frank, wanting to fill the silence as much as anything, added, "You know I'm your friend. I'll be your friend tomorrow, no matter what you do here today. I just won't be very proud of it." Frank turned and started to walk back toward Janice, who had been standing motionless a half-block away, watching the scene.

Jonathan raised himself up to his elbows, then called out, "Hey!" Frank stopped and turned. Jonathan managed to struggle up to a sitting position. "Nobody talks to me like that – except my father."

Frank pursed his lips into a straight, emotionless line, then replied, "Please don't ever tell me I'm anything like your father."

Jonathan nodded slightly. "OK. Deal. Just do me a favor. Wait up for a minute." Jonathan lurched to his feet, brushed the street dirt off the back of his trousers, and started to walk toward Janice. He didn't say anything. The two men reached the waiting woman and spread out to take either side.

They walked in silence toward the end of the block, where the protesters were standing. A few yards before the corner, they were met by a cheerful young woman wearing an orange vest – the kind that highway workers wear for safety. She asked if they wanted an escort into the clinic, past the protesters. Frank thanked her, but said they could manage by themselves. They walked forward, finding themselves suddenly engulfed in a swirl of bodies, seemingly more than the six or seven protesters they had seen. They were mostly young men, but there were a few women as well. They reached out, shoving papers toward Janice's face bearing photographs of fetuses and slogans like "Every Fetus Feels Pain" and "Don't Kill Your Baby." Frank and Jonathan pushed the pamphlets away and hurried Janice through the gauntlet.

Frank lagged behind the other two as they ascended the three stone steps into the clinic. He looked back at the angry faces – not pleading, or disappointed, but truly enraged. He looked back toward Janice and Jonathan, who had kept his face away from the protesters. He also had donned a black fur hat, with flaps that hung down over his ears. Even Frank would have been hard-pressed to recognize him as he swept up the stairs with Janice and into the building.

Twenty minutes later, a petite Asian woman wearing a smock that must have once been white, but which now was a streaked gray, came into the dingy waiting room carrying a clipboard. She scanned the small area, cluttered with foam-padded chairs with steel arms pushed next to each other like so many marching soldiers, their ranks broken only by battered end tables after every fourth seat piled with out-of-date magazines.

There were a dozen other people in the room, but Janice, Frank, and Jonathan stood out like Hasidic Jews at a Christening. Every eye in the room turned to the nurse, who called out, "Stanton" and waited for a response. Janice turned to Frank, who squeezed her hand. Jonathan reached out his hand also and received a soft slide of her skin against his as she brushed past. She disappeared around the corner toward what Jonathan could only imagine was a sparsely appointed operating room. He once again mused about Mt. Sinai before stuffing his hands back into the pockets of his jacket, which he continued to wear owing to the chilly air of the waiting room and his continuing hope that nobody would recognize him.

Across from Jonathan sat a young Hispanic girl who looked no more than fifteen. She was with a large woman with arms the size of rolling pins, who Jonathan surmised must be her mother. The girl was silent, but the mother kept whispering to her, loudly enough for the entire waiting room to hear. She gesticulated with her arms, sending waves of flesh cascading from where her triceps muscles should have been. The girl's name was Marcella, and her no-good deadbeat boyfriend's name was Hector.

From what Jonathan could gather, Hector was a good deal older and had been making noises about wanting Marcella to keep the baby and drop out of high school and that he would support them both on his job as an auto mechanic. Marcella's mother was not keen on the plan. She had moved to the shithole apartment where they lived solely so Marcella and her younger sister could attend a better public school than the one they had in the Bronx and she was going to be damned if her girls were going to drop out before they got their diplomas. Jonathan was sure from the conversation that Marcella was the oldest of the two daughters, but he also got the distinct impression that the mother had been to the clinic before, with the other sister.

Jonathan got up to stretch his legs and wandered toward a set of French doors at the back of the waiting room. Outside was a small balcony, the same width as the doors and barely three feet deep. The balcony was protected by a wrought-iron railing, depicting the swirling branches from an unknown tree. The ironwork had been painted white in some past decade and now was peeling away around the edges. The balcony overlooked a shabby courtyard that had once contained a garden. A few overgrown forsythia bushes were spreading out along one side, engulfing what may have once been a well-tended flower bed.

An ancient peach tree stretched out its tentacle branches on the opposite side, near a brick wall separating the courtyard from its twin attached to the adjoining building. The warm weather of the past week had nudged the first bulges of impending buds out of the ends of the twisted branches. Jonathan was formulating an analogy between the potential fruit of the tree and the soon-to-be aborted life within the clinic when his attention was interrupted.

"Got a light?" a young Black girl said, holding out her left hand with a cigarette between two fingers. She was fully a foot shorter than Jonathan, and so had to reach upward to present her request. Jonathan noticed that her fingernails were polished, but several were broken and poorly filed. Her dark fingers were slender, and her wrist was encircled by dozens of thin bracelets, which slid down her tiny forearm almost to the elbow as she raised her arm. She had jet-black hair which Jonathan thought needed a good conditioning. She looked up at him with fuzzy eyes – neither brown nor green, but something in between. She wore far too much eye makeup. He noticed her multiple ear piercings, along with one eyebrow sporting a small gold ball on its extremity. She wore dark lipstick, more brown than red.

"Do you think it's a good idea to be smoking here?" Jonathan replied matter-of-factly, without moving his hands toward the lighter he always kept in his pocket. His father had told him to always be prepared for the request of a light, from a woman or a potential political ally or donor. Be prepared, like a good Scout. He looked away from the Black girl, who couldn't have been more than seventeen, and mused about whether his father would consider this an appropriate occasion to take advantage of his sage advice.

"Ha!" the girl spewed out a laugh. "You gotta be kidding, right? Like I'm going to harm the baby or something at this point?" She stepped back a foot or so, lowering her outstretched hand and planting her right fist squarely on her hip. She cocked her head and shifted her weight, causing the other hip to jut out sensually as she surveyed Jonathan. "I figured you were out here for a smoke, but I guess I was wrong, huh?"

Jonathan forced his attention back to the girl. She was not unattractive, he supposed, although he had never much considered the attractiveness of Black girls. He had been schooled from an early age not to be attracted to women who could only get him in trouble. He found himself wondering, in a detached way, whether he could, in another life, find such a girl interesting. He gave her a thorough once-over with his eyes. Her jeans were faded and had a hole in one knee, but fit snugly down her thighs. He could see a sliver of light between her legs and speculated that she probably had a nice ass, although he could not see it from this angle. She wore a bulky sweater that covered her belly loosely, but contoured well around her medium-sized breasts. He forced a weak smile and reached for his pocket. "No, I suppose that's not a consideration, although you do know that smoking is bad for you."

"Lots of things are fucking bad for me," the girl replied casually, "including having a kid. I'm not doing drugs, so what the fuck – a butt isn't going to kill me." She stared at Jonathan defiantly, waiting to see whether his hand was going to emerge from his pocket with a match. When Jonathan finally provided the flame, she placed the cigarette between her lips and stood on tip toes, leaning in to receive the gift of fire. Then she immediately stepped back a step, puffing out the first wave of blue-gray smoke over the railing.

"Thanks," she said simply, losing a little of the edginess from her voice, "my name's Charlene." She didn't extend a hand the way everyone else in his life had done when introducing themselves to Jonathan. He smiled. It was a first, to be remembered.

"Jon," he returned the introduction without outward motion.

"Your girlfriend inside?"

Jonathan missed a beat. "I'm sorry?"

Charlene turned and stared up at him, lips pursed and cigarette dangling from her fingers, which were casually perched beside her face. "Well I know damn well you don't work here, so the only thing to get a guy like you in here is a knocked-up girlfriend. Am I about right?"

Jonathan laughed out loud and smiled broadly. "A fine bit of deductive reasoning. Charlene, right?"

"Uh-huh," she nodded. "Don't let the looks of this shit-hole fool you. Inside, the doctors are damn good. It's clean and proper. She'll be fine."

Jonathan's brow furrowed involuntarily as he puzzled over the statement. "Thanks. Do you know someone who works here?"

"They know me alright. Been in before, so I guess I'm on the frequent flyer plan."

Jonathan turned toward the girl, studying her face. He concluded that his original estimate of seventeen was still about right and cast a disapproving look toward Charlene. "Look, it's not my business, but maybe a little family planning would be a better alternative than the frequent flyer plan at this clinic."

Charlene's face flashed anger for a split second, but then she slumped against the railing, resting both forearms on the old iron and staring out over the dreary courtyard. She took a long drag on the cigarette, letting out the smoke in a thin line like the exhaust of a fighter jet. "You know what, Jon. It's Jon, right?" He nodded. "Jon, you are absolutely right. I told that boy to wear a fucking condom the first time I got knocked, but he was in too much of a fucking hurry and I blame myself for that one. I should have known better but I was too young and stupid."

"How young were you?" Jonathan found himself asking before he realized it was probably an inappropriately personal question.

"Fifteen." Charlene replied without taking any offense while she took another puff, this time hanging her head over the rail and blowing the smoke down toward the frosty ground. "My momma said I had to finish school and couldn't be havin' no baby, so she took me here. It wasn't so bad. So now I'm a smart bitch, right? I know fucking everything. You'd think I'd know better than to let it happen again, huh? That what you think?"

The edge was coming back to Charlene's voice. Jonathan wasn't sure whether she was getting angry at him for asking, or angry at whatever situation brought her back to this clinic for the second time.

"I'm – I'm sorry," he stammered, "I didn't mean to be critical."

"Oh, you ain't critical. Not like my momma. She would be so pissed off if I told her I had to come back here again. Ha! This time I made him wear a condom. Oh, yeah, I was Little Miss Prepared. Had one in my purse and everything." Charlene was staring into space now, the ash from her cigarette burning low without her noticing. Her voice started to crack a little as a tear formed in the corner of her left eye and trickled slowly down her cheek. "Too bad his fucking slimeball buddy didn't have one."

Jonathan stood silently, not knowing what to do or say. Finally the silence was too much for him and he blurted out, "You mean, that wasn't—?"

"He's such a prick," she stood up, wiping the tear away and flicking the burned butt over the rail. "Momma was right about him. What kinda boyfriend invites his friend to hide in the closet and watch? Huh? You're a guy. What makes a guy do something fucking sick like that?"

Jonathan shrugged. "I couldn't begin to speculate."

"Ha!" Charlene spat out the laugh, then paused, looking up at Jonathan thoughtfully. "Hell, you probably can't. How's a rich white boy like you gonna know what goes on inside LeRoy's tiny fucking brain."

"Why would you think I'm rich?" Jonathan asked, now wary of whether Charlene had somehow recognized him.

Charlene looked him up and down with an expression like a mother surveying a child found with cookie crumbs on his fingers. She shook her head slightly. "Jon, that jacket is London Fog, that watch is Movado, and those are two-hundred-dollar shoes or I'm Oprah Winfrey." She smiled at the dumfounded look on Jonathan's face. "I work cosmetics counter at Bloomingdale's on weekends," she explained. "I'm gonna be goin' to FIT in the fall. That's why I can't be havin' no baby, even if I wanted the motherfucker's baby in me."

Jonathan glanced down at his watch and shoes. It had not occurred to him to wear cheaper shoes or leave his watch at home for this excursion into Harlem. "Well, Miss Charlene, I hope things go well for you." Jonathan smiled his best politician smile, flashing bright white teeth and extending his hand. Charlene took the hand reluctantly and offered a weak squeeze before pulling back. "Don't worry, I'm not trying to hit on you," he added, stepping back a half step.

Jonathan turned toward the French doors and saw Frank walking quickly in his direction. When Frank saw that Jonathan was looking, he waved him back inside. Jonathan turned quickly back to Charlene and said, "I have to go now. Good luck." He spun on his heel and walked through the French doors, without looking back.

The walk back to campus was slow and quiet. Janice was not talkative, and after a few efforts, Frank stopped trying to make small talk. Jonathan was withdrawn, not so much because of Janice as because of Charlene. He thought about this young girl, having her second abortion. He had been drilled from childhood that abortion was evil and morally wrong in all circumstances. He had been told, and had espoused to anyone who would listen, that girls who got pregnant should have their babies. Give them up for adoption if they don't want to or can't raise them. It was their fault for getting themselves pregnant in the first place.

But what of Charlene? Would she be able to keep her job at the cosmetics counter at Bloomingdales if she were a 17-year-old pregnant Black girl? She seemed smart, and said she was going to college in the fall. Fashion school, perhaps, but still a potential career. And what about the young girl in the waiting room with her mother, who wanted her to finish high school? What if she tried to have the baby? She couldn't have been more than fifteen. Was it right for them to have their babies? Charlene had been raped, or at least put into a situation with a boy who she did not intend to have sex with. Was it so wrong for them to give up their babies before their babies ruined their lives? These were thoughts he had never been permitted to have. They were like Charlene – something that could only get him in trouble.

The next day, Jonathan was walking back toward his dorm after a mid-morning class when he saw Frank and Janice, sitting together on a sofa in the Hartley Hall foyer. They were talking, although Jonathan could not hear the words. Jonathan thought Janice looked a little pale. He waved casually as he passed by, making no attempt to stop and talk with them.

They both waved back. Jonathan nodded at Frank. Frank nodded back. It was done. They would never speak of it. He would never be associated with it. He would also never sleep with Janice again.

Chapter 31

THE FOLLOWING FRIDAY NIGHT, Jonathan was back in New York City. Considering that he was a senator from Connecticut, it never ceased to amuse him how often he stood on high floors of Manhattan buildings, looking northward toward his constituency, while attending fundraising events in New York. *As long as the whiskey is good*, he thought, looking down at his crystal glass.

He watched the lights of a jet liner approaching its landing at JFK airport and mused about the people on that plane. Several hundred people, each with an individual story and a personal history. Each with a family, and a lifetime of friends and memories. Each with a basket of personal troubles. Some coming home from business trips on a Friday night, some headed for a weekend of fun in the Big Apple. Some his constituents; perhaps even some whom he knew or with whom he had corresponded over the years. So many people. What was ever the right choice for all of them?

A stroke of soft skin against his hand broke him out of the daydream. It was Donna, who had accompanied him to the event in Gwen's absence. Officially, Gwen had been diagnosed with anemia and was resting at home with her mother while receiving treatment that was expected to have her back in tip-top shape within a few weeks. The children were being cared for there in southern Maryland, since Jonathan's schedule really didn't allow him enough time to look after them properly, even with a nanny. It was a good story. Everyone believed it. They had no reason not to, since Jonathan and Gwen had always been the perfect couple.

Tonight Donna was wearing a floor-length black satin evening gown, with one bare shoulder. Her hair was tied back and a long diamond earring dripped from her lobe, nearly brushing against the bare skin of her shoulder when she leaned to her left. The gown had a very high neckline, yet it seemed almost more revealing than many of the cleavage-enhancing numbers being worn elsewhere around the room. There was simply nothing that didn't look good on Donna.

She guided Jonathan smoothly back into the crowd and to a waiting klatch of executives from the fashion industry who were particularly concerned about rumors concerning increased import tariffs on clothing manufactured in Asia. Jonathan smiled, nodded, expressed concern and sympathy, and explained how maintaining free trade was essential to the long-term growth of the economy. He had repeated the same mini-speech so many times that he sometimes forgot where he was and repeated the same sentence twice if he didn't pay attention.

After handshakes all around he excused himself for a refill, motioning toward his glass, which now held only melting ice cubes. Donna laced her arm through his elbow and escorted him from the group, whispering a small complement about how well he had handled them.

Donna spent the evening as Jonathan's chaperone and arm jewelry. She alternated him between Black Label and sugar-free iced tea, which looked about the same in the crystal tumbler. She laughed demurely at the appropriate jokes and smiled shyly when one of the semi-inebriated old coots in attendance said something off color. She looked everyone in the eye, and ignored the fact that most of the men had their eyes focused somewhat lower than her face. She kept her body next to Jonathan's most of the time, but never made any move that would have been seen as anything other than a political colleague and subordinate.

When the official photographer came around to take the obligatory pictures of Jonathan standing individually with each paying guest, she slid out of the way without notice. She was magnificent.

After Jonathan gave a brief speech from a podium hastily rolled into the ballroom for the occasion, the event started to thin out. The bars around the room closed up and waiters scoured the room, snatching away plates and glasses that weren't being guarded securely enough. Jonathan was shaking hands with possibly the last contributor of the night when he saw a familiar but out-of-place face lurking beyond the circle of well-wishers. The man's suit was more wrinkled than the real guests', and he was not holding a drink in his hand. Jonathan recognized him as one of Max Foster's lieutenants, by the name of McGreavey.

When the opportunity presented itself, McGreavey sidled up to Jonathan and said in a low voice that Max wanted Jonathan to come to his office after the affair was over. It was just a few blocks away. A car would be waiting downstairs on the curb in front of the hotel. He then left quickly and quietly, not waiting for a response, since the invitation was not really a request, but a summons. For a few moments, Jonathan thought about declining the invitation, but he didn't want to deal with the inevitable fallout afterwards and so he accepted by failing to say anything. The default was to comply.

Jonathan escorted Donna downstairs and saw to it she was delivered to a black Lincoln Town Car that would take her back to the airport Marriott, where they would stay – in separate rooms – for the night before flying back to Washington the next morning. Once Donna was safely away,

Jonathan joined McGreavey in the black Mercedes sedan, which drove them all of four city blocks to Foster's office building. Jonathan mused that he could have walked, but McGreavey only grunted, "Yeah, sure" in response.

It was well after midnight when Jonathan walked through the entrance doors into the outer office of The Foster Group. McGreavey had not accompanied him. As he ascended to the twenty-seventh floor, Jonathan felt like he was going to a private audience with the Pope.

The office lights were dimmed – no doubt a power-saving protocol at this hour – but Jonathan knew the way to Max's office well enough to have walked the corridor blindfolded. He reached the carved maple double-door to Max's private office and stopped within knocking distance. He removed his jacket, draping it over his left arm, and ran his hand through his hair before giving the door a sharp rap once, then reaching for the handle without waiting for a reply from within.

The looming figure of Max Foster stood silhouetted against the light coming through the huge window behind his desk. He turned when Jonathan entered and smiled like a wise old uncle greeting a wayward teenager. Jonathan hung his jacket on the mahogany rack near the door and took a familiar seat on the over-stuffed leather sofa opposite Max's desk, while loosening his necktie.

"Hello, Max," he said with a sigh, sinking into the softness of the sofa and for the first time all evening feeling the effects of the blended scotch he had been drinking off and on since eight o'clock. He shook his head quickly, trying to clear the cobwebs. He knew he always had to be sharp when sparring with Max. "I'm sure this must be important for you to call for me so late."

"Important is probably an understatement, Jonathan," Max's voice was low and mellow. "I'm afraid 'urgent' might be a better choice. You see, I have been hearing some rumblings that are disturbing and I wanted to make sure we head off any problems before they get started."

"What kind of rumblings?" Jonathan inquired, trying to maintain a detached approach. "Surely you don't mean more fallout from that article?"

Max waved a hand dismissively, "Oh, no, no, no. We did a nice job of deflecting all of that nonsense. The numbers are very good in that regard, if you haven't seen them. Overall approval ratings in core constituency areas are back up to ninety percent, overall approval is above sixty-five, and only a quarter of those polled, even among the Democrats, were even able to identify you as being linked to the *Journal* article. It's disappearing into the ether, as we knew it would, and the shoes will have totally forgotten it by your next re-election campaign, although it will get dredged up by whomever the Dems set up against you." Max checked himself, realizing he was rolling along on a topic other than what he intended. "But, no, Jonathan, this is not about that, although I suppose it might be related."

"What is it, then?"

"I am hearing you are starting to go soft on blocking the Menendez nomination. Is it true? If it is, then I'm worried about you, Jon. Next thing you know you'll be making some stray comment about a woman's right to choose to kill unborn babies. I'm sure you know consistency and solidarity with the Party here are critical to your future. And so I'm left to wonder what's happening. But first I want to hear from you – personally – that it's not true. Tell me it's not true, Jonathan." Max had walked around his desk as he spoke, and he was now leaning back against it, his massive buttocks engulfing the ornamentally carved rim that ran all around the front.

Jonathan furrowed his brow and looked past Max at the sparkling lights of New York City through the window beyond. "Max, I'm not sure what you're talking about, specifically. I have not made any public or private statement in support of confirming Menendez."

"Don't bullshit me," Max spat out, now raising his voice slightly, pushing his bulk away from the desk and landing in an enormous leather-covered chair positioned horizontally to the sofa on which Jonathan sat. "That's crap you can feed your staff and the press, but not me, Jon. Remember to whom you are speaking. Senator Stevens called the Whip personally and told him that you withheld your full support to the vote on blocking Menendez. You and I both know that's hokum for the fact that your support is wandering."

"Well, I suppose it might be misinterpreted like that, Max, but it's not at all what I intended."

Max stared at Jonathan for a full thirty seconds of awkward silence, considering his next move. "Jonathan, that's a very clever answer. I'm frankly proud of you for being able to come up with that on your own, at fucking midnight after a long night of bullshitting your contributors. I've taught you well. But remember, I'm the teacher, not the student. I've had many students before you, and I'll have many more before I'm through. But you may be the one with the best chance of seeing the inside of the White House, so I care very much about your future. But it's still a line of hokum and you know it. However you intended it to be interpreted, it was interpreted as a lack of full support for the correct side of the issue, and that has some people nervous, including me."

Jonathan started to lean back, but then changed his mind and inched forward to the edge of the sofa, uncrossing his legs and placing both feet firmly on the floor. "Max, I'll confide in you that I'm having some doubts about whether the Party's position is really correct. I have not broken ranks. I have done nothing to undermine the Party. I have said nothing to suggest I am going to change my vote. If I'm hesitating to confirm full support, then that's what it is – only hesitation, not reversal. I will admit, however, that I worry about the precedent of refusing to confirm the President's nominee without solid grounds. That may come back to haunt the Party."

Max stood up and began pacing. "There is a fabric to it all, Jon. You know that. The shoes need to hear you loudly and clearly all the time. They don't want to question the truth. They need you to confirm to them that you know the truth. You can't give them reason to doubt you. You can have all the doubts you want in private, but you can't do anything to suggest that you don't know what your position is. You're the leader, Jon. You have a chance to be the ultimate leader. They don't want a leader wracked with doubt and self-examination. They want instruction about what they should think."

"What about the truth?" Jonathan barked back.

"Truth!? What's truth? The only truth that matters is what the shoes will vote for."

"But there is truth in the world. Facts are facts. What's right is right. Just because you can convince a majority of registered voters that something is true doesn't make it so."

"That's where you're wrong," Max replied calmly.

"I don't believe it."

"But you see, it doesn't matter what you think or what you believe, because reality is what we make it, and that's the truth. If we say Iraq is a hotbed of terrorist activity and the press reports it and the polls show the people believe it, then when we invade in the name of suppressing terrorism we have that justification. It's truth. It doesn't matter if there's a single terrorist in the entire stinking country – it's still true. And if we secure future oil production along the way, that's just a collateral benefit of what was a noble cause."

Max's eyes were shining. Jonathan had never seen him so animated. He was in his pulpit, preaching the gospel. "And the opposite is also true, Jon. Don't you know that by now? It doesn't matter if millions of poor bastards are being slaughtered in Darfur. If we say the ruling government is democratically elected and an ally to the United States and that the rumors about ethnic cleansing are overblown, and if the media picks up our version of the story and if a majority of the people believe it, then it's true. We have no moral imperative to change things in that country, because there is not a problem. Jonathan, I'm surprised you haven't figured that out yet."

"I know full well that's how you work, Max," Jonathan was working hard to control his emotions, but he was clenching his fists so tightly that his fingernails were digging into his palms. "You manipulate the media and you manipulate the voters. That's what you do, and you are damned good at it. But don't lose sight of the real truth along the way. Don't start believing your own propaganda."

Max's lip curled into a hint of a smile. Then he threw his head back and let out a full belly-laugh, his jowls fluttering with the convulsions of his body. "Woo, boy, Son you don't ever have to worry about that with me. Who do you think I am, Reverend Hawkins? But I got news for you – he doesn't believe his own hokum either. You think he thinks he's going to Heaven? Ha! He's a player and he plays his flock like the pied piper and they follow him wherever he leads. And I tell him where to lead. And he leads them to you, my dear senator. He leads his millions of shoes into the voting booths with your face before their eyes and his words ringing in their ears and they vote for you because that's what I want them to do."

"I wish you wouldn't call them that."

"What?"

"Shoes. It's demeaning."

"No, Jon, it's enlightening. You tell me not to forget the real truth. Don't you forget the essential truths of being a politician. You want to be president some day? You need the shoes. You need them to pound the pavement for you and run the rallies for you and hand out the flyers for you and hang the lawn signs for you, and you need them to walk into those booths for you. Don't get hung up on the names, Jon. The names change, but you'll always need the shoes. They don't have brains, Jon. They don't have feelings. When the soles wear out, you replace them. They serve you. Without them, you have no support, but you choose them, and you can change them. I like the image, Jon. It took me years to find the right simile."

"I still find it offensive. These are people, Max. They have real lives and real problems and sometimes they need our help."

"And they get our help whenever we decide it's in the best interests of the greater good."

"You mean your own best interest, don't you Max?"

"It's the same thing. Haven't you been listening? We decide what's in their best interest, and they believe it because we tell them it's so, which makes them happy – to know what they should want."

"You're right about one thing, Max. It's hokum."

Max leaned forward slightly. Jonathan watched a drop of sweat release from Max's eyebrow and splash onto the reflective surface of his black loafers. Max had been working hard for the past few minutes – his body was not used to such stress. When he spoke, he truly did sound like God Almighty. "Hear me, Jonathan, and don't ever forget this. You are what I made you, and but for my grace and that of your father you would *be* one of the shoes. So, you can stay on course here, or you can leave the path of truth and find your own way in the wilderness. But without me to guide you, you will be lost, Jon. And that's the truth."

The large man leaned back into a normally erect posture, or at least as much as Max Foster was ever able to achieve. He pulled down on the vest of his three-piece suit, reached into his breast pocket for a white handkerchief, and wiped the sweat from his forehead and face as he walked to the door of his office and held it open for Jonathan. The audience was over, and Jonathan knew the drill. He got up from the leather sofa, collected his jacket from the rack near the door and draped it over his left arm, leaving his right free for the exit handshake. It was mechanical and automatic. He did it without thinking. He walked to the door and extended his hand toward Max Foster, but Max made no move to reciprocate.

"You see," Max said slyly, "that's part of your hokum, Jon. Do you *really* want to shake my hand right now? Are you happy to have been here? Are we parting as friends? If not, then you should not shake my hand, unless you are trying to fool me into thinking you really do think I'm your friend and that we're parting on cordial terms. Is that what you're doing, Jon? Trying to make be believe something that isn't true?"

Jonathan lowered his hand but stopped half way, then realized how awkward he looked and tried to compensate by raising his hand to his face to scratch an imaginary itch under his right ear while he thought about his reply. "Max, you and I have worked together for many years now. I owe you a debt of gratitude no matter what I may think of you professionally, and no matter whether I plan to heed your advice today or not. I can respect you and disagree with you at the same time. That's why I offer to shake your hand, as a matter of courtesy and respect." Jonathan once again extended his hand, as he had done millions of times before without thinking. Max took the offer this time and gave him a firm, brief shake.

"Bullshit," the big man said simply. "But extremely well-delivered bullshit." Jonathan smiled, turned, and walked through the smoked glass doors of the outer office toward the elevator, without another word and without looking back.

Chapter 32

November, 1988

PROFESSOR WALLACE GRAY'S BARITONE boomed through the small seminar room in Hamilton Hall. "Four weeks, gentlemen. Four."

It was a gray, cloudy, chilly day outside the slightly grimy window, and nearly as drab inside the room. It certainly had not been painted in twenty; no, thirty years. Brown streaks ran down over what had once been ornate carved wooden molding, staining the paint where the heating pipes leaked hot water during the winter months. The iron radiator under the window hissed occasionally during class to remind the students they sat in the same room, with the same hissing radiator, where Lionel Trilling had first taught *Ulysses* to eager boys in tweed jackets. Wallace Gray had been one of them, and now he was teaching another generation of philosopher kings, only Joyce was not on the fall semester reading list for Contemporary Civilizations.

Plato's *Republic* was, although the memories of it were fading in the minds of the ten young men and five young women sitting in silence before the gray-haired professor.

Only four weeks until the semester exam. A thousand pages left to read, and three thousand behind them to review.

Wallace Gray was an icon. Chairman of the English department, professor for over twenty years. His Senior seminars and upper-class lecture classes on Elliot, Joyce, and Pound were always oversubscribed. English majors battled to have him for an advisor. Yet he still relished the opportunity to teach freshmen and sophomores in the "core curriculum" classes of Literature Humanities and Contemporary Civilizations. The great works of literature, philosophy, politics, and economics. The basis of Western civilization. They were the bedrock of the Columbia education and brutal courses for young students, no matter how well prepared they were in high school. Professor Gray was molding minds, shaping the courses of lives. He loved every minute of it.

He was a few inches short of six feet, with a paunch developed over many years of teaching. White hair flowed across his brow and was always in need of a cut, as were his bushy eyebrows. His suit jacket came in rumpled and was quickly discarded after class began, as he rolled up the sleeves of his white cotton dress shirt and loosened his thin, drab necktie. If you looked up "college professor" in the dictionary, Wally Gray's picture would be there.

Gray prowled the front of the crowded room, making eye contact with each student, pouring ideas into their minds like fine wine into a two-week-old jack-o-lantern. Jonathan and Frank sat next to each other on either side of the far corner of the long rectangular conference table: as far from Gray's roving eyes as possible. This ran counter to Frank's usual custom of being close to the professor, but he wanted to stay with Jonathan, who had insisted on these seats.

"What is the point of *The Prince*?" Professor Gray scanned the pool of down-turned eyes before him. "Mr. Prescott?"

Frank's eyes, which had been among the few not looking at the names carved into the table top, swiveled toward his friend. Jonathan lifted his head, and his eyes widened. He looked down at his notebook. No help there. He reached his left hand toward the cover of his copy of Machiavelli's masterwork. The pages were neatly stacked, the binding uncreased. He laid his hand on the book, as if willing some knowledge to seep through his skin and into his brain. Nobody breathed for ten seconds or so, during which Professor Gray's eyes never wavered from Jonathan's face. At last, Jonathan looked up and met Gray's gaze.

"I'm not sure, Sir," He said as forcefully as he could muster, which Frank thought was pretty good under the circumstances.

"Well, what do you think of this narrator?" Gray responded, leaning down on the table with both hands and boring into Jonathan with his eyes. The students sitting at that end of the table leaned away to make room for their mentor.

"I think he'd probably make a good politician in this century, Sir, or I guess a political advisor."

"And why is that?" Gray smiled as he posed this question, removed his hands from the table, and resumed pacing, now scanning the faces of the other students.

"Because he has a specific agenda, and he will do anything to achieve it, which would make it easy for him to get political and financial support from people in whose interest it would be for him to achieve his objective."

Gray stopped his pacing and returned his eyes to Jonathan. "Ah, but do you agree with his objective and his methods?"

"His objective is the same as any politician – to maintain power. His methods are whatever is necessary. Sure, I would agree."

Gray looked hard into Jonathan's face. "Spoken like a true Republican." The group of students sucked in their collective breath for a few seconds, and then saw Gray's mouth curl into a smile, at which point fourteen voices chuckled in unison.

Jonathan sat, impassive and unsmiling. "But you'll have to do better than the Cliff's Notes on your exam, Mr. Prescott."

The remaining laughter stopped in a heartbeat.

"I realize you have other classes, and that there are other distractions for all of you, but your obligation is to actually read the books, ladies and gentlemen. If you think you will be able to get by on the summaries come exam time, you will find yourselves quite disappointed. I've been reading blue books for CC exams since before any of you were born, so I suggest you find some time to do the reading. The point of the class is for you to actually read these works – to gain some basic understanding of them, to be sure, but to have that understanding born from personal exposure, not second-hand. I'd like to think all of you will find the time, later in life, to read these books again, and that you will find additional understanding and insight then that you will lack now. But you may be surprised, someday, to find that there is some value, some wisdom you will have taken from them. You can't get that from the Cliff's Notes; only from the books. You're lucky we don't make you read them in the original language anymore." The last comment drew some polite laughter, but many heads were down, including Jonathan's.

Ninety minutes later, Jonathan and Frank walked together down the stone steps of Hamilton Hall and across the plaza toward the dining room in John Jay Hall. Frank looked up at the imposing figure of Alexander Hamilton, frozen in bronze on a high pedestal and staring down at another generation of Columbia undergrads. Jonathan muttered, half to himself, but loud enough for Frank to hear, "I'm fucked."

"Nonsense," came Frank's bright reply, "merely mildly screwed. C'mon, he probably gives that speech to every class. Not to worry, buddy."

"Sure, easy for you to say. You've been doing the reading." Jonathan gave a half-hearted chuckle, trying to convince himself he had said something funny.

"You've done some of the reading, right?"

"If almost none is some, then yes. I figured I could get away with reading the first chapter and the last chapter, and then fill in with the Cliff's Notes. It always worked for me in prep school."

"So, this is not so different, right? You'll get by."

Jonathan shrugged, but said nothing. Later that night in their dorm room, the two freshmen were both studying when Jonathan closed his copy of *The Communist Manifesto* and looked over at Frank, who was lying on his bed with his book propped open on the pillow in front of him. "Frank?" he said softly, not wanting to startle his roommate, who was obviously deep into the reading. When Frank looked up, Jonathan continued. "I really am worried about my CC grade."

Frank sighed and sat up on the bed. "Hey, I know you're nervous here, but we're all in the same boat. Heck, you went to prep school – there must have been courses like this for you there, right?"

"Right," Jonathan responded dully. "But the teachers mostly cut me a break, and I always had a tutor when I needed help."

"So, get a tutor now – I've seen dozens of ads around campus for CC tutors. What's the big deal?"

Jonathan looked down at the floor as he replied. "Because I told my father – and myself – that I could handle Columbia on my own and that I need to stand on my own two feet. If I go back and ask for him to pay for a tutor now, I will have failed in my first year." Jonathan gave Frank a pitiful look.

"OK, so you arrange for a tutor, but you don't tell your old man about it. How hard is that?"

"It's actually pretty hard," Jonathan replied, shifting from his chair down to the linoleum floor of the dorm room. "I get a fixed allowance and if I ask for more money I'd need a reason."

"Oh right, like you don't have enough walking-around money in your pocket you couldn't spare a few bucks for a tutor." Frank waved a hand at Jonathan dismissively and started to settle back into his studying position, but Jonathan wasn't finished.

"I could spare a few bucks, of course, but I was thinking maybe *you* could help me here. I mean, I'd be glad to pay you some, and we could work it out so I could pay you more this summer, when I'll have more available cash and it won't arouse suspicion. You know this stuff – I see it in class. You're the one Gray always calls on when nobody is prepared. You are always offering up your insights that aren't in the Cliff's Notes. You could help me."

Frank returned to a sitting position and pondered the suggestion. "Jon, we're classmates and roommates. I'm happy to study with you, and help. You don't have to pay me for that."

"But I know you're working two jobs and barely have enough time for your own studies. I know it would be an imposition on your time if you spend it helping me. I'd like to at least pay you a little from my allowance." It seemed to Frank that this was the most sincere thing he had ever heard Jonathan say.

"I tell you what, Buddy, why don't we just do the studying and figure out the payment, if any, at the end? I think working with you will probably help me remember the material better anyway. You're doing me a favor by forming a study group."

Jonathan smiled. "That's bullshit, but I appreciate it. Don't worry, I always pay my debts. My father taught me that – always take care of the people who do you favors."

Frank laughed. "Well, let's see whether it's really a favor first."

Over the next four weeks, Jonathan and Frank spent blocks of ninety minutes barricaded in their room, going over each of the books covered in the CC class. Frank made Jonathan read passages aloud, which Frank had already highlighted in his copy. They debated points that had been covered in class, and found some new ones to think about. A few times, Frank was late coming back from his student job in the library, but Jonathan made it a point to not be impatient – which was hard for him. He was used to having his way, and having people wait for him.

Jonathan continued to be terrified of the prospect of getting a C in the class. A gentleman's B would be fine, but if he failed to maintain at least a 3.0 grade point average, his father would be pissed, and he would be in danger of being in the bottom half of the class. He didn't need to be the class valedictorian in order to have succeeded in college, but he needed not to trail the field. A middle-of-the-pack finish was fine, and a B average would be entirely acceptable.

By the day of the exam, Jonathan was reasonably comfortable that his studying with Frank would pay off. The students arrived at the exam room – not their regular seminar room – and were surprised to find a student proctor, not Professor Gray, there to administer the exam. They received their blue books, recorded their names, and then the proctors handed out the exam. There were two questions, each of which elicited references to many of the texts they had covered, and each of which could easily have taken up the entire three-hour test period.

Jonathan looked over at Frank, across the empty chair separating them, to prevent cheating, and smiled weakly. Frank gave him a clenched fist signal of strength and dove into his own exam book. Jonathan took a deep breath and started to make notes on a blank sheet of scrap paper, outlining the points he wanted to make.

Three hours later, after they had both turned in their exam books, Jonathan and Frank staggered across Broadway to The West End and collapsed into a booth. Frank started to ask Jonathan about his exam approach, but got a raised hand from his roommate. "No. No talk about the damned exam. I think it was fine. I think I made it through. Thank you, Frank. I don't think I could have done as well without you – even if I had a tutor. But that's it. It's over. Let's not talk about it."

They shared a large mound of fries. Jonathan paid, and Frank did not object. Other students buzzed around the restaurant discussing different exams that had just occurred, or which were on the immediate horizon. Everyone was excited. Jonathan was simply relieved.

When the semester grades came out, Jonathan was almost afraid to open the envelope. He left the mail room on the ground floor of the dorm and walked north on campus, past the dome of Low Library and into the courtyard next to the chapel, watched over by Rodin's "The Thinker." He stepped over the low chain protecting a patch of grass around the marble base from wandering feet, and sat down with his back against the statue.

He blew out a frosty breath into the January air and ripped open the envelope. There was one C – in Biology. He could live with that, since it was not at all related to his presumed Political Science major. He had to satisfy the science requirement, and he had thought Bio would be an easy class for him, since he had taken AP Biology at prep school just the year before. It turned out not to be such a good call, since the class was filled with pre-meds who were cut-throat about their grades. The material was mostly different from prep school, and he had struggled. He was not surprised at the C. The rest were all fine.

He had pulled a B in Contemporary Civilizations, a B+ in French, where his prep school classes had actually helped him be prepared for a change, and an A in microeconomics. He knew he had the economics down cold – a subject he really loved. His GPA was above 3.0. He was safe.

When Frank got the news, he gave Jonathan a sincere hug and the friends shared several high-fives. Jonathan said "Thank you" so many times that Frank begged him to stop.

"What can I pay you, Frank?" Jonathan asked for the third time that night in the cafeteria over dinner.

"Don't worry about it," Frank replied – also for the third time. "It worked out. I did well in the class partly as a result of our study time together. You really don't need to pay me anything."

"But I want to."

"I said don't worry about it. It was my pleasure."

"Well," Jonathan finally relented, "someday I will make it up to you. I always repay my debts."

"OK," Frank replied, trying to end the conversation. "We'll see what happens down the line."

Chapter 33

THE FOLLOWING SATURDAY, Senator Jonathan Prescott III was one of four featured speakers on the final day of a four-day gathering of the Daughters of the American Revolution in Washington, D.C. The convention was an enclave of conservative stalwarts, fundamentalist Christian leadership, anti-abortion activists, and gun regulation opponents. Any liberal thinker was sniffed out and turned away at the door to the Fairmont Convention Center. FOX News was hosting its studio shows live from the event all weekend. CNN had a crew doing interviews for its Sunday morning political talk show. The major networks stayed away, but the local affiliates in D.C. sent crews to monitor the major speeches. Max was counting on a good reception for Jonathan, whose poll numbers were rebounding among conservatives as the fury of The Article started to die down. The Foster Group's speech writers had come up with fifteen minutes of flame-fanning that were sure to draw a series of standing ovations. Max had sent his own film crew to capture the speech and reactions from the crowd with an eye toward future campaign ads.

Jonathan was waiting in the green room with Donna and Ed Edwards. The stage manager for the event, a harried-looking woman of about fifty with white hair, a bright red dress, and an American flag pin the size of a small Frisbee, chirped incessantly into her headset as she checked off notes on a clipboard. She told Jonathan for the fifth time in the last twenty minutes that he was scheduled to go on third, after the President of the National Rifle Association. The program was running approximately three minutes behind schedule. Ten minutes earlier, she had announced the program was running *four* minutes late, so she was feeling very pleased with herself that she had somehow miraculously managed to shave a full minute off the deficit. Donna was chatting amicably with a young man who was an assistant to the convention organizer and who was so smitten by his proximity to the sensuous older woman that he appeared to be actually drooling.

Jonathan was both bored and apprehensive. The speech covered only familiar themes, but the text was new and he was a little nervous about the cameras recording this one for use in future campaign spots. He got up from the uncomfortable, stiff-backed chair in which he had been sitting and excused himself, going outside into the dimly lit area behind the temporary stage. It had the feel of a warehouse, with thick, dark drapes hanging down from the rafters some two hundred feet above, flanking the back of the stage and sheltering the backstage area. There were seats all around the floor of the arena, but the back quarter of the oval was cordoned off and empty in the area behind the stage. Jonathan could hear the applause and the amplified sounds of the speech being delivered at that moment by some dignitary from one of the sponsoring organizations who was owed the honor, but who was no public speaker.

As Jonathan paced through the open space, rehearsing his speech in a whispered voice, he was distracted by a commotion near the door leading to the green room. A knot of people crowded around the doorway and there were a few voices raised and a few arms gesturing expressively. Jonathan could not distinguish enough words to figure out what was happening, so he turned away and resumed his rehearsal. He was just getting to the transition between praise for the memory of fallen veterans of the past and support for all the current troops abroad when a voice startled him out of his concentration.

"Say there, Senator Prescott," drawled the familiar voice, "you think you might have just a moment or two for an old preacher?"

Jonathan turned and looked into the deep, dark eyes of the Reverend Abraham Hawkins. Although Jonathan had argued with presidents and met with heads of state and celebrities of all varieties, he was momentarily flustered by the sight of the icon standing before him, without any entourage or choir. He recalled seeing the reverend speak at the Riverside Church when Hawkins was a younger firebrand and Jonathan was a college student. Jonathan had seen him give speeches on television since then, and had heard clips on the news hundreds of times, but he had never actually met the man. After only a small hesitation, Jonathan's political reflexes kicked in, and he extended his hand heartily and smiled. "Reverend! It is truly a pleasure to meet you, Sir."

Hawkins took the offered hand with a brisk pump as he waved his left hand in Jonathan's direction. "Aw, now Senator, it's nobody's pleasure to meet an old man like me. But I wonder if I could bend your ear for a minute or two?"

Jonathan actually felt himself blush slightly, although the reverend could not have noticed in the dim lighting. In the close quarters, Jonathan thought he detected the scent of whiskey, mixed with mint, on the older man's breath. "Of course, Reverend Hawkins, what can I do for you?"

"Well, Son," Hawkins began, now speaking with an air of superiority and wisdom that was a marked change from his 'aw, shucks' introduction, "I've had my eye on you a bit. We have some of the same constituents, you and me, you know.

Walkin' down the same path, you might say. And you know, Son, I can tell you there have been a few times in my life when I've strayed from the straight and true path – a bit."

Jonathan raised an eyebrow and curled his lip in a tiny smile, "Is that so? Well, you know, come to think of it I believe I might have heard a few rumors about something like that, along the way."

"Heh, heh, well, you know you would not be the first one to have heard that," Hawkins gave a self-deprecating laugh and reached out to place a weathered hand on Jonathan's shoulder. Jonathan could smell the perfume of the reverend's hand lotion. "I just want you to know, Son, that if you follow the Lord and stay true to His will you will always be able to right your ship and get yourself back on the right course."

"By 'the Lord,' do you mean Jesus Christ or Max Foster?"

The reverend smiled broadly and laughed more loudly. "Well, Son, I'm not sure there's a difference there, unless you know something I don't know about Jesus Christ."

Now Jonathan joined in the laughter. "Max has told me the two of you have worked together. He told me he got you to say some nice things about me on your television show, so thank you."

"Aw, now don't you worry 'bout that at all. I'm sure there'll be plenty of times for you to thank me in a multitude of different ways, my boy. In fact, I think the two of us may be able to help each other out quite a bit."

"How do you mean?"

"Well, now, I know you've had yourself a little spot of trouble recently and perhaps you could use a little image rebuilding."

"And you think you can help me with that?" Jonathan asked as innocently as he could muster.

"Well, now, I think I just might, Senator. You know there have been quite a few folks in positions like yourself who have had to repent and ask forgiveness in order for people to see how sincere they are about changing their ways."

"You mean on your television show?"

"Yes, indeed, that is the place where the Lord shines the brightest." Hawkins flashed his best toothpaste commercial smile.

"Well, Reverend, I appreciate the thought, but you realize the sins for which I would be repenting happened more than twenty-five years ago?"

"Of course, of course, I understand, Senator. But still, it's the act of contrition that matters to the people. It don't matter none that you've lived a flawless life for three decades or three hundred, what matters is that they see how sincere you are today and associate you with goodness and light and the Holy Spirit."

Jonathan pondered his next response, and was getting a little annoyed that his rehearsal for his impending speech had been interrupted for so long. "Reverend, is there some particular reason why you want me to appear on your broadcast?"

The reverend chuckled. "Now you know I can always use a little ratings booster. A senator is a tremendous draw, and your name is very well known. Just think how you can increase your profile in the Black community." He winked at Jonathan as he finished.

"Have you discussed this with Max?"

"No, now I don't always discuss every move I make with the great Mr. Foster. I'm sure you don't either."

Jonathan smiled and lowered his head, thinking about some of those times, but knowing this would not be one of them. "I'm afraid I'm not sure that this would be the right time, Reverend. I've been dealing with the situation and I'm told the public's memory of the incident is already fading – I'm pretty sure bringing more publicity to it at this point in the curve would not be the proper approach."

The reverend looked visibly disappointed, but composed himself quickly. "You know, Son, the right path and the Max Foster political machine focus group poll results path are not always the same thing." He paused to make sure Jonathan was still listening. "Do you think I do everything Max Foster tells me to do?"

Jonathan raised an eyebrow before responding. "You seem like a man who cuts his own path in life, Reverend."

Hawkins smiled. "You have that right, my friend. You have that right. I can tell you my daddy set me on my course, like yours did for you, but my daddy never dreamed of what I've done. I can't say for sure whether my father the country preacher would approve of everything I've done, but a boy has to chart his own course through the sea of life. I have given away more money to more deserving people than my whole home town ever earned in their entire lives. I have helped educate more poor Black children than anyone in this country outside of the NAACP College Fund." Hawkins beamed at his own accolade. "If I had done only what my daddy told me to do, or only what Max Foster tells me to do, then I would not have accomplished all I have."

"Well, we all have a different arc through our lives, Reverend," Jonathan offered, hoping to end the conversation and get back to his speech.

"Now you listen to me, Son. I'm telling you something important here." Hawkins' eyes grew wide and he leaned in close to Jonathan. "I want you to know I understand how you feel in a way you can't possibly know. I know you never had a son of your own, and neither did I. It is one of my greatest disappointments. What you don't know – what nobody knows – is that I had a chance to have a boy of my own." The reverend stared over Jonathan's shoulder, lost in his thoughts.

"The baby you lost? It would have been a boy?" Jonathan asked.

Hawkins nodded his head slightly, then looked back into Jonathan's eyes. "I was gone a lot, leaving my angel bride home alone for long stretches. I guess I was not a great husband. She was alone too much. I never dreamed that I would only have one chance. I was away when it happened. She started bleeding, but she did not want to call an ambulance right away. She didn't want to cause a fuss or any publicity. If I had been home, I could have gotten her to a hospital sooner. I might have saved my baby. I might have saved her. I know that regret, Son. I know what it's like to lose the son you could have had."

"That's why you are so passionate about abortion, isn't it?" Jonathan asked softly.

Hawkins paused in thought. "When the Lord took my son from me, and then ten days later the Supreme Court issued its insidious decision, I knew God had given me His mission. I have to save those other unborn sons for their fathers."

"Thank you for sharing that with me, Reverend Hawkins. I appreciate it."

"Well, now, Senator, there is also one other thing I want to share with you. I know I'm no saint and I've had my share of sins in this life, but the Lord knows the good works you do, and that's what counts. Not your sins, Boy – not your sins – your blessings. You go make up your own mind about what is right. The man once said, 'To thine own self be true,' you know?"

Jonathan chuckled to himself, while keeping eye contact with the reverend. "My father once told me that, but he meant it the way Polonius meant it when he told his son to be true to himself. He meant to be selfish and to do what was best for his business. I think you mean it differently."

Hawkins looked puzzled. "Now, I don't know about that, Son, but what I mean is that you got to do what you think is right in this world. I know there are folks like Max Foster who think you could be president someday. I don't know if they're right, but I know anybody who wants to sit in that chair needs to know how he got there and needs to know where he's going. And he needs to know he's done good in the world in the eyes of the Lord. I hope you can say you are a man of good works, Senator."

Hawkins held out a well-manicured hand for Jonathan to shake, which he did reflexively. The reverend turned and walked back to the green room, while Jonathan went back to his run-through. As much as he tried to focus, he kept thinking about what Hawkins had said about being true to himself. He recalled his father telling him the same thing when he was twenty years old. He had convinced himself that he really had made up his own mind to follow the path laid out by his father. He had decided.

Following his father's advice, and Max Foster's advice, had served him well. It had always been good advice, and he was in his present position because he had followed that path. He had been true to himself. Hawkins didn't know him. But he couldn't shake the line from *Hamlet*. He strained his memory for the exact lines.

> *This above all: to thine own self be true,*
> *And it must follow, as the night the day,*
> *Thou canst not then be false to any man.*

By the time Jonathan got back to the green room, the reverend was with his entourage preparing for his own appearance, sipping on a cup of coffee. The conference organizer hustled Jonathan to the waiting area on the side of the stage so he would be ready to go on at exactly the right time. The two men did not speak again that night.

Chapter 34

THE TIRES OF THE BMW 380I CRUNCHED across the smooth gravel driveway leading up to the Prescott Estate. Jonathan had traversed this route a thousand times, always with a sense of anticipation that his home and all its comforts awaited him. During his college years, he always looked forward to the warmth and softness of his bed, and the way his mother doted on him and saw to his every need when he came home for a visit. The liquor cabinet and the fridge were always full. Since his marriage, the visits had been fewer; holidays and family events, mainly. Still, this house was a refuge from any troubles the world could throw his way.

Today, his stomach churned. He hadn't felt like this since the night he went to visit Janice – the day he found out about the baby. Funny, he thought, that he would connect that event with this one. This was his first visit home since The Article.

His mother greeted him as always with a long hug, after which she brought both her hands to his face, held him between her palms, and looked into his eyes. Normally, this was followed by a kiss on each cheek, for which he had to bend his knees to allow his mother's lips to reach him. Today, he didn't bend down, and she had to settle for a peck on the chin. As she stepped back, her brow furrowed.

"What's wrong, Honey?" her voice wavered with genuine concern. "Something bothering you?" She clasped her hands in front of her red-and-white checked skirt. Jonathan always thought she dressed every day as if company were coming over. He noticed her gold cross dangling from a thick necklace. Her auburn hair was pulled into an impossibly tight bun, emphasizing her taut cheeks and the length of her neck. All Jonathan could see in her eyes was worry. "When you called, I could tell something was the matter. Is it Gwen? Is she alright?"

"It's not Gwen, Mother," he said softly, and brushed past her into the house. "Did you tell him I was coming?"

"No, he hasn't called."

"Good," Jonathan exhaled and turned away. He hadn't realized he was holding his breath. He checked his watch. Six fifteen. "Mother, do you mind if I go upstairs and lie down for a few minutes?"

"You see, I knew you weren't feeling well. Come here and let me feel your head."

"Mother," Jonathan scolded mildly. "I feel fine, I'm just a little tired."

Sylvia Prescott gave her son a look that, when he was eight years old, would have caused him to bow his head and march straight to his mother so she could kiss his forehead to see whether he had a fever. Today it wasn't working. "Fine, then, you run upstairs and rest. I already told Hilda you were coming and she's making up something special for supper."

Jonathan held back a protest about making a special dinner. He knew nights like this were what Hilda lived for – showing off how she could whip up a gourmet meal without notice. He climbed the stairs, sliding his hand along the polished but well-worn banister. The step second from the top squeaked, he remembered, so he skipped it and lunged up the last two steps in one quad thrust. He turned, resting a hand on the shining mahogany railing, and called down to his mother, "When will the senator be home?"

"I expect him by seven," she called back. "Dinner at eight. Are you sure you're feeling all right?"

"Yes, Mother. I'm fine. Please let me know when he arrives." He closed the bedroom door behind him and snapped the lock in place. He didn't want to face his father. Not yet. He walked to the window and threw up the sash, allowing some of the warm July air to filter into the musty space.

His room was perpetually in suspended animation, it seemed, waiting for the next visit. He noticed a wrapped stick of chewing gum lying on the dresser, in the exact spot where he had left it. The bed had been neatly made, all the surfaces dusted or vacuumed and all the clothes neatly replaced in their drawers. He scanned the pictures on the walls: Jonathan and his father when Jonathan had received the most valuable player award after his last year on the football team at prep school; Jonathan and his father with Ronald Reagan at a fundraising dinner; Jonathan wearing his graduation robes, with his father's arm around his shoulders. His father was smiling so broadly in all of them. Not the practiced smile of the seasoned politician, but an honest, genuine, happy smile. There were no pictures of his mother in his bedroom. He tried to think if he had ever seen a picture of himself with only his mother – without his father. No, he was pretty sure there weren't any.

He laid down on the bed. He perceived the light dimming outside. He heard the rattle and bang of Hilda in the kitchen working away at a festive Friday night supper. A rare occasion these days – both Jonathan III and the senator home for dinner.

A light knock on the door roused him from the nap he didn't realize he was taking. "Mmm. Yeah?" he managed, sitting up stiffly on the bed and smacking his dry lips together in an attempt to generate some saliva.

"Dinner in ten minutes, dear," his mother's voice came through the door.

"Okay," he replied as if he had cotton balls stuffed into each cheek. He tucked in his shirt and walked unsteadily down the hall to the bathroom to splash some water on his face and comb his hair. By the time he reached the dining room, he was more or less fully awake. He cursed himself for sleeping. He had wanted to catch his father as soon as he arrived home, without waiting for dinner. That plan was already out the window.

The senator was already seated at the head of the long dining room table. It sat twelve comfortably, but tonight was set for only three, although the place settings looked as though they were for an inauguration ball. No matter how many years passed, each time he walked into a room where his father was, he felt like a teenager who had been caught with a condom in the pocket of the pants he had put through the wash. There was always something he didn't want his father to know, it seemed.

The elder senator unfolded a linen napkin and began arranging his silverware and drinking glasses. After forty years, Hilda insisted on setting the table according to Miss Manners' accepted protocol, even knowing that the senator liked his water glass on his left and his bread plate pushed out behind his dinner plate. Jonathan smiled at the ritual. Old habits were hard to break.

The dinner was light on conversation, but heavy on gravy. Hilda had decided to make up a Thanksgiving dinner for the occasion. Chestnut stuffing and mashed potatoes were smothered in rich turkey gravy and homemade cranberry sauce with walnuts. Water chestnuts, carved into the shape of flowers, decorated every plate. Jonathan enjoyed the food, despite his growing anxiety about the after-dinner conversation.

"You're awfully quiet tonight, Son," the senator observed, hoping to entice a response.

"Sorry, Sir," Jonathan replied stiffly. "I've had a lot on my mind lately. I'd like to have some time with you and mother, after dinner."

"What about?"

"After dinner, please," Jonathan responded softly, looking at his mother. His eyes pleaded for some support, which he knew he would get.

"Yes, Dear, after dinner would be fine. Would you like some more of the green beans?" The senior senator set his mouth in a hard line, disappointed not to get an answer to his question, but knowing that his wife's preemptive strike could not be countermanded without a significant effort that didn't seem warranted. He swirled the pinot noir in his crystal glass before draining the last mouthful, then reached for the bottle for a new pour. He smiled at his wife and his son, but his brow remained furrowed. He had been in the Senate twenty-four years and he prided himself on being able to feel when dangerous sailing lay ahead. His intuition was telling him to be on alert, and his intuition seldom failed him.

After dinner, the three adjourned to the library. Jonathan closed the oversized double doors to the room, sealing them off from Hilda's inquisitive ears. The library had no telephone, and had long ago been sound-proofed to be a refuge within the house. Maple bookshelves rose to the ceiling around three sides of the space, with two-story windows covering the fourth wall that overlooked the woods and the western sky. A plush, Persian rug covered most of the hardwood floor, muffling all sounds that were not already absorbed by the rows and rows of hard-cover books, many of them first editions or rare collector's pieces. In the center of the rug, three plush maroon leather easy chairs, separated by small wooden end tables, stood ready to engulf visitors. The chairs were opposed by a long couch of the same material, with end tables on each side on which Tiffany lamps glowed softly.

The senator had a glass of brandy, his wife a cup of decaffeinated tea. Jonathan ushered them to the couch, and he eased himself back onto the edge of one of the opposite chairs, but then stood up again, nervously.

"What is it, Boy," the senator barked out, impatient with Jonathan's hesitation. He never appreciated that some people had difficulty getting a conversation started. Directness was never a problem for Jonathan Prescott, Jr.

Jonathan licked his lips and began. "You know there was a story written about me. About you . . . us . . . the family."

"Aw, hell, Son. Is that what's bothering you?" The senator kicked out one leg and reached for his snifter. "Boy, when are you going to learn not to listen to tripe like that? You're a target, Son. You'll be a target as long as you're a Prescott. You have to ignore the assassins in the media. Come on, now, it's not like this is the first time you've seen some hatchet-job story in a newspaper." Jonathan's father sat back on the couch, crossing his legs dismissively.

"In this case, I know the woman who wrote the story," Jonathan plunged ahead, ignoring the senator's dismissal. "I also participated, to some degree, in the research that went into it. I can't ignore these facts. I can't help but want to know for sure. The truth. Truth is always important, right? You told me that." Jonathan looked directly at the elder Prescott and held his gaze. He was forty-seven. He was his own man, with his own wife, and his own career. He stared into his father's eyes and he didn't blink or look away. It struck him that this was the first time in his life he had looked at this man as his equal.

"I want to put this story to rest once and for all. A DNA test is simple and conclusive. It should not be a problem. All I need is a blood or hair sample and I'll take care of the details."

The senator shot to his feet with surprising quickness. "The Hell I will!" His eyes blazed in a way Jonathan had never seen. He slopped some of his brandy onto the rug, but paid it no attention. "We do not let some media whore blackmail us into submission. We do not justify ourselves to anyone. You hear me, Boy?!"

Jonathan looked from the rage of his father to his mother, sitting quietly on the sofa, her left hand raised to her mouth as she stared at her husband. She did not look at Jonathan. "But why?" he asked, with more cheek than he intended. "We have nothing to hide. Why not put the issue to rest? Unless there is, in fact, something to hide."

Jonathan Prescott, Jr. took two large steps and slapped his son across the face with the palm of his right hand. The force of the blow, along with its surprise factor, knocked Jonathan off balance. He fell sideways, catching himself on the arm of one of the easy chairs. He shook his head, blood rushing to his face, and instinctively rose back up, fist clenched and weight shifting to his opposite foot. He saw his father's face, still a mask of rage.

"Stop!" Sylvia Prescott's voice sliced through the room, freezing both men. "Enough! Both of you. My God, look at you!" She had risen from the sofa and crossed to her husband's side. She was holding his arm, weighing it down to prevent another strike.

"Jonathan," she was pleading now, a tear forming in her eye, "please." The senior senator dropped his arm to his side and stepped back. Sylvia entwined her arms around his waist and looked up into his eyes. "It's time, my darling."

"No! Hell no!" he spat, pushing her away.

"Then I will." She cast a steely stare at her husband.

"No, you won't."

"Won't what? What, Mother?" Jonathan had shrunk down into the chair and was watching the drama unfold in front of him. He lowered his voice to nearly a whisper. " What?"

Jonathan's mother wiped the tear away from her cheek and walked back to the couch, where she settled herself carefully, smoothing out the pleats of her skirt. The senator had crossed over to the window and was looking outside, able to see his wife in the reflection of the dark glass, but unwilling to look directly at either her or his son. Sylvia took a sip of her tea, and then looked into the clear blue eyes of her only child.

"Jonathan, dear, it was very different back then. I know you think of those days as wild times when everyone was 'live and let live' but in our social circles, we were very constrained by conventions. And the science wasn't nearly as well developed as it is now, you see, so you can understand that it wasn't easy." She paused and looked at Jonathan for some sign of understanding.

"What wasn't easy, Mother?"

"Well, dear, it wasn't easy becoming pregnant. You see, sweetheart, your father–"

"DON'T!" boomed the senator's voice from across the room. "Do not blame me like you always did." His voice trailed off, and he continued to stare into the nothingness of the window glass.

Sylvia re-composed herself, then continued. "Well, dear, we – your father and I – we had some difficulty becoming pregnant after we were married. We tried for several years without any success. Not even a miscarriage. We thought it might be me; that I might be unable to bear a child. But the doctors said they couldn't find anything wrong with me. I wanted your father to get tested, but—"

"But masturbating into a cup so they could examine my sperm under a microscope was not something this senator was going to do for anybody," the elder Prescott's voice rose again from the window.

"You were a congressman, then, Jonathan," Sylvia noted softly. "You weren't elected to the Senate until after Jonathan was born."

"Well fine, then," mocked the senator. "It was not something *I* was going to do."

"So, you see, Dear," Sylvia continued, "we wanted so much to have a child, and something like in vitro fertilization was so new and so controversial, well, it was out of the question for us. Your father's political enemies would have crucified him had they known. He was opposed to it, you see, on moral grounds. It was a very different time.

"And so we kept trying, but your father was away in Washington so much, and I was here – well, actually in our old house in New Greenwich – and I wanted so much to give Jonathan a son. Oh, it was the most important thing in the world to him. To me. To us. You must understand. I had to. It was my duty. My most sacred and profound duty was to provide an heir, a son. Someone who would carry on the family name and my Lord we were blessed. We were so blessed to have you. We were so happy. You made us so happy. And we are so proud of you, Jon. We are so proud." She paused to clear away another tear.

Jonathan sat, puzzled. He closed his eyes and tried to make sense of what he had just heard. "So, I'm not sure I follow. You were able to get pregnant, right? I mean, you gave birth to me, right?"

"Yes, my son. I bore you. I carried you. I cried and cried in the hospital when they put you in my arms. We were so happy you were a boy; a son. Yes, Son. Yes." She held out her hand toward Jonathan, and he galloped across the span separating them, taking his mother's hand in his own and pressing it against his cheek.

"So, if I'm your son, I don't understand why it's such a problem to prove it to the world."

Sylvia squeezed Jonathan's hand with hers. "Because, while I am certainly your mother, there is a very good likelihood that your father is not your biological father." She allowed the words to hang in the air for only a moment before rushing forward. "But that's not what matters, Jon. I bore you. We raised you. You have been our son since you were born. You are every bit a Prescott."

"But, if father – the senator – is not my real father, then who is?"

"I am your father, boy!" The elder Prescott finally turned to face his wife. "Don't let her tell you otherwise. Don't let her fill your mind with possibilities and speculation. It's as good as lies. All dirty, filthy lies. I am your father. Don't you doubt that."

Jonathan looked from his father to his mother. Her head was bowed, and now she was weeping openly, not making any attempt to brush away the tears. "I tried, Son. I really, really did. I'm sorry. I was weak. I was desperate. There was a man I met at a fundraiser when your father was in Washington. I had a few glasses of wine, and he was as tall as your father and I... I let him... I needed to be pregnant. I had to be pregnant." Her sobs became too heavy for her to continue speaking. She shook for a moment, drawing in breath as if in great pain and battling to hold it in. "I suppose I knew I might be able to conceive. I did conceive. I am ashamed of what I did, but I did it for us, for your father. For you."

Jonathan stared blankly for a moment, trying to absorb what he was hearing. His father's voice filled the void. "And I made love to you during that same time, Sylvia. Jonathan may still be my son. He could be my son. Damn it, he is my son and nothing you can say will change that!"

"So, why not be certain?" Jonathan asked the man he had always considered his father.

Senator Prescott's face paled, and he slumped down onto the sofa next to his wife. "I don't want to be certain!" he mumbled, without making eye contact with his son. "Uncertainly is all I have. As long as you could be my son, then you are my son."

Jonathan turned back to his mother. "Is that why I never had a brother?"

"Yes, Dear," she said, now under control with the tears properly reined in. "We still tried to get pregnant. We never used any birth control. But we were never able. I never allowed any other man to touch me again. I swear it. But we were never able to have another child."

"Well, that seems like pretty compelling evidence. But what if I need to know? What if I need to know for sure? Will you let me do the DNA test? Confidentially? Only we need to know the results."

"No," the senator said softly. "I will not. What you need, Boy, is to be a Prescott. Being a Prescott is what you are. You don't need to mess with that. You are my son, as sure as the sun sets in the West. I don't need any test to tell me that."

Jonathan stood up. He hugged his mother and softly said, "Thank you," into her ear. He walked to the doors and opened one side, then stopped. He turned to his father – the man he had always called his father. "What I need is to be who I am, and not who you are. I'm not you. I'm not even the next generation of you. I'm me. I guess I already knew that before I got here. Now all I have to do is figure out what being me really means."

He turned and walked through the door, closing it quietly behind him. He left them in the library. He walked out the front door, got into the BMW with vanity plates reading "PRSCT III", and drove away without looking back.

Chapter 34

JONATHAN STAYED LATE TO WORK the Monday after his brief trip home to Connecticut. Gwen and the kids were still at Gwen's mother's house. Everyone else had gone home. He had to order Donna to leave or she would have kept responding to emails from donors as long as he kept working. It was a surprise when the phone rang and his display told him the call was coming from the Majority Whip, Angelo Cruz from Florida. He said he wanted to meet with Jonathan in person, if he had a few minutes.

Jonathan replied that he did have a few minutes, but that he had not had dinner and was starving. Jonathan suggested meeting in the Senate cafeteria, where he could get a sandwich even after the normal dinner hour. Cruz agreed. Jonathan was happy to have the meeting on neutral ground, rather than in the Whip's office. He quickly poured himself a half shot of Black Label from the crystal carafe on his credenza, then popped an Altoid before heading out.

When Jonathan reached the entrance to the cavernous cafeteria, he marveled at the size of the room, now nearly empty. The space provided breakfast and lunch to not only the senators and their staffs, but also the swarm of workers, security guards, and the working press who were present each day in the Capitol building. At noon time, the floor would be teeming with activity and the long tables would be filled with clattering trays and boisterous talking. At nine o'clock at night, it was a ghost town, except for a small knot of men sitting in a corner near the entrance at a dimly lit table. Jonathan noticed the men were all dressed in blue overalls, signifying that they were janitorial staff, probably taking a break from emptying trash cans and polishing the corridor floors. He doubted that these men would intrude on his upcoming conversation, but he nevertheless found a table on the opposite side of the room after securing a tuna salad sandwich and a Diet Coke from the self-service shelves.

Senator Cruz arrived before Jonathan had taken his second bite, a paper coffee cup in his left hand. He offered no handshake in deference to Jonathan's handful of tuna sandwich, and instead got right down to business. Cruz was a small man who had a hunched posture most of the time, making him seem even shorter. His weathered face carried a perpetual scowl. He was known to be a bulldog on conservative issues and a staunch party supporter. He was happy to do the grunt work of organizing the Republican caucus, sending out agendas, and herding the senators when it was time for an important vote. He was liked by almost nobody.

"Jonathan, thanks for meeting with me at his late hour," Cruz began, then took a swig of his coffee. "I just needed to have a quick check-in with you in person on Menendez. I already spoke with Max Foster and he assured me you were solid and could be counted on as always, but just to be absolutely sure I just wanted to hear it directly from you." Cruz looked across the pitted table top at Jonathan expectantly, putting down his cup as if the conversation was already over.

"Angelo, you know I've always been reliable." Jonathan stated this as fact, not really expecting or wanting a response. "So why the question now?"

Cruz dropped his eyes before speaking, which was typical for him. "Jon, don't read anything into it, it's not as if I'm worried about you."

"Then what is it?" Jonathan snapped back, more harshly than he intended. A speck of white bread shot across the table and bounced off Cruz's coffee cup. "And frankly, Angelo, what if I were not as solid on this as I always am on everything else? Would the party fall to pieces if the President's nominee is confirmed? Do you not think he's qualified and intellectually capable?" Jonathan glared at his colleague.

"Now, Jon, you know it's not about being qualified. I'm sure the guy is smart and all that, but he's turned out to be so liberal – we can't let this seat get filled. That's the strategy, and we've all agreed on that, right?"

"You know I went to school with him, right?"

Cruz hesitated, grabbing for his coffee to stall for time as he took a slow sip. "Yeah, I know. It's common knowledge. But what, it's a college buddy issue for you? Is that the problem?"

"Did I say there was a problem?" Jonathan retorted. "I don't recall saying anything about there being a problem – I was just posing a question."

Cruz frowned, puzzled by Jonathan's rhetoric. "It's late, Senator Prescott. I'm not up for an academic discussion. Just tell me you're voting no."

Jonathan chewed his sandwich slowly before responding. "I'm interested in hearing your answer to the question, Angelo. Do you think the man is not qualified?"

"I'm not saying that."

"So," Jonathan continued, "what decisions has he written that you find offensive to conservative values?"

Cruz looked annoyed. "Jon, I didn't bring my briefing book with me, but you know as well as I do that the point isn't whether he's qualified, it's that we want somebody else."

Jonathan nodded his head. "You are absolutely right, Angelo. I have the same briefing book as you. I'm sure it's well researched, although I have looked at a few of the cases and I'm not in total agreement with the conclusions about the affronts to conservative values. But the recommendation is to vote against, right?"

"Right," Cruz agreed, looking confused.

"So, if that's the party instruction then you can expect all good Republican senators to go along and vote the way we are all told, right?"

"Right," Cruz again agreed, nodding, but not sure what was coming next.

"And I am a senator who can be counted on to always follow along and vote the way I'm told to vote, right?"

"Jon, you always have been."

"So," Jonathan put down the last quarter of his sandwich and took a sip of his soda, "what in the world do you think you have to worry about?"

Cruz frowned slightly. "Nothing, Jonathan. Right? Nothing to worry about."

"So, no problem, then," Jonathan concluded, getting up from his seat and collecting his Styrofoam container and soiled napkin.

"Great," Cruz mumbled, struggling up from his bench and grabbing his cup. "Great. I'm glad to hear it. I'll see you on the floor tomorrow then, for the budget bill vote."

"Fine," Jonathan replied, standing still and waiting for Cruz to pass him and lead toward the exit. He let the Whip get several paces ahead of him before meandering toward the garbage can, depositing his trash, and then walking in the direction of the group of custodial employees, who were still gathered at the table near the door. Cruz had disappeared around the corner already, leaving Jonathan alone with his thoughts. Cruz figured he was solid, because he was always solid. So why ask? Did the party needed Cruz to bully him back into submission. Like always. Was he that easy? And what had Cruz's arguments been? Nothing. Like always. The will of the Party. Don't question. Wasn't he supposed to question things?

He walked toward the door, not really noticing the men in the blue overalls, lost in his own thoughts. One of the men then spoke. "Ev'nin', Senator."

Jonathan was roused from his inner discussion by the salutation. He looked up and reflexively responded, "Good evening." He looked at the man to see if he recognized him at all. The man was Black, tall, and thin, with calloused hands and wrinkle lines around his eyes, but he was smiling sincerely toward Jonathan. His blue work uniform was stained and frayed around the cuffs, and his black shoes had not been shined in months. Jonathan could not place him, and so did not attempt to call him by name. He merely smiled and waved in the man's general direction. As he did, Jonathan noticed the rest of the group. All were minorities – three Black men and two Hispanic. All but one of them were looking up at Jonathan, and he nodded acknowledgement toward them.

One man was not paying any attention to Jonathan. He was at the end of the table, one knee propped against the edge, on which he held a folded magazine. He had black, wide-rimmed glasses and sported a thin moustache. He looked younger than the other men, but Jonathan had trouble judging the ages of Black people. The man's hair was clipped short and showed no trace of grey. Jonathan guessed he was under thirty. His eyes were turned down and hidden from Jonathan's view. He held a stubby pencil in his right hand as he studied the paper in front of him, engrossed beyond being distracted by the appearance of a senator. As Jonathan passed the group and walked through the doorway, he peeked over his shoulder at the bespectacled man and saw that on his knee was a crossword puzzle, with the spaces on the left-hand side filled in.

Jonathan walked briskly toward his office, trying to define in his own mind why the conversation with Cruz had made him so agitated. The Whip was just doing his job, confirming votes. Why should he not expect Jonathan to tow the party line, like always? He walked, and wondered what would have to happen for him to ever not follow his instructions. When was it appropriate for a senator to break ranks?

He continued toward his office and as he reached the outer door, he stopped. He thought about the Black man in the blue overalls with the crossword puzzle. He turned around and walked briskly back toward the cafeteria, then hopped down the steps toward the cafeteria two at a time. He arrived at the doorway and stopped short. The custodians were no longer at the table near the door. There was no sign of them in the room. Jonathan thought about searching the hallways, but dismissed the idea as too unbecoming of a senator.

He went back to his office and sat at his desk, reviewing his briefing books and sending off a few emails. Within an hour, he heard a soft knock at the door. "'Scuse me, Sir – I'm gonna take the trash." The custodian slowly opened the door and silently went about the process of emptying the trash cans from the office before departing without another word. Jonathan recognized him as the same man who had greeted him in the cafeteria. Jonathan wondered to himself why he had not greeted the custodian, acknowledged his presence and thanked him for his service. It would have been so simple and easy – but it was not expected. It was not part of the accepted protocol, and Jonathan followed the protocol as he always did.

Jonathan packed up his briefcase and left the building, oddly bothered by the night's events, but unable to come to a conclusion about exactly why.

Chapter 35

ON THE FRIDAY BEFORE THE VOTE to confirm the Supreme Court nomination of Ricky Menendez, Jonathan returned home earlier than usual and relieved their nanny in the middle of feeding dinner to the children. Gwen had returned home with the girls. Gwen had meetings scheduled with several of her charity organizations that she could not miss. The groups were in the final stages of planning for fall events and typically elected new officers before the August lull in Washington. Gwen had been chilly toward Jonathan, but they had settled back into the routine of their lives – taking care of the girls, Gwen's social obligations, Jonathan's Senate schedule, and the hectic pace of Washington.

Jonathan poured himself a glass of red wine and sat at the butcher block table in the kitchen listening to the snippets of news about their respective school days that the girls could get in between bites and sibling interruptions. He smiled at the similarity to debates on the Senate floor. Gwen was due home by 6:30. He had stopped by the gourmet grocery on the way home and had her favorite dinner ready to pop into the microwave – veal Marsala with garlic mashed potatoes and grilled asparagus. He was hoping for a quiet dinner together, a simple pleasure they seldom shared because of his hectic schedule and her cluttered social calendar.

He shooed the girls through their baths and had them in pajamas and huddled in front of *The Lion King* by six twenty-five. Finding silver candle sticks that had been a wedding present tucked in a white box in the corner of the china cabinet and two slender white candles in a nearby drawer, he set the table in the dining room. Then he re-filled his wine glass and one for Gwen and started nuking the dinner, which would have been nearly ready on time if Gwen had arrived with her usual punctuality. By 6:45, the dinner was languishing in the microwave and the candles had burned half way down. Jonathan extinguished the flames so there would still be something left for his wife and drained the remainder of his wine glass. He sat in the semi-darkness holding an empty glass, and heard muffled giggles from upstairs along with bouncy music he identified as "I Just Can't Wait to be King." The empty glass in his hand and the empty chair next to him at the table were juxtaposed against the happy laughter from above.

Was this his life now? He wondered silently whether waiting so long to have children had been a good idea. Jonathan had not felt ready to be a father until he had established himself in a career, and while Gwen certainly would have been happy to have kids, she had deferred to Jonathan's hesitancy. Plus, Max had figured that having teenage children at the time of a presidential run would be a good way to show he was still young and virile. At times like this, when he was home alone with two pre-teen girls, he felt lost and helpless as far as his parenting skills.

Jonathan was just popping the cork on the next bottle of pinot noir when he heard the key in the front door lock and the sound of his wife dropping her purse on the hardwood floor. "Hello, darling," he called out cheerily as he punched buttons on the microwave to re-heat the dinner. He rounded the corner from the kitchen into the dining room, bottle in hand, but stopped short when he saw Gwen leaning against the small hallway table, crying softly. "What happened?" he asked as he placed the bottle on the table and put his arms around her waist from behind.

She shook her head wordlessly, reaching up to wipe the tears from her cheeks. "You set the table," she said simply.

He spun her around gently to face him. She was wearing a smart maroon-and-gold skirt suit with a string of pearls around her neck and matching earrings hanging from her lobes, which were emphasized by her hair being pulled back behind her head. On Barbara Bush, it would have looked grandmotherly, but on Gwen it was simple and elegant. She looked up at him with soft, moist eyes, but didn't speak.

"I got your favorite from DaVinci's. It'll be ready in a jiffy. Will that make you feel better?"

She nodded and buried her face in his chest, squeezing him close with both arms. "Oh, Jonathan, just tell me we'll get past all this soon."

"Get past what?"

She pulled back and steadied herself against the table. "I'll light the candles, you get the food," she said. "We can talk over dinner."

After her first half-glass of wine, Gwen related the story of her meeting with the planning committee. The Daughters of the American Revolution held an annual Gala dinner every fall to raise money for supporting troops abroad and for historical preservation of American monuments and battlegrounds. She had been on the organizing committee for the last two years, and was vice-chairman for this year's upcoming event. It had been taking up a significant amount of her time and put her in close quarters with the highest strata of Washington's conservative wife corps. This year's chairwoman was the wife of the senior senator from North Carolina, Edward "Ebb" Birdsong, who was nearing the completion of his seventh term and seriously talking about a re-election campaign at the age of eighty-eight.

"They asked me to defer. Can you believe that? Defer! Me!" Gwen's voice went up an octave as she recounted the events.

"Did they say why?" Jonathan asked calmly, trying not to escalate the emotional temperature and to keep Gwen from crying again.

"They didn't even tell me that there was going to be a meeting to discuss it. Charmaine – ooh, how I loathe that woman – told me the other members of the Executive Board met informally and decided that it was best if I did not serve as chairwoman for next year, even though it was my turn. She said I would remain vice-chair for next year and after that they would *consider* whether it would be *appropriate* for me to chair the following year. Do you get that? Consider? You know damned well the vice-chair is *always* appointed chair the following year. It's tradition. They totally screwed me, Jon, and they did it all behind my back."

Jonathan sat motionless, listening to the saga. On one level, he did not share his wife's sense of outrage merely because he did not consider the chairwomanship of the DAR Gala to be a big enough deal to warrant this kind of emotion compared to the kinds of issues he dealt with daily in the Senate. But he understood on an emotional level that this was critically important to Gwen, and so he nodded his head and soothingly agreed with her on all points.

From the day they were married – even before that – her world revolved around social circles and invitations. Where she was seated at a dinner party meant more to her than whatever charity happened to be the beneficiary of the event. There was apparently a pecking order among the women of her circle – a ladder to be climbed that was as important to them as which committee seats and chairmanships were awarded to a senator. It was politics on a different level, and it meant everything to Gwen. As he listened, he recalled how devastated she had been when someone – he could not recall who it was – cancelled an accepted invitation to a party Gwen had arranged shortly after they were married. Even before moving to Washington, where the social scene was magnified, Gwen had wanted to move in the top rings of the society circles. This was a blow to her and Jonathan knew it, even if he didn't fully understand it. "Is there anything I can do?" he inquired innocently, genuinely wanting to help.

"Ha!" she sputtered, halting her wine glass in mid-air and sloshing the dark liquid within its large-bowled glass. She shook her head and looked at the candle, now nearly burned out in front of her at eye level atop its silver stem. "You really don't get it, do you, Jon?"

Jonathan stared into her eyes, utterly clueless. "I guess not."

"You can't help here, Jon. You are the problem. Don't you see it? They don't want me to chair the Gala because of *you*."

"Me?"

"Because of Janice-the-Bitch and that article and the abortion and the scandal and the newspapers and the whole thing. I'm suddenly too *controversial* and not *suitable* to be the face of the organization for the Gala – even *next year's* Gala. Oh, I could just kill her."

"Charmaine?"

"No, Jon – Janice Stanton!"

"Oh," Jonathan stammered, leaving a heavy silence at the table. He took a deep breath, then said what he had been thinking during the entire conversation, and in fact had been thinking for years but had kept to himself. "Darling, if those women are so petty and ungracious then why not just say 'to Hell with them' and find some other causes or other friends who'll be loyal no matter what? These people who let you twist in the wind just because they don't want to be associated with any bad press? They aren't your real friends. Why do you care so much?"

Gwen's hand flew toward the table, slamming down with an impact that jarred every dish and utensil and knocked over one of the candles, spilling hot wax onto the table's polished surface. "You don't understand, Jonathan!" she screamed. "This is what I have. This is what I've always had. I have you, and the girls, and then I have what I get as Jonathan Prescott's wife, and that's it! And it has always been good, and that's what I want. And it's not just for me – it's for you, too. Don't you realize how important it is when you accompany me to the Gala, or sit on the dais at the Cancer Society ball? It's all part of your image, Jon. Our image. I put up with it because it's important!"

She was crying again, but too agitated for Jonathan to think about comforting her. "I can get through this, Jon, I'm just angry and frustrated because it took so long to build up and now it's falling down so fast. But you'll come through this, right? You aren't going to have any more scandals. You're going to be president someday, and then I'll make them all grovel."

"It's not about making them grovel, Dear. It can't be just about that."

She flashed her eyes at him, wiping the tears again. "You just don't understand."

"No," he admitted, "I guess I don't. I understand that I want us to be happy. I want you to be happy. I want the girls to be happy. Just tell me what I can do to make that happen."

"Just be the man I married," she said softly, no longer crying but still red and puffy around her eyes. "Just be the Jonathan Prescott that everyone wants you to be. He's a very good man."

"But what if I were not that man, Gwen? What if I were a plumber from Indianapolis and the only thing you were the chairwoman of was the pie baking competition at the county fair? Wouldn't you still love me, and wouldn't we still be happy?"

"You really don't understand," she said, getting up and dropping her napkin on her chair. She walked away around the corner and up the stairs, leaving Jonathan sitting alone, the light of a single candle trying desperately to illuminate the space. Jonathan could hear the upstairs door open as the music from *The Lion King* briefly got louder, then was muffled again by the closing door. He really did not understand her sometimes.

Chapter 36

FRANK ELKHARDT LEANED CASUALLY against the worn wooden podium, glancing down at the typed pages neatly organized in the three-ring binder in front of him, but shielded from the view of the jury. The courtroom, on the fifth floor of the federal courts building in lower Manhattan, was mostly empty. The case was not high profile and had not drawn a gallery or press coverage. The only witnesses to the events were the judge, the jury, the court personnel, the parties, and one reporter from *The Wall Street Journal*. Janice had slipped into the courtroom during the direct examination of the regional director for Omni-Mart's northeastern stores. Frank had not noticed her. As she watched, she realized she had never seen him in action, even on the college debate team. She was trying to piece together the case based on the testimony as she listened.

"Mr. Cousineau, isn't it true that you oversee the company's training program for store managers?" Frank asked with no apparent emotion.

"Yes," came the monotone response from the witness stand. Peter Cousineau was not an imposing figure. He was slightly overweight, with slightly thinning, wispy hair. His square chin matched his square framed glasses. He wore a nondescript brown suit and an equally forgettable brown-and-orange striped tie. He was sweating lightly around his forehead.

Frank held out his left arm in the direction of the counsel table as he took a step in that direction, away from the podium. His assistant at the table was already holding out a spiral-bound bundle of papers with a bright yellow evidence tag affixed in its lower-left corner. Frank accepted the package and then walked in the direction of the witness stand. "Your Honor, may I approach the witness?"

"You may," came the somewhat bored response from the judge.

"Mr. Cousineau, I am handing you a document marked as Plaintiff's Exhibit 19. Can you tell me whether you recognize that document?"

"Yes."

"And is it, in fact, the training manual that was in use at your corporate management training facility in Norwich, Connecticut during the years 2005 through 2011?"

"Yes, it is." Cousineau flipped through the pages of the document as if scanning for some indication that the document was not what it purported to be, but after he was satisfied, he placed it on the ledge of the witness box in front of him.

Frank had returned to the podium, positioned so the jury could see him and also the witness. "Now, Mr. Cousineau, would you agree that during management training for store assistant managers, there is a significant emphasis on efficiency?"

"Yes, that's true. We try to maximize efficiency at all times," the manager proudly spouted the company's mantra for employees.

"Great," Frank quickly replied, "and isn't it also true that, in the name of efficiency, whenever there are more than three customers in a checkout line the assistant manager is supposed to direct the fourth customer to a checkout line that has fewer people?"

"Yes, that is the standard operating procedure."

"And isn't it also true, Mr. Cousineau," Frank pressed forward, "that if there is no checkout line with fewer customers, then the assistant manager is supposed to open a new register to keep the lines shorter than three customers? Isn't that the instruction to assistant managers?"

"Well, yes, that is the goal, to make sure customers don't wait in checkout lines too long. That is our customer service objective." Janice thought the manager was doing a good job of marketing the company to the jury, but was not sure where the questioning was going.

Frank again extended his arm and received another, somewhat smaller document from his assistant. This time, he merely nodded at the judge before approaching the witness and handing him the document. "Mr. Cousineau, this document is marked as Plaintiff's Exhibit 20. Let me again ask you if you recognize this document?"

This time, the witness puzzled over the document and carefully looked at the first few pages before flipping through the rest with a frown on his face. Frank stood by patiently, giving no appearance of being concerned by the delay. Finally, Cousineau said, "I'm not entirely sure whether I have seen this document before." He handed the document back to Frank, as if not wanting to keep touching it.

"Well, Mr. Cousineau, as the regional director, isn't it correct that you get monthly efficiency reports on all your stores from the home office?"

"Yes."

"And isn't it also true that one of the metrics reported by your in-house statistical team is the number of customers processed per minute by cashiers?"

"Yes."

"And when those statistics are reported, they include the total number of customers handled and with the amount of time that the cashier is logged into the register, right? In order to calculate customers per minute, you need to know the total number of customers and also the total number of minutes, right?"

"Right."

"And if you look at the cover page of that report, Mr. Cousineau, doesn't it say that the report is the statistical efficiency report for the Bronx location for the first quarter of 2010?"

"It does say that."

"OK, Mr. Cousineau, then let's look at page seventy-two of this report." Frank flipped to a page marked with a sticky note and handed the open report back to the witness. "Right there, on page seventy-two, is the statistical information for the first quarter of 2010 for all the cashiers who worked in the Bronx plant, isn't that right?"

"Well, there are names and numbers on the page here, but I can't say for sure whether this is accurate information for that location for that time period." Cousineau again glanced in the direction of his lawyers, looking worried. Janice noticed the lawyer giving him a hand signal that seemed to say, "Stay calm."

Frank kept up the pace of questions. He meticulously walked his witness through additional reports showing that all the assistant managers worked more than ten thousand minutes per quarter staffing the registers.

When the judge called for a lunch break, Frank spent two minutes consulting with the young associate who was assisting with the trial, then walked to the back of the courtroom to greet Janice.

"What was all that about the minutes?" She asked before Frank said anything.

"Well," Frank responded, "if you assume a 40-hour work week, and an assistant manager is spending 11,000 minutes working the register, that's about forty percent of their time – or about thirty percent if you figure they really work 50-60 hours per week. When you combine that with the time they spend stocking shelves and assisting customers and even sweeping floors, we will be arguing that their primary duties in the store are really not management – so they should be receiving overtime."

Janice shook her head. "How much money is at stake?"

"For the entire class of assistant managers in the northeast region, it's in the neighborhood of one hundred million dollars, before liquidated damages and attorneys' fees," Frank rattled off the numbers without any apparent excitement.

Janice whistled softly, which echoed in the empty courtroom. "Well, that will pay a few bills, won't it?"

Frank lowered his chin and blushed slightly. "It's a lot of people, Janice. Each one will receive only a fraction of that, and I expect even if we win the trial, the company will appeal and we'll end up settling for something less. But yes, it's a lot of money that's at stake."

Janice gathered up her things and they walked down the stairs to the ground floor and out into the mid-day heat of Manhattan. They walked north into Chinatown, then east, winding through narrow streets choked with merchandise from the sidewalk vendors until they reached Doyers Street. They sat in a dingy booth at the Nam Wah Tea Parlor, ordered a variety of Chinese dumplings and rice balls, and talked.

"Working on anything confidential that you want to tell me about, Jan?" Frank ribbed his old friend.

"Just the fate of the world hanging on my golden pen, as always." Janice suppressed a smile as she tried to deadpan her reply. "Truth is that I'm working on several things, Frank, but that's not why I wanted to meet with you."

"I kinda figured you were not hoping to do an expose on Omni-Mart and its systematic exploitation of its assistant store managers. So, what's the story, morning glory?"

Janice smiled again, then tried to reclaim her game face. "I'm thinking about leaving *The Journal*."

Frank perked up just as their waiter brought the first three plates of dim sum, arranged on china dishes with different colored flowers depending on the price. At the end of the meal, the waiter would add up the value of the empty plates to determine the amount of the check. As he deftly secured a steamed pork bun with his chopsticks, he asked, "Writer's remorse?"

"No. Well, maybe a little," Janice conceded, scooping up a sticky rice ball. "I mean, I'm not sorry I wrote the story. I guess I was expecting it to have more impact. Like always, it just rolled off Jon like water off a duck and now it's forgotten. It didn't really generate the kind of discussion about the issues I had hoped."

Frank pursed his lips while he finished chewing. "Jan, first of all I think you underestimate the damage to Jon – and Gwen. It may not come out publicly much, but behind the scenes there was impact."

"Have you spoken to Gwen?"

"Yes. I can't really say anything about that, but let's just say there was a personal toll."

Janice lowered her eyes and pushed the remnants of her sticky rice ball around her plate. "And do you think the article advanced the national discussion about abortion?"

"I think you exposed the duplicity of some conservatives, who are willing to say one thing publicly about their view of how other people should act, while acting contrary to their stated high moral values when their own ass is on the line. That hits not only Jon, who may not have been all that vociferous on the abortion subject anyway – if you noticed – but also by association other conservatives. It plants some doubt. You accomplished that." Frank looked across the table impassively.

"Is that enough?" Janice said pleadingly, seeking Frank's affirmation.

"I don't know, Jan. Only you can decide. It's your conscience that feels guilty."

Janice pouted, then reached for her cup of tea and took a sip. "I feel so – I mean, it's such an important issue and I feel like I want to do more, like I want to be more of an advocate and a strong voice – but in my job I have to be objective and I can't be editorializing and writing slanted pieces."

"Have you thought about writing a book, or ghost writing some articles?"

"I'm not allowed to publish anything under a different name, so that's out. I could take a book leave and try to write the definitive book about the abortion issue in American politics. Did you know they changed the Bible?"

"What?" Frank asked. "What do you mean?"

"I mean the conservative anti-abortion lobby had the book publishers change the words in the Bible to take out the passage that supports abortion rights and replaced it with the opposite meaning. You didn't know?"

Frank looked puzzled. "You mean Exodus twenty-one? How can you change the Bible? What? How?"

Janice smiled to herself that she was more in the know on the subject than Frank. "It's not well-publicized, but between 1977 and 1995, after the *Roe v. Wade* decision and the rise of the religious fervor over abortion rights, many of the English-language book publishers who were putting out editions of the Bible changed the words of the verse in Exodus. Instead of saying that a man is to be fined if he causes a miscarriage, they changed it to say that if a man strikes a pregnant woman and causes her to have a "premature delivery," then he is to be fined, but if there is harm done to the baby, then the punishment is an eye-for-an-eye et cetera. It totally changed the meaning and gave the anti-abortion advocates some Biblical support when there had been just the opposite."

"How did they think they could get away with that?" Frank asked incredulously.

"Well, it seems they did, because nobody noticed – not even you, Frank. Nobody actually reads the Bible, unless they're fishing around for something to support whatever political position they're taking. That could be a whole chapter in the history of abortion in America. Do you think it would sell?" Janice looked up expectantly, but Frank was not giving anything away, as usual.

"I'm not a publisher, Jan. It's not a terrible idea. Could you take that kind of a leave?"

"Yes, I would be allowed to take a book leave for up to a year, but any chance of getting the Washington Bureau Chief job would go out the window – not that it seems likely anymore anyway."

Frank now looked puzzled. "I thought they were grooming you for that job. What happened?"

Janice choked out a rueful laugh. "Well, it turns out that if politicians are unwilling to talk to you, your chances of success as a journalist in that city are somewhat diminished."

"Oh," Frank nodded. "I guess that was not something you thought about before you published, huh?"

"I thought about it, but I hadn't been in Washington very long. I didn't know the Democrats would be just as afraid of me as the Republicans. Sometimes it turns out they *can* have bipartisan consensus."

Frank chuckled sincerely. "You see, you have accomplished something nobody thought was possible. Unintended consequences."

"Sure, there are always unintended consequences," Janice mumbled, half to herself. "So, do you think the book idea might work?"

"I think it is a plausible idea, Jan. If I were you, I would find an editor at a legitimate publishing house and explore the concept to see whether it has legs. Give it a shot and see where it leads. If you feel passionately about it, then go with that."

Janice smiled. "I haven't really felt passionately about anything since the Hawkins story died."

"Well, get back to that feeling, however you can." Frank encouraged, pointing his chopsticks vigorously in her direction. "Is that what you came down here to ask me – whether I thought you should leave *The Journal* and write a book?"

"I'm not sure. Maybe. Maybe I just needed to see a supporting face for a change."

Frank put down his chopsticks and reached out his hand, putting it on top of hers on the checkered plastic tablecloth. She made no effort to pull away, but also didn't make any move to hold his hand back. "I'll always be there for you, Jan. You know that. Any time." Frank withdrew his hand, and broke out into song.

"You just call out my name, and you know, wherever I am, I'll come running – to see you again. Winter spring summer or fall – all you have to do is call and I'll be there, yes I will."

Frank paused, looking across the table at Janice's smiling face. He held out his hands, palms up, entreating her to join in the final line. She reached out and took his left hand in her right as they finished together, *"You've got a friend."* Frank embellished the final note, drawing stares from the other diners. He and Janice then broke out in loud laughter, still clasping hands.

They finished their dim sum. Frank paid the bill in cash and headed back toward the courthouse, dropping Janice off at the subway entrance. When they parted, Janice hung on to

Frank's hand as he pulled away, as if not wanting to let him go. Then she finally released him and waved as she descended the stairs.

Chapter 37

ON MONDAY, JONATHAN VISITED the office of McKenzie "Mack" Jackson, the senior senator from Michigan and the Minority Leader for the Democrats in the senate. The visit was unannounced and not on Mack's calendar, but Jonathan had collected intelligence through the secretarial network and established that Mack had no appointments between 11:15 and 12:30. Jonathan arrived at 11:20. "Tell him it's important," he instructed Jackson's personal secretary.

Two minutes later he was sitting on a blue sofa, sipping a cup of Earl Grey and admiring the original oil painting of a bald eagle on the wall of Jackson's office. Jackson was in his fourth term and was settled into the position of wielding power within the Senate without having any aspirations for higher office. He had hair as white as a winter rabbit and lines around his eyes suggesting a perpetual smile. He was everyone's grandfather, but Jonathan also knew he was a shrewd politician and would carefully guard his turf.

"Word is," Jonathan began in a guarded voice, "Spellman will vote for confirmation when the chips go down, but that still leaves you one short. Am I right, Mack?"

"Now, Jonathan, you and I both know you can't always believe every rumor you hear. I think you may be surprised who supports this effort when the cameras come on."

"You may be right, of course," Jonathan parried, "but my sources say they are pretty certain you don't have anyone else. The other fifty-one votes will sink the nomination." Jackson stared blankly, keeping his poker face. Jonathan wasn't telling him anything he didn't already know. "I want you to yield me fifteen minutes of floor time on Wednesday before the vote."

Jonathan's request came out of nowhere and clearly caught Jackson by surprise. Jackson, as the minority leader, controlled two hours of floor time leading up to the vote. It was formally listed as "debate" on the nomination, but true floor debate was long since a thing of the past in the Senate. The time was allocated to speakers who would make prepared statements for the C-SPAN cameras. The speeches seldom changed anyone's vote, but made for good sound bites. Real discussion about the merits of a bill, or a nomination, were reserved for subcommittees and lunch meetings.

"Why don't you ask Harry?" Mack asked. Harry Reid, the Republican majority leader, controlled the other two hours of floor time leading up to the vote. "I'm sure he would cut you some time."

"I don't want to give Harry an advance copy of the text, Mack. And I don't want to lie to him." Jonathan fixed *his* poker face at the more senior senator, not betraying any emotion.

Jackson sat forward in his chair, sensing an opportunity being handed to him, but still cautious. "I don't suppose you're going to give me an advance text either, eh?" He raised an eyebrow, hoping to get a response from Jonathan.

"No, Mack. I can't give you an advance copy because, to tell you the truth, it's not written yet."

"But you wouldn't be asking me if you were going to vote with the party, right?" Jackson gave Jonathan an opening to crack, but he held his blank expression.

"Mack, when I get back to my office, I expect to hear through the grapevine that I had a meeting with you to talk about the vote on next week's Education Bill. If I hear anything else, or if any rumor leaks that I might be wavering on Menendez, then forget the whole thing. I'll say only that I'm considering my position here, but I'll take a lot of heat for it if I move. I'll tell you now, though, if you yield me the time and I decide I'm still voting against, I'll decline the time and I won't embarrass you."

Jackson sat back and scratched his chin, thinking of what angles Jonathan might be playing. "Is this straight up?"

"Straight up," Jonathan replied without smiling.

"OK, then. The last slot before the vote is my time, but who in hell is going to listen to me who hasn't already? But I don't want to even call you unless it's a go. You leave a message with my secretary from Mister Wade if you want the time."

Jonathan smiled at Mack's quick wit in referencing the seminal Supreme Court decision the Republican party hoped one day to have the Court overturn. "Fair enough, Mack." Jonathan put down his tea cup and stood to leave.

The men shook hands and Jackson said, "I served with your father, Jonathan. I know him pretty well. Is this something you've discussed with him?"

Jonathan hesitated, grasping the older man's hand. "I'm not my father," he replied simply, disengaging his handshake and turning to leave.

Tuesday night, Jonathan donned his raincoat at nine-thirty and announced he was going for a walk to clear his head. He headed briskly down the street and entered a Starbucks, where he ordered a venti skinny vanilla decaf latte and settled into a small table in the corner. He reached into his inner pocket, extracted six typed pages of text, and set to work reading and editing with a ballpoint pen. He thought about his father and his mother, whom he knew would survive anything he did in his life because they were so solid together in their own world.

He had always done what his father wanted of him. His father was a wise man. His father, and Max Foster, could make him president someday if he continued to play the role of obedient offspring. He thought about Gwen and the girls. Gwen's whole life was geared toward being a politician's spouse and strolling in the light cast by his star. The brighter his light, the happier her life. Was it fair to her to dim himself? And the girls – did he owe them the same life he was given by his parents? Should he take that away from them? Would he, or would their lives be better down a different path?

He thought about himself. He had always taken the easy road. His stomach knotted and his hand shook as he underlined a word in the draft of his speech, creating a wavering line like a wave on an ocean drawn by a second-grader. He took a mental count of everyone he knew and what they would tell him to do if they were assembled in the Starbucks at that moment. He mentally sorted them – the right side of the house telling him not to throw away his career and all he and his family had worked for; the left side of the house telling him that he could only truly live with himself by following his heart and doing what he believed was right, no matter what his father or his political advisers told him to do.

In his mental opinion poll, the right side of the house was crowded with familiar faces. On the left were only a few. He had never been a lone wolf. People always told him he was a leader, but he had always waited to follow the crowd, and only when somebody else was telling him where to go.

Jonathan finished his editing and tossed his empty cup, stuffing the papers back into his breast pocket, folded down the middle. The walk back up the hill toward home was slow.

It had started to drizzle. He looked out toward the Capitol, which was obscured by trees. He could see the top of the Washington monument, brightly lit with mist hovering around its pinnacle. George Washington. Would Washington follow the directives of his political handlers? Would Hamilton? Would Jefferson? He tried to remember all the names of the signers of the Declaration of Independence – an exercise he remembered from high school. He couldn't recall them all. There was no Prescott.

If he had been there, in Philadelphia in 1776, with a conviction for treason and certain hanging awaiting him unless the rebels could somehow defeat the much larger and better armed British army, would he have signed? Did he have that kind of courage?

Later, when he turned out the light and rolled over in bed, he put his arms gently around his wife, snuggling up against her and feeling her round bottom pressing against his groin. He kissed her bare shoulder lightly and said, "I love you, Gwen. I will always love you."

She squirmed herself backwards, against his body, and murmured, "I love you, too, Honey." She rolled toward him and they made love, gently and slowly. Afterwards, she lay in the crook of his arm, her head on his chest and his arm under her neck. "That was nice," she purred. "We haven't done that enough lately."

"I know, and I'm sorry, Sweetheart. I want you to know that no matter what happens in our lives, I'll always be there for you."

"What's going to happen?" she said with alarm in her voice, propping herself up on one elbow. "Is something the matter?"

"No, Dear," he replied, pressing her back down onto his chest. "Nothing is wrong. In fact, I think things are going to be much better."

"I hope so," Gwen said sleepily, snuggling closer to him.

"So do I," he said, allowing himself to slip off to sleep, still holding her and feeling the warmth of her body against his.

Chapter 38

March, 1991

AT THE TAIL END OF WINTER IN 1991, Jonathan Prescott III received in the mail of his dormitory a fat envelope bearing a King's Crown in blue ink next to the return address of the Columbia Law School. It wasn't that anyone ever doubted Jonathan would be admitted to Columbia Law, but still the concrete reality of the acceptance letter was cause for a celebration. Frank, Gwen, and Janice all toasted Jonathan's accomplishment with beers at The West End, and gently ribbed their friend with comments about how he'd probably never practice law a day in his life. He was bound to end up in politics, like his father. Jonathan protested, but without much enthusiasm.

"Did you hear from Columbia Law?" Janice asked Frank, assuming that the answer was no, or he would have already said something.

"Actually, I did. I was not admitted – not that I really thought I would be, considering my grades and LSAT score."

"What do you mean?" Janice protested. "Your grades are great, and you tested well – just about the same as Jonathan, as I recall."

"Yes, well, not quite as well as Jon. Considering my inherent disadvantage – in that my father is not a U.S. senator – that difference is somewhat magnified. But it's fine. I'm not hugely disappointed. I'm admitted at GW and BU and I'm still waiting to hear from NYU, so I'll be fine."

Janice and Gwen exchanged a glance in which both silently pleaded with the other to change the subject. Gwen jumped in to rescue the situation. "You are probably lucky to be getting out of this city for a while, Frank. I just adore Boston, and I've always loved visiting Washington. Wouldn't it be ironic if you went to George Washington Law and ended up in politics while Jon here stayed in New York and ended up slaving away in a big sweat-shop law firm for years and years?"

"Ha!" Frank burst out laughing. "Right. I don't think so. I haven't got the slightest interest in politics – well, I mean, not the slightest interest in being a politician. That's not who I am."

"So, who are you, Counselor?" Jonathan was also happy to move the conversation in a new direction.

Frank took a long sip of his beer before answering. "I suppose on some level, my view of being a lawyer is not much different from my view of being a good politician. If we are fortunate to be put into a position where we have the ability to shape the world, through the making of laws or the enforcement of them, and to make the world a better place, then we should be happy and seize that opportunity. We are the Philosopher Kings Plato theorized – we control the fate of the world. We can change the world. That's what I intend to do – change the world." Frank sat back, satisfied with his little speech, and nodded at Jonathan as if to yield the floor to him.

"Well, it's good to see that you're humble," Jonathan joked, eliciting a chuckle from the other three. "I certainly agree that we have an awesome responsibility to the world. Not just me, and you, but all of us who are fortunate enough to be in positions of power and authority – even if none of us have reached that level quite yet."

"But you will, certainly," Gwen beamed.

"Well, let's say I have high hopes, just like Frank. I think the world will be a better place in the future and I certainly hope to contribute to making it so."

"Wow – alert the media – I believe Jonathan Prescott the Third just said something almost modest about his future!" Frank called out to the mostly student population of The West End. "Ladies and Gentlemen, gather 'round and take note that this man right here," and he stood and pointed down at Jonathan's head, "will probably be the President of the United States someday, and yet he is humble and only wants to make the world a better place." Frank raised his beer glass and looked around for a spontaneous burst of applause, but instead found nobody in the bar paying him the slightest attention.

"What a guy," Janice quipped. "I hope the two of you are very happy together."

"I think I would prefer just Jon and me," Gwen said, trying to keep a straight face.

Frank leaned toward Jonathan and asked, "Jon, why should we believe you would ever take a position as a politician that isn't exactly what your father wants you to take?"

"You don't think I can think for myself? That I can't independently determine what is the right choice on issues of political significance?"

"No," Frank and Janice said simultaneously, both shaking their heads, then bursting out in a joint giggle.

"I am offended," Jonathan said mockingly. "I think I have shown you over the past four years that I am not just my father's clone. I have a mind of my own. I am not as conservative as you think I am."

"That's a pretty low bar," Janice offered.

"Seriously, though, Jon, do you really think you're going to be an agent for change? Do you see yourself in Congress someday sponsoring a bill to preserve the environment, or aid hungry children in Africa?" Frank was playing, but was also half serious.

Jonathan got a little defensive in reply. "Mr. Elkhardt, what you fail to realize is that changing the world and making it a better place includes ensuring we have a strong economy, which will drive growth in food production and exports to aid the citizens of the rest of the world. It includes ensuring that citizens are free to innovate and build wealth without excessive taxation, and that everyone is able to reach their own dreams. I also would expect to balance the value of preserving the natural beauty of the Earth, but without excessive government regulation."

"Spoken like a true Republican," Janice chimed in. "Change the world as long as the change supports the status quo and protects the currently wealthy and powerful."

"Hey, who do you think contributes money to all your liberal causes if not those who have wealth and power?"

Frank then jumped back into the discussion. "The problem, my friend, is that while some of those currently in power and those who have wealth in the world do good with their money, too often the rich get richer while the poor get poorer and the gap widens all the time. We have an obligation to close that gap and to help those who have less find ways to get more. Wouldn't you agree, Senator Prescott?"

"Give me a specific example, Mr. Chief Justice Elkhardt," Jonathan returned the serve, buying time.

"OK, Senator. Let's talk minimum wage. Wouldn't you agree that the current federal minimum wage is insufficient to allow workers at that level to build any actual wealth, while the owners of businesses who pay the minimum wage reap the benefits of low-wage workers – in a way exploiting their labor for the owner's benefit? And couldn't the government rebalance the distribution of wealth in a minor way by increasing the minimum wage in order to more fairly compensate the working class for their contribution to the wealth they create for the owners?"

Jonathan leaned into the table and smiled. "My esteemed colleague, you have posited a simplistic formula that excludes many important economic factors, including the tendency of business owners to either reduce staff when facing higher labor costs, or to raise prices to the consumers in response, which in turn drives up inflation and reduces the buying power of the poorer classes. An increase in the minimum wage often causes increased unemployment and lower buying power, which actually harms the poor rather than helping them. It is important to factor all this into any attempt to legislate wages or the redistribution of wealth and to understand that allowing the free market to function naturally, without excessive government regulation, is the best solution in the long run."

"But, as Keynes said, in the long run, we're all dead," Janice deadpanned.

The four all laughed and the girls declared the debate a draw so they could avoid a series of rebuttals. "Let's just leave it at this," Gwen offered. "Frank is going to change the world, and Jon is going to preserve that which is good and proper, leaving the change to necessarily involve only that which is bad and needs to change." The four all toasted to that and Jonathan waved to their waitress for another round. He was in a good mood and nothing was going to alter it.

"Seriously, Frank," Jonathan said, "are you telling me that if I offered you a great job after you graduate law school with a six-figure salary and a nice apartment and a quick route toward paying off your student loans, but you have to work for a law firm that represents big corporations against lawsuits from disgruntled workers and activist environmentalists – you'd turn it down?"

Frank looked gravely at his former roommate. "Yes, Jon. I would. I have a vision for what I want to do with my life, and being a corporate lawyer is not what I have in mind."

"Seriously?"

"Seriously, Dude. That's my future. If I get to be a lawyer for Greenpeace, or the Sierra Club, I would be very happy."

"And very poor," Jonathan said matter-of-factly. "I think you'll change your mind.

"What do you want to bet?" Frank asked.

"A million dollars."

"Will you take an IOU?"

Jonathan laughed again as he took a pen out of his pocket, grabbed a napkin off the table and started scribbling. He held out the slightly damp paper to Frank, bearing the words, "I O U one million dollars ($1,000,000.00) – Frank Elkhardt, professional do-gooder." Frank studied the napkin, then took the pen from Jonathan and added to the document, "To be paid upon selling out to the Man." He then signed the napkin and handed it back to Jonathan, proudly.

"What do I get if I win the bet?" Frank asked.

"I promise to appoint you to the Supreme Court, if I am ever elected president."

"You'll put that in writing?"

"Not necessary." Jonathan stuck out his hand toward Frank. "I'm a man of my word, and you have two witnesses." Frank laughed and firmly grasped Jonathan's hand, then gave it one firm shake.

"Fine," Janice announced. "I'm the arbiter of disputes. I'll check in with both of you in thirty years and see who wins the bet."

"I'll drink to that," Jonathan grinned, raising his glass again. They drank, and laughed, and talked about their plans and dreams for the future. It was almost spring, and they were only a few months away from graduation.

When Jonathan got back to his dorm he undressed, removing his wallet and key from his pants pocket, along with a crumpled napkin, which he tossed into the trash.

Chapter 39

ON WEDNESDAY AFTERNOON, Harry Reid pounded his gavel against the wooden lectern and asked for order for the ninth or tenth time in the last hour. The floor debates over the nomination of Ricardo Menendez had been winding down and tempers were short. Two senators had exchanged words on the floor that would get them censured later and would provide fodder for late-night talk shows for weeks to come. There were twenty minutes left before the formal end of debate – actually ahead of the planned schedule because one of the Democrats who had planned to speak cancelled at the last minute. He had assured Mack Jackson that his voice was gone from the prior night's arguments over a different bill and that his silence did not suggest any change in position.

Reid called on Mack Jackson to announce how he intended to allocate his remaining time. Jackson stood at his podium, looking around at the deep colors of the carpeting and the rich wood of the Senate chamber. In his hand was a pink message slip, handed to him by an aide fifteen minutes earlier. It was a message from a Mr. Wade regarding "principle trumps partisanship." He smiled and glanced toward Jonathan's seat. It was empty. He looked to the side of the chamber and saw

Jonathan there, a few steps away from the lectern used by floor speakers, holding a leather folio.

Jackson once again banged his gavel and shouted into the microphone. "The chair yields twenty minutes to the junior senator from Connecticut." The buzz around the room stopped suddenly, replaced by a murmur of confusion. Had Jackson said *junior* senator? Before anyone could raise the volume level, Jonathan strode to the podium, placed his folio on it, and began speaking, looking directly into the C-SPAN camera.

"The vote currently under consideration is about power, and the exercise of power in a way contrary to the Constitution. The elected President has the power and the obligation to fill vacancies on the Supreme Court. That power is subject to the advice and consent of the senate. If we exercise the consent power to reject a jurist who is as highly qualified as Ricky Menendez, what is our rationale? What is our explanation to constituents who ask us?

"I have known Judge Menendez for many years and I have followed his career and his decisions. I know he is a man of integrity, and a jurist who applies the law consistently and logically. He is a careful writer, and explains his decisions in simple terms that anyone can understand. When evolution in the law is needed in response to unique facts, he understands that such change should be slow and incremental. He is a superior intellect and an exemplary human being. And still, I have been told he must be stopped. Why?

"My party has given me its collective justification – presented by consultants who seem to control our actions and our positions. They say that, if elevated to the Supreme Court, Judge Menendez would be more likely to side with environmentalists against the interests of businesses. They say he would be likely to side with individual rights against government regulation. He would side with the rights of workers and those unfairly discriminated against rather than with employers. He would side with women who want to choose whether to bear children and would not reverse the now-venerable precedent of *Roe. v. Wade* that has set the constitutional standard for more than forty years.

"These are his sins, according to the Republican party. I am told that if I am to remain a good Republican, I must vote against his nomination. But this is the insidious disease to which our politics have succumbed. We have stripped our leaders of their right to independent thought – our right to dissent and question and challenge. We have allowed the party and those behind-the-scenes who raise the money that is now so essential to our ambitions of power to make all the decisions. We are but lambs who must vote as we are told, lest we be branded a heretic and retaliated against. I am told my support for the wisdom of the party cannot waver. That is not leadership; it is servitude.

"If we are to lead this diverse nation into a prosperous future, we must think for ourselves. We must have our own ideas. Mine may be different from yours on some issues, but we must embrace those differences and use them to forge better policies and better laws, rather than steamroll over each other based on sheer power when we have it, only to watch those one-sided views reversed the next time the other party wins a majority in some future election. This is no way to run a country as great as the United States. I am here today to denounce that system and to urge all of you to denounce it with me.

"But if I am not to parrot the positions and talking points given to me by my party leaders, then what will I say? What do I believe, independently from my briefing books and my press notes? What is my vision for this country, and my state, and myself? To whom will I listen when I am unsure which path to travel on a particular issue?

"In my life I have been influenced by many people. To a great extent I am the amalgamation of all the people who have shaped me and taught me and pointed me in the direction my life has taken. The most significant of those influences has been my father. My father is a great man, who has done great things. Since I was old enough to understand his words, my father has been telling me I am a Prescott. 'You are a Prescott,' he would say, 'you have a responsibility to uphold the family name and tradition.' 'You are a Prescott, act like one.' I love my father, and my mother, and I have a deep appreciation for how fortunate I am to be their son.

"But what does it mean, that I am a Prescott? Does it mean that as a right of birth I have greater potential than other men? Does it mean I have a greater capacity to learn, a greater understanding of the world around me, or a superior ability to make decisions? No. It means none of that. We all come into the world as a lump of clay, ready to be molded, or as sponge, ready to soak up the world around us. Certainly our genes, passed down from our parents, determine important characteristics of our physical selves. They may carry diseases from which we cannot escape, or physical deformities we must overcome. They may inflict upon us a learning disability that inhibits us, or infuse us with genius to be cultivated. But ultimately those issues do not define us, any more than we are defined by our skin color, or our place of birth.

"What I understand now, more clearly than I have ever understood anything, is that I am not defined by who my parents are, but by what kind of man I make myself. To be a Prescott means I have been given a unique opportunity in the world – an opportunity to act in a way that makes me proud of who I am, and allows my children to be proud of me. I want their lives to be positively influenced by what they see me do with my life. It is not enough for me to provide them with comfort and material possessions; I must be for them an example of the kind of person they should aspire to become.

"And to be that person, I can no longer exclusively listen to the many people who have for years told me what my obligations are. I have been told by leaders of faith that I must follow a particular course, to be consistent with Divine will. But there seem to be as many different interpretations of Divine will as there are leaders of faith. With so many people listening to God, it's amazing that the messages they hear are so different from one another. I cannot be defined by them, nor led by them. Those who claim to speak for God, yet speak for their own agenda, shall no doubt have a special place in Hell. While religion can provide inspiration, and comfort, and hope, it cannot direct our lives, nor tell us which battles to fight or which side to be on.

"I have been told by leaders of industry that they understand what is best for the nation, and how serving their interests will also be in the interests of the greater good, to foster a healthy economy, and to provide the foundation for a strong nation and society. And they are right; but they can be narrow-minded in their focus on the accumulation of wealth, and on the perpetuation of their own status quo. There are other issues, including the effects their industries have on the environment, and on the people who toil day by day to generate the vast wealth of this country, which is controlled by so few. Things are never quite as simple as they would have me believe.

"I have been told by the spokespersons for many groups about how their causes are just and true and how important it is that I place a priority on their interests. I have been told by those who claim great power and privilege that they understand what is right and that I should follow a course supporting their interests. But there are so many interests, all perpetually in conflict.

"I have been told by my political advisors what is in my own best interest, as a senator and as a possible candidate for president someday. I have been counseled to follow the words of Polonius in *Hamlet* – 'To thine own self be true.' Except that those who repeat the line seldom remember its true meaning. I believe I must be true to myself – to the man I want to be. But if I have learned nothing else in the past few years, it is that a course designed to maximize my own personal best interest is seldom the proper path.

"I am left alone, pulled to the north and to the south by equal magnetic forces. The conclusion I reach is that I must make my own choice. The people of Connecticut elected me to exercise my judgment, and I intend to. So make no mistake; my decision is my own. It has not been purchased nor influenced. I am my own man. I am not controlled by those who fund my campaign, or by those who claim to be able to influence the outcome of my re-election.

"A man is not defined by the amount of wealth or power he accumulates, but by how he uses the wealth and power he has, whether large or small, when called upon to act. In every life, the time will come when you must decide – when you define who you are – and that time for me is now.

"In many prior generations, the events of the world thrust people into situations that tested their metal. Ordinary citizens were called to the service of their country in war, or thrust into crisis on home soil – whether civil war or the fight for civil rights. They knew their duty, and they bravely faced it. Many died in the effort. Many, I am certain, fled from their duty, but history seldom records their cowardice. These were ordinary citizens; Americans in every way. But in my generation, there have been no such crises. We have not been forced to confront ourselves and to decide what kind of men and women we are, or want to be. We have been left to find our own trials.

"I have faced some trials in my personal life over the years, and I wish I could say I faced them bravely and with honor. I am ashamed to say that more often than not, I acted with cowardice and selfish motivation. More times than I care to admit, I ran from responsibility for my actions. I was weak, and I allowed others to tell me how I should act rather than making my own decisions.

"History records the great works of men, and the great tragedies. History remembers those who took risks and succeeded, as well as those who brought pain and grief upon others for their own gain. How will history record us? How will future generations recall this year, this day, this moment? Will I be remembered as a senator who led by example and who followed through on his principles, or as an anonymous vote in support of the status quo, controlled by power brokers and chained to the history of his family?

"I choose my own path. I am not a self-made man. I did not overcome a childhood of poverty. I did not struggle. My family did not struggle to support me or to provide for an education and a world of opportunity for me. My life has not included hardship, pain, and disappointment – at least not by the measure of most Americans. I have had my own pain, and those who know me well may understand this, but by the standards of most Americans I have led a life of privilege and comfort.

"What do I know of the plight of the family that wonders where the next month's rent will come from? What empathy can I offer to the worker whose job is downsized or outsourced, or the single mother who labors to provide for her child with little regard for her personal well-being? Today, I tell you here I cannot. I cannot know. I cannot know the anguish of a young mother who gives up her child for adoption because she cannot provide for him, and the act of excruciating love that parts her from him. I cannot know the despair of the father who, when called upon to face his own test of character, runs from it, leaving his lover and child to fend for themselves. But I do understand that, but for the grace of God, I could have been in their shoes. I could have lived a life not knowing whether the end of the month would be the end of my days. Wondering not whether I would achieve honors scores on a literature test, but whether I would be shot in the streets on my way home from an inner-city school. It could have been me, but providence provided for me a different fate.

"What I know is we are all of the same cloth. Each one of us could have been born into wealth or poverty. Each one could have been nurtured or tortured. Each one of us shares the same basic fabric, and we each struggle to provide a better future for ourselves, our children, and our grandchildren.

"I can no longer turn a blind eye to the oppression of those whom I was taught to ignore. I was taught what is important in life is what is important to my family, and their friends, and their business associates. We – they – are the rulers of the status quo and seek to maintain it. I can no longer rationalize that existence. No matter what the price, I must look inside myself and see the man I can be, and see the world I know can still exist. I choose the more difficult path – the one leading me away from my supporters, my protectors, my family, and many of my friends.

"I have no brothers or sisters. I have many cousins – an extended family stretching across the country. Today, I choose to consider every American a cousin. Every White family, every Black family; every Hispanic and every Asian family; every immigrant to this land and every Native American. You are my family. I have a responsibility to you. We, together, have a responsibility to each other. From this moment forward, my focus will be on doing what I can to make the life of every one of my cousins better, so their children and grandchildren can live in a better world and in a better country.

"As a government, this is our true mission. This is what I choose to think is the will of Alexander Hamilton and Thomas Jefferson and George Washington. This is what I choose to believe is the will of God, in whatever form God may take. I choose to support the agenda of the wealthy and powerful only when it is consistent with the agenda of the weak and poor. I choose to define myself in those terms. I cannot save the world single-handedly, but I have been blessed with the opportunity to be in a position to make a difference, and I do not intend to waste it.

"But let there be no mistake about what I believe. I do not agree with the panderers of entitlement. Just as no person should think they are entitled to power, or wealth, or opportunity solely by virtue of the happenstance of their birth, neither do I believe that those who have the misfortune of being born into a situation of need should think they have a right to be supported by their neighbors or by the government without any personal responsibility. Everyone deserves an opportunity to succeed, but opportunity does not imply that this government, nor any private organization, should do for you what you should be doing for yourself.

"This is a country founded on hard work – on sweat and blood and tears. No one should believe they should be granted the privileges of citizenship without working for them, without fighting for them. Let no man tell me they deserve assistance from the government merely because they need it. The politics of need are as malformed and perilous as the politics of birthright and the perpetuation of power. Make no mistake.

"Those who are willing to work – those who are willing to put forth their effort and their toil and their whole self in order to scratch and claw their way upward toward their goal – these are the people who are true Americans. These are the people who deserve an assist, an opportunity, and the support of their government as they work toward bettering their lives and the lives of their children. We should put no unnecessary obstacles in their path, and should provide a level playing field so they can succeed as their merit dictates.

"Those looking to scam the system, or who are able-bodied and sound of mind, but who prefer a handout over a hard day's work – to them I offer nothing. You shall not receive benefits you have not earned. Your neighbors and your community will help you when you are in need only when you participate constructively in the community, and earn the right to receive aid.

"I think back to my college years, when I had the good fortune to become friends with a man named Frank Elkhardt. Frank was from a middle-class family. He worked his way through a college his family could not afford. Nobody gave him anything – he earned everything he got. I offered him money, but he refused to take a hand-out, even from a friend. He would tell me to find someone else who needed the money more. He is an example of a man I wish I was. Perhaps I still can be.

"My mission, my meaning, my definition is now clear to me. To my people – to all the people who struggle and who aspire and who climb rung by perilous rung the ladder of hope – to you I pledge my support and my loyalty. To my country, which I know can be a place where all people of any race or heritage can work together for the betterment of themselves and their community, to you I pledge my allegiance. To the hope, to the dream, to this future reality, I will dedicate myself. And to those who seek only to protect their own wealth at the expense of the opportunity of others, to you I say, beware the wrath of Jonathan Prescott.

"There is an education Bill on the horizon that seeks to extend financial assistance to worthy students who have worked hard and who have ambition and ability, but for whom higher education is beyond their financial reach. The Bill is flawed as written, but its intent is correct. I will work with my colleagues to revise the Bill, but despite my party's opposition, I will support it.

"Dr. Martin Luther King, Jr. once said, 'The ultimate measure of a man is not where he stands in moments of comfort and convenience, but where he stands at times of challenge and controversy.' We all must face the question of where we stand. For me, I am facing that point today.

"I will vote as one man – as the independent representative of the people of Connecticut. I will not seek affiliation with either current political party, for I believe both are corrupt and neither reflects the true American values of which I speak today. I am hereafter an Independent senator, and this Independent will vote 'yes' to confirm this nomination."

Chapter 40

AT 11:58 P.M., THE PRODUCTION ASSOCIATE on the live remote from CNN gave the "cut" signal. The red light faded to black. One technician shut down the blindingly hot set light as another started tearing down the blue drapes that had been the backdrop for the shoot in the vestibule of Senator Jonathan Prescott's office. Jonathan had been speaking via remote link to Wolf Blitzer in the studio, so there was no reporter on site. He unclipped the tiny microphone on his tie, popped his earpiece out like a veteran television anchor, detached himself from the cords, and walked unsteadily away from the improvised studio toward his inner office.

He mopped the sweat from his forehead with his handkerchief, then furrowed his brows as he puzzled over the brown stain in his hand until he remembered the make-up girl who had forced him to put on base and powder before the Nightline segment on ABC half an hour earlier. It was slightly less than ten hours since he had stepped away from the podium in the Senate chamber, to wild applause from the public gallery, a standing ovation from the Democratic side of the floor, and stunned silence mixed with glares of outrage from his Republican former colleagues.

Angelo Cruz, the organizer of the opposition to the Menendez nomination had grabbed his arm before he could get back to his chair and asked him what the fuck he thought he was doing. The lip readers watching C-SPAN and the writers on *The Daily Show* had a field day with that one. Jonathan had simply removed the Whip's hand and kept walking, picking up his battered maroon leather brief case and returned to his seat without saying another word.

Harry Reid attempted to postpone the vote so he could try to work on Howard Spellman, who was widely expected to vote with the Democrats because of pressure in his home state. He was up for re-election and trailing slightly in the polls. But the vote on the motion to table the confirmation vote was the same as the vote on the confirmation itself: 50-50, with the Democratic Vice-President casting the tie-breaking vote.

Since the speech, Jonathan had done three live television interviews for the national networks (only FOX eschewed a live feed), seven radio interviews by telephone, six telephone spots for local television stations in Washington, Hartford, and New York, one press conference for all the Capitol Hill correspondents from the major newspapers, one private interview for *The Wall Street Journal*, and now three live remotes for the late-night news shows and CNN's daily wrap-up.

C-SPAN had the whole speech on tape, and was busy distributing the clips to all who requested them. His staff had already distributed the transcript via email to everyone on his list of contributors and key constituents. Donna also put it up on Jonathan's private website, but within an hour the site had mysteriously gone dark. It was hosted on servers maintained by the Republican National Committee. Somebody at the RNC had apparently decided Senator Prescott's page needed some routine maintenance. Donna already had a request in to move the site to a different host server.

The message on Twitter went out when he was still speaking on the floor, followed by the link to the video on Facebook and Instagram. His staff had cut off commentary on the posts after an hour and forwarded several death threats to the FBI.

There were at least twenty telephone messages on his desk he would not get to that day. He didn't expect he would get to all the telephone messages tomorrow, either. His staff had drafted canned responses to all incoming emails: one for the positive, supporting emails, which asked for the sender to consider becoming a donor to the senator's new Independent re-election campaign; one for the angry Republicans who were pissed off at him, but who had never contributed to his campaign; and one very carefully drafted response to his friends and supporters who were likely to be his *former* supporters, if not also his former friends, who now considered him to be a lying, backstabbing, ungrateful dirt bag, or sometimes something worse.

Jonathan poured himself a small scotch, loosened his tie, and sat down wearily on his maroon leather sofa. It certainly had been a busy and eventful day. A day Jonathan would not soon forget. As he sat alone and exhausted, recalling some of the more colorful comments hurled at him by various right-wing spokespersons and analysts during the day, it occurred to him that he didn't feel bad about those insults. He actually felt pretty good about himself. He didn't have the empty feeling in his stomach he so often remembered having after television appearances or news conferences. He felt ... contented. He was glad he had stepped off the cliff. He hoped the worst of the fallout was over. That was perhaps the only act of self-delusion in which he engaged the whole day.

Then he thought about heading home and his stomach sank. He had called Gwen before heading for the Senate chamber. Since the speech, she had not answered her phone. He hoped she would understand, but wondered whether she would ever really get over the fact that he had not confided in her before taking such a huge step. He questioned whether he should have. It was too late for regrets. It was time to move forward.

Chapter 41

THURSDAY MORNING, the mood in Jonathan's office was somber. Donna was there, wearing an ultra-conservative two-piece grey suit with a knee-length skirt. Jonathan smiled to himself that Donna would pick this moment to dress like a conservative. Two of his aides, who were actually on the payroll of the RNC and not on his Senate payroll, were nowhere to be seen. When he reached his desk, there was a pile of additional messages. Jonathan sorted through them slowly, putting aside two. The first was from Mack Jackson, who wanted to meet with Jonathan if he had time that day. Jonathan could guess he would be asked to join the Democratic caucus as an Independent. The second was from Frank Elkhardt. His message was written out in Harriett's neat handwriting:

Who hath made man's mouth? Or who maketh a man dumb, or deaf, or seeing, or blind? Is it not I the Lord? Now therefore go, and I will be with thy mouth and teach thee what thou shalt speak.
—Exodus 4:11-12

Jonathan smiled. Leave it to Frank to find scripture to quote to a conservative politician who had stepped off the straight and narrow road. He asked Harriett to see if she could get Frank on the line. She buzzed back before Jonathan finished a first read through the remaining messages.

"Frank, you old rascal. Let me guess, you were actually watching C-SPAN live yesterday and want to tell me how good I looked on camera."

"Let's just say I saw the highlights – and you looked mahvelous," Frank laughed. "I just wanted to call to make sure you hadn't been fed to the lions yet."

"I believe that honor is scheduled for Monday at nine o'clock, live on FOX," Jonathan quipped back. "I may not have a staff left by then, but as far as I know I still get a vote on the floor."

"Well, old friend, you just let me know if you need a hand along the way. I can always take some time off."

"I appreciate that, Frank. I really do."

"I'm proud of you, Jon. You did what you thought was right for a change."

"Thanks," Jonathan choked out, feeling actually constricted with emotion at the comment. "I'll talk to you." He hung up the phone and sat down, swinging his chair around to look out the window. He wondered why, after so many years, he felt emotionally uplifted by Frank's praise when he had never – ever – felt that way when he received the same comments from his father, or Max, or any of his political mentors and supporters. He wondered how long the feeling might last.

As it turned out, the feeling lasted about ten hours. All day Thursday Jonathan received congratulations and accolades from politicians who had been some of his staunchest detractors. He gave a few more media interviews and he accepted Mack Jackson's invitation to caucus with the

Democrats, although he reserved his prerogative to continue to support conservative positions.

He shook hands with Tom Markey from Vermont, the lone Independent senator before Jonathan's bombshell. Markey caucused with the Democrats, but only because he had no other option, given his positions. He and Markey then visited the office of Howard Spellman of Washington. He was not willing to resign his party affiliation, although he was worried about being expelled from the Republican caucus – if he retained his seat.

Jonathan and Markey agreed to have a monthly lunch meeting and call it the Independent Caucus. Considering how split the senate was now – 50-48-2 – the two independents actually could wield considerable power if the partisan split was still razor thin after the upcoming election. For the moment, they could be deal-makers.

When he walked down the hallways of the Senate office building, all eyes turned to him and voices spoke in hushed whispers. He got death stares from his Republican former allies and nods from the Democrats.

When he returned to the townhouse, the euphoria of the day came to a crashing end. Gwen had left him a note, which she had printed out from the computer. *Not even the personalization of handwriting*, Jonathan thought wryly. It was not a lengthy diatribe or even a heartfelt explanation. Just a simple bit of information.

"I've taken the girls to stay with my mother. Please don't call."

Jonathan walked through the empty space, his footsteps echoing off the walls. He could recall few times when he was in the townhouse when it was empty. Sure, there had been middle-of-the-night roaming, with the children sleeping quietly, and there were a few times before when Gwen had taken the children away for a weekend, but those usually corresponded with times when he was traveling or otherwise working late and not at home anyway. Here he was, rummaging through the fridge looking for something to eat, but with no company.

He inspected their bedroom, finding that Gwen had taken two large suitcases and had cleared out half her closet along with at least ten pairs of shoes. He couldn't bring himself to do the same inspection of the girls' rooms, which he left closed. He thought about calling Donna to see if she was free for dinner, but thought better of it. He had come close to succumbing to Donna's charms once, and that had happened accidentally. He didn't plan for it. He really did love Gwen, and wished she were there to stand with him during this time of intense emotion and profound change in his life. He wasn't going to give up on her. He hoped she wouldn't give up on him.

He poured himself a glass of red wine and turned on Vivaldi's *Four Seasons* – his favorite piece of music, which normally calmed him down when he was tense. Tonight, it only made him sad to think he was reduced to listening to Vivaldi because his wife had left him. When he finished his wine, he went to bed and hoped for sleep, which didn't come.

By five o'clock, he was up and out jogging the empty streets, hoping that a little sweat would make him feel better. He felt physically good after his shower, but still had a knot in his stomach. He wanted to throw himself into his work, but wondered what his legislative agenda was going to be. He spent his day making lists and doing his own vote counts – looking for bills where the Independent Caucus could have some weight as the swing votes.

On Monday, he called the private school where the girls attended to report that they would not be in class, only to be told that Gwen had already called. He trudged into the office and asked Harriett to go over his schedule for the week. "I have a lunch speech on Wednesday in Baltimore. What do I have today and tomorrow?"

She gave him an odd look, licked her lipstick, and grabbed her calendar. "Actually, Boss, the Wednesday speech has been cancelled," Harriett began. "They called this morning. Said it was no longer appropriate for you to address the group."

Jonathan frowned, but then shrugged and said, "Oh, well, I hate giving those tired speeches anyway. No problem. I'm sure there will be plenty of others coming up."

"Well..." Harriett stammered, "since you mention it, Senator, you have received several calls asking for your availability, but I have not wanted to give them much encouragement."

"Really?"

"Well, Sir, these are not the kinds of groups you would want to be associated with. I mean, Gay Rights Alliance, Sierra Club, the ACLU, for crying out loud. It's not like I'm going to be making room on your schedule for that lot! But you are going to have some room, because you have had more than a few cancellations. It's like we're erasing everything and starting over from scratch."

"We are starting over, Harriett." Jonathan smiled at her, attempting to project an it-will-all-be-all-right demeanor. "This is a fresh beginning. It's a new page in a blank book."

"Sir, no disrespect intended, but I'm not sure I'm ready for all that." Harriett had been his personal secretary since he came to Washington as a congressman. He thought about it and realized that Max had recommended her. She had worked for a Republican senator from Nebraska for many years, but he had retired and his replacement brought his own staff to Washington. Harriett had been grateful for the position. Had Jonathan even interviewed her? Of course, but only after Max told him he would love her, which he did.

"Well, Harriett I certainly am not going to do anything to stand in your way if you want to look around for another position. I will give you only the highest possible recommendation."

"Thank you, Senator. I appreciate that. It's just – I know all the people on this side of the aisle. I think I'd be more useful for somebody else."

"When did Max call this morning?" Jonathan asked nonchalantly.

"Oh, it was very early, Sir, only a few minutes after I arrived at seven." Harriett stopped herself, making eye contact with Jonathan and then blushing and putting her head down.

"Don't worry. I still won't hold it against you. You owe your job to Max. I understand. You have more time with Max than with me."

"I'm sorry, Senator. He told me that if I stayed, I would never get a recommendation from him again, and he said you'd never be re-elected as an Independent and that I'd be done in two years unless I move now. I feel just awful."

Jonathan smiled at her and put a hand on her shoulder, an act of unusual personal contact between them. "Like I said, I understand. But can you give me two weeks' notice and help me find a replacement?"

She brightened. "Yes, Sir. That's the least I can do. Thank you." She spun on one heel and headed back to her desk. By noon Jonathan had three resumes on his desk for personal secretaries who came highly recommended by the staff grapevine. All had worked for congressmen who had lost their seats in the last election. All those congressmen were Democrats.

Donna said she would vet the candidates.

"Will you still be here in a month?"

"Boss, I'll be here for you as long as you have an office."

Chapter 42

THE LOBBY OF THE HYATT HOTEL in Memphis was a sleepy place at eleven-thirty in the morning on a Thursday in August. This meeting was outside of the normally scheduled quarterly sequence and had been arranged hastily, leaving Max's security team little opportunity to scope out the venue Abraham Hawkins had suggested to coincide with his rather cramped speaking schedule. Max had lobbied for a meeting in New York, but Hawkins couldn't make it, and the two had long since agreed they would never hold meetings by telephone.

Max arrived first and took a seat in an overstuffed chair in a corner next to a large potted palm tree. There was a sufficient amount of background noise to mask any conversation, and Max's advance crew had moved away all other seats in the general vicinity except for the one other chair arranged opposite Max's perch. The big man checked his watch and pulled out his phone to check whether there were any urgent messages.

Max had reviewed only four emails before he heard the whistle from Earl, signaling the arrival of the reverend. Hawkins loped over to where Max was sitting and plopped himself down into the facing chair. "No drinks?" He drawled indignantly.

"Not today, Rev. Too early for me, and this is a quick meeting. No organizational report."

Hawkins pursed his lips and nodded, glancing around the nearly empty lobby. "Alright, so why the emergency meeting?"

"I assume you heard about the rather unexpected change of colors by Senator Jonathan Prescott?"

Hawkins took his time before nodding his understanding. "Uh, huh. I believe I did catch that news report."

"Well." Max sat forward in his chair in order to be able to use a lower volume. "You remember, I'm sure, that Senator Prescott was the man I asked you to start talking up a bit, to give him some positive references, because I was anticipating a presidential run from him. Now, of course, those plans are no longer in play, so you can back off on support for the now-independent senator."

Hawkins looked impassively at the man who was his benefactor and colleague. "You don't think the man might eventually come back around? No chance of a reconciliation?"

Max smiled ruefully and shook his head. "No, I'm afraid this lamb has left the flock permanently. I don't see any chance of him returning to the fold."

"Now, that is just too bad," Hawkins lamented. "I was thinking maybe I could still manage a little influence with the boy. He'll need some help now, especially. Maybe if I were to lend him a hand, he might eventually understand he has chosen a particularly difficult path and I might be able to help direct him toward the proper light. And who knows, maybe an independent candidate can be president someday – somebody who can be a bridge between the polarized national parties?"

Max worked hard to prevent his face from showing his annoyance with the reverend's reticence. This was supposed to be a quick meeting. "Abe, this is not the time to speculate.

I'm going to be working on a new candidate for this Senate seat, and keeping it red will be a huge priority. We need to be on the same page here, and that means giving no quarter to traitors."

Hawkins smiled and bowed his head slightly, acknowledging the point. "I understand, Max. I understand. I'm just looking at the long term here."

"You should be thinking about the short term, since in the long term you're not likely to be around to see what happens." Max chuckled as he said this, but in his eyes Reverend Hawkins saw that he was quite serious.

"Well, now," Hawkins drawled, stalling for time while he considered his next response, "you let me know who your next man is. The last man, you told me, had a chance to be the President of the United States someday and we would both have a piece of that action. As sorry as I am that your prediction turned out to be somewhat inaccurate, I'm even more sorry you also told me that our lost sheep was the best horse in your stable, which doesn't give me a lot of hope that the last-minute stand-in is going to be a good bet. So I will wait for you to give me the information, but I'm also going to keep all my options open, just in case." Hawkins sat back in his chair, satisfied that he had parried the fat man's attack and made a thrust of his own.

Max pursed his lips, but held his tongue. No point in creating a scene and alienating the reverend before he even had a plan in place. "Abe, you are a shrewd customer, and I admire the fact that you always have your eyes on your own selfish interests. It's the sign of a good politician and a good businessman."

"Well, I can honestly say, Max, that I have a much greater focus in that area after years of working with you than I ever had before, so I have you to thank."

Max smiled genuinely. "Well, please keep in mind that in order to continue the program of study, we need to stay in the same classroom. I expect you to come to New York for the next quarterly meeting, yes?"

"Of course," Hawkins replied smoothly. "I always look forward to our get-togethers." Hawkins stood up, steadied himself on the arm of the chair, and signaled to his driver that he was ready to leave. He turned and gave a two-finger salute to Max, who was still seated, and then turned and walked slowly to the door and disappeared.

Max sat for a few minutes, contemplating the conversation and wondering how much control he really had over the reverend. As long as their interests were aligned, he supposed he would be able to get Hawkins to travel the course Max set out for him. He knew most of the reverend's secrets – at least the financial ones. He could wield that leverage if necessary, although he never wanted to have to resort to threats. That would not make his other clients feel comfortable about his discretion and loyalty. Still, if push ever came to shove, there were arrows in his quiver.

He shook his head slightly, clearing his thoughts. The first order of business was to find a new horse to put into the Connecticut Derby. Jonathan had left him in a difficult spot, but one that represented a great challenge, and Max always relished a new challenge.

Max stood up and walked toward Earl, who was leaning on the hotel bar, half-sitting on a stool as he observed the discussion in the corner. "How'd it go, Boss?" Earl casually asked.

"Fine. Fine. Let's go make my plane."

Earl led the way out the door and into the waiting car, which took him to the airport for the flight back to New York. Max returned to his email and tapped out a few responses to suggestions coming in from his business contacts and Republican sources about possible successors to the Prescott seat in the Senate. He frowned to himself because none of them were close to being as promising as the candidate he thought he had in Jonathan Prescott III.

Chapter 43

ON SEPTEMBER 15TH, *The New York Times* ran a lengthy article in the Opinion section describing the difficulties Senator Jonathan Prescott III had encountered since declaring himself an Independent. The article was not nearly as sensational as *The Wall Street Journal* piece from earlier in the year, but it subtly made the point that Jonathan had jumped off the Republican Party cliff without a parachute. "He has not fully embraced the Democrats by changing party affiliation, and has not fully embraced most Democratic party positions. He is still, at base, mostly conservative, which makes it difficult for true liberals to support him, but he has burned nearly all his bridges with the Right."

The writer was affiliated with a liberal advocacy organization – they preferred to avoid the term Political Action Committee – but the point was on target. Jonathan was a nomad. He could not count on support from the Left or the Right. The best he could hope for was a Senate so hopelessly divided and partisan that the Independent Caucus could swing the balance of major votes. This might happen frequently in the short term, but in the long term he had a re-election fight looming in two years.

The following Monday just before noon, his new secretary, Michelle, buzzed him to say that he had an unannounced visitor and asked whether he would see a mister Frank Elkhardt. Jonathan bounded from his desk chair and into his waiting area to greet Frank with a bear hug and a surprised smile. "What the hell are you doing here?"

"Well, old pal, I was reading *The Times* the other day and was reminded about how difficult it is for an Independent politician to make it in this heavily partisan environment, and I was thinking you might be interested in some volunteer support with fundraising and speech writing."

"From whom?" Jonathan asked sincerely.

"From *me*, you dolt."

Jonathan stood with a confused expression for a few moments before picking up on the idea that Frank was being serious. "What, you're going to quit your law practice and come work for me?"

Frank stood with a deadpan expression and said, "That's exactly what I'm saying."

"But . . . why?" Jonathan asked, still confused.

"Because you're my friend. Because I admire what you have done. And because I owe you."

"You don't owe me anything, Frank."

"Oh, sure, like you don't remember."

"Remember what?" Jonathan was still genuinely flummoxed.

"You win the bet."

"What bet?"

"Don't tell me you lost the contract?"

"What the hell are you talking about, Frank?"

Frank shook his head and smiled. "I thought a good politician never forgot when he had a chit to call in. But I guess you are not that good a politician. Allow me to remind you. Senior year, at The West End. I gave you an I-O-U that I would pay you one million dollars."

Jonathan frowned, trying desperately to remember. "You mean the napkin? Bro, you were half-drunk, and I don't even remember what it was that you were going to do, or not do, for me to collect on that marker. What was it?"

"Well," Frank lied, but only a little. "The way I remember it, I was going to pay you a million dollars if you ever stopped being a Republican."

Jonathan furrowed his brow and tried to recall that night twenty-five years before. "Old buddy, I seem to recall something about you having to sell out and take a high-paying corporate law job in order for me to win that bet. Am I misremembering?"

"Yes," Frank stated, as if that ended the discussion. "You are mistaken. I am here to start working off my debt. When we get to the point where you would have paid me a million dollars in wages, then we're even."

"What's your imaginary annual salary going to be?" Jonathan was sure this was a joke, so he decided to play along.

"Hey, I'm very good, so I'm thinking two hundred and fifty K per year sounds about right."

Jonathan smiled again. "Have you ever in your legal career had a year when you declared net income of a quarter-million?"

"Yes," Frank replied quickly. "Once. We had a very big settlement and all the partners shared a little more than two million in total fees, which netted me out at about four hundred thousand."

"OK," Jonathan stated firmly, "you're hired. You get a salary of $250,000 per year, but you owe it all to me and so for the next four years you are my slave and I get all your services for free. Done deal." Jonathan smiled broadly. "Do you want a drink, Slave?"

"It's a little early in the day for me," Frank responded. "Besides, there's no time, since you're taking me to lunch."

"Oh, really?" Jonathan asked incredulously. "You really think you can just waltz in here and that I'd be free to take you to lunch?"

Frank turned to Michelle and winked. Michelle looked up and said as sweetly as she could manage, "Boss, you don't have any appointments until 3:00. You are free for lunch." She smiled at Jonathan, then at Frank.

"You put her up to this, didn't you?"

"I have no idea what you're talking about," Frank said through a Cheshire Cat grin as he motioned toward the door.

Jonathan looked at his secretary and frowned playfully. "You are in cahoots with this liberal freak, aren't you?" Michelle shrugged and turned toward her computer terminal.

Frank led Jonathan out of the building and down Independence Avenue toward the Washington Monument. There was a chill in the air as the calendar moved toward autumn. Frank made a turn up 4th Street and ducked into a deli. Jonathan followed reluctantly, conscious of his lack of security and not really knowing what Frank was up to. They stood in line at the counter and ordered sandwiches and sodas, then walked up a narrow stairway to an upstairs seating area, past a haggard-looking man who was probably homeless and who was enjoying the warmth of the heating vent next to the garbage can. There were small tables for two lining the middle of the upstairs room. Only a few tables were occupied. Frank walked to the back of the room where a woman sat with her back toward Jonathan. Frank turned around and sat down opposite the woman, leaving room for Jonathan to sit next to her.

"Well, hello, Senator," Janice said matter-of-factly, smiling sincerely at Jonathan and Frank.

Jonathan stopped in his tracks, stunned at seeing Janice. "You have a big pair, Ms. Stanton," he said, still standing. "What is this, an intervention?"

"Not exactly," Janice responded, picking at a salad on the plate in front of her. "It's an apology, sort of, and an offer of services."

"My lucky day," Jonathan replied dryly.

"Hear her out," Frank said, sitting down and unwrapping his sandwich.

Jonathan reluctantly took a seat in a wobbly chair, but made no effort to eat his lunch.

Janice placed her plastic fork on her plate and looked up. "I know you have no reason to trust me, and no reason to even like me anymore. I acknowledge that what I did in my article hurt you, and although that was not my intention, I know it was a breach of a trust and you'll probably never forgive me for it. I put my own career ahead of keeping my word. I was being selfish."

"That has always been your problem, Jan – you were never selfish enough." Jonathan wasn't smiling, but the comment made Frank chuckle.

Frank attempted to advance the discussion. "Jon, I'm here because I think what you are doing is very brave and I want to support you. Jan's here for the same reason."

Jonathan scoffed. "How can you ever be sure she's not really here as a reporter for *The Wall Street Journal*?"

"Because I quit *The Journal*," Janice said softly.

"What?" Jonathan was genuinely surprised and leaned forward, causing the table to tip toward him and sending pieces of blue cheese tumbling off of Janice's plate. "What do you mean?"

"I mean, Jon, that I decided *The Journal* was not really where I wanted to be. I thought it was, and I thought I was about to reach the pinnacle of my career as a journalist, but when I really asked myself whether I was happy and whether I was doing something I thought was important with my life, I couldn't truthfully say that I was. I've been chasing stories for the wrong reasons – including the story about you. I regret it now. I'm sorry. I know that will never be an adequate apology. What I want to do now is help you. Like Frank said, we're both really proud of you. You have taken a step we never thought you could. You are trying to do something important. I want to help."

"Help?" Jonathan blurted out. "How do you think you could help at this point? I think it's a little too late for a retraction."

"True," Janice pushed forward, "but I'm not talking about a retraction. I'm talking about the future. I want to help you be the best independent senator ever. I want to chronicle your extraordinary journey. I want to help write your speeches, and I want to write a book about you. A good one. A positive one. One you will have total editorial control over. An autobiography that will have only you listed as the author. Your story is remarkable. It will be a guaranteed best-seller and will make a ton of cash for your campaign war-chest. It will be an inspiration to millions of young people in this country as they struggle with their own difficulties and hard decisions in their lives. I think your story needs to be told and I want to be the one to help you tell it."

Janice paused and looked from Jonathan to Frank, hopeful for some encouragement. "I have nothing but time on my hands. I've got a bunch of money saved away and no commitments or obligations. I'm a free agent. I want to do this."

Jonathan turned to Frank. "You put her up to this, didn't you?"

"Actually," Frank shrugged, "she put me up to it. Jan came to me with the idea. I was already thinking about offering to help you, and when she called me, I thought it was really a great idea. But I also told her she had burned her bridge with you and that you probably wouldn't agree to it."

Jonathan looked at his old friends, then stared out the second-floor window of the little deli. He could see the top of the Washington Monument beyond the building across the street. So much had changed in his life over the past few months. "I'm going to have to think about it," he replied, without showing much emotion.

"So," Frank offered, "then that is *not* a no?"

Jonathan smiled. "No, it is not a no. It is an 'I'll think about it.'"

"Good enough for me," Frank said cheerfully. "Now eat your sandwich, for Christ's sake." That got a genuine laugh from both Janice and Jonathan. "An olive branch has been offered. All you have to do now is take it."

"I said I'll think about it. Fine. You have ganged up on me, just like always. Congratulations. Now, Frank, when are you heading back to New York?"

Frank gave a puzzled look. "What do you mean? I'm not going back. Remember, I'm your slave and I'm staying here to work with you. I'm planning to start looking for an apartment this afternoon."

"C'mon, Frank. Don't keep up the act. It was a good ruse to get me to come to lunch and meet with Jan, here. No need to keep it up."

"It's no act," Frank responded seriously. "I'm here to work for you. I am as serious as a heart attack." He stared at his old friend without blinking.

"No shit?"

"Yup. No shit. I'm totally here for you. I really do think you're going down a great, uncharted road and I don't want to miss the ride."

Jonathan sat back, causing the little chair to tilt a bit. He ran his left hand through his hair and shook his head slowly from side to side. "Why do I think the two of you are pulling one over on me here?"

"Because," Janice interjected, "you are paranoid and generally incapable of accepting the genuine love and affection of others."

"Really? Is that it?" Jonathan grinned.

"Oh, absolutely," Frank jumped in. "You have to consider your situation here. You are without significant political allies, without any fundraising machinery, lacking in support from either major party, facing what will no doubt be a brutal re-election campaign when your seat comes up, and you can't even really figure out what your positions are without someone from the Party to give you a briefing book. You have blown all prospects of ever being elected president – which means I now have zero chance of ever being nominated for a seat on the Supreme Court. Bro, you need all the help you can get, and the two of us are both offering you help. My advice is to take it."

Jonathan looked at Frank's sincere face, then at Janice's apologetic eyes. "Do I have a choice?"

"Not really," Janice chimed in. "You need us. I need to feel like I'm doing something worthwhile, and I need to do something to make it up to you, a bit."

"Oh, be honest, Jan, you're doing it to soothe your guilt and make yourself feel better."

"Well, maybe a little bit of that, but also because I really do believe in what you did, and what you're doing."

"Thanks," Jonathan conceded weakly. "And if you really are going to stay here, Frank, you're going to bunk with me and not find some fleabag apartment on a moment's notice. I have plenty of room – since I have no wife or kids to clutter up my townhouse."

Jonathan bowed his head, while Janice turned away. "We're really sorry about that, Jonathan. I'm sure Gwen will come around. She's not gone for good."

Jonathan pursed his lips. "I'm not so sure. She's had a tough time. I'm not sure she'll be able to handle things here. At least not for a while."

The three sat in silence, the mood suddenly not as jovial as it had been moments before. Janice broke the silence. "Give it some time, Jon. I know Gwen really does love you. She's as loyal as anyone I've ever met."

"You are right about that," Jonathan said softly. "She's a far better wife for me than you would have been."

"You would have never married me."

"I don't know what I would have done if you had decided to keep that baby."

Janice was flustered and sat in silence for a moment. "Well, I guess neither of us will ever really know for sure, but I'm glad it worked out as it did. You and Gwen were meant for each other."

"Gwen was meant for the man she thought I was. The man I thought I was. I'm not sure she's meant for the man I am now. I'm not sure of much anymore."

"I'm sure," Frank said. "I'm sure that Gwen loves you. She'll come back. But you need to go get her back."

"I hope you're right."

Later that night, Frank and Janice came to Jonathan's home. Jonathan had not specifically accepted Janice's offer of assistance, nor her proposal to ghost-write an autobiography for him. But he had offered her a glass of wine and even allowed her to pick out the bottle from his extensive wine rack. After the second bottle, Jonathan acknowledged Janice's apology, although he didn't say he accepted it.

Before Janice got into the cab to go back to her own apartment, she suggested that maybe she could call his new secretary to schedule an appointment to start the series of interviews that she would need to conduct in order to get started on the book. Jonathan said it would probably be a bad idea for her to come to his office, but they could arrange for some evenings in the apartment – as long as Frank was willing to chaperone. Janice agreed and blew him a kiss as she wobbled into the back seat of the taxi. Frank and Jonathan stood on the stoop of Jonathan's Georgetown brownstone and watched the car turn the corner and disappear into the night.

"Just us guys, eh? Like old times," Frank said as he nudged Jonathan's ribs with his elbow. "Maybe we should put on some tunes and cram for that poli sci final you have tomorrow."

"Thanks," Jonathan replied warmly. "I can always use a study partner. I've got a lot of work to do if I'm going to make it on my own, without the Prescott/Foster political machine to prop me up."

"Don't sell yourself short, Jonathan. There's more to you than you think there is. And you're not on your own. You've got me, and Jan, and no matter what you may think, you still have Gwen and the girls. And I suspect that out there in Liberal Land there are a lot more Jonathan Prescott supporters than you think. Who knows, there may even be some Republicans out there who might vote for you when push comes to shove. You did the right thing."

"For once in my life?"

"No way! I'm sure you have done the right thing dozens of times in your life before now." Frank looked at Jonathan, deadpan, and held the pose for nearly ten seconds before breaking into a broad grin.

"You never let me get away with anything, do you?"

"It's my job, Boss. I'm here to keep you honest."

Jonathan looked his old friend in the eyes and said, "The one thing I think I am at this point, Bro, is honest. I used to think I knew exactly who I was and where I was going and how I was going to get there. I had no doubts, no fears. Now, I look in the mirror every morning and I see a man who has no idea who he is, and I have no idea where I'm going or how I'm going to get there. I have a million doubts, and I'm terrified that I'll fail and be a laughing stock. But I know I've finally stopped lying to myself, and to everyone around me. Honesty sucks."

"Fear not, my son," Frank intoned as if imitating the preacher Abraham Hawkins, "tread the path on which I lead you, and I will show you the way. Open your heart to the message of truth and righteousness and I will put the words in your mouth and teach you what to say."

"I'm not worried about what to say, I'm worried about who is going to pay for the television time for me to say it."

Frank slapped Jonathan on the back as they turned and walked into the apartment. "Have faith, Jon. It's a great country, and the people will flock to a good message."

"I used to think I didn't need those people."

"Well, those people used to think they had no use for you, and that you had no use for them. It's up to you to change their minds."

"That's going to be a high mountain to climb," Jonathan said somberly.

Frank nodded. "One step at a time, Boss. One step at a time."

Jonathan stopped in the doorway, looking out at the quiet street. "I just hope I'm not Sisyphus in this epic; rolling my boulder up the mountain one tortured step at a time, but never reaching the summit."

He closed the door, and he and Frank quickly cleaned up the dirty glasses and empty Chinese food containers. Frank pulled out the sofa bed while Jonathan dragged extra linens from the closet. Frank had declined the invitation to sleep in one of the girls' beds, saying he wanted them to stay undisturbed for when they came back home. As Jonathan said "Good night," Frank reached out and placed a hand on his shoulder.

"You're not Sisyphus, Jon. You're Odysseus. The battle of Troy is over; now you have to navigate yourself home. Your

Odyssey is just beginning, and when you reach Athens, your wife will be there waiting for you."

Jonathan nodded, then walked up the stairs to the master bedroom. On the night table, next to the Tiffany lamp, he saw the silver picture frame with the smiling faces of a younger version of himself and his bride on the day of their wedding. His eyes were bright, and there were no wrinkles around the edges. Gwen was beaming and waving to someone in the distance.

He realized Gwen had not chosen to pack that photo when she left for her mother's house, and wondered if she didn't want to be reminded of the happy day, or if she wanted him to be able to see her happy face every night before he went to sleep. If he thought like Frank, he would assume the latter. He wondered if he could ever learn to think like Frank.

When the light went out, soft moonlight through the window provided just enough illumination for him to see Gwen's youthful smile. She seemed so hopeful about the future – their future. He rolled over and closed his eyes.

He dreamed about mountains – and boulders.

The End

Thank you for reading *A Legacy of One*. I truly enjoy hearing from readers about their reactions to my characters and stories. I welcome critical comments and suggestions that can help me improve my writing and urge every reader to **please leave a review**. Even a few words will go a long way and I will be grateful. Post on Amazon, Goodreads and/or BookBub to let other readers know what you think. And send me an email directly via my website at www.kevingchapman.com to tell me your thoughts about this book.

And please tell your friends (and book club members) about this book. As an independent author, I need all the word-of-mouth plugs I can get. Keep reading books by indie authors; there are a lot of great writers out there just waiting for you.

Kevin G. Chapman
June 2021

Book Club discussion questions for *A Legacy of One*

1. Did Jonathan make the right choices? Would you have made different choices in his shoes? Why?
2. Did Janice make the right choice to publish the article? Should she have limited the article to the issue of Jonathan's biological parentage, or was it appropriate for her to include the information about the abortion?
3. Did Janice's choice to publish the article make you feel differently about her character? Why?
4. How do you feel about Gwen in the end? Did she have a right to expect Jonathan to make different choices? Did she have the right to know in advance what Jonathan was going to do?
5. Did Jonathan's father do anything wrong in his decision not to tell Jonathan the truth about his ambiguous paternity? Should his mother have told him?
6. Does it matter whether Jonathan was the biological son of his father or not? Why?
7. Do you think Jonathan would have made different choices if it turned out that he really was his father's biological child?
8. Is Max Foster a villain? Why? What did he do to make you feel that way about him?
9. If you were in Frank's shoes, would you help Jonathan?
10. What do you think will happen next? Will Jonathan be able to hold his Senate seat as an independent? Will his actions have any impact on his colleagues in Congress? How do you think his constituents will feel about what he did?

ABOUT THE AUTHOR

Kevin G. Chapman is a labor & employment attorney for a major national media company. Kevin lives in central New Jersey with his wife, Sharon. Sharon was a student at Barnard College when Kevin attended Columbia, but any similarities between them and the characters in *A Legacy of One* end there.

Kevin is the author of the Mike Stoneman Thriller series, a very different kind of fiction, featuring NYPD Homicide detective Mike Stoneman. You can find Kevin's crime-thrillers at amazon.com or in audiobook format at all major audiobook retailers.

Kevin and Sharon both still call New York City home, despite living in New Jersey. Kevin is an avid golfer and tournament poker player and can often be found at Citi Field cheering on his beloved New York Mets.

ACKNOWLEDGEMENTS

This novel was a long time in the writing – and then a longer time before this revised edition. Many people assisted and contributed, for which I am extremely grateful. My wife, Sharon, not only provided the images for the original cover (and author's photo), but she read chapters and contributed significant feedback and suggestions all along the way. Her common sense and intelligent commentary helped positively shape the story and characters. My son, Ross (CC '18) undertook a complete read-and-edit project during his summer break from school in 2019 and offered many very cogent observations in addition to spotting numerous technical issues. The final draft owes much to Ross's efforts. Jeanne Klockers also provided valuable proofreading and saved me from several embarrassing mistakes that were in the original page proofs. Other friends and colleagues provided helpful input on both content and presentation, including Gail Shields, Carol Keller, and Roy Pomerantz. And the typokillers from AuthorsXP were terrific, particularly Darla Meyer.

Keeping it in the family, my daughter Samantha, who is a professional freelance editor (find her at samanthachapmanediting.com) did a complete edit before the publication of this revised edition.

And, of course, I owe a great debt to my classmates in the Columbia College class of 1983, many of whom formed the creative foundations for some of the characters and scenes in the story. I only regret that I didn't finish the book fifteen years earlier so Jonathan Prescott could have been a fictional member of our class.

And thanks to my teachers at Columbia who inspired me and fanned my creative flames through the years. In particular, thanks go to George Stade, for whom I did my first real fiction writing; Kenneth Koch, who taught me to love poetry; and the great Wallace Gray, who taught me and all his students at Columbia to aim high, dig deeply into the words, and enjoy the ride.

Note about the 2021 edition

In 2016, after ten years of working on it, I self-published *A Legacy of One*. I was attempting to write the Great American Novel. It included some wonderful scenes that illustrated specific points about the characters and about the world. It followed a structure that included allusions to the ten commandments. It had parallels between all the major characters. It had stand-alone chapters full of new characters who populated them as independent short stories. It was epic. It was also 160,000 words. No wonder few people bought it.

I also discovered that, as much as I had tried to proofread and edit it myself, there were flaws and mistakes that needed to be cleaned up. And, if I wanted it to be a readable novel and not merely a personal opus, I needed to cut it down.

So, I first sent the manuscript to my editor. Now that I've been writing and publishing books for a while, I have one! Then, like a director trying to cut a 3-hour movie down to a 2-hour time slot, I started evaluating each scene. Some were just not necessary to the story. It's like "killing your babies" as Ken Levine says, but it cut 40,000 words and thirteen chapters off the text by the time I was finished.

I also updated the politics and time line a bit. I cut out the main legislative issue from the original story and focused on the confirmation of a Supreme Court Justice – which turned out to be very topical both in 2016 and 2020.

Now, I have a more manageable second edition, which I hope you enjoyed. If you ever want to read the unabridged first edition – just send me an email. I have plenty of printed copies that never got sold, or I can send you the e-book version.

In its current form, is this book better than *The Great Gatsby*? I'll leave that to my future readers. It is intended to be a book that sparks thought, discussion, argument, and contemplation. If you were Jonathan, what would you do? It is always easy to take the safe route, to satisfy your understandable desire for security, comfort, and opportunity for your children. It is easy to follow the voices around you, telling you what you should do because it is in your best interests and will make your family happy and comfortable. The safe course. The path of least resistance. Why take a risk and mess up the perfect world that is right there in front of you?

And yet, we recognize that a hero is the person who takes the risk, who walks the more difficult path, who takes on evil in the world despite the personal risk. Someone with nothing to lose risks little, but someone with everything to lose is the real risk-taker. Would you make the same choices that Jonathan makes? I hope reading this book makes you think.

After I completed *A Legacy of One*, I decided to go in a different direction and write something less serious – more fun. I wrote *Righteous Assassin (A Mike Stoneman Thriller)*. This crime thriller features Mike Stoneman, a New York Homicide Detective, and is a serial killer chase. If you find *A Legacy of One* too heavy, you might prefer the Mike Stoneman thriller series, which as of this date is comprised of 4 books, with book 5 in production. You can view a preview of *Righteous Assassin* on amazon.com here: https://www.amazon.com/dp/B07JJDZZC1.

KGC (June, 2021)

Other novels by Kevin G. Chapman

The Mike Stoneman Thriller Series

Righteous Assassin (Mike Stoneman #1)
Deadly Enterprise (Mike Stoneman #2)
Lethal Voyage (Mike Stoneman #3)
Fatal Infraction (Mike Stoneman #4)
Fool Me Twice (A Mike Stoneman Short Story)

coming soon:
Perilous Gambit (Mike Stoneman #5)

Visit me at www.KevinGChapman.com

Made in the USA
Middletown, DE
02 July 2021